I0648110

IMMORTOPIA

THE THIRD BOOK IN THE DOMINANT SPECIES SAGA

by

Kingsley Pilgrim

Grosvenor House
Publishing Limited

All rights reserved
Copyright © Kingsley Pilgrim, 2018

The right of Kingsley Pilgrim to be identified as the author of this
work has been asserted in accordance with Section 78
of the Copyright, Designs and Patents Act 1988

The book cover picture is copyright to Sanjay Charlton

This book is published by
Grosvenor House Publishing Ltd
Link House
140 The Broadway, Tolworth, Surrey, KT6 7HT.
www.grosvenorhousepublishing.co.uk

This book is sold subject to the conditions that it shall not, by way of
trade or otherwise, be lent, resold, hired out or otherwise circulated
without the author's or publisher's prior consent in any form of binding or
cover other than that in which it is published and
without a similar condition including this condition being imposed
on the subsequent purchaser.

A CIP record for this book
is available from the British Library

ISBN 978-1-78623-084-3

"You are untrustworthy and pure evil, but we can work with that."

DEDICATION

This book is dedicated

to

Marie Maguire
Gerard Higham
and
Chloe Pilgrim

Thank you for bringing me into the world and raising me with love and respect for others.

You have always stood beside me with so much patience.

It is the ride of a lifetime being your son, one I will never forget.

I will always love you.

ACKNOWLEDGEMENTS

Can't quite remember when I started this book, but it was fun and different to write, even though it took longer to finish due to me producing a short film whilst writing it.

It's basically the same roll call as the last book, but let's add some more names to spice it up a bit.

Well, the family as always have continued to support me in my little ventures and I thank them for that and thanks to the following people who helped out this 'Silly Goose'.

Dexter 'Rudy' Roberts for his tech support, midwifery terms from Tara Billinge, my editor Natasha Wagner.

Also, the whole duration crew (Saturdays wouldn't be the same without at least one of you turning up!), Beehive Illustrators, Sanjay Charlton, Louise Winther, the doctors and nurses at Milton Keynes hospital.

Plus Daniel Alexander and all the cast and crew of the 'Dominant Species' film, thank you so much for bringing all these characters to life, from script to screen.

Cheers to all the people who paid good money to read my books, I really do appreciate the support from you.

ABOUT THE AUTHOR

Kingsley Pilgrim lives in Milton Keynes and no longer considers himself an actor, as all of his agents have finally left him. When he isn't writing he likes to produce short films, watch cartoons early on Saturday mornings and eat cheese and red onion sandwiches

CONTACT

Kingsleypilgrim.co.uk

Twitter:@Kingsleyland

Guess. Try. Hope.

ALSO BY THE AUTHOR

In the Dominant Species Saga

Paintshark
Glimmerfin

PROLOGUE

Planet Rayash

The planet was beautiful with enormous forests and vast vegetation. Its oceans had the weirdest and most wonderful creatures swimming in its waters.

Magnificent buildings across hundreds of cities touched the tops of the sky, grand in every sense of the word. Rayash was truly a great world filled with sentient beings, loving the life they led and working hard to provide a better life for all their families.

But all that didn't matter now as the planet was on the verge of shaking itself apart. Giant, winged creatures tried in vain to haul themselves away from the crumbling forestry; it wasn't the falling branches that halted their escape, they were overcome from the now noxious gasses creeping out from deep inside the planet itself. They fell down, crashing into the trees they once called home.

The planet was falling apart, breaking up from the inside, countless earthquakes and volcanic eruptions sent seismic waves of energy travelling through layers upon layers of the planet's crust. Rayash was doomed.

Solar plasma flares from the sun it orbited had become more frequent. Rings of plasma occasionally reached Rayash, which at first only slightly interrupted the technology. But now the plasma flares were erupting from the sun's surface at a tremendous rate and they rained down on the planet.

The destruction of the planet wasn't the first of the problems for its inhabitants – that was the virus. Nobody knew why it had happened, but it started with the rats in the city of Kornush. People said that two huge rats appeared from the forest first with glowing red eyes. They scuttled out from the trees completely changed, their eyes were bright and had a haunted feel to them. Their movement was strange and unconvincing, eyes bulging and tongues protruding wildly, and they infected the city rats.

Curious children bent down to look at the odd, moving creatures and were instantly attacked, the rats swarmed around them and bit and chewed at their tiny legs. Some larger rats found the remarkable ability to jump, which they did with ease, viciously tearing at the crying children's cheeks. The rats clung fast as their skin was pulled away. There was a turning point with the children, as they were bitten by the hordes of rats. Foam appeared at their mouths and they had to be restrained by fearful adults as they were overcome by a violent rage. They kicked and punched and found any weapon to kill anybody close by, which in most cases were their parents, murdering with fits of extreme anger.

Crowds ran in panic as the children turned into violent, unthinking animals; people were trampled to death, trying to escape as the age range of the victims grew and adults entered the fray of extreme anger. The hospitals of Kornush were filled with violent patients, both adults and children strapped down to trolleys and beds for their own safety and the safety of the doctors and nurses around them.

The people who had suffered rat bites became ill very quickly, their eyes changed colour and they needed to cause violence and destroy, but after a while they stopped fighting, stopped caving in the heads of their loved ones and neighbours, because they died. The infected just collapsed to the ground or went silent whilst pinned to the hospital trolleys. But shortly afterwards, they were awake again. They came back to life no longer craving violence, this time they needed to feed, and just like the rats, they needed blood.

Nobody ever saw those two giant rats again, some people say that they were perched on the shoulders of a bloodied, naked lady, who was biting people and laughing as she did so. Everybody was attacking people at the same time and some were indeed naked as they did so, but only one was laughing.

CHAPTER ONE:

Magic to Tragic

Earth 65: Heffernan City underground tube station, Central line, 25 miles away. One day after the virus broke out in Olympia City.

It was late and the passengers were tired, the old-style train rumbled along the rough, battered tracks, shaking more than it should be due to the lack of maintenance on the rails. The train had seven carriages, dirty on the outside and even worse inside. It had been another hot day and the night wasn't that much cooler, the stench from the day of sweaty passengers hung in the air for the unfortunate nightshift.

Commuters were on their way home from jobs they hated, they worked even longer hours now due to boredom more than anything else, plus nothing to go home to; the TV ban wasn't in force like in Olympia, but there was still nothing much on to watch and internet restrictions had been upgraded.

The most popular entertainment people now was placing bets to see who could break through the walls of Big Man's Messiah complex first, hundreds of people used to gather outside with picnic baskets and cans of cheap beer and just sit and watch others launch stones and other projectiles at the impenetrable building.

Quite a few of the passengers had just come back from the complex and were tired and desperate to get home before the wilder inhabitants of Olympia joined their train. Heffernan City neighboured Olympia, a much smaller city, but the influence of Big Man and his game show still poured over its residents.

A balding man with sweat patches underneath his armpits wiped his brow and shuffled uneasily in his suit, keeping his briefcase close to his chest, nervously eying up his fellow travellers.

A woman with her friend sat close together as she discussed intimate details about her date the night before; they giggled and pointed at the pictures she had on her phone. Two teenage lovers were wrapped around each other on one of the far seats. They wriggled around in each other's arms like two octopi trapped in a fishermen's net.

The girl's tongue easily probed inside the mouth of her boyfriend as she pulled him even closer to her, kissing him fiercely, she pulled away only to stroke her lover's hair and look dreamily into his eyes.

"Love you."

"Love you more," he replied quickly as not to earn a rebuke from his girlfriend.

"Thank you," she said, "Thank you for taking care of me."

He gave her a long, loving look and put his finger to her lips.

"You don't have to say thank you, I love you with everything I have."

The girl pulled in a deep breath and closed her eyes, clenching her tiny fists with her boyfriend's shirt as she hauled him closer to her.

"Correct answer, mister."

She left his embrace and straddled on top of him, sitting happily on his lap.

"Let's see what's in here," she said, slowly unbuttoning his trousers.

The other passengers tried to look away, embarrassed by the lovesick antics of the teenagers, only a few with voyeuristic tendencies kept watch.

The door at the other end of the carriage opened and some more youths breezed through. Looking up from her boyfriend. The girl heard the door snap shut as the group walked through. A youth, massive in size, led his friends into the train, two girls and two boys followed the dark-skinned boy as he weaved his way in between the legs of the weary passengers, who tried to withdraw them quickly as not to cause trouble, apart from the lovers who went on kissing.

Tripping over the boyfriend's outstretched legs, the big kid raised his hands.

"HEY! PUT YOUR FEET IN, MAN!"

The young lover held up a hand as if to silence the leader of the gang, which enraged him further, his voice, older than his years, boomed through the train.

"WHAT? YOU THINK YOU'RE FUNNY NOW, PUNK?"

Slowly shifting his girlfriend to one side, the boyfriend spoke.

"Sorry? You talking to me?"

The rest of the carriage anticipated trouble and moved away quickly, as did the girlfriend.

"Just leave it, Kane."

Lacy, the girlfriend, turned to the group.

"Please, we don't want any trouble."

The gang leader slicked his hand over his short black hair, looking at the girl through shades.

"I'm sorry, but lover boy here has really pissed me off."

His stare returned to Kane.

"Think you're a bad boy now? Want me to mess you up?"

The crowd of kids behind him grew rowdier.

Cameo, a jaw-dropping, stunning blonde girl, dressed from head to toe in black leather, snarled at the couple.

"Mess him up, Achilles."

"Stomp on him, man," hissed Harley, a tall boy with a ginger mohawk.

Another girl with long black hair and a hint of authority tried to stand with her arms folded, but couldn't as the carriage rocked from side to side; Sully sucked her teeth in annoyance, bored of the whole scenario.

"Just beat him up and let's be done with this, Achilles."

Poxon, a larger boy, bit down hungrily on a chocolate bar, a piece fell from the packet on to the train floor, he greedily stooped down to pick it up and eyed up Lacy's fearful face as he rammed the remains into his mouth.

"I think we should keep the girl for ourselves, teach the bitch a lesson."

He scratched at his neck after he spoke, a rash was appearing.

Tears began to trickle down Lacy's face, she shivered from the fright that now crawled over her body.

"Please don't," she pleaded again.

Achilles, the strapping leader, whispered to the sniffling girl, "Sorry girl, once we sort out your boyfriend, we'll sort you out too."

Kane rose from his seat and looked at the young giant, his eyes barely meeting Achilles' chin.

"You lay one hand on her head and I'll kill you, stupid prick."

The big teenager stared long and hard at Kane.

"What did you call me?"

Lacy was crying harder now, "PLEASE LEAVE US ALONE!"

"Shut her up please."

Cameo grabbed the hysterical girl with force and pulled her away from her lover. Before Kane could react Achilles reached for his neck and lifted him off his feet with terrifying ease, "I repeat the question, what did you call me?"

Kane squirmed in Achilles' grasp and kicked at the huge boy, his blows coming to nothing against Achilles' muscled legs, he managed a breathless gasp.

"I called you a prick, I called you a stupid prick!"

Achilles grinned and responded in a quieter voice than Kane.

"Time to die then."

He didn't blink, he just casually threw Kane hard onto the dirty train floor, he eased his massive frame on top of him and began to punch his face.

"STOP IT! GET OFF OF HIM!" Lacy screamed.

Achilles' fists continued to rain down on Kane as Lacy struggled in Cameo's grasp.

"WHO'S THE PRICK NOW EH? WHO'S THE PRICK?"

The frightened passengers fled their seats, some ran back through the closest doors to them on the train, whilst the others were eager to witness the free entertainment and stayed to watch.

"GET OFF OF ME!" Kane shouted.

Achilles didn't respond, he just increased his punching speed on Kane's face.

"YOU'RE HURTING ME!" Kane implored. Achilles continued his blows, "STOP HURTING ME!" he continued.

Lacy screamed and tried to rush forward, but Cameo's grip was firm and quite deceiving for her slender frame.

Sully looked at her watch, bored, "Hurry up and finish him."

"OW! OW! OW! PLEASE GET OFF!"

Kane's words slowed down and then he finally stopped and held a frightened stare at Achilles as the huge fist hesitated, trembling before the final blow. The passengers looked on scared and intrigued in equal measure. Suddenly Kane burst out laughing, "Sorry, sorry I can't hold this shit in anymore!" Achilles rolled off of Kane and brushed himself down, "Look at the state of my trousers," he moaned. All the girls were giggling, including Sully who forced a smile.

The passengers knew from the smiles of the teenagers that they had been duped as Kane rolled around the seat in hysterics. The gang hadn't asked for money or tried to rob them and it did make the laborious trip home slightly more interesting.

Achilles ushered the others around him and made them all stand in a line between the isles and cleared his throat, "Thank you for showing an interest in our little demonstration tonight, but the show is over and I want your cash credits as soon as I finish speaking or else there will be trouble." This bought gasps of shock from the crowd with looks of frightened concern thrown in, "Just kidding, folks." Achilles waved his hands in the air to calm down the early panic, "I'm messing with you."

Cameo, an immaculately beautiful girl, slunk in between Lacy and Poxon, her voice a cool relaxed calm.

"Excuse my friend, he can be such a tease." She felt the cheek of Achilles with her palm and rubbed it teasingly, "What he was trying to say is that you have been lucky enough to catch a show from the young Heffernan Players, we're a drama group based on the north side and we spend our nights entertaining the weary travellers on the tube home from a hectic day at work, all we ask in return for a distraction from your daily grind is a small donation." The crowd moaned again as Cameo continued, "You can give as little or as much as you like, but our labour is merely entertaining our Heffernan brothers and sisters."

Achilles bent down and whispered into Kane's ear, "Heffernan brothers and sisters?"

"Yeah, she's been reading and rehearsing new lines, got them from the new drama teacher."

"Bet that's not all he's been giving her," Achilles grinned.

The friends bumped fists as Cameo bought her speech to an end.

"My friends will be going down the carriage for your most grateful donations, so it just remains for me to say thank you once more for enjoying a night of urban theatre from the new Heffernan Players."

On her last word, they walked forward to link hands, looking proudly at each other from their night's work, Achilles, Cameo, Kane, Lacy, Poxon, Harley and Sully all bowed to the left, right and centre to their train audience and then just let Poxon wander through the train to collect the money, using his hat as a collection bowl.

Sully let the crowd continue to huff amongst themselves and pulled Achilles aside.

"How long do we have to keep this up? Wasting our nights collecting shrapnel from the walking dead?"

"Don't call them that, they're just tired from travelling up and down the city for work, Olympia still hasn't recovered from Big Man's fallout."

Sully pulled her long hair up and began tying it, "So why the sudden show of concern?"

Achilles looked in her eyes unflinchingly, "Because it was these same people, the same 'walking dead' who funded our college trip, how long ago did we know about it? Six months ago maybe? So we had to do this charade every night along every underground line in all the districts until we had enough money."

Sully responded slowly, "I know, it's a shame that none of our parents could raise that cash for us."

Achilles shook his head, "I miss them too, but they were put in Gommerstall Prison, nobody has heard from them in years."

"No, they escaped, remember? They destroyed the prison and got out."

Achilles raised an eyebrow, "We don't know if they got out, we saw footage of the plane leave the prison and then it exploded, we were kids back then but I know what we saw."

"DON'T SAY THAT!" Sully's outburst shocked the whole carriage, Poxon raised his head from collecting the money.

"Everything ok?" he asked.

Both Achilles and Sully looked to the floor sheepishly, "We're fine, we're sorry."

Poxon grumbled and went back to counting the credits in his hat. Achilles took Sully aside, her demeanour made him think that she didn't want to talk or listen anymore, but he made her anyway.

"Look, I miss my parents too, we all do, and there's nothing I want more than to see my mum and dad back here but they're not, and we are! We took care of ourselves, we dodged the authorities who wanted us fostered, we are all the family we need right now, and by putting on crummy shows, that cash for that college trip on the spaceship might just be possible."

Sully relented.

"We will get to the spaceship won't we, Achilles? I really want to go on that zoo trip."

Achilles answered loudly, whilst putting a huge arm around her shoulder, "You see us? All of us? We're all going on that trip tomorrow." He pointed to the others, "Every one of those kids has been through hell and back since we all lost our parents to Big Man's shit, but we got through it."

Sully smiled and nodded her head in a slight relief, "You really know how to say the right things to a girl."

Achilles' own smile was pensive when returned, "Didn't work with Jess, did it? No matter how hard I tried."

"I don't know why you're still trying to win her back you know."

Achilles shrugged, "Fair heart never won a maiden, some might say."

Sully wasn't convinced, "Others might say she's a virus with cheap shoes, plus there is that other girl, Sayles, sniffing around you."

"I like Sayles, I'm going to ask her out after we get back if things don't work out with Jess."

Sully chewed at her right thumbnail and found herself hesitating, "Jess dumped you, chances are it's over."

Achilles' eyes flicked to his friend's and then back to Sully, they squinted slowly as Sully began coughing with her head bent down.

"You ok?"

Sully gave the 'thumbs up' whilst still hacking a nasty cough, "Just a summer cold probably, I'll be fine." Achilles wasn't sure but carried on regardless.

"You never liked Jess, did you?"

"Not after the way she treated you and you still run around her like a lovesick puppy, just hope you haven't invited her."

"Nope," Achilles sighed.

"Good, because if we can raise the money, I'll ask my cousins Echo and Enya to come."

"The redheads?"

Sully nodded and coughed slightly again.

"Well shit," Achilles said with a grin, "Why didn't you say so?"

Rayash

Dozens of figures entered the National Headquarters of Pure Science at Kornush.

They strode purposely through the great halls clad in combat attire with laser rifles raised in attack anticipation. Leading the men was a man wearing an old, battered leather jacket adorned with knives of various shapes. He wore a scarf wrapped tightly around his neck. As he walked forward in deep strides with his group, another figure stepped out in front of him.

It was a middle-aged man who didn't move right, his steps were awkward and unsure and there was a vacant look in his eyes. He started to blink rapidly and stumbled forward.

The group stopped and observed that the man lumbering forward was almost nude, apart from a pair of bloodied running shoes. The left part of his jaw was missing as well as most of his left arm, his right arm swung softly like a child's garden swing in a summer's breeze, although its hand was missing.

As soon as the stumbling creature spotted the group, its strange steps turned more bizarre as it tried to hurry itself towards the pack of men.

The leader of the group began to unravel his long scarf, it was a gift from his wife for his birthday. She got it from the finest silk shop in Kornush, and it did look good with his leather jacket, which she also bought for him from a flea market as he forgot her own birthday the week before.

The fine scarf was meant to protect him from the dense smoke which was appearing all over Rayash thanks to the plasma flares, but it was now hampering his breathing and he was almost done removing it.

With effortless calm he got up close to the stumbling being and wrapped the scarf around the creature's neck, pulling it hard and turning it around. His men looked on as they watched their boss choke the life out of the poor creature; whether it was already dead or just heavily infected with the virus, the men saw what little life slip away from the creature. There was a frightened look in the creature's eyes as the man tightened the scarf around the infected being and snapped its neck.

"Excuse me," he muttered as he unraveled his scarf from the infected man's neck and wrapped it around his own, he rubbed his hands down on his leather jacket and spoke without looking back at his soldiers, "You ready, boys?" All of the soldiers nodded in unison, "Ok, let's go."

The men sidestepped around the body and continued their walk further towards the science centre, when they were met with more company.

The woman lay in her birthing chamber, breathing heavily, as her husband stood by her side holding her hand while his wife thrashed around in pain.

A midwife adjusted her position as the baby was about to come, as another watched nervously nearby.

"Easy Tashar, breathe easy and push." the first midwife called to the second, "She's in second stage right now, head is low."

The younger midwife just nodded and then softly spoke, "I'll check her obs."

"Ok, this baby is coming now," said the older midwife.

"SCREW YOU!" was the expected reply.

The nurse was used to such outbursts and carried on regardless, "Almost there, Tashar, just keep breathing, vertex visible."

The first midwife's face dropped for a moment, "Ok, FHR is dropping, your baby needs to come now, you're struggling, so pull your knees to your chest, take a deep breath and push."

Tashar strained through gritted teeth, and with an almighty effort pushed and screamed until there was silence, which was only broken by the sound of a baby crying. A terrific smile beamed upon her husband's face.

"IT'S A GIRL! WE HAVE A BABY GIRL!"

The midwife carefully handed the precious baby to the man and he turned his new daughter to his wife, "Look at her Tashar, isn't she lovely?"

Through extreme exhaustion, his wife managed a smile, "She's beautiful, just beautiful, Kozak."

The midwife took the baby away from the father.

"It's time to run the tests, Kozak, we have to make sure the baby is the potential."

The science centre rocked from another explosion, the fires were becoming more intense. Kozak covered his ears and then went to hold his wife's hand, he stroked it tenderly.

"Kozak?" The midwife called again.

"Ok, do it," he answered not even looking up at her.

She nodded and reached into her pocket for her phone and spoke into it, "Could you come now please?"

After a slight pause, the voice on the other line finally spoke and the midwife nodded again and stood back. There was suddenly a sound like a mini thunderclap and another figure materialized into the room shrouded in thick blue smoke. As the smoke cleared, it was another midwife, who wore her pure white nurse's outfit with blue dreadlocked hair hanging behind her back. The smoke revealed a dark skin and piercing blue eyes aimed straight at the first midwife, her voice was calm and soft.

"Ok, I'm here."

The first midwife coughed and waved her hand in front of her face, trying to fan the smoke, "We don't need three midwives here, it's kind of strange."

The second midwife hurried out of the room, pausing slightly to look at Tashar, her face was confused and she nodded her head to the new girl and then to the direction of Tashar before exiting, the first midwife coughed again.

"Do you have to bring so much smoke with you, Silo? We do have a baby here."

Silo's eyes narrowed at her colleague as she began to tie up her loose blue hair, "I'm a Vanisher, Bailey, we teleport and when we do, smoke appears, it's part of the deal."

Vanishers were a race of beings on Rayash, they were teleporters who were mostly the minority on the planet.

Rayash was filled with many strange beings, not only teleporters but Changers as well; changers were essentially shapeshifters, with the ability to take the form of any person that they had already come into contact with.

Both Vanishers and Changers studied sorcery and were quite adept, but Bailey and Silo were midwives and very good at their jobs, even as the planet crumbled around them, their main concern was for the welfare and health of this baby girl.

Silo was slightly younger than Bailey, but both girls were in their twenties, Silo early and Bailey mid.

Bailey handed the baby to Silo and pressed some buttons on the wall behind her. A blue three dimensional display of the room appeared from a small beam of light at the other end of the birthing chamber. The second young midwife returned, entering from a side door, looking flustered and tired.

"What are you doing back, Tobin?" Bailey asked sternly, "Silo is here, I don't need you."

"Sorry, I have family problems and have nowhere else to go, I just wanted to help, I just want to learn."

Bailey's eyes closed with frustration, "Ok, you can stay but don't let it happen again, young lady."

"No miss."

Tobin again nodded to Silo, who vanished again and reappeared. Silo carefully placed the baby into a medical scanner tube. Tobin joined Bailey as all three midwives got down to work with the health checks.

The light then honed in on the baby and began to make its way up and down the tube. As the diagnostic readouts flashed up on the computer screens attached to the scanner, another explosion made everyone stumble, Tashar clung hard to the bed rails.

"That wasn't a plasma flare, we're under attack."

Kozak listened to Bailey and took a step closer to one of the surveillance monitors.

"What is it?" his wife asked.

Kozak's eyes never left the screen as he replied, "Trouble."

Outside the front doors of the science centre more of the horrific creatures were gathered; they had a yellowish complexion, but most of their faces were smeared with blood.

Their clothes were ragged and torn, it was difficult to see where the clothes ended and the skin began, some stumbled along with missing arms, whilst others dragged themselves along as their stumps left a bloody trail.

Leg stumps weren't the only thing leaving a blood trail on the ground, intestines oozed out of bloated torn bodies and were stamped harder into the already bloody ground.

Kozak let out a tired sigh as laser fire and hand grenades exploding cut through the swarm of lumbering infected and the troops pressed on, shooting down any surveillance camera attached to the front of the building.

Tashar tried to ease herself from her bed as the explosions grew closer, "Is that guns I can hear outside?" she asked.

Kozak span around to her and bit his lip nervously, "Like I said, it's trouble."

The leader of the armed men made his way through the charred bodies of the infected.

"Even though I don't like killing my own people, we must do whatever it takes to preserve the life of everybody on Rayash." He gave a look to the people still in flames, "But I think it's too late for these poor bastards." Anger flashed across his skin and he closed his eyes and clenched his fists, after a few controlled deep breaths, he opened his eyes again, "I won't lie to you boys, what's happening to our planet is scaring the shit out of me."

His men looked away in embarrassment at their leader's choice language.

"Does this bother you? Me swearing? Not being a sergeant major type? Not commanding respect from you? Well sod that, those days are over, we haven't much time and I'm not going to lie to you, what lies beyond those doors and what we must do to protect and preserve our people is worrying and unnerving."

He gaped at the scene of the dead and rubbed the bridge of his nose due to extreme tiredness, "Anybody who doesn't want to enter these doors is free to turn around and venture back into the solar flares that are making our beloved planet crumble, they are welcome to take their chances with our brothers and sisters who have succumbed to that cruel rat virus that courses through their veins, now I don't believe any more than you do that you can truly turn the tide and hide from the sun or cure thousands of the infected, but you're welcome to try with my blessing."

He looked at his men and gave a half smile, "Was that a bit too dramatic?"

Mason, a new recruit in the squad, usually very quiet, turned for a reaction from his colleagues, when none came, a foolish grin slowly appeared on his face, "Just a little bit sir," he smiled.

"Thought as much."

The leader took out a parcel from his leather jacket and unravelled it, "You see this? This is from my wife: it's her homemade fairy cake. It's a bit big and is as hard as rocks, but I love it because she made it for me; it's a symbol of our love as she made some fairy cakes for me on our first picnic." He shook his head sorrowfully, "She isn't here with me now, so I'll take a bite to remind me of our love and when I've finished? I know all hope is lost."

He looked again at Mason after taking a small bite from the cake and put it back in his pocket, "Was that speech a bit mushy?"

"Pretty much, sir."

"Ok, we'll crack on, as I was saying, if you want to leave and not enter the science centre or temple or whatever it is, then off you go."

The leader walked through the remains of the infected and his men and to the back of the group, he made a 'parting motion' with his hands and the men moved with their backs towards the walls.

"Anybody?"

The man in charge made a face when one of his men politely put his hand up.

"Yes lad?"

The solider with intense blonde hair and a pattern of freckles on his face spoke up, "I'm afraid sir, I'm afraid and I don't want to go in there, I know we're fighting to preserve our people, but I'd rather take my chances back in my home town if it's all the same to you. My family is there, my friends are there and if these are to be the final days of Rayash, then I'd rather be with them." The solider hesitated, wondering how his boss would react.

"It's a dangerous world we find ourselves in, solider, are you really sure that this is what you want?"

Trembling slightly, the young solider struggled with his reply, "Yes please."

An uneasy quiet fell over the whole platoon and especially their leader, who shrugged his shoulders and asked for a towel from another soldier, who quickly passed it to the man in charge.

He buried his head in the towel and wiped away a face full of sweat, "Then you can go, I don't like the fact that you're leaving this crew, but never let it be said that I'll pressure any of my men to do something that they're not entirely happy with, so yes, you can go and do what you feel is right."

The freckled soldier waited a while during the awkward silence and then bolted, pushing hurriedly through his teammates.

As the soldier fled like a startled spider, a rifle fired from the group, the laser blast cut into the man's head; his legs kept running, but his head was missing. After what seemed an eternity, the body finally toppled over, his remains had splattered all over his former colleagues, bits of brain and nose were wiped away in disgust.

The leader reared back in shock as well as most of the platoon. He looked to see who had fired and saw the smoking rifle from another young recruit, his chest rose as he breathed heavily from shock.

"WHAT DID YOU DO?!" screamed the leader.

"I shot him, sir," was the earnest reply from the young assassin.

The leader threw his hands up in the air, exasperated, "WHY WOULD YOU DO THAT?"

"Because he was going to leave us, sir."

"I KNOW! BECAUSE I SAID HE COULD GO!"

Giving his leader a dour look, the youngster raised his little eyebrows, "But you said, 'You must do what you feel is right,' so I assumed that was code for 'If somebody wants to escape, shoot them.'"

"No, I said, 'You must do what you feel is right' because I meant, 'You must do what you feel is right.' I wasn't bullshitting the lad and you've just murdered one of your own comrades, I really could have done without this." His hands tightened a bit more.

Stay focused, he told himself. *They're losing it, you're losing it, you're in charge not them, guide them and free them.*

The leader released a humourless laugh and breathed out hard, "Fine, it's done now, I'm not going to kill you, we will lose many more lives until we are finally free."

The man's voice had changed, it went back to the clinical detached tone he started out with, "We haven't much time, so please be quiet and try not to kill anybody unless they're already dead." Realising his platoon's nervousness at the situation, he cut short his words, "Let's go gentlemen, we have a world to save." A sneeze stopped him from continuing as a soldier wiped his nose, "I think my hay fever has started sir."

Earth 65

Sully sat upright in her bed, the curtains were drawn, trying to keep out the daylight. She was surrounded by an assortment of cuddly toys, which had been her bedtime companions for years. Her mother used to tell her that she was 'too old' for stuffed toys and that she should get rid of them. Sully had always gone against her wishes with regards to her furry friends, either fishing them out of the rubbish bins after her mother had cleaned her room and thrown them out, or hiding them elsewhere in the house when her mother threatened to do it again.

It wasn't the fact that her mother was opposed to her family of stuffed zoo animals cluttering up her bed, it was the fact that she had instilled in her daughter to never get too attached to anything.

Everything was fine when Sully was a young girl, both her parents were fun-loving and had a completely relaxed attitude with her and the upbringing they gave her; they were schoolteachers and were good at their jobs.

Classical music concerts, museums, and art galleries were a constant in her childhood, as were her parents' smiles and laughter.

That was before the 'Game Show' and before Big Man; that was before all teachers, poets, artists, musicians, and comedians were chosen to be the next pawns in his devious, yet premature plans.

They were hunted down all over the giant capital city, Olympia, nobody could hide from Big Man's crooked police force.

It was teachers mostly who felt the full brunt of Big Man's wickedness, as he herded them all up like troublesome cattle to fight for their lives in the most horrific of ways for a poor taste in entertainment. Their schools were shut down and teachers fled.

That was when things changed for Sully. It was the morning her dad woke her up and coolly and calmly asked her to pack the bare essentials in the car, she had barely time to wipe the sleep from her eyes before they had hit the road.

Sully watched the town she grew up in whiz by in a sweet blur of colours, not knowing if she'd ever hear the sounds of her beautiful town again. Obviously she didn't think it was beautiful at the time, she thought it was full of self-indulgent idiots, but those were the views of a know-it-all teenage girl.

"Don't worry honey, you'll like this new place."

That's what her Dad told her, he told her to 'Buckle up and stay calm' as 'This place is cool'.

"Daddy, where are we going?" she recalled asking.

"A better place, a safer place."

At first Sully thought he genuinely meant it as her mother tenderly squeezed his lap in support as they drove away, as she sank back into her seat and twiddled with the eyes of her cuddly toy.

In time she had grown to hear those words often, words which eventually meant nothing after each time they were said. She had to duck and cover in the night and move away yet again from another town she was beginning to feel safe in.

Sully usually pressed her head forlornly against the window of the back seat of the car each time they moved away.

She watched the various brown leaves from the trees fall to the ground as she remembered they were green when she first arrived at each town.

Every town they passed through, Sully's parents tried to make idle chit-chat to her to take her mind off the new move.

"Look at that fox in the road sweetie, isn't he silly, Sully?" said her father.

"Silly Sully! That's a good one, honey," her mum chipped in with the useless humour.

Sully didn't answer, she wasn't speaking to either of them as once again she'd had to leave a new town she was just getting used to through the fault of her parents.

Every new friend she had met and grew close to, she had to blank out of her mind and forget them when her family went on the run Sully knew that she'd never see them again; it was becoming more and more difficult to start again.

After another move to a town she didn't really care about, Sully finally flipped. She tried to bite her lip and contain her anger but it was to no avail.

"YET AGAIN YOU'VE LET ME DOWN! EVERY TIME I FEEL SAFE, EVERY TIME I'VE FELT WANTED, YOU HAVE TO DRAG ME AWAY, ALL BECAUSE OF YOUR STUPID JOBS, JUST DO ME A FAVOUR AND STAY AWAY FROM ME!"

"I'm sorry, Sully," her father replied. His daughter made a gesture to him that he would never forget, "One day I hope you can forgive your mother and me."

Sully started to drift away in her headphones in what was to be her final trip in the back of the family car, she looked up and gave her father a false smile from the back seat.

"Drop dead, Dad."

Her father sighed heavily and carried on driving to their temporary home. Sully barely spoke to him afterwards, only just to put him down again. The insults that followed over the next few weeks made him long for memories of a young, kinder Sully, this new teenager was harder to bear.

Soon both he and his wife would settle down and find a job they'd hate just to get by, but they longed to teach; it was the only job they wanted to do and the job they always did well.

But they couldn't outrun Big Man's hatred for teachers and they were tired of running, tired of being scared and tired of being unable to trust anybody.

For one final move they returned to Heffernan City and settled into a district just outside of the city, just in time for Big Man's rage to finally catch up with them.

Sully returned home from yet another school she didn't really care about, but some of her new classmates she found to be slightly amusing. Her new friends and annoying school instantly left her mind as she walked up to the front door; it was ajar.

Her parents never left the door open, even before they were hounded by Big Man's cronies, safety was always a concern.

Sully felt a creeping sensation of fear as she entered her home.

"Hello? Mum? Dad? You there?"

Her skin prickled as she walked further into the house, the furniture in the living room had been overturned and broken table lamps were strewn all over the floor. The signs of a violent struggle were evident all around the house as, room by room, Sully's face grew white and paler, "Is there anybody in here?" Each passing moment of silence made her face become blank and devoid of emotion. Sully slowly cleared her throat as her eyes wandered, "Please answer me?" She drew a long hard breath as the silence continued.

The small bungalow had been completely turned over and Sully walked back into her parents' bedroom just to make sure she hadn't missed anything.

Pulling back the closed curtains, her knees buckled at what she saw on her parents' window.

Sprawled out in big letters was a message. Sweating now and breathing hard, Sully walked over and gently touched the writing on the gleaming window. It was blood, dried blood now as the evening sun had done its job well:

WE'VE HELPED OURSELVES TO SOME
TEA AND BISCUITS
AND TAKEN YOUR PARENTS
CHEERS FOR THE CUSTARD CREAMS.

"NOOOOOOOO!!!!" Sully screamed a massive cry of terror as she read the words. Spinning around she pounded her ringed fists against the wall, "YOU BASTARDS! GIVE ME BACK MY PARENTS!"

The sad teenager sank to her knees as the tears she held back for so long finally appeared, "MUM, DAD, PLEASE COME BACK," she cried. "I need to see you." Sully whispered.

But she never did, her parents were taken along with many other teachers around the city to Gommerstall Prison.

Six years later and Sully remained at the house, which had become derelict and run down and was ignored by the proper authorities. She had stayed there oblivious to the teaching association who thought her parents were still living at the address.

As the years went by she forged documents and dodged various parents' evenings, only to return home to an empty house every day, nobody—except her aunties and uncles—knew her parents were missing.

Her cousin Enya talked about trying to get a job in Big Man's complex to see if she could get some information on where Sully's parents were. The whole country tuned in to see the great prison escape from Gommerstall Prison but when the ship crashed, not even Big Man knew what happened to the escaped convicts.

Apart from her family, the only thing that kept Sully sane was the friends she had met in the school she'd hated.

Some of them were rich, others lost teacher parents to Big Man's regime too. Things had turned bleaker than they should have and the school was suffering with most of the teachers missing.

Her new friends kept her spirits up and made her feel slightly alive again, but the one thing that kept their mind off their missing parents was the thought of going on the new zoo ship, *Utopia*.

Its first major voyage was to hover above the earth's atmosphere with some college kids on board to observe the effect the floating space ship would have on the animals.

It would be an expensive trip and the kids without parents had to find other means to fund their trip.

So they entertained commuters on the various networks of trains below the cities of Heffernan, Olympia and other districts.

Through acting and songs they managed to raise enough money to book themselves on the spaceship, the college would leave tomorrow morning. That was before her condition.

She had been suffering flu-like symptoms for a few hours now. She slumped back down and rolled over to check the time on her clock. Everything seemed to stand still since the group got back from the underground. Sully had felt ill and restless and was burning up from a quick fever, she had a tightness in her chest and groaned uneasily in pain.

Sully unsteadily rose to her feet and made her way to her bedroom window. Screams erupting from the back garden drew her closer to the glass. Her fingers were shaking as she drew back her curtains which reminded her of the time she saw the message of her parents' disappearance years ago.

Even from her viewpoint she could see a tall, smart-clothed man drenched in sweat and shivering uncontrollably, his skin was cracked and bloody. The man had a teenage boy in his arms and was pounding his fists repeatedly in the young boy's face, the only emotion coming from the older man's face was pure rage and nothing else.

Sully looked once again at the suited man smashing the teenage boy's face to a pulp and turned away from her bedroom window, she didn't want to respond. She sat silently on her bed and looked around her bedroom walls, her house had been too silent since her parents had been taken.

Sully was ill and getting worse, she had no idea how and no idea why, but she could feel her own rage inside starting to build. Outside her window, more and more people with strange sudden outbursts of rage gathered around the fallen boy and joined in the savage beating.

She pulled forward on her bed and reached out and picked up one of her precious stuffed toys, visibly shaking at the sight of it. She tore the head off her beloved stuffed friend, and in a frenzy of blurred motion and anger she destroyed all of her stuffed toys without a second thought.

People with uncontrollable fits of rage were roaming outside Sully's window and unbeknownst to the poor, sick girl, she was ready to join them.

Chapter Two:

Blood Sweat And Fears

Rayash

Tobin fiddled frantically at the controls and another hologram shone around the room.

Tashar struggled to rise from her birthing chamber, but managed to show her concern.

"How is my baby? What are her signs?"

Tobin wiped her sweaty hands on her skirt and glanced back at the worried Tashar.

"The signs are through the roof!"

Bailey struck her a hard look, "Sorry Tashar, I meant the results are phenomenal."

Still wiping her hands, Tobin pressed on, her fellow midwife Silo played with her blue hair as she watched Tobin fiddle with the holographic panel, "Your baby is a teleporter and according to the scales she is a class 100."

Tashar was crying, the tears sparkled in her eyes and then began to slowly make their way down her cheeks. She composed herself and glanced around her birthing chamber in an uncertain manner.

"Class 100? That cannot be?"

Tobin nodded her head excitedly, "SHE IS! FOR GOD'S SAKE, SHE IS THE ONE!"

"Calm yourself, Tobin," snapped Bailey.

"NO, I CAN'T!" Tobin said in frustration.

"Tashar, your daughter is a class 100 teleporter, no one has ever seen the likes of a being that powerful. She has the potential to be able to teleport this whole city, this whole country away from the sun's flares, SHE CAN SAVE US!"

Silo kept playing with her hair as she answered.

"She's a baby, how can she teleport us? She doesn't even know what day it is?"

Tobin complied with an answer right away, "This baby potentially has the ability to teleport this whole planet to another galaxy. We find an uninhabited planet, with a breathable atmosphere and let the baby take us there. She can save us, she can save everybody."

Bailey sighed and looked to her young companion Silo, as the blue-haired youngster shook her head in dismay, "So you want a newborn baby to teleport eight billion people and possibly all our planet's architecture to a new planet? All at once?"

"Yes," Tobin nodded with force.

"So what will happen to the baby after it teleports the whole planet away?"

Tobin felt increasingly nervous from Silo's questions, she looked up and shook her head to silence her, "The strain will probably kill her."

"ARE YOU OUT OF YOUR MIND?!" roared Kozak, "YOU WANT ME TO SACRIFICE MY DAUGHTER? MY NEWBORN BABY? FOR THE SAKE OF YOU, TOBIN!"

"IT'S NOT JUST ME, KOZAK, IT'S YOUR PEOPLE, YOUR KIN, YOU CAN DO THE RIGHT THING AND SAVE OUR WORLD!"

"AT THE RISK OF KILLING MY BABY?"

Tobin was not regretting what she'd said and carried on, trying to calm him down.

"This is bigger than you now, Kozak, it's about sacrificing your only child for the sake of a saving a whole race of people, *your* people, one child for a billion."

Kozak hesitated for a reply, but his wife beat him to it.

"DROP DEAD, TOBIN!" screamed Tashar.

The new mother had managed to get herself out from her birthing chamber and stood trembling at the foot of the bed.

"IF YOU DARE COME NEAR MY BABY, I'LL DROP YOU WHERE YOU STAND."

The anger returned to Tobin and her teeth rattled, "DON'T YOU GET IT, TASHAR? OUR PLANET IS DYING, OUR PEOPLE ARE DYING. IF IT'S NOT JUST WITH THE SUN'S SOLAR FLARES, IT'S WITH THIS DISGUSTING RAT VIRUS, SO WE'RE DEAD EITHER WAY UNLESS WE USE YOUR DAUGHTER."

Kozak turned away, the look he gave his wife was that he was now determined to leave.

"Silo is a teleporter, she can teleport us out of here from harm's way."

Tobin threw her arms up in desperation, "Silo is only a class 20 Vanisher, she can only teleport a few miles away. We can't escape our planet's death."

Silo recognised the sharp tone in her friend's voice and nodded, "She's right, I can only teleport a few miles away, not too good in our situation."

Tobin nodded, quite pleased with herself and ran to Silo and grabbed her with both arms, "SO YOU AGREE WITH ME? WE MUST TAKE THIS BABY AND MAKE HER TELEPORT US AWAY?"

Silo pulled back and grimaced, "Dude, at the end of the day, which seems like right now, I'm a midwife, you're a midwife, our job is to take care of the baby and mother and keep them safe to the best of our abilities."

"What?" Tobin spat angrily, trying hard to concentrate, "You would happily die, for the sake of your job?

Silo had begun to feel increasingly uneasy in Tobin's presence, but she simply yawned and stretched her arms out, "The baby comes first, no matter what, my cousin."

Her boss, Bailey, gave a slight proud smile. Tobin's once sweet face turned into a hideous scowl, "Then you have dammed us all, who do you think will save us? *You* Bailey? A sad old sorceress or your stupid midwife apprentice Silo who can only teleport a few miles? You're all PATHETIC!"

Kozak slowly made his way to his wife. He was now holding his baby and beckoned to Bailey and Silo as the pretty young Tobin grew more unstable.

"SO WHERE ARE WE GOING TO GO, KOZAK? YOU'RE THE LEADER OF THE SCIENCE COUNCIL, SO WHAT DO WE DO?"

Bailey looked around the room cautiously at the possible escape routes and tried to calm down her young student, "Listen Tobin, I don't know what's come over you, I don't know why you're saying such things, but please just relax and join us."

Tobin's cute face had been flushed out with anger, but she kept her growing rage in check to grunt an answer.

"Where?"

Tashar groaned as she shifted to her side on her bed. Kozak put the baby back into the incubator and held his wife's hand.

"There is an escape shuttle underneath this building, I designed it, well modified it from an old mining ship, it's a crude design but…"

Tashar squeezed her husband's hand, urging him to carry on and save the ramblings for another time.

"We're going to fly to the planet of Lodi, there's a settlement there, a secret one, many of my fellow scientists have fled there. We hid our plans from the generals as I knew they would never have accepted this." Kozak wiped his brow and continued, "The midwives are coming with us, they're our friends, as are you Tobin, come with us, join us, I can't promise you safety but we will try, I assure you."

Tobin glared at him before she responded, "Take us with you."

Kozak smiled, thinking that he'd finally won over Tobin's stubbornness, "We were never going to leave you, of course you can come."

Tobin spoke through gritted teeth, "I meant take the *whole* planet with you."

"You know we can't do that, Tobin, the strain would kill my child. We discussed this."

Tobin held her glare, then backed away to the front of the room, "Then I'm afraid I can't let you leave, not just yet."

Her voice had gradually turned old and gritty, betraying her tender years. She reached into her apron pocket and pulled out a mini communicator, keeping her eyes on the people at the back of the room, she spoke softly into the device, "I think you'd better come in now."

Bailey raised a tired eyebrow suspiciously, "What have you done, Tobin?"

Tobin continued to back away until the steel door stopped her. She shook her head forlornly.

"I am sorry."

Bailey cocked her head, "WHAT HAVE YOU DONE?"

"I'm securing our people's future."

The young girl turned around and pressed the release button on the door behind her.

The huge steel doors slid open to reveal the soldiers and their leader at the front.

General Orion paused before looking everywhere around the room. He bent down and kissed Tobin on the cheek.

"Good girl, you've done well."

Bailey wasn't impressed, "So this was the 'family problems' you spoke of, Tobin?"

"Don't be hard on her," Orion's smile wavered slightly, "She was only trying to save her race."

The rest of the men followed Orion as he stepped purposely forward, "Thanks to Tobin bugging this establishment I know how powerful the child is and what she can do."

Kozak still clutched Tashar's hand as Bailey and Silo provided protection from the front. Orion scratched his earlobe gently, "It just leaves me to say congratulations to you, Kozak, my old friend, my heart warms as I know you and Tashar have always wanted a child." He finished on his ear and gave Kozak a cutting look, "So if you don't mind, we'll be taking the baby and be on our way."

Earth 65

Before last night, Sully was looking forward to the college trip, getting away and seeing the amazing animals in a gigantic floating zoo, something to take her mind off the loss of her parents. But something happened between the final night at the underground tube station and this new day.

She had an anger burning inside of her, which made the simple fact of making her bed more of a begrudging pain. She looked at the scattered, torn up bodies of her stuffed toys. Turning away again, Sully stuffed some clothes into a small overnight bag, hurriedly scooping up more useless items; her anger had slowly surpassed for the moment.

Sully used to come downstairs to the breakfast her parents had made. Nobody would call the smell of scrambled eggs and bacon beautiful, but the way her dad cooked them was tremendous; a smell and taste she longed to have again.

Sitting in the kitchen, she drank some tea from her father's favourite mug. Breathing hard, she put down the mug and wiped the trails of tea from her mouth and chin.

As the rest dribbled onto her lap, she brushed it off and sighed heavily. Grabbing her bag, Sully made her way to the front door.

She stopped suddenly as she saw the door handle wriggle and shake. Sully tensed and dropped her bag, anticipating either an attack from the creeps outside or her parents. Then the door opened and a figure with a crisp and clean white outfit entered. Before the man could even speak, his head bounced back against the hallway wall, as Sully shoved him hard against it. The man tried to break free from Sully's grasp, but her nails dug deep into his skin, his pitiful struggles increased.

To silence the man, Sully simply released him. His body hung forward and with speed and savagery, she back-handed him and his head rocked against the wall again.

"WHO ARE YOU?" she screamed.

She glared when no reply came from the battered man, puffing out her chest she tried again, "WHAT HAVE YOU DONE WITH MY PARENTS?!" Their noses almost touched and Sully hissed, "Answer me now!"

The man's sorry eyes looked up and he grumbled, "Milk."

"WHAT?" Sully barked.

"I'm the milkman."

Sully chewed her bottom lip suspiciously, "You're who?"

The man, still dazed, opened his eyes and spluttered some more, "There's some strange looking people wandering around on the streets this morning, I thought I'd better knock to give you your milk as they might steal it."

Sully stood back and adjusted the man's crumpled collar, "You startled me, I'm sorry." She tried to smile, he could not and swayed badly.

"You've got some serious problems, lady."

The act of staying on his feet was becoming a struggle for the milkman, and Sully, with a touch of guilt, tried to keep him steady.

"Do you make an habit of breaking and entering people's houses?"

He finally laughed, a gravely throaty sound, "Do you make a habit of beating people up who do?"

"Wouldn't you if it was your house?"

Sully's answer made him think as they finally made full eye contact, "Good point."

The milkman painfully shifted his position and handed Sully a pint of orange juice and milk, before slowly heading out the front door, rubbing his head as he left, "Be careful out there," he said.

A reluctant Sully flashed acknowledgement and struggled to raise a smile, "You too, if you don't get attacked by odd bods whilst trying to deliver my milk."

Out the corner of his eye the milkman saw something that made him slowly, dolefully shake his head and start to quicken his step.

"Take care," came his eventual response.

With the two bottles in her hands, Sully closed the front door with her foot and headed towards her kitchen fridge.

The milkman rolled his head around until he heard it give a satisfying click.

He knew this customer was a rude and arrogant girl and so he kept his quick pace up and made his way up the road. Whatever the milkman saw at a swift earlier glance, was almost upon him. He fearfully looked behind him and shuffled down an alleyway, before a large shape leapt onto his back and sent him crashing to the floor.

More shapes appeared from out of nowhere. Men, women and children joined the melee on the back of the milkman. They were bloodied and horribly disfigured, bloodshot eyes wide, enjoying the fascination of fear from their next victim. They extended their grotesque, torn hands into the body of the crying milkman.

Slashing and biting away at the poor man's back, they began to tear him limb from limb. The milkman screamed at first, but as his arms were torn from his sockets, he could only offer a muted cry of despair.

When the creatures had finished feeding on him, they tossed away body parts like a spoilt child with unwanted gifts on their birthday.

Sully reappeared soon afterwards with her bag over her shoulder and slammed the front door shut, walking into the soft shine of morning sunlight gleaming off the neighbourhood cars.

As she set off to college to meet up with her friends and board the waiting spaceship, Sully threw a cautious look behind to see if she had truly shut her front door. Her gaze concentrated on her house for a while. Once satisfied, she walked up the road past the alleyway, unaware as the new blood-hungry creatures picked off what skin was left from the milkman's bones.

Rayash

"You're not taking my daughter, Orion."

Kozak had a comfortable glare aimed at the general, "I didn't know the subject was up for discussion, my old friend. Your daughter can potentially save the existence of your race, so she'll be safe with me and my troops, end of."

"I'm going to have to pass on that, giving my firstborn daughter up to a power hungry nut is not an option."

Orion's eyes focused hard on the young midwife Silo as she moved slowly towards the baby.

He shook his head in sorrow when he noticed her movements.

"I'm sorry it's come to this, Kozak, but you leave me with no choice; the sake of our very existence is in your daughter's tiny hands, our very existence shall be sorted by..." Orion paused slightly, "I've already said that haven't I? The whole 'existence speech'."

Kozak nodded, "You have always been quite predictable, Orion."

"When it's my people at stake, I guess I am." Orion raised his eyebrows, "Why are you killing your race? Our planet is doomed so at least save those who walked on it with pride."

Kozak's mind was flushed with anxiety, but tried to remain calm, "My daughter is my priority now, so if you don't mind we'll be taking our seats in this shuttle and my family and friends will be flying away from this, and away from you and your silly army."

Orion kept his eyebrows high and concentrated on the young midwife, "Silo isn't it? Midwife and a circus freak, can you stand away from the baby please? Both you and Bailey if you don't mind?"

Bailey closed ranks around the baby unit, holding hands with Silo. Tobin walked up to the sleeping baby unit and looked at her: "A creature so beautiful, yet so powerful, this child could be the beginning of our future. Please listen to Orion, he means to save us all."

Tobin turned to Bailey and offered her hand. Bailey shooed it away, "You've made your choice, young lady," she said coldly.

Tobin angrily brushed the two women aside and ran towards Orion.

Kozak closed his eyes and yelled, "NOW!"

Bailey put her hands in the air and wriggled her wrists.

A flash of magical bright light came from her palms, blinding the soldiers. The armed men staggered and rubbed their eyes, in the confusion Kozak shouted again, "GET TO THE SHUTTLE!" He ushered the midwives towards him. A scream came from the middle of the men.

"OPEN FIRE!"

The soldiers raised their rifles in panic and pulled hard on the triggers. Laser fire erupted around the complex. They cut down Tobin who was caught in the middle, her body came apart like a cheaply constructed child's toy, her lower jaw fell to the floor, followed by her head, her eyes forever preserved in terror.

"NO!" Silo and Bailey screamed together.

"WHO'S FIRING?!" Orion yelled.

The blasts from the soldiers' weapons zipped above the heads of the midwives:

"Ok, two can play." Bailey muttered.

With her hands still glowing white the sorceress Bailey shook them hard again and they changed from white to blue. She uttered something under her breath and threw her hands towards the armed soldiers.

Blue streams of energy shot out from her palms and slammed into the chests of the soldiers, knocking them down on impact and rendering them unconscious.

"GET MY BABY AND WIFE OUT OF HERE, SILO!" Kozak screamed.

"WHAT ABOUT YOU?"

Kozak threw a baleful look at the army of young soldiers, trying to harm his family.

"I'M TAKING THESE BASTARDS DOWN."

He felt his hands against the wall and slammed his fist hard on to a tiny hatch.

It flipped open to reveal a hidden compartment, which contained two laser pistols.

There was an unquestionable confidence in the way he took one out and started firing back at the men.

He picked his targets carefully, picking off the army one by one. Bailey was using her mystical powers to stun her opponents, the midwife in her was not ready to take a life just yet. Kozak had no such issues, these men were threatening his family, his friends; the scientist in him was long gone, this was war.

"CEASE FIRE!" Orion still yelled, but his men ignored him in the fire fight, trying to stop the scientist from killing them.

Silo bounced from wall to wall with her heightened agility, avoiding the laser blasts.

She reached a couple of the soldiers firing the most frantically and held on to their flak jackets tightly and then she vanished with them. Silo appeared again in an instant, shrouded in black smoke around her, mid-air, outside the complex.

All three were hurtling towards the ground at a tremendous rate as the men screamed.

Silo calmly spoke to the men still clutched in her grasp, "Can you hear that sound, babes?"

"WHAT SOUND?" the smallest man spat with fear.

"That's the sound of me leaving you."

Silo disappeared again reappearing inside the complex next to Kozak, as the two soldiers fell through her blue signature teleportation smoke and landed hard on to the ground; if the men were to survive the planet's destruction, they would have to do so with a few broken bones. Kozak looked to her, "GET TASHAR AND THE BABY INTO THE ROCKET, BAILEY AND I WILL HOLD THEM OFF."

"WHAT ABOUT YOU?" Silo shouted back, her words aimed more at her mentor Bailey than Kozak.

"DON'T WORRY ABOUT US."

Bailey gave a stern but reassuring nod to her young ward as Kozak continued, "JUST MAKE SURE THE CHILD IS STRAPPED IN AND SECURE."

"BEEN THERE AND DONE THAT," was the reply, but it wasn't Silo.

Another laser beam struck a solider right between the eyes as the group looked to see who had fired the shot.

Tashar staggered up close to her husband with the other pistol in her shaking hands, "They will not take my baby while I have an inch of fight in my body."

Kozak slowly lowered his weapon and tenderly stroked his wife's head. Bailey upped the firepower from her hands as it was only her now on the defensive.

"Please my love, get into the ship, I'll be along as soon as Bailey, Silo and I take care of these idiots."

Tashar gave a gentle frown, "At least you're a better shot than you are a liar, I know you too well my love, as soon you retaliated with the girls, you had no intention of making it."

Kozak grimaced a smile, trying to cut out the cries of Orion still screaming at his men to stop.

"Tashar please get to the shuttle, make a new life with our baby with the other settlers. Rayash is dead, you have a chance to get away."

Tashar shook her head violently and her beautiful face was etched with anger and quick disappointment.

"No, no, no! How could you think for one moment I could ever leave you?"

She stopped in mid-sentence to fire off a few more rounds from her gun and then turned back to Kozak, "Whatever you do, wherever you go, I will always love you."

Kozak watched again in awe as his brilliant wife stopped talking to take down some more soldiers with her expert marksmanship. She spoke as she fired again:

"You're the fantastic man who gave me my family, you're the cleverest man who told us all that our planet is dying, you're the brilliant man who I gave my heart to and I will—"

A flash of laser fire came between them, which made Tashar's body shudder. She fluttered her eyelids and looked down to the hole where her stomach had been, "Wow! Would you look at that?" she said in amazement, she died next.

Kozak tried to catch his wife as she collapsed to the ground. His mouth was agape and he stared at her in shock, shaking her body gently with hope that she was still alive. Bailey looked behind her, her head trembling with sadness as she saw Tashar's limp body.

Kozak's beautiful wife had a gaze transfixed on something else, a gaze Kozak looked painfully at, trying desperately hard to understand why. He carefully closed her eyelids; they would never open again. His own eyes began to fill with tears as he dragged her body out of the line of fire.

Orion witnessed the death of Tashar and finally got his men to cease firing. The sight of a new mother's death was probably the only way these trained, scared men would stop shooting. Orion shook his head mournfully, "I didn't mean for this to happen my friend, I'm so sorry, please forgive me." The leader of the soldiers dropped his rifle and slowly walked forward, with his hands held in surrender, "This wasn't meant to happen."

"But it did," growled Kozak. He stood upright after tending to his dead wife, and reached over and picked up

Tashar's laser pistol. He looked directly into the eyes of Bailey and Silo.

"Take my little girl, take my darling baby and you make her safe, you get her away from here and you keep her safe and tell her about me, tell her about her mother and tell her she was loved, tell her she will always be loved."

Silo kept a tearful gaze on Kozak, "What are you going to do?" she asked between sniffs.

Kozak carefully pulled Bailey and Silo closer to him and kissed them both tenderly on their foreheads, hands still clenching the weapons, "I'm going to end this."

Pulse racing and a forehead dripping with sweat, Kozak roared like an unleashed caged animal and began firing with both pistols at the gathered army. Orion and his men ducked for cover as Kozak ran at them like a man possessed. He managed to take more soldiers down in a blind rage than he did when he'd picked his targets off carefully earlier.

Orion could only afford a glance of pure horror and disbelief as his men concentrated their fires on Kozak and finally cut him down in a fury of laser fire as he stepped out from the shadows.

"NOOO DON'T!!"

Orion's cries came too late as he saw his best friend and his best enemy fall into a crumpled heap, his body riddled with holes. Silo's face had changed from fear to pure anger, her blue eyes blazed inhumanly. Furious, she stormed towards the baby in her ship. Bailey grabbed her arm and Silo spun round to face her, "WHAT NOW?! HAVE YOU SEEN WHAT THEY'VE DONE?"

The head midwife looked at Orion cradling the body of Kozak and then back to her young apprentice, her own anger beginning to swell inside.

"Take the child," Bailey said slowly.

"Promise me that you will make it to the ship and do whatever you can."

Silo tried to laugh, a nervous giggle escaped, "I'm a midwife, not a pilot; Kozak was going to fly the ship."

"Well I think he has other things on his mind, dying being one of them."

Silo was shocked by Bailey's observation, "Get it started, get it in the air and I'll meet you at the front of the complex."

"That's quite an ask," Silo said.

"You've done better," Bailey replied half-heartedly.

"Listen, I will lead them away from you and it may take a moment, but I'll get to you, so long as I'm alive, just wait like I said."

Silo's eyes widened in surprise and then squinted quickly as she spoke, "So don't die then."

Bailey swung another quick look to Orion and Kozak, "I don't intend to, not yet anyway."

A hideous groan came from Kozak as Bailey kept her stare, "Go now Silo, take the baby and run." Silo's heart hammered, "What are you going to do?"

Bailey replied through gritted teeth, "Finish this." Bailey's palms glowed blue again and in an intense fury unleashed a volley of plasma balls at the remaining men. She wasn't gentle with them this time as her mystic energies cut right through them.

Silo turned away and in an instant disappeared.

Orion cradled the severely wounded Kozak, "It didn't have to be like this, my friend," Orion whispered.

Kozak coughed up blood over Orion's jacket and gently smiled, "Yes it did, we both knew this was always going to happen."

"I'm going to have to find your daughter my friend, she's the only one who can save this planet."

Kozak tried to haul himself up using Orion's collar, "I know you will find her, but she will save you Orion, she will save you from yourself."

The smile stayed on his face, the last expression that came from him. Orion lowered his dead friend's head to the ground and turned towards Bailey, who was cutting down his troops. Aware that he was running out of options, he shouted at the woman, "BAILEY!"

His voice carried authority, but unlike before, everybody stopped, his men and Bailey listened.

"I KNOW YOUR ROLE IS TO PROTECT THAT BABY AND THAT IS HONOURABLE, BUT I'M GOING TO STOP THAT SHIP AND SAVE OUR PLANET."

Bailey yawned like a bored housecat, "You know what? I'm actually quite bored of that line now, it's all I've heard ever since you came here, can't you waffle on about something else for a change? Maybe like how the price of milk has gone up or how music sounded much better in your day."

Bailey saw in the corner of her eye Silo re-appear into the shuttle cockpit, the baby was already strapped in safely. She saw Silo desperately struggling with the controls and tried to stall Orion some more.

"I mean most people have a 'to do' list when they start the day, do you have a moan list which you tick off after each miserable act you do?"

Orion shouted, "MUSIC WAS BETTER IN MY DAY AND—" His face was like a spoilt child throwing a tantrum, when he suddenly stopped and snorted with derisive laughter, "Oh ok, I see what you're doing, trying to keep me talking, eh?"

A tremendous roar of jet engines boomed around the complex, as the escape shuttle steadily rose into the air.

The shuttle shuddered forward and skimmed the heads of the troops, who then ducked for cover as a terrified Silo punched every button on the control panel.

"Clever girl," Orion's expression showed that he was quite impressed.

Silo was struggling even more as the plane continued to surge forward. Bailey watched as the shuttle soared above her. She arched her back and made a terrific leap for the bottom of the craft. Her jump was perfect and she clung on desperately, aided by a mystic touch.

Orion watched as the shuttle crashed through the fortress, wincing at the sound of metal scraping against metal. The ship gained altitude as Bailey clung on desperately to the underside.

"MASON!" Orion roared, "Get the rocket launchers ready."

Mason rallied the remaining troops to hold their giant firearms high, "Ready sir," he replied to his boss.

Orion's body arched forward, looking at the gigantic hole in the building caused by the escaping shuttle, eyes gleaming, he spoke softly to Mason.

"Take out the ship's thrusters, don't destroy the ship, it still has the child on board and don't hit Bailey."

"Why not sir?"

"Just don't."

Orion paused and flicked his tongue on his bottom teeth, "Let them know we really mean business."

The troops struggled with the heavy weapons on their shoulders, but they concentrated just for a moment and pressed hard on their triggers, releasing the rockets.

The rockets spat out from the launchers and slithered into the sky to find their target.

Concentrating with all her might and a little help from her magic, Bailey held on to the ship with one hand and swung from underneath the plane. She released her trademark pulse beams from her remaining hand and shot down some of the trailing missiles, but one missile evaded her beams.

Inside the cockpit, Silo could only watch in horror as the beeps from the radar got louder as the final missile honed in on its target. Bailey struggled to look behind her hanging with one hand, but she could hear the missile coming closer. She needed a decent vantage point to destroy it, but would have to use her other hand to do so, "Shit," she mouthed silently.

Releasing only a little scream Bailey let go of the shuttle and tumbled down towards the ground, she quickly tried to stabilise herself and concentrate on the missile, putting her left hand around her right, making a 'gun' and released her beams, destroying the missile instantly. Bailey felt an uneasy sense of satisfaction as she plummeted. The shuttle wobbled away higher into the sky, making its escape with a panic-stricken Silo at the controls, trying to save the baby.

Laughing hysterically as the ground approached, Bailey wasn't sure if her sorceress powers would protect her from the fall, but as gravity had a firm grip on her, she was about to find out.

"This is going to hurt," she whispered after her laughing fit, "I'll find you," were her next words as the ship disappeared from sight.

Orion's eyes had long adapted to the darkness, but even he had to squint as he saw Bailey crash into the ground some distance away from him.

Orion gave Mason a stern look, "YOU FIND HER! MAKE SURE SHE'S ALIVE, SHE KNOWS WHERE THAT SHUTTLE IS GOING, SHE KNOWS HOW TO FIND THAT BABY!"

He then began frantically pointing to the dead body of Kozak, "YOU BURY THAT MAN AND HIS WIFE, GIVE THEM FULL HONOURS THEY DESERVE."

The solar flares that rained down on the planet had stopped briefly and Orion knew this had given him some time.

"Can I have the binoculars please?" he asked a private standing close by.

Holding them up high, Orion saw a faint rocket trail from the ship as it finally disappeared, "Thank you," he said softly handing them back to his soldier, "Mason, track the trajectory of that shuttle and get our own craft ready."

Orion's eyes grew despondent as he turned to what little men he had left, "WE ARE GOING TO TRY AND FOLLOW THAT SHUTTLE WITH THAT BABY ON BOARD, IT'S THE ONLY WAY WE CAN SAVE OUT PLANET,

WE WILL BE GONE FOR A VERY LONG TIME, SO SAY GOODBYE TO YOUR LOVED ONES BY SCREEN OR PHONE, ANYBODY WHO DOESN'T WANT TO COME CAN STAY HERE AND DIE."

Mason put his hand on Orion's shoulder as his commander continued, "WHO'S WITH ME?" The air was filled with a triumphant roar of approval from his men, "Good, find Bailey, gear up and man up, this is going to take a long time."

Silo was fighting hard to take full control of the shuttle, she wanted to teleport to check on the baby, but she had never done it in a vessel travelling at such a speed and wondered if she would vanish outside of the shuttle.

The baby was crying and that was at least a cold comfort for Silo. All she wanted to do was find the auto pilot button, so pushing every button in view was still her only option. Suddenly in an abnormal fashion the shuttle manoeuvred abruptly and fell into a flat spin. The ship jerked back and forth throwing Silo against each side of the cockpit. She wasn't strapped in but didn't have time to curse her mistake. Alarms were sounding and the control board was flashing like a set of party lights for a rave.

The engines wailed and spluttered but they continued to work with some sort of defiance. She didn't take her eyes off the panel and every muscle in her arms tensed as she tried to pull hard on the control wheel from her position on the floor to see if it would stop the ship's jerks.

It seemed it would take a minor miracle to halt the shuttle's bizarre new flight plan, but another worry came crashing into her mind. The only sound she could hear was the ship's chaotic engines, there was nothing from the baby. Silo's heart skipped a beat and she looked quizzically down the shuttle's corridor. *I can't teleport, I can't do it, I might die,* she thought. Her small nostrils twitched and she hesitated again. *No, not this time.*

Not willing to take the chance on possibly teleporting outside of the ship, Silo bolted down the slim corridor of the shuttle to reach the baby.

The youngest child of Rayash slowly twisted around in her incubator, her eyes fixed onto the concerned face of Silo. The baby cooed, which was strange for a newborn.

She attempted to move her hands and that's when Silo noticed a multihued glow appear from them. The colours swirled around the body of the baby and she smiled and waved her hands trying to grab them as they began to dance around her. Bright colours snaked their way further down the baby, who was oblivious to it all.

Swallowing hard, Silo watched as the baby managed to create more coloured lights around her, which completely covered the child. She wriggled her legs and then disappeared. Silo shifted her stance and rolled her eyes.

"Ohhh-kaayy."

Her eyes focused on the spot where the baby once lay. *That wasn't supposed to happen,* she thought. Frantically searching through the incubator, Silo spun round with a sharp quickness, "BABY! BABY WHERE ARE YOU?" *Stupid, it's a baby, she can't talk.*

Silo's chest tightened with fear as the realisation that the baby was gone began to sink in. *She teleported, ok, what do I do now?* Silo's face swept from panic to confusion.

As the ship slowly steadied itself, she ran back to the main control panel and quickly familiarised herself with it. Her fingers slid slightly over the surface bringing up a holographic image of all the planets in the sector. Hundreds appeared on countless monitors around her and Silo knew the baby could be on any one of them. Her brow furrowed. *Why should I care about this baby? She's not mine. Bailey is probably dead, Rayash is in flames, why should I try to find her? I should just leave and find a new life.*

But Silo knew she couldn't do this, she was assigned to protect the baby by her mentor, Bailey, and she would not let her down, alive or not. Silo thought hard and made a chewing motion as if she had tobacco in her mouth. She banged her fists hard on to the control panel hoping for a reaction and was surprised when the computer spoke to her.

"Voice authorization activated, proceed when ready."

Excited, Silo spoke quickly into the computer, "Computer, latch onto projectile leaving shuttle."

"Unable to compute," was the reply from the panel.

Silo gave an indulgent look to the computer and tried again, "Computer, locate the baby who left this ship."

"Unable to compute."

Tilting back her head, Silo stared at the ship's roof, "Computer, just piss off!"

"Unable to piss off."

Silo scoffed at the computer and shook her head. The baby somehow had teleported to a unknown planet and Silo had to find her, but it was probably going to take years, many years, she swallowed hard and licked her lips.

There was no spit left in her mouth, "Computer, are you able to fly this ship?"

"Unable to compute."

"Ok, let's try something else, computer engage secondary auto pilot capabilities."

"Status-searching- autopilot capabilities online."

The computer's ability to finally co-operate knocked the wind out of Silo and she slumped back into her chair.

"Computer, please scan and review the probabilities of sentient life forms on all planets in this sector."

"*Status-searching-searching-searching-search incomplete-searching-searching-searching.*"

Silo replied with a groan, "I need some sleep."

CHAPTER THREE:

The Animals Went In Two By Two

Earth 65 – Typhon Space Cruiser
Utopia Class
Animal Loading Bay

"HURRY UP WILL YA! YOU'RE AS SLOW AS TURTLE SHIT TODAY!"

An old man heard the shout from his younger colleague and tried to move faster, hurting his back in the process. The young man had a slightly guilty look on his face when he saw the older man rub his back in pain. He held back for a moment and then spoke, "You ok, man?"

"Yeah, just really getting too old for all this shit, a man my age humping around these cages."

The young man stretched his unhurt back and yawned, "Do you know how much money we're getting paid for this, Larry?"

Larry was a man in his late fifties with a large stomach, which his vest was desperately clinging onto, and a big hooked nose. He shrugged his shoulders; his workmate, Dickson, was considerably younger and fitter.

"We're getting *a lot* of money for this because it's the first of its kind, nobody has ever done this before and I'm proud to take part."

"Proud? Really? You're loading animals, exotic they may be, but it's still lugging cages filled with smelly animals on to a stupid ship."

Dickson blinked and pushed a creature into its cage with a little bit more force than was necessary.

"Look at this ship, Larry, it's beautiful."

Pulling his vest over his exposed stomach, Larry took a step back to fully take in the impressive sight of the Typhon ship, the *Utopia* was a new ship in its range with new dreams and beginnings.

There was a mass of activity from construction workers walking high atop scaffolds still attached to the ship, making final preparations.

Soon the scaffolds would be dropped and the ship would be able to take off for its maiden voyage in space.

The crew were making their way on board, carrying or dragging suitcases towards their temporary accommodation, which would serve as home for a few months.

The idea for the floating zoo was to have children from various schools and colleges join them for one day of study of glorious creatures from around the planet, then drop them off and pick up a new batch of children and animals.

For once Larry stood back and took in the impressive sight of the new starship and for the first time a trickle of jealousy ran from his head; he wanted to be one of the college kids embarking on a fantastic day out in space. He wasn't cut out for studying as his mother constantly told him, forever ramming home the point that he was '*Too stupid*' to go to college. It was a collection of brain numbing, soul destroying jobs that were to carry Larry to this current point, collecting animals and putting them into cages. A hint of depression hit Larry's voice as he finally spoke back, which he tried hard to disguise.

"Kid, I really don't care about a crummy space zoo for rich kids."

"They're not rich, the kids are local. Like you and me."

This wasn't the job Dickson wanted, he'd thought he would breeze into a job after finishing university, but that wasn't the case. All his job applications for the work he wanted to do were unsuccessful. He did find work with a removals company, a company who claimed *'They could get rid of anything from mountains to mothers-in-law'*.

It was only meant to be a stop-gap but that was six years ago, now at twenty-seven he thought life was passing him by. He loved working with Larry, it was Larry who showed him the ropes when he had first joined the company.

Larry was an enjoyable friend to be around, funny, charming, but the job was making him become a borderline alcoholic. Larry considered himself to be a complete failure in life, his wife was having an affair and his two sons gave him no respect as a father.

It was at work where Larry found some brief respite from his life, especially with Dickson, who was a breath of fresh air. He enjoyed the banter between them, it kept his mind off of what was happening back home.

"Come on old man, let's keep at it," Dickson said to his friend.

"Old people have their place in society too you know."

"Yes, it's called a coffin, now step to it!"

Dickson looked like he was expecting Larry to challenge him, but the old man smiled and just went over to the huge conveyer belt transporting larger creatures into the ship.

Larry had missed Dickson smile back with respect.

"Ok, what have we got going in next?"

Dickson kept his eyes focused on Larry and shouted to the other workers to come and join them, ignoring Larry's bored stance, "GUYS, LET'S HURRY THIS UP! LET'S GET THESE CREATURES ON BOARD NOW!"

The tired men listened to the young worker and began to push the huge crates properly onto the conveyer belt. The belt continued to work and a succession of creatures rolled into the massive craft. Suddenly the belt shuddered to a halt, the workers looked at each hoping a shocked stare would get the machine started again.

"BLOODY HELL! WHAT'S HAPPENING NOW?"

The shout came from the boss of the removal firm, Mr Bears, an arrogant balding man with a constant morose look on his face. He barged his way through the rest of the workers, his face turning redder by the second, "WHY'S THIS CONVEYER BELT NOT WORKING?"

"I'm not sure, sir," replied Dickson.

The man in charge ran his fingers through his thinning hair and sighed loudly, "WELL FIND OUT WHAT IT IS WILL YA? I'M LOSING MONEY HERE!"

Dickson fiddled with the controls on the side of the closed cage, "It seems the ground locks from the container have attached themselves to the conveyer belt."

"Well can you fix it?"

The university graduate caught the hard stare of the owner and began to climb up the top of the container via a side ladder.

"I CAN DISABLE THE LOCKS FROM THE OVERRIDE SYSTEM FROM THE TOP OF THE CONTAINER," Dickson shouted.

Mr Bears threw his hands up in annoyance and looked at his watch, "WELL DON'T WASTE TIME TALKING TO ME DUMBASS, FIX IT!"

Dickson looked uncomfortable as he looked at the lock configuration. He fiddled around at the controls before shouting down again, "WELL, THE MAIN LOCK IS STUCK BUT I—"

Before Dickson could finish his sentence, the top hatch doors dropped and he tumbled into the cage below.

"DICKSONNNN!!!"

Larry screamed as his friend and colleague disappeared from view, "GET HIM OUT OF THERE!" Larry yelled to his boss.

"He'll be fine," Mr Bears chuckled.

"What's in there anyway? Chickens? Ducks maybe?"

"It's a sway lizard," Larry whispered.

Mr Bears shuddered when he heard Larry's reply, "Shit, someone go in there and get him."

His request was met with terrified silence from the crew, Mr Bears repeated Larry's earlier cry, "I SAID GET HIM OUT OF THERE NOW!"

Dickson got slowly to his feet in the massive container, his left leg was hurting, but he knew it wasn't broken; he did learn *something* from university.

The smell from the container was horrific. The sun was heating up the dry straw and faeces inside and it was already becoming unbearable for Dickson, more than the pain in his leg.

There was no sign of the creature and Dickson felt slightly relieved. The top hatch was still swinging and there were ladders attached all around the inside.

He wanted to shout for help, but knew any sound from him could bring attention from the inhabitant of the container. *Sod it* he thought, "GUYS! I'M OK, MY LEFT LEG IS SPRAINED BUT NOT BROKEN, I'M CLIMBING OUT NOW."

Larry glanced nervously at the top of the container, "JUST GET OUT OF THERE, MATE, CLIMB SAFELY, DON'T PANIC, BUT PLEASE MOVE IT."

The tone in Larry's voice made Dickson more concerned.

"What's in the container?"

"JUST CLIMB, DICKSON!"

"I SAID WHAT'S IN THE CONTAINER?"

Larry yelled as loud as his old voice would allow, "THERE'S A SWAY LIZARD IN THERE WITH YOU!"

Dickson went quiet and suddenly became very frightened. He turned around and hobbled towards the ladder when the creature stepped out from the darkness and Dickson instantly froze in fear.

It stood about eight feet tall, it's huge head swayed gently from left to right, sizing up Dickson. Its colour was like a setting sun, reddish brown with shades of yellow peeking through. The creature's neck was elongated like a leathery ostrich and its body resembled the same except a huge, lizard-like tail swayed gently behind and seemed to keep it stable. Its head was reptilian with red intelligent eyes locked solely onto Dickson. Rows of razor-sharp teeth were revealed when the creature opened its mouth. It had two claws on each forelimb, but its arms were smaller in relation to the rest of its body. The legs were shaped like a cat's hind legs with claws larger than its forelimbs. Dickson's heart pounded as he and the creature stared at each other. He reacted first and made a grab for the ladder, climbing for dear life. The lizard watched for a moment and then emitted a powerful shriek, leaping up to Dickson with ease and snatching him down with its jaws. The creature bit into Dickson's side and swallowed a part of it as he fell heavily to the ground.

Lying on his back Dickson was unaware he was bleeding to death, he just felt content and unafraid. The lizard opened up Dickson's stomach with ease with its forelegs slicing through his flesh like a hot knife through butter. Dickson's final view was the lizard stooping over him, its powerful jaws gently picked up his head in them and beginning to squeeze. Dickson knew nothing more after that.

"I CAN'T HEAR ANYTHING!" Larry was becoming more frantic.

"I know, not good," Mr Bears said under his breath.

The silence was too much for Larry, "DICKSON! ANSWER ME!"

Suddenly a ferocious scratching could be heard from inside the container. As all of the work crew listened intently, the sound began to rise.

"Oh my god," mouthed Larry.

"It's climbing out," he finished, rather too slowly.

"GET THAT ROOF SHUT NOW!" ordered Mr Bears.

The men rushed around the controls on the front of the unit, pressing and sliding every device on show.

"THE GROUND LOCKS ARE STILL STUCK ON THE BELT!"

"DO YOU THINK SO?" Mr Bears' sarcasm was deeply misplaced on Larry.

The scratching was near the top, it dropped a few times as the lizard lost its footing.

It could obviously see the gap where the unfortunate Dickson fell through. Larry yelled out to his fellow workers, "EVERYBODY, GRAB A BAR AND HELP ME PRISE THE COGS FREE!"

All of Dickson's colleagues grabbed what tools they could to try and shift the stuck container with Larry at the front. He jammed an iron bar in to the cog, digging both legs firmly into the ground. Pulling with his all his might, the pain racing through his body. The muscles in his arms tensed and he tried hard not to lose his grip, "MOVE IT, MOVE IT!" he cried.

Everyone tried just as hard as Larry to get the container moved, the scratching had now reached the top of the huge crate and suddenly all eyes nervously watched the sway lizard struggle to climb out with its feebly short forearms. Its head poked up from the gap and it hurriedly tried to escape.

Larry didn't care about his bleeding hands or the fact that his right arm was throbbing.

His heart was beating like a jackhammer but he couldn't lose his grip and fall. The sound of a triumphant bellow from the top of the container sliced through the morning and silenced the whole crew, the creature was now on top of the container, standing awkwardly on the metal surface.

"NOW!" roared Larry.

The huge cog clicked back into place on the conveyer belt and the container shuddered forward, slowly moving into the space shuttle.

An angry screech followed from the lizard, and, unable to keep its balance, it toppled back into the cage after trying so hard to free itself. Moving slowly into the zoo's storage compartment, the sway lizard's cage rumbled out of sight. As the men lay in a heap on the ground, Mr Bears' blank expression didn't change as he heard the scratching from the creature continue, albeit from the container's bottom.

"Get that cage locked down into the shuttle."

"Sir, we can lock the container into the craft, but we can't close the lid, sooner or later that creature will escape."

Mr Bears' blasé look continued, unconcerned by Larry's views, "Your point being?"

"My point being that soon that ship will blast off into space with hundreds of college kids on board, that creature will escape and kill them all."

Mr Bears arched his neck and interrupted, "Like I said, your point being?"

Larry forgot himself and shouted at his boss, "FOR GOD'S SAKE! THERE ARE KIDS ABOUT TO GO ON THAT SHIP! I'M NOT GOING TO STEP OVER THAT LINE!"

Mr Bears rolled his eyes, "The only line you'll be stepping over is the unemployment line if you don't keep your mouth shut, yeah there are kids on that ship, but none of them are mine, so I really don't care."

"YOU BASTARD! I'M GOING TO–"

Before Larry could continue he slumped to the floor clutching his left arm.

"You're going to do what? Roll around the floor and shit yourself?" Mr Bears sneered.

"HE'S HAVING A HEART ATTACK, YOU DICK," another colleague yelled.

Larry tried to stand but couldn't, the crushing pain in his chest was getting worse, he called out weakly for help but before anybody could help, he went silent for good.

"Larry? LARRY?" His now former colleague shook his lifeless body in vain, "He's dead, we have to get an ambulance."

"Bit late for that don't you think?"

"You know what I mean, he has to be taken away."

Mr Bears remained calm and muttered to the next employee in line with guts, "Reece is it? Before you call the doctor, let's get our stories straight. I'll contact the ship and its captain and inform them that we've had a fatality on our site." The foreman paused for a moment, "Actually, wait until the ship has blasted off before we inform the authorities and under no circumstances do we mention the loose dinosaur on board, that way we may walk away from this with our jobs, agreed?"

Reece wiped sweat from his eyes and paused, "I'm not sure, sir."

"Not sure? Do you know how hard it is to get work in this city? And if you or any one of you mention what *really* happened here, I'll make it my life's work to make sure that you never work here or any other city on this planet...again, so I'll ask you once more, is everybody here agreed?"

Reece looked around for assurance from his colleagues, when none came forward, he slowly nodded his head, "Agreed."

Mr Bears sighed loudly and looked at the body of Larry and thought about the probable death of Dickson in the container, "Let's just see how this day goes and hope there aren't any more surprises."

Earth 13

The powerful waves pushed Katherine further underwater and she knew she was going to drown. She had gasped for air so many times as the cruel water kept a tight hold of her ten-year old body. She thought she was a good swimmer but it wasn't working, splashing away when the tide was low was one thing, but swimming in the sea with a high tide was something completely different and it seemed she was going to pay for her ill judgement with her life.

Her little muscles ached with the pain as she kicked and struggled against the tide. Katherine didn't know how long she'd been fighting against the water, but she began to feel tired; the more she screamed and shouted for help, the more her lungs filled with salt water.

She was tiring out quickly and was tempted just to close her eyes and let the water finish the job it had already started and take her young life and keep her beneath the waves forever. She felt snug and relaxed now and stopped kicking, the water had wrapped itself around her like the fine blankets in her bed, the bed she shared with her cousins who she'd now never see again. It was time to sleep now as unconsciousness began to take hold.

Suddenly Katherine's eyes were open and as alert as possible as the salt water stung them. Her back arched and her head tilted backwards as she was slowly lifted out of the water. She tried to struggle in fear as some unseen force had plucked her from her impending watery grave and made her gradually float towards the safety of the shore.

Katherine became completely immobilised, the fear of dying she could handle, but this new fate was different. She found what little strength she had to throw her head and torso back to let out a gurgled shout, and then, lying flat, she passed out as the strange beam carried her up to the beach.

Katherine's body settled softly and safely on the morning beach as the source of the energy beam relaxed.

A hand returned from being a fist to its open palmed familiar self and the beam which had carried Katherine from the sea to the beach switched off.

The hand belonged to a woman in a battered old brown leather jacket. She had blue dreadlocked hair which was slightly covered by an equally old hat and completely out of place for the beach. She knelt down.

The gloved hand hovered over the little girl's body, she wasn't breathing and her frame remained still. The figure in the coat summoned up some more of her energy and a fiery bolt shot out of her hand and into Katherine's chest. Her body shuddered and slowly her heart began to rise again, she coughed and breathed again.

"Easy now, take it easy," the stranger's soothing voice said.

Katherine suddenly bolted upright, trembling with fear she looked up at her saviour's face and screamed as if she was back in the water.

"WOAHH! Calm it down, kid, what's the matter with you?" The stranger inclined her head back.

Katherine staggered her words out, still breathing heavy, "My lady, your face!"

"What about it?" the stranger asked, touching it gently.

The ten-year old coughed wildly and looked out at to sea and then back at the woman, "I offer you my thanks for rescuing me from those terrible waters, my lady."

"But?"

"Your face is as dark as a midnight sky."

"Shouldn't you be in bed at that time?" the woman asked.

"Your hair is the same as the sea which tried to claim my life."

The woman paused slightly and then continued with her gentle voice.

"You mean my hair is blue?" she chuckled.

Katherine didn't answer, she just looked hard into the woman's face as a confused image flashed upon her own, her eyes shrank slowly and then began to widen in fascination.

"Still looking at my face aren't you?"

"Can it rub off? Is it some source of trickery as to why you are so dark?"

A slight weariness hit the older woman and she shrugged it off with a smile, "No I can't rub it off, it's who I am."

"Why?"

"I don't know."

"Why?"

"It's just one of those things."

"Why?"

"Listen could you stop that please? I'm black, so deal with it."

"Black? Is that your name? Hello 'Black' my name is Katherine."

The woman dumbly shook her head, "No, *I'm* black, but my name isn't Black."

It was Katherine's turn to look confused as she slowly got to her feet, her legs as weak as a newborn foal.

"I'm sorry my lady, I don't understand."

"Don't worry about it kid, thousands of years from now idiots will still be making a fuss over the colour of one's skin."

Katherine's face still drew a blank, the woman sighed and held out her hand, "My name is Silo and after all this time I've finally found you."

Still slightly fearful of the woman, Katherine hesitated with her arms by her side.

"Oh yeah, I forgot," Silo huffed. She took a step back and curtsied, "My lady Katherine, Silo at your service."

Katherine wobbled on her feet but replied in kind with her own curtsy.

"Katherine, at your service, my lady."

"I know who you are young lady, I've known for years."

"How would you know of my name, my lady?" Katherine asked cautiously.

Silo was silent, she walked forward to Katherine and stopped, "You are too young to understand the words that I'm about to say to you, but I know of you Katherine, daughter of the late Edmund. You are a sorceress and I had a feeling you'd be struggling here on the beach today because we are connected. I have travelled here from a place far away because you hold the key to the survival of the whole universe. You are now my ward. I am your sorceress protector, I am your secret guardian of the many worlds, I am your loco parentis, I am your survivor surveyor, any questions?"

Katherine blinked, slowly, "Yes, and you're also black?"

Chapter Four:

Gods And Robbers

The Hunters

The young girl had been running for too long, her heart felt as if it was going to explode from her chest. She had chosen many different directions to run in but it was to no avail, her pursuers were still on her trail.

Her legs felt sluggish, after ages of keeping her alive they finally began to betray her with their now painfully slow movements. She didn't know where she was, but had taken a detour through a forest. The ground was wet and muddy and she now had to begin to trudge her way to safety. Creatures of the night scurried around in the branches above her and some others foraged for food in the bushes below, each new movement from any of the animals freaked the girl out even more. The harsh wind bit at her body, slowly nipping away at her bones. Panting for breath for the umpteenth time that night, she wiped away the trickle of sweat which began to appear from beneath her headband.

Something heavier than a nocturnal mammal snapped a twig on the ground nearby, forcing her to spin wildly. The girl knew it would be a waste of time to shout to see if she was alone.

"WHAT DO YOU WANT WITH ME?" she screamed.

There was no answer, only the trees replied as the unforgiving wind rustled through their leaves. Her breath made sharp rasping sounds as she took out her phone and held it aloft, "COME ON PLEASE! COME ON!"

Pulling down the phone she frantically slid various screens across as it illuminated the forest clearing. Raising her eyes skywards, she waited a couple of seconds and tried again with her hands trembling. Still nothing from her phone. The frightened girl saw that the path she was on split in two and she automatically chose the high road.

Running hard up the gruelling forest incline, she managed a look behind and saw nothing to immediately alarm her. Tired of fleeing and with seemingly nowhere else to run, she stopped and bent forward with her head by her knees. She whispered to the ground, her voice was thick and swallowing was an effort, "Please leave me alone."

"Sorry love, no can do."

The gruff male voice made her jump more so than any of the night sounds she'd heard previously. The terrified girl rolled onto her back and looked up at the many faces peering down at her, all men with flashlights blinding her, she tried to shield her eyes but it did no good.

"You gave us a good chase, girly, but you should have stayed in the city, you could have been safe with the crowds around you, but you've signed your own death warrant hiding in the forest."

She trembled with fear more than cold from the night, "Who are you? I haven't done anything to you."

"No you haven't sweetheart, but you should really know who we."

"Please leave me alone, I'm begging you!"

The man who spoke to her had a long black beard and slicked back hair which ended in a ponytail she could make out in the moonlight. He had an athletic build and definitely worked out.

On his person was a whole arsenal of weaponry and knives underneath a brown leather jacket. His men had an equal look, but didn't carry it off as well as the man leaning down at the front.

He stroked his magnificent beard a few times before answering, "Now you know we can't do that, Bailey. You would have thought that after years on the run you would have had the common sense to change your name. Saying that, it has taken us many years to find you, do you know how many planets we had to jump in order to find you?"

Her anguish bought more talk from the bearded man, "Would you like some coffee?"

"WHAT?!" The girl spat, her fingers rigid with fear.

"It's freezing out here, bring out the thermos and give this girl a cup of coffee."

The man with the beard ushered one of his team forward, the henchman smiled slightly and offered his thermos to his boss who took it with thanks and poured out some coffee and offered it to the girl who he still stood above, "Here you go."

"PISS OFF!" She knocked the thermos cup from out of the bearded man's hands, the coffee trickled easily down the hill, which she had so much trouble getting a grip on, not before most of it went on to the jacket of the bearded man. The boss man stroked his cheek with a perfectly manicured fingertip, "That wasn't very nice was it? Here's me trying to make your death more pleasant and you go and spill coffee on my new jacket?

That's just mean!" He stared at her in a soft sad manner, "You sure you have no idea who we are?"

The girl looked directly into his eyes, "No."

"Really? You have no idea who we are?"

The bearded man looked to his team, back to the girl and then to his team again, "You see? I told you that we should have got decent PR."

He gestured firmly to his team, waving his hand frantically so they all understood him, they all slowly raised their guns to the girl. The prospect of death had already unbalanced her as the bearded man continued, "Look, I know you know who we are and I know you know what's going to happen to you," scratching his chin, he carried on, "Looking good though, I mean how long have you been on the run now? How many years have you been hiding? Your sorcery hides your true age well, but you are hiding the girl and you have to die, you and your kind have led us on a merry dance. Sorry, nothing personal it's just what we have to do you. Tell me where the girl is and then you die, oh wait…" The bearded man turned behind him to face his crew and back to the girl, "Did that sound racist to you? It wasn't meant to, 'You and your kind?' I meant nothing against sorcerers, black ones, brown ones…" He looked to his men for support, "You know I'm not a racist bigot don't you, boys?"

They nodded in agreement and mumbled their various positive replies, the man looked back to the shivering young girl, "Sorry kid, but you've known me long enough to know that I'm not a racist."

"I don't know what you mean, you dick," the girl rolled her blue eyes.

She knew pleading for her life wasn't going to help and let the man in charge prattle on.

"You've failed girl, now I can make your death easier if you simply tell me where the girl is and her protector. We know she has her and we know that you know where she is, hold on..." He thought for a moment, "Not again! Wait, yeah that makes sense." The man raised a bushy eyebrow, "This is getting extremely tiresome, you sorcerers never learn, do you?"

The girl, who had been running all night and according to the bearded man running for years, gained a grin on her now confident face, her voice sounded deeper and deliciously husky.

"As a matter fact my love, we do."

The bearded man waved his right hand, a signal to his team, but before anybody could react, the young teenager's features began to ripple and then bubble like a blowtorch heating up the paint on an old windowsill.

Her pale face changed features and blonde hair turned black, a smooth look appeared as if she'd been carved in perfect ebony.

The dark hue surrounded her face, it was a face of beauty, with firm red lips and her eyes went from blue to a bright yellow.

The sorceress's transformation was complete; what was once a frightened teenager shivering on the ground was now a strong woman with bright eyes and a sense of aristocratic confidence. The men all jumped back in shock as the woman gracefully stood to her feet as the men cautiously backed away.

"There was a saying from one of the many planets I went to whilst on the run from you guys which I think fits this occasion quite well." Her voice carried strength as she curtsied theatrically, "Voila!"

The bearded man whispered, "Bailey, it *is* you."

A strong sense of power suddenly filled the mouth of the new identity of the sorceress, her mouth was filled with a red energy source, her body stiffened as a surge of red flame left her mouth.

"MOVE!" the boss man screamed.

The fires had engulfed some of his team in a scarlet flame as they rolled on the ground in pure agony.

"Don't worry, their pain won't last for long," she said to the boss, slightly tired.

Breathing back in the fire, she rolled the energy around like a sweet in her mouth and then spat out the glowing orb, aiming for the middle of the flaming men. The sphere bounced like a schoolboy's rubber ball, coming to a rest in the centre.

"I'd duck if I were you, lover."

Suddenly there was a scurry of movement from the bearded man and his lieutenant as they dived for cover in the sparse shrubbery.

A pulse of white hot energy exploded deep into the huddle of injured soldiers, killing them all.

Bailey collapsed on to the ground, completely spent of energy and concentration.

The bearded man rose to his feet slowly, wiping off the remains of his men from his body, "MY BOYS! YOU KILLED ALL MY BOYS! TONIGHT WAS OUR POKER NIGHT AND YOU KILLED THEM!"

Bailey's eyes misted over and acknowledged the bearded man's rant.

"Them first and then me."

The bearded man shook his head, refocusing on the carnage, "It didn't have to be like this."

Bailey coughed as a corner of her mouth lifted with a faint smile, "It did, you know it did, it was inevitable that you were finally going to catch up with me and end this...Orion."

His forehead creased and the bearded man known as Orion the Hunter bent down over Bailey.

"Just tell me where the girl is, you've used up all your of your power and you're too tired to fight, I'll let you live if you tell me."

Bailey stifled a sound of pain, "We both know that's not going to happen Orion, you poor fool."

"WHERE IS SHE?" he screamed down her throat.

"I know you will find her, it's inevitable, I'm just slowing you down a little."

Bailey strained a smile as her strength weakened further, "She's somewhere you'll never find her demon, just get on with it, the shit storm is about to begin."

Orion held Bailey's head in his hands and stroked her forehead tenderly, "I'm sorry," he said very slowly. He kissed Bailey gently on her cheek and then turned away, closing his eyes as he snapped her neck, the sound was like a twig breaking. Orion didn't look at the body afterwards.

One surviving private brushed himself down and walked over to Orion who now sat by the forest edge away from Bailey's body, "Boss, all the men are dead."

Orion nodded, "I know, Bailey was always good at her job."

"So what do we do now sir, with no men I mean?"

The boss scratched his head, "How many planets have we got left?"

"There's two or three which we haven't been to yet where the key could be hiding."

Orion made a sound of frustration as he got to his feet, "Ok, what planet is next on the list?"

The private swiped the screen on his tech glove and a holographic image shone from his hand, illuminating the closed forest with planet schematic readouts.

"We could try Earth 42, we haven't been to that planet yet."

Orion cleared his throat and studied the illuminated planets, "Fair enough, Earth 42 it is then."

He gave the solider a long, considered look.

"I'm sorry lieutenant?"

"I'm not a lieutenant, I'm a private."

Orion stared at the charred bodies of his troops and then back to the private, "You're a lieutenant now son, you're the only one left, what's your name?"

"Mason sir, Lieutenant Mason."

Orion looked dull-eyed and pale.

"Well, looks like you and me are going to Earth 65."

"Earth 42 sir."

"That's the one, get the jump equipment ready, we leave in five minutes."

Mason's expression softened.

"Forgive me for asking sir, but that sorceress dead on the ground…"

"Bailey, her name is…was Bailey," Orion mumbled.

Mason squeezed his eyes shut apologetically, "Yeah Bailey, well what do we do with her? I mean we've been trailing her for years and now she's dead, do we just leave her here?"

Orion weighed up his minimal options and breathed hard, "No, we call in the back-up team, if we can, and if they can find us and arrange for them to give her a full burial, no expense spared, I don't care that she's a sorceress, I want to give her the greatest burial money can buy."

Mason fiddled with the big piece of 'planet jump' equipment attempting to get it ready for the next journey.

"That's very accommodating of you sir, to sort out that woman's funeral like that."

Orion's head bent wearily towards Mason, "It's the least I could do, I mean she *was* my wife."

Earth 65

Lacy rotated her left arm anticlockwise and gently rubbed her sore scars. The tattoos were fresh and stinging but she still lifted her arm up into the sunlight coming through the car window to see more of the magnificent prints forever imprinted on her body. Kane looked quizzically at her and emitted the heaviest of sighs, "Are you sure you like it? I mean it's going to stay with you for life, you do know that don't you?"

Lacy turned hard to look at her boyfriend, "Don't you like it?"

"It's a little permanent isn't it? I mean it covers your whole arm."

"That's the whole idea, don't you like tattoos on girls?"

Kane slowly drove his car into an empty bay in the college car park and turned off the engine, "Listen, I get it, I don't mind the tattoos, it's just they look pretty now but what about years down the line? You're going to be an old woman with saggy arms and tattoos, you're going to look stupid."

Lacy puffed out her full red lips at Kane, "It takes money to look this good you know."

Kane gave her an assessing look, "Well, if you get fat in the future, you can tattoo a picture of a thinner arm on your arm, that would come in handy. I just don't see the point of having tattoos on you now, look you have the fittest body on any girl I've seen."

"Kane!" Lacy said slightly embarrassed.

"No babes I mean it, why have a tattoo now on a young beautiful body. Why not wait until you have an old body with wrinkles when no one cares what you look like?"

"That's a bit harsh isn't it? Making fun of old people like that?"

"Not really," Kane continued, "Nothing can make your body worse when you're old, so why not? If you've got false teeth, put glitter on them to make them look sparkly, or if you've got big blue varicose veins running down your leg; just tattoo monkeys on them make it look like vines."

Lacy gave a humourless, self-deprecating laugh, "Fine, don't worry about it," she crossed her arms and puffed out her chest in annoyance.

Kane leaned in for a kiss and Lacy pulled away.

"You're pissed off with me aren't you?" Kane asked, his eyes guilty like a naughty puppy.

Lacy cleared her throat, "I really wanted you to like these tattoos."

"I do, just not on you that's all, but I don't mind if you get your teeth whitened though."

She smiled back, all teeth, "Who said romance is dead?"

The handle of the car door was stuck. She pushed her shoulder hard against the glass and heaved, the door swung open and Lacy collapsed into a heap on the ground. Kane leaned over to her from his own seat, "I guess I should have opened the door for you."

Lacy cursed herself and then at her boyfriend under her breath.

"Sorry hun," he smiled. Lacy looked flustered, "You ok?"

She slid her shades down her tanned elegant nose and pushed up her expensive breast implants."

"So, you don't like my tattoos, but you don't mind *these*?"

Kane immediately unbuckled his belt and slid over to the passenger side door. He rolled out clumsily to the ground next to his girlfriend, shuffled up closer and made a grab for her chest, "Because I can have more fun with these then I can with reading words on your arm."

Lacy swatted his hand away and gave him a cold imperious look, "No, you had your chance of some fun with me, but you blew it when you said my tattoos were shit."

"I didn't say that they were shit, just that I didn't like them."

Lacy had mastered the art form of manipulation as well as applying expensive imported make up; this was all too easy.

"Well the next time you want to insult me or my tats, why not do something vaguely more interesting like getting the hell away from me and walking into some traffic."

Kane looked hurt, "You're a bit harsh, hun."

She finally rose to her feet and brushed herself down, "I know, so what happens now?"

Deflated, Kane looked around the college car park, "The others haven't arrived yet, I think we're the first ones here."

Lacy looked at him blankly and sighed heavily, "Remind me why we're doing this again? In college on our day off? It's 'Apology Day' too, you know, Big Man's parties are to die for, only a few of the city's finest get an invite."

"Are you serious? Don't you keep up with current events? Big Man has been holed up in his complex for years, remember? For wrecking half the city?"

The girl completely removed her shades and squinted her rock and roll eyes in the morning sun and looked bemused, "Really?"

"Yes, really."

Lacy replied with a hardened grunt, "So I have to go up on that spaceship with all those filthy animals?"

"Yes, in order to get the credits we need to get our college diploma, we need to spend the day on that zoo spaceship with filthy animals in cages."

"Animals in cages? What are you talking about?"

Kane rubbed at his throat slowly, "We're going to a zoo? With filthy animals?"

Lacy looked at him impassively, "Actually I was talking about our classmates."

Kane smiled and held it in place as another vehicle pulled up next to them. It was a big people carrier with seven seats, the engine was purring smoothly. The driver held his foot on the accelerator and revved the engine to prove a show-off point, the noise drowned out the other sounds of cars arriving at the car park. Lacy banged her tiny fists against the blacked out driver's side window, "HEY EXCUSE ME?! DO YOU MIND TURNING THE ENGINE OFF?" The engine roared even louder, making Lacy bang harder, "I SAID TURN IT OFF!"

Her shouts finally had the desired effect and the driver quieted down the engine before turning it off completely, "THANK YOU"! Lacy shouted sarcastically.

She gave one last bang on the glass before the door finally opened. Lacy gave the driver a stern look as he unbuckled himself from his seatbelt and stepped out, "Dickhead," she hissed at him.

The huge driver, Achilles smiled like a kid with a new toy, "Love you too, babes."

The side door opened and two teenage boys, Harley and Poxon, tumbled out excitedly.

"WHAT'S UP BITCHES?" The two waved their hands excitedly in the air like kids seeing a clown at a birthday party.

"COLLEGE TRIP BITCHES!" yelled Poxon.

Lacy gave them a sentence-stopping stare, "Stop saying that."

Kane glared at all three of his newly arrived friends, "WHAT THE BLOODY HELL IS THIS?!"

Achilles pointed to the van and sniffed the air which still had lingering gas fumes from the massive exhaust, "Oh this? This is my brother's van, I borrowed it because my car is in the repair garage."

Achilles could almost hear Kane's mind ticking away, he knew how his friend's brain worked and just watched silently as Kane walked around the van, examining it as if he was a doctor dealing with a new patient. He finally stopped when he came to the van's bumper sticker: *Don't come a-knocking if you see this van a-rocking.*

Achilles grinned as Kane read out the sticker message, "Like I said, it's my brother's van, I don't know what he gets up to."

"I think we all know what he gets up to in that," Lacy quipped and looked at Harley and Poxon, "You guys were sitting in that as well, that's totally gross."

Poxon wiped his hands on Harley in a comedic manner who returned the gesture.

"Ridiculous," Lacy huffed.

"Is this all of us?" Harley asked.

"Nope, Cameo isn't here yet," said Kane.

Achilles looked down at his shoes with a cheeky smile, "I wonder who she is on now then?"

Lacy slapped him on the arm with a force that betrayed the look of her little frame, "Don't be so mean, she just messaged me to say she's running late."

"But from whose bedroom did she text from?"

Another slap from Lacy didn't change Achilles' smirk, "I told you, don't be so mean."

She held back from slapping Achilles again, her hand began to ache.

"What about Sully?"

"She's ill apparently," Achilles said, rubbing his arm; Lacy's slap did have an effect on him after all.

"I forgot to say, when I dropped her off, she was looking like shit."

"She always does," smiled Poxon.

"No, worse than usual, I think she has some sort of virus? When she turned to say 'Goodbye' she looked like the walking dead. She's not replying to my texts so I guess we leave her, which is a shame really as she said she was going to try and get her two gorgeous cousins to come, Enya and Echo?"

"Did she really say gorgeous cousins?"

"Nope, that was just me."

Lacy saw a lump of disappointment appear on Achilles' face, but spoke again anyway, pressing her chin into Kane's shoulder, "How would they be able to come to the zoo if they're not registered from our college?"

Achilles leaned in, separating the couple excitedly, "We have a substitute teacher coming on the trip today, they wouldn't know everybody in the class."

"What do you mean?"

"I mean we take the names of two people who are sick today and give them to Echo and Enya, the teacher isn't going to know who they are."

Lacy wrinkled her nose and gave Achilles an arched look, "The teacher has an image register notepad, he or she will know exactly who is missing and what they look like."

Achilles looked puzzled, "Really? I chose class 642, the classroom next to us, who is off in that class?"

Lacy rolled her tongue out in desperation and deep thought, "Samantha and Stevie Lovejoy from class 642 have been both ill recently and not in class."

Achilles clapped his hands excitedly, "You see! Echo and Enya can take their names and profiles and come on board."

Lacy shook her head, "No, Samantha and Stevie are twins."

Achilles grinned, "Echo and Enya can play twins."

"And they're black," Lacy said with a tinge of sarcasm.

Achilles gave her a dour look, "Oh, maybe not then."

Earth 13

"Two chickens in white wine sauce, no, a duck maybe stuffed in a goose with three bottles of wine, maybe with a steak?"

Katherine looked up at her rescuer as she walked cautiously behind her along the beach front.

"What are you doing? I believe you were having a conversation with yourself?"

Silo looked thoughtfully up at the sky and then behind to Katherine, "I was just thinking if I actually get you out alive from here, what I would eat for a relaxing meal when it's all over."

"But my lady, you already have rescued me from the sea and you forever have my gratitude but there is nothing more you can do, except escort me to my house."

Silo tried to sound casual but her voice became strained, "Did you not hear a word I said to you earlier?"

"I did my lady, but your words made no sense. I held my tongue as I believed you to be insane."

"Wow! I forgot how freaky you guys spoke, did nothing I say get through to you?"

Katherine hitched up her little dress and struggled to keep up, "What is a 'Wow'?"

"Forget it," Silo huffed.

"Freaky? I've never heard of such an utterance."

Silo stopped walking and turned around to the perplexed little girl, "Do I have to speak like a nerd in order to get my point across to you?"

"I am known as a nerd now? Should I be proud of this?"

"Never in a million years, but that's another story. Look, you must listen and understand the words coming out of my mouth."

Katherine stood still, her eyes wanted more information but she remained quiet, which was a good thing to Silo.

"Look, there's no easy way to say this, but I've been searching a long time and all across the many lands for you."

Katherine's eyes closed slowly like an alarmed clam, "Many lands? And you failed to try Lambeth first?"

"This is serious..."

"Yet you say? But you have not explained who you are and why you need me?"

Silo scratched at her dreadlocks, "Oh yeah, sorry I don't think I explained everything properly to you."

"Well I would be interested if you would."

Katherine paused, unsure if her next word would make sense, "Enlighten me on how I can make things better for you and easier, if you let me, I'm quite reasonable?"

"That's quite a sentence."

"I heard it from one of the girls behind the market place, there are a lot of ladies there who take men in their house and then after a few minutes, the men come out again with no money, yet they are smiling."

Silo's eyes grew and then stopped. She wasn't completely drained, but slightly tired from her rescue, she stared hard at the little girl, "Well for a start you can tell me how you actually got into the sea?"

The little girl gazed at her, "I don't understand what you mean?"

"Well looking at your clothes, your boots, your skirt, your top, well the fact that you're wearing clothes full stop is a bit of a giveaway for a trip into the deep blue sea." Her eyes dipped slightly, "I'll ask again, how did you find yourself in the sea, young lady?"

Katherine shrugged her shoulders like a bored teenager, which she did well, seeing as she wasn't quite one yet.

"Trust me," Silo added.

An unsure movement from her tongue probed Katherine's lips, "My lady, what time of the year is this?"

"I'm sorry?"

"Which season is upon us?"

Silo gave a long assessing look, "This is summer I believe."

Katherine looked out to the sea and then back to Silo, "My lady I have been here before, but not today. My uncle was delivering dead peasants to the people who want to buy them off of him."

"Wait? Your uncle was selling peasants to people?"

"Yes indeed, my lady."

Silo's eyes widened and a bizarre expression appeared on her face, "Why would he do such a horrible thing?"

"Horrible? I would not call it such a thing, my lady."

"What would he do with these peasants?"

"We would set traps for them and when they enter, we string them up and snap their necks for the people who want to buy them."

There was an awkward silence, which Silo finally broke angrily, "I CANNOT BELIEVE YOU'VE BECOME SUCH AN EVIL YOUNG WOMAN!"

Katherine made a face, "My lady, can I ask you for the reason why you have yourself become such a beast towards me?"

"BECAUSE YOU'RE KILLING PEOPLE, PLUS YOUR CALLING THEM PEASANTS? THE CLASS SYSTEM OBVIOUSLY SUCKS IN THIS TIME."

"My lady, I have no idea on what the words you uttered mean."

Horrified, Silo clutched her cheeks, "Murdering people?"

"My lady? People? We're killing peasants, but we don't pluck their wings though; we leave that to the people who want to buy them."

Silo blinked rapidly and shook her head, still slightly confused, "Peasants? Don't you mean pheasants? As in the bird?"

"My lady, that is what I said, peasants."

Silo had a guilty look on her face, which Katherine picked up on, "My lady, is there anything wrong?"

Katherine's innocent face put her own to shame and Silo offered her an awkward smile.

"Just noticed your lisp, sweetheart."

"Is that what they are called? Yes, we had customers and he took me along, we rode together on his cart to deliver our catch. We live in a small village and sell our birds to the kitchens of noblemen. Anyway, this day, I think, or a day before? I was on his cart and fell asleep, it was a long day and I was tired then I had a dream. I dreamt about the beach and swimming in the sea and when I awoke..." Katherine paused, unsure.

"Go on," said Silo, still smiling.

"When I awoke, I was actually in the sea and I was drowning. I don't know how I got there and then you came and my uncle is gone and..."

Silo saw the girl struggling and whispered, "It's ok, it's ok."

"I don't know what happened to me, how I got here or who you are?"

Katherine was beginning to cry and Silo needed to distract her. Silo spotted something ahead of her, eyes excitedly squinting, she grabbed Katherine and pulled her over towards it.

"Ice cream! Everybody likes ice cream, do you want some?"

The little girl opened her mouth but no sound came out, "Good, I take that as a 'yes'."

"What is this 'creamed ice' you speak about?"

Silo gave the sweetest most revolting smile, "You've never had ice cream before?"

Katherine felt a slight unease, "I'm not familiar with this term."

Silo looked at the ice cream van and its driver, reading the name on the van boldly, "Big Man's ice cream? Sounds good, anyway can I have two '99s please?"

The ice cream man was shivering in the back and not because of the ice, he was afraid of something.

"Hello? Can I have an ice cream please?" Silo asked again.

"What's your name, sir?"

"Edward," he stammered.

Edward got up slowly, still shaking nervously and wiped his hands on his apron, which covering a tartan suit which had begun to fray at the cuffs. He pulled a lever and pure white ice cream oozed out from a slim nozzle into a wafer cone, "Where am I?" he asked. He handed it to Silo and started with the second one, "I asked where am I, woman?"

Silo looked perplexed and ignored him, "Try this," she said, passing it over to the cautious eyes of Katherine.

"I don't think it's wise I should be tasting food from a stranger." She glared at the driver, "Even this horseless carriage looks strange."

"Just taste it," Silo said, looking hideously cheerful. Katherine took the cone from Silo, still trying to keep her guard up, "Don't think about it, just do it."

A little tongue slipped out and probed the cone, it shot back in when it licked the cream.

"It's cold."

"It's called ice cream for a reason, honey."

Katherine slowly closed her eyes, mouth open and she slurped some more, "I think…I think I like ice cream?"

Silo chuckled and then took a piece from her own ice cream, "Right, now back to more pressing matters." Her brown eyes rolled around slowly, "Edward, do you have a moment?" The ice cream man reappeared at the window.

"Please help me, I don't know where I am."

She swept off her hat and curtsied to him, "What are you doing? Who does that?

"So they don't curtsy where you come from?" Silo asked.

"Nobody does."

"Where do you think you are?"

Edward blinked a couple of times, "I was sitting in my van, waiting to go on my next round and then the next minute there was this black spinning hole, it looked like a whirlpool and it sucked my van in. I tried to start the engine and drive away but before I could, everything went dark and I ended up here on this beach."

Silo cast beseeching eyes at Edward, "So you have no idea where you are?"

"I just said that," Edward said, his voice deepening with anxiety.

Silo cleared her throat, "Let's just keep our voices down and keep this away from the child."

"I DON'T GIVE A DAMM ABOUT THE GIRL OR THE ICE CREAM! I JUST WANT TO GO HOME!"

Katherine raised her head from her ice cream for a moment to hear the outburst and then went back to slurping. Frowning, Silo shuddered slightly, "You're in the wrong time, you shouldn't be here, you could ruin everything."

"TIME? WHAT ARE YOU TALKING ABOUT?! I DON'T KNOW ANYTHING ABOUT TIME!"

Silo checked behind to see how Katherine was. Satisfied she was fine, she kept a completely serious face to Edward and entered the van. Edward stepped back with caution, his way was blocked with boxes of ice cream cones.

"I'm sorry you're here, there must have been a disruption in the time line continuum and somehow when there was an abrupt teleportation, you ended up here, in a place where you can't stay, if you do? It may destroy time itself if anybody sees you."

"You look different from the people I've seen here already, why are you still here?"

"I'm working on it, I shouldn't be here either." Silo stopped and straightened herself, "So people have seen you in your van in this land?"

"Yes, I gave some kids ice cream, they liked it." Edward calmed down but was still nervous.

"I don't want to stay here."

"I can help you," Silo said, her voice tinged with sadness.

"How?" Edward asked, his eyebrows raised very high.

"I can send you home."

Suddenly, her blue eyes turned red and she placed her right hand back on the chest of Edward and slid it over his heart, "Just relax, this won't hurt."

The ice cream van glowed blue and rocked slightly. Katherine jumped at the sound of a pure plasma energy blast and went to investigate. As she walked up to the van, Silo stepped out, her face forlorn and she wiped away the tears which were rolling down her cheek, she ushered Katherine away from the van.

"Don't go in there," Silo said solemnly.

"Where is the man?" Katherine asked.

"I sent him home."

Silo's tone had changed, she was sad and Katherine noticed.

"Are you ok, my lady?"

Silo's happy face began to seep away, "Yes, but there is something I should show you."

She lifted her right arm in the air and spun her wrist around, suddenly a blue mist appeared around her hand and gently hovered around it before making its way into the sky. Silo only smiled as she waved her hand higher and more smoke emerged from her wrist.

Katherine's heart thudded rapidly, scared half to death, "WHAT MANNER OF TRICKERY IS THIS? YOU'RE A WITCH! GOD PRESEVE US YOU'RE A WITCH!" she cried.

"God, I love the way you talk," Silo grinned.

"WITCH! WITCH! YOU ARE AN UNRULY SPIRIT!" Katherine cried.

Silo shook her head and licked her dry lips, "Calm down, child."

"NO, NO I WILL NOT! YOU ARE CURSED BY THE DEVIL HIMSELF AND I WANT NO PART IN THIS!"

Silo reached out to the little girl, "You're quite loud for a ten-year-old, you do remember I saved your life and this is all the thanks I get."

"NO MY LADY! YOU ARE MUDDLING WORDS TO ME! YOU ARE CURSED AND YOU WILL BRING YOUR CURSE DOWN ON ME AS WELL!"

Katherine only stopped shouting to throw up over her little feet, the stench almost overpowered her.

Silo eyed up the frantic girl compassionately, "I know you're frightened, you don't know me and I know what happened here wasn't a nice thing to view."

"I didn't see anything, my lady."

Silo paused, looking back to the ice cream and then carried on, "That blue energy you saw? I was taught to use it by my mentor, Bailey, she was powerful and cool but..." Silo studied the little face of Katherine, "Sometimes being all powerful isn't all it's cracked up to be." Katherine nodded but didn't say anything, "You have this power too, that's how you ended up in the sea."

Katherine's little hands were clenched, "I don't want it my lady! I don't want to be like you."

"You are like me, there's nothing you can do about that." Silo went to hold Katherine's hand and she pulled it away, "You must believe me when I tell you that you will grow up to be somebody more powerful than me, more powerful than you can possibly imagine, and one day you will save thousands of lives with the energy that will eventually surge through your body, but you need training to help you with your powers and I can help you."

"No, why can't you just leave me alone?"

"Because I can't," Silo said flatly, "I can't," she repeated, this time with sadness, "I travelled to find you from a far-off land and I can't get back home; I've nowhere else to go and I have to help you."

"What do you mean, my lady?" Katherine asked anxiously. Silo's slight flapping had worked on Katherine, "This power I have—" She corrected herself, "This power we have, we must use it to protect and never attack. When it is the only option available, then possibly, but we never think like that, as there are many who would wish to bring harm on you and force you to use your powers for evil. Many will come looking for you and they will find you and after they get what they want? They will kill you."

"But why?" Katherine sniffed.

"If you trust me, and I mean really trust me, I will protect you and save your life and I will teach you Kitty, because hopefully one day I hope you'll do the same for me, do you mind if I call you Kitty?"

"Nobody calls me that except my uncle."

"Where is he now?"

"Drunk somewhere I think, my lady."

"Would he not be out looking for you?"

"Sometimes I think he doesn't know I'm there."

"Perfect," smiled Silo. Kitty vomited again as Silo tried hard not to gag, "That's a lot of sick for a ten-year-old."

Kitty suddenly froze, "What if you are one of those people who want me to use my power for evil?"

"I saved you from drowning, why would I do that?" Kitty shrugged, "Do you want to die?" Silo asked with a sad smile.

"My lady, of course I don't want to die."

"Well, chances are your family think you are playing hide and seek or something, giving us a chance to begin your training."

Kitty was still frozen at the sound of Silo's comment, "Training my lady, but I do not understand, can't I return to my family?"

"Trust me and come with me. I'm not kidnapping you, I will return you to your family as soon as your training is finished. In fact, don't think of it as training, just imagine we're going on a magical adventure. I'll explain it all to you on the way."

Kitty's sharp eyes looked up at Silo.

"But I am torn between fear and excitement, my lady, your words to save me sound so delicious but I am still afraid."

"Just stay with me and I'll keep you alive, just stay out of trouble, ok?"

Kitty sighed and curtsied.

"My lady, then I am your humble servant, you devil wench black lady."

"Let's just stick with Silo for the time being shall we, kiddo?"

Kitty nodded eagerly. Silo offered a smile and put her hands on Kitty's shoulders and then slowly pulled her into a hug. The little girl struggled at first and then relented and allowed herself to be drawn forward. Silo pulled back, the embrace would have been longer if it wasn't for the puke covering Kitty, "Let's go then, young Kitty sorceress." Silo walked away from the wrecked van as Kitty still stood there, "You coming?" Silo asked.

The ten-year-old Kitty ran back to the broken ice cream van, "Wait my lady, there is something I want from inside this horseless cart."

"WAIT!" Silo shouted, "Don't go in there yet."

Silo climbed back into the van and rummaged around and found a blanket in one of the overhead cupboards and laid it over Edward, covering him whole. Satisfied he was completely obscured from sight, she made her way out.

"Remember what I said about having to defend, no matter the cost?"

"Yes my lady, I remember."

"Don't look in the back, Katherine."

On hearing Silo say her full name, Kitty tilted her head, her mouth opened a little, "I cannot make myself understand what you are talking about my lady, but I will try."

She then climbed into the stricken vehicle, ignoring the blanket on Silo's request.

"What are you doing?" Silo's eyes narrowed as she asked.

"My lady, please be patient with me," came the reply as the little girl scrambled deeper into the van, her hands were a blur of motion as she fiddled with and prodded with various pumps, head down beneath the van's insides.

"We don't really have time for this," Silo added.

Kitty pulled herself upright from the wreckage with her hands, wobbling carrying wafer cones. She breathed a little easier and managed a smile when she straightened her hands high into the air, "My Lady, I bought some creamed ice for the journey."

Silo shook her head and raised her eyebrows uncertainly.

Kitty bit her lip and wiped some more vomit from it, a hard skill whilst carrying ice cream cones, "I'm sorry, I meant ice cream, my lady." Silo took one longingly sad look at the ice cream van, knowing she could never come back from what she had just done, "My lady, are you well?"

Silo raised her face, "Sorry Kitty, what did you say?"

The young girl gave a shy smile and handed one cone to Silo, who wiped away another tear and sniffed loudly, "Thank you."

Silo gave her face one more wipe with the side of her hand, taking care with the nose and eyes especially.

She offered the same hand out to Kitty who tentatively held it. Silo looked down to her, "Ok kiddo, let's get ready for an adventure."

"Yayyy!" Kitty's hand gripped Silo's harder as her nerves began to disappear. The two headed off, swinging each other's arms merrily and licking away at their cones.

The Hunters

The rain hammered down on the two figures who had given up looking around for proper shelter, and crouched down in a broken-down garage, "Why is it we never get a gig in warmer climates?"

"Why is it you never shut up?"

Mason looked to his boss, intent on speaking on, but thought better of it. Orion offered a glare back and muttered to Mason, "So do we have any information on what's happening here?" Mason kept quiet, "Did you hear me?" Mason's rain-soaked expression turned serious.

"I thought you wanted me to 'shut up'?"

Orion smiled, all wet teeth, "Mason old buddy, I'm just joshing with you, having some fun, that's all,"

"Are you sure there's nothing else bothering you?"

Orion's smile turned thin, "The fact that we're at another location on a mud ball of a planet trying to find a needle in the mother of all haystacks and have been for years now, my wife has gone and hope is fading fast to save our planet…other than that? I'm peachy keen."

The rain made Mason blink too frequently and he wiped the water from his eyes.

"Oh, I just thought because you threatened to kill me six times on the way over here, you may have something on your mind?"

Orion failed to answer, looking more morose in the driving rain. Mason's eyelids drifted slightly through the rain again, yet he tried to lift the dour mood.

"So I have threats of violence and a disrespectful commanding officer? This is the exact reason why I joined the planet core army."

The man in charge tilted his head slightly to let the rain make another path down his face as he ignored his colleague. Mason tried another tactic.

"I married a camel when I was eighteen years old, we got a place together."

Orion's eyebrows raised and he paid attention, "You married a camel?"

"Yeah, that's right, we got married, booked a hall and everything."

A slim sigh came from Orion's lips, "You what? It's not the point that you got married to a camel which bothers me. It's the point that you never cared to invite me."

Mason's gaze hardened, "I would have invited you, but my missus doesn't like you, in fact if I'd invited you, she would have got…"

Orion could clearly see where this was going and joined in to end Mason's sentence, they finished simultaneously, "The right hump."

"The old gags are the best eh, boss?"

Orion shrugged and brushed long wet hair off his shoulder, "Not really, just being polite to you with your unfunny gag."

Mason unbuttoned his body armour and wiped more rain from his face with his shirt, "I'm starting to see why everyone wants to kill you everywhere we go, sir."

Shivering, Orion gave a slow, bitter laugh, "What can I do to improve the situation then, Mason?"

"Well personally, I agree with all the inhabitants of every world we've been to: a bullet to the head can do wonders for someone's personality."

Orion took off his right glove and began to pick at his fingernails, "Looks like my 'Boss of the Year' award will have to wait for another year."

"Well it was between you and General Magno from the Guyuan quadrant? He's the one who found out one of his platoon was having an affair with his wife, he didn't know which one it was, so he drugged them all and buried them alive after breakfast."

Orion continued to pick at his nails, "So how come I'm behind this guy then?"

"He killed everybody after breakfast. He served up a massive fry up before he poisoned them which puts you on worse odds really."

Orion frowned, "So this guy gives his crew a big fry up breakfast, poisons them, buries them alive and he's still more popular than me?"

"Pretty much."

"Figures, and here's me thinking serving you guys alphabet soup was a treat."

The rain continued to hammer down and the drops increased in size and amount, there was a riot of howling winds.

"With regards to your earlier question and information on our location?" Mason tapped at his left glove with his rain-soaked right, it was a mini keyboard which lit up co-ordinates onto a tiny screen. The inanimate shapes of construction vehicles were laid out across the landscape. Giant cranes, excavators and tractors lay abandoned on a unfinished housing complex site. Smaller vehicles and machines were clustered around the building site with craters filling up with water dotted around the site. His eyes strolled past the various machinery, "Well the air is breathable and it seems to be some industrial site or something."

Orion looked around at all the machinery scattered around the landscape, "An industrial site, really?"

Mason ignored his superior's attempt at sarcasm and continued scanning the area with his glove, Orion took the time to continue as he squinted his tired eyes and was slightly flustered.

"So I can see why all this machinery is here, as whoever it belongs to—or hired it—is in the process of building some flats." Mason nodded, beginning to curl up is arms and shivering slightly at the foot of the garage, "But what gets me..." Orion stood up and held his hips, rolling his neck from left to right and then wiped more rain from his face, "What gets me, in this industrial wasteland with all these construction vehicles..."

Mason turned off his glove and looked to his boss, anticipating his next question, "What the hell are *they* doing here?!"

A herd of Brontosaurs made their way towards the largest of the puddles, a low dull cry echoed around the half-built garages as the head dinosaur bought the others to a stand still. Their huge graceful necks swung side to side, glistening in the driving rain. Huge tails lazily moved back and forth as their giant heads bent down to drink. Younger Brontosaurs weaved their way in-between the larger adults' legs as they reached the watering hole, which was a giant puddle in front of a new housing complex.

"Why are there dinosaurs drinking outside a block of flats in the pouring rain?"

"Not exactly sure sir," replied Mason.

"What planet is this?"

Silence followed and then Mason finally answered.

"It's Earth 19, I believe? Prehistoric life forms with an inflated property market."

Orion heard the buzz of large wings flapping and looked up to see a flight of Pterodactyls soaring above him. For a moment he was confused, unsure about what was real and what he was imagining from having no sleep. He rubbed his knees and rose slowly. The grey forms of the Pterodactyl were beginning to plummet for food, making Orion turn quickly to his assistant, "The girl isn't here, is she?"

Mason was getting prepared to duck his head from the Pterodactyls, "No, I don't think she's here."

A tremendous high-pitched shriek hit the building site as the flying dinosaurs dropped closer, extending their necks to the men on the ground. Orion sighed as the birds flew closer, "Go and pack."

"We're leaving sir?" Mason asked.

Orion simply pointed at the dive-bombing Pterodactyl, "Yeah, I think it's a pretty good time to leave, don't you think?"

Mason looked at the flying reptiles and rubbed his chin, "We need a new ship, we're low on supplies and have no crew."

Rubbing his hands into his now thick beard, Orion leaned forward, ignoring the flying terror, "So we need a ship with supplies, yes?"

"That's what I said, boss."

"So you did," the general said, interested.

"How long can we last with our current transport?"

An uneasy quiet fell above them before Mason answered, "Water is at 20%, oxygen is at 39% on the ship, medical supplies are at an all-time low, just basic field dressings left and antibiotics."

"So I take it the tangy BBQ nuts are finished?"

"Went on the first day, sir," Mason tried a cheery smile.

"Ok let's get serious, how long can we survive on this current transport and situation?"

Mason shifted around behind to reach into his backpack he pulled out his mini screen computer and plugged it into his battery pack attached to his arm, grimacing as he did so, his pain didn't go unnoticed.

"You ok there solider?" Orion asked slowly.

"After all this time and you still find it hard to communicate with me?"

"I'm still your commanding officer, solider, no matter what we've been through."

Mason shook his head, "Communication? Is that why your wife left you? Lack of communication?" From the look on Orion's face, he considered the possibility that he'd overstepped the mark.

"Watch your mouth, soldier, don't you mention my wife again."

"Your 'wife' tried to kill me and killed all of our men recently, did that escape your attention? One of the women we've been tracking for years who may know where the child is who could save our planet, which is probably dead by now...happens to be you wife!"

"Cowgirl."

Mason's train of thought tumbled off the rails, "What did you say?"

Orion replied in an unregimented normal voice, "Bailey worked on a farm years ago, it was her father's I think? Anyway, one day I was going to some convention about how to train kittens in the army or some other shit and my cheap second-hand car broke down outside her farm. I knocked on the door for help and suddenly this gorgeous creature opened it and stepped out, both of our planets suns lighted up her beauty, she was wearing a short skirt with these beautiful legs tucked into knee high boots."

Mason rubbed his lips together, picturing the image, "You have a good memory of what she was wearing that day, sir."

Grinning broadly, Orion continued, "Actually it was Bailey's sister who opened the door first, god she was hot! But Bailey was standing behind her, shy, quiet girl she was kind of geeky really, but there was something about her, something cute and unassuming. Neither one of them could fix a car but I knew I had to see her again."

"How old were you?"

"I was twenty, she was eighteen, about twenty-five years now."

Mason shook his head, confused, "But how come she looks..." He corrected himself, "Looked so young."

A frown appeared on Orion's face, "I sold that car, bought a cheaper one, and after making some 'adjustments' to the engine and driving it back the next week, the car did what I expected it to do and broke down outside her house. Bailey would come out and wait with me until the breakdown van turned up, I would always say that each week I was going to a new army convention and every time she would just smile, knowing that I was lying. We would talk for hours about everything and everyone and she was great." A small laugh surprisingly escaped from his lips, "I called her 'cowgirl' as that was the only animal they didn't have on the farm, which I thought was quite odd. We dated for a while and one thing led to another and then we got married."

Mason rubbed his aching side, beginning to become disinterested in how they met, his voice turning colder, "So like I said, how did she look so young?"

"Sorcery, she began to study at a young age. I mean technically she was born a sorceress, but she really got into it when she hit her twenties and that's when her personality changed."

"What do you mean?" Mason asked.

"The magic made her cold, more arrogant, she became obsessed with the 'Prophecy' and what she could do to defend the child."

A scowl emerged on Mason's face, "Excuse me? You're the reason why I'm stuck here on this planet because you believe in the same prophecy, you're the one who dragged me and the men all around the galaxy and now they're dead because of you, so don't go blaming your ex-wife because of your beliefs."

"Wife."

"I'm sorry?"

"She was my wife, not-ex, we didn't split up, we had issues, but we didn't split."

"Maybe you should have."

"Maybe you should mind your own business."

Mason arched his back and rubbed his side, "It seems to me that you and your wife should have spilt up years ago, I think you were hanging on to a dead relationship."

Orion waited for the flying reptiles to fly over, before he spoke, "You seem to be very opinionated on my marriage, does it concern you?"

"No, what concerns me sir is that your obsession with the child has cost the lives of so many men you believed to care for, men you were supposed to save as well as our planet."

"Unfortunately they were casualties of war, it was a shame for my brothers in arms to lose their lives, but they knew the dangers of what we were about to face."

Orion watched Mason play with his wedding ring on his left hand, "You really miss your wife, don't you?" Mason played with his lip, listening to his boss.

"Does it show? She had a body like an adventure playground, full of bumps and curves and fun to play with and I miss her, more than you know."

Orion smiled politely, "You blame me for this, don't you?"

"I don't know how your marriage was, but mine was fine and whatever little time our planet has, I could have spent it with my loved one and not you."

Cocking his head to one side, Orion had a say, "Staying with me may save our planet and your wife too."

Mason shrugged, "Yeah, probably, but would have been nice to have been given the choice."

Orion stared down and whispered, "I'm sorry for taking you and our brothers away from our loved ones, but let's find a new ship and find the 'Chosen One' to save our planet."

Mason went quiet, unconcerned about Orion's words, "I know we are low on medical supplies," Orion continued, "But do we have any beer left in that bag of yours?"

Mason smiled patiently at him again and grimacing with pain, reached into his bag and pulled out two bottles of beer, handing one to Orion.

"Your side still hurt?" Orion asked, thanking Mason with his eyes.

"Yeah, ever since your wife blew herself up next to me, my side hurts and apparently I now have issues with authority."

Orion narrowed his eyes and raised his drinking hand up in the air with a salute, "Let's raise a toast to our lost wives and find this new ship, you have no idea how I miss her."

Mason mirrored the arm salute with his drink and took a small sip of beer, "Lying bastard," he muttered softly under his breath.

CHAPTER FIVE:

The Identity Grief

Earth 65

"Hooray! Here she is, finally made it, have we?"

Sully ignored the sarcasm from Poxon and took her place at the registration. When Achilles saw that Sully failed to react to Poxon's semi-joke, he stepped in, "You ok? You didn't look that good yesterday."

"I'm fine."

"Are you sure? I mean…"

"I SAID I'M FINE!" Sully snapped. Eyes grim and head down, she composed herself in front of her shocked friends, "I'm sorry." She slowly turned to Achilles, "I'm sorry, didn't get much sleep, I really don't need this stupid trip."

Achilles didn't know what to say, he'd never seen Sully so angry before; she was miserable at the best of times, but never shouted. He gently put his arm around her and said nothing.

"I wish I'd thought of that," grinned Poxon, "Could have scored me some major babe points."

Sully raised a smile and playfully thumped Poxon on his arm, "You're a dick, do you know that?"

Poxon rubbed his arm with a fake grimace, "I know."

Kane unwrapped his arms from around Lacy and seemed satisfied that the situation had been resolved,

"Now that you've finished kissing and making up, we can make our way to the shuttle, is that ok?"

Achilles was unsure about Sully, but nodded anyway, "Ok, let's make our way inside." He turned to the stunning blonde, Cameo, sitting quietly to his left, slightly startled, "When did you get here? I didn't see you turn up."

The beautiful girl put her phone away and smiled, backed up with a sweet stare, "You'll find I'm full of surprises."

"You ready to go then?"

"Yep, let's go," Cameo smiled.

The college students gathered around the huge shuttle and waited for their form tutor to read out the registration list.

The main hangar was awash with frenzied students rushing around and joining their tutors in lining up and queuing at various doors to enter the huge shuttle.

Strange animals were still being loaded in at the cargo bay. The shuttle was so big that none of the teaching personnel were aware of the fatalities that'd happened earlier. Maintenance teams carried out final safety checks, preparing for the launch. The anxious teenagers waited in line and watched late equipment being loaded.

"This is going to be so cool!" Poxon nudged Achilles.

"Dude, I know! It's going to be so epic."

Cameo lifted her head from her phone with a hint of superiority, "My god! Could you two be any nerdier?"

Poxon scratched his ear slowly, "Sorry, 'Miss not-over-yourself-yet' when are you leaving us to play a human trampoline on some homeless bum?"

"I'll let you know when I've finished with your dad," Cameo said not missing a beat.

Poxon went silent, knowing that all of their parents were missing. Nevertheless, it was a good joke; Cameo smelt lovely and he let it slide with a tainted smile.

"Good one."

She looked around with fake concern, "What happened to the other nerd?"

Poxon and Achilles traded glances and looked back at her, "What are you talking about?"

Cameo looked down at her elbow and scratched it gently, "Fat man is usually joined at the hip by another loser, Harley, I haven't seen him today."

Achilles let his leadership mantle drop and began to snigger with Poxon, "He's not here, he's over there."

Cameo followed where Achilles' hand was pointing and looked at the space cruiser, she lifted her top lip from her teeth to produce a curious smile, "He's on there? He snuck onto the ship?"

Achilles and Poxon nodded in exited unison, "Yep, he's on board, he smuggled on about ten minutes ago." Poxon smiled.

"Why would he do that?"

Poxon looked as if it was like the first time Cameo had asked such a stupid question, "Really? This is Harley we're talking about here, he can scope some info about anything he wants to and feed it back to us, nothing will get by him."

"So, he's snuck onto the ship for what reason again? Is he getting ready for a date with a girl or something?"

Achilles looked uneasy, "No, he hasn't been the same since the girl he meant online blew herself up in that science experiment, it cut him up quite bad."

"Her too, I'd expect."

"CAMEO!" Achilles shouted.

"That's bang out of order, he really liked that girl."

"'Bang' out of order, Achilles? Strange choice of words."

"Damn," Achilles muttered.

Sully quietly moved past the kissing-again couple of Lacy and Kane and sat next to Cameo and spoke softly, "You certainly get around, Kane."

Lacy pulled away from her boyfriend, "What does she mean by that?"

Kane simply shrugged his shoulders, "Don't know."

Lacy wasn't convinced, "What did she mean saying, 'You get around' then?"

Kane put his hands up in defence, "I have no idea what she's talking about."

"What did she mean?" Lacy turned to Sully, "What did you mean, Sully? Take it back."

"No."

Sully left the bickering lovebirds to it and spoke softly again, but tight with authority.

"I'm not apologising for anything anymore, I've said, Kane is a bigger tramp than Cameo and Harley is a big boy and once we board the ship and go through all the shit introductions with the zoo staff and listen to their shit, we can go and find Harley, mourn about his dumb girlfriend who should have 'cut the blue wire' if I'm honest, have a tour and look at the stupid animals and then get off this pissing stupid space zoo."

Achilles sized up Sully and looked to Cameo, "Was she talking to you?"

Cameo shook her head and studied Sully who began to suddenly start coughing uncontrollably. Sully's sudden grim mouth produced more and more blood, which decorated the tough grass near the landing bay.

Cameo looked at the blood on the ground, making sure that none had landed on her. Unconcerned, she looked into her oversized handbag and pulled out a nail file, "Think she was talking to you, babes."

Earth 13: One Month Later

Kitty stared, puzzled at the list in her hand. She could read quite well for a girl of her age, but was having trouble working out what some of the words meant. She turned the piece of paper upside down to make some sort of headway, but it wasn't working, "My lady black, I cannot understand the words on this paper."

Silo sighed loudly, "For the last time, it's Silo!"

"Forgive me, my lady black?"

"My name is Silo, not black." She glanced at the numbers on her wristwatch and found Kitty's eyes burning a hole at her, one more sigh made her stop, "What is it now, Kitty?"

The young girl looked around, there wasn't anybody looking at them anymore; all the other people who stared at them as they walked through the packed market place, were *still* in the market place.

The faces, which looked slightly ashen as the dark woman with striking blue hair strolled confidently past with a little blonde girl in tow, all looked like little ants now as Silo and Kitty walked on top of a huge church roof.

"Everybody was looking at us."

"No, everybody was looking at me."

"Why would they do such a thing?" Kitty asked.

Silo's voice went quiet with bored control, "What did I tell you?"

Kitty looked to the near, dull sky and remembered, slightly uncertain, "Because they are...?"

She struggled hard with the question, "Dickheads? Is that the term?"

Silo smiled, "No, but close, try again."

"Ignorant?"

"Sort of, but I need more."

Kitty's little tongue poked out the side of her mouth in concentration, "Scared of..."

"Go on..."

"Scared of what they don't understand?"

"Good girl."

"Thank you, my lady."

Kitty returned to the perplexing list in her hands, "I am yours to command as you saved my life my lady, but as you have said many times since our introduction, it's 'doing my head in'?"

"All in good time," Silo said.

It was Kitty's turn to sigh now, "I do not take kindly to these tales of witchcraft with which you have betided me."

"We've been through this before, Kitty: you have a remarkable ability, one which none of this world have ever seen or understand. You have to see that ability, believe in yourself, before we can carry on. Are you hungry?"

Kitty shook her head, "No thank you, my lady."

"Where do you go to find a decent steak around here?" The blank look on Kitty's face answered it for her, "Ok, well read out what we have on the list."

"Why my lady? And what is the purpose of us being upon this place of worship?"

Silo was getting too used to Kitty's whining, "Just read out the list please? Or better yet, just go through the bag and show me what you've got."

Kitty grumbled as she rummaged through the bag, "My lady, there are four strawberries, sugar, lime juice, bat wings, snake blood, a bowl and…" She held up two separate bottles, "My lady, I cannot recall us purchasing such bottles as these from those market traders, what is inside them?"

Silo gave a reflective smile and took them from the confused girl, "These, kiddo, are my own personal stash which I hid in my shuttle."

"My lady?"

"We have strawberry liquor and a glorious bottle of white rum."

"My lady?"

"Do you have to keep saying that?"

Kitty stopped walking and tapped her foot, "My lady, do you have to keep calling me kiddo? Whatever that title means?"

Before Silo could answer Kitty continued walking, "Stalemate…my lady?"

Silo bit her bottom lip as another smile was forcing its way through. She placed the bottles on the church roof and went through the rest of the ingredients putting all but the bat wings and snake blood in the wooden bowl. She mashed them all together and poured the result into a small cup which was also in the bag.

"Ok kiddo, sorry Kitty, this potion is called a daiquiri and it well help you to teleport, which, before you ask again, is how you left your uncle's cart and ended up in the sea, in fact it's actually how you ended up on this planet in the first place."

"What do you mean, my lady?"

"Shit!" Silo breathed in, "Doesn't matter, stand there please," Silo said indicating to a gap on the roof.

"Why my lady?"

"It's time for you to step up and embrace your sorceress heritage," Silo began to usher the scared little girl to the edge of the roof.

"My lady, I don't understand."

"Basically, drinking this magic potion will help you teleport."

Silo gave the cup to the shivering little girl and took a step back.

"Drink it and then concentrate, think of the other side of the roof and you should teleport and reappear over there."

Kitty hesitated and raised a little eyebrow, "Go on," Silo pressed.

Kitty slowly took a sip and spat it out immediately, "Yuck! This drink is disgusting!"

"Don't care, just close your eyes and concentrate."

Silo's voice was starting to sound hard, which Kitty wasn't used to. She kept her eyes shut and trembled about the height and for the first time. Silo changed her tone:

"Keep them shut, don't look at me, just try to imagine yourself on the other side of the roof." Silo's tone was sounding more superfluous by the second, "I won't ask you again Kitty, just think about where you want to go and you should appear there."

Kitty looked down at the little people on the ground below, some had now taken the time to look at the girl wobbling atop the church roof. She heard Silo's voice growing louder behind her. Kitty wasn't as strong as her, the blue-haired woman had a stomach as strong as a bull, while at the moment her own stomach twisted like snakes.

"THE OTHER SIDE OF THE ROOF, KITTY! TELEPORT NOW!"

Genuine terror was spread all over Kitty's face and tears soon followed, "MY LADY, FOR THE LOVE OF GOD I CANNOT DO IT."

Silo's eyes grew large and animated, "I SAID DO IT!"

"PLEASE MY LADY! I CAN'T!"

The sight of Kitty crying and balancing precariously on the church edge finally made Silo stop shouting and walk over. She took the little girl's hand in hers and held her small blonde head with her other.

"I'm sorry Kitty, I thought you were ready to teleport again."

Kitty raised her head between gasping sobs and spluttered out a reply, "My lady, I can't do it, I tried to disappear like you said, I really can't! That is something I cannot do."

Silo picked up the cup of alcohol strawberry drink from the ground and straightened up whilst taking a sip and smiled at Kitty.

"Don't worry kiddo, it's fine."

She rolled her head from side to side and gave Kitty a little shove off the roof.

Watching the screaming girl plummet to the ground, Silo took another sip from her gorgeous drink, "That tastes bloody lovely."

Earth 65

Harley walked through what seemed to be another endless corridor in the space zoo.

He was quite impressed by the layout; the schematics of the medical bay was what he was most impressed by. The design crew found it necessary to put diagrams of the ship's quarters all over massive screens illuminating from the ceilings. Making his way through the massive ship, Harley wanted to find the cargo hold to see some of the animals but had somehow managed to end up in one of the medical bays instead.

Most of the crew were still outside awaiting their orders and stations before the ship blasted off, so Harley knew he didn't have much time to snoop around to find something which could prove his worth to his friends. He sat down behind a remarkably clean desk and tapped the controls in a makeshift sequence on a computer panel. He looked intensely at the data streaming across the screen. '*Wow! How can they do that?*' he thought, his fingers caressed the keyboard as he sought out more information about the cargo.

He pressed more buttons on the keyboard and suddenly and slowly some small cryogenic tubes rose from small gaps from within the control desk. Looking at the time on a clock on the wall, Harley checked his own watch and huffed, knowing he didn't have much time to search the rest of the room. Swiping his watch face, Harley's fingers typed in the phone mode and rung Achilles.

Nervously waiting, he breathed a sigh of relief when Achilles answered.

"Where are you, Harley? We are about to board the ship."

"Just shut up a minute and listen to me."

Harley had interrupted him, which was something he wouldn't have normally done and waited for a rebuke from the other line, the silence meant he was in the clear and he carried on, "Look, I'm going to send you pictures of what I can see in this ship, it's amazing."

"What do you mean?" Achilles' voice crackled from the other end.

"There's creatures in here, all sorts."

"Of course there's creatures in there, it's a zoo," Achilles said dismissively.

He could tell by the tone in Harley's voice that it was something important to him, so he breathed in and let Harley finish, "Go on."

Harley nervously rubbed his mouth, "I think they're creating something, lots of test tubes here, not just one single specimen but many."

Achilles began to finally show interest, "Many what?"

Harley shrugged his shoulders, a force of habit even when he was alone in a room, "I'm not sure who these people in this zoo are? But computer simulations show that they are trying out genetic experiments on pure, healthy organisms."

Achilles' eyes changed from rolling around lazily to darting about nervously, "I'm not going to ask you again Harley, what does it all mean?"

"Hold on mate, I think someone's coming."

Harley ended the conversation prematurely but kept the camera on his watch. He suddenly turned around to face his intruder and then wished he had never stepped foot on the *Utopia* space shuttle.

It took a matter of seconds for Harvey's eyes to adjust to what had entered the room. A giant turkey-like creature ambled into his sight. It had a big head and a long neck with huge blinking eyes that glowed in the reflected light; there were no feathers on its body, just a leathery reptilian hide; it had razor-sharp claws on each hand and a giant snakelike tail kept it balanced.

Harley stared at the giant lizard. He recognised it immediately as a sway lizard; he'd seen pictures of them as a child in books and later on various documentary shows on television.

Heffernan City wasn't governed by the same laws as Olympia, so television wasn't banned. Harley was always fascinated by these classic creatures of prey, but this beast wasn't on a nature programme; it was standing in front of him and he didn't have the comfort of a television screen to keep him safe.

He kept on staring at its unreadable eyes, ignoring the pee that began to run down his leg. The sway lizard reacted first and let out an ear-piercing shriek and launched itself at the frightened teenager. Harley got up and made a dash behind him back to the door he came through, running frantically down the next corridor.

The bigger creature was on the boy in a few quick bounds knocking his back and sending him flying across the room. Harley twisted around and scuttled on his back.

As the lizard moved in for the kill, Harley pressed the camera device on his watch in a horrific panic. The flash blinded the creature and it recoiled away in shock, and bellowed its annoyance.

The camera watch flashed on as the lizard rolled its head to the side as the clicks continued. Harley kept on pressing, knowing his life depended on it, knowing as soon as the flashes stopped his life would end too. But the creature was backing away, the camera watch was working. *I'm doing it! The nerd is doing it! The nerd is winning!* Harley thought. The sway lizard hissed menacingly at Harley as it moved backwards, becoming more and more confused. The teenager knew this was now his only chance to escape; as his confidence grew he began to walk towards the giant lizard, ignoring running in the opposite direction and feeling he needed to keep forcing the creature back. He was winning against a magnificent beast and finally felt so good about it. This was his moment to shine and it was a shame that nobody else was around to see it; none of his friends were around to watch his moment of glory. Not his nerd partner in crime Poxon, the slutty Cameo, the constantly moody Sully and even the self-appointed boss Achilles, so eager to stamp his urban street ideas on everything, most of the time; they were all missing out on the lowly geek guy taking down such a vicious, dangerous lizard.

As thoughts of premature glory filled his head, Harley failed to notice the sway lizard lowering its own. With its shoulders hunched like a bitter old man, it suddenly spun its whole body round with alarming speed. The whip-like tail knocked Harley down again and this time the lizard was upon him before he could press his camera watch. As he lay defenceless on his back, not even the sound of his chest being crushed by the heavy clawed leg of the lizard could change the final words in his mind. *Stupid nerd,* he thought.

Earth 13

Kitty had seen a giant catapult once, from a distance outside a castle grounds. She had wondered sometimes what it would feel like to be shot from a catapult, to soar through the air like a graceful swan, but now excitement had been overtaken by horror as she hurtled towards the ground. The screams from the people on the floor watching her fall, drowned out her own, she had stopped whining now. She kept her hands on her heart and it was pounding hard against her chest. She just had enough time to think why Silo had pushed her off the roof in the first place, it would be the last thing to go through her mind, probably the second last thing as soon as she hit the pavement.

Suddenly, a wave of black smoke quickly swirled about her, it encased her whole body and wouldn't leave Kitty and was followed by a quick blue flash of light. The people on the ground screamed as the little girl, who was falling with frightening speed towards them, suddenly disappeared in front of their eyes.

Kitty reappeared back on the roof and slammed with incredible force straight into Silo. The impact sent both of them spinning across the delicate church top and crashing against the side.

"OH MY GOD! OH MY GOD! OH MY GOD! MAY GOD PRESERVE ME, MY LADY!" Silo wearily stood to her feet and checked herself for broken bones as the excited Kitty continued, "MY LADY! HOW DID YOU KNOW THAT THE WITCHES' BREW YOU MADE WOULD SAVE MY LIFE?"

Silo blinked hard and rocked her head from side to side, still checking for injuries. Once she had convinced herself she was fine, she rubbed her broken fingernails against her palm, "I didn't."

Kitty's little eyes narrowed, "Pardon me, my lady?"

Clearing her phlegm-filled throat, Silo turned her head and looked up at Kitty, "I had no idea that you were going to teleport from that drop, fair play to you kiddo, who knew?"

Kitty's eyes kept their stare on Silo and she spoke quietly, "I'm still trying to come to terms with some of your words you speak, my lady, but I don't understand what 'Who knew' means?"

"It means that I didn't know that you'd survive that fall."

"Really, my lady?"

Silo looked past her, "Yes."

"LIAR!"

Kitty closed her eyes and concentrated and then disappeared into a mess of blue smoke and materialised directly above Silo. She struck Silo with an unlikely blow to the face and disappeared again leaving only her now signature smoke. Silo rubbed her aching jaw and her face hardened as she waiting for another surprise attack – the wait wasn't long. Kitty reappeared before the smoke had cleared and landed a somewhat feeble kick to the back of Silo's head. There was nothing Silo could do and grimaced as the little blow still sent her forward.

"KIDDO! CUT IT OUT!" The young girl kept quiet and materialised on the other side of the roof, panting heavily, "YOU DON'T HAVE TO DO THIS, KIDDO," Silo shouted.

"YOU LIED TO ME, MY LADY, SO I'M AFRAID I DO."

Kitty charged at Silo and vanished before Silo could react, reappearing yet again above her head. She was getting the hang of her new found teleporting powers and again and again she punched and vanished before Silo could do anything.

The church roof was filled with blue smoke, with a fist and a little leg striking its target and then bouncing off the sides to teleport and strike Silo again. Finally Silo was knocked to the ground due to the frenzied attack of Kitty.

"ENOUGH!" Silo shouted.

Kitty paused and flashed a strange grin, "No, my lady."

"YES!" Silo yelled again and slowly got to her feet and raised her hands in surrender. Kitty ignored her and spoke softly, body still trembling.

"In the name of God, I will lift you from this church and drop you to the people below, my lady."

Silo began to smile and it kept rising as she took her breath back, "Well done kiddo, you've passed lesson one."

"Forgive me, my lady?"

Rubbing her eyes, Silo continued, "I took a chance on your powers re-emerging as soon as they did, but your multiple teleporting actions? That came as quite a surprise, I take my hat off to you." Silo bent down to pick her hat from off the roof, "No need now." An anguished look crept on to Kitty's face, but Silo didn't stop, "Plus those were some pretty neat punches you threw, with a little guidance we could have you being a proper little boxer."

"What nonsense do you speak of, my lady?"

"Like I said, I took a chance and it paid off."

Kitty's head dropped and she arched her shoulders, "So I take it to believe that you were not sure that I would survive that drop, my lady?"

Silo blinked a few times, still groggy from her attack and then replied, "Pretty much."

Kitty dropped into a curtsey and rose slowly, "Very well, my lady."

With lighting speed, Kitty grabbed Silo tight around the neck and with no effort at all had lifted her off the ground, Silo struggled in her grasp, "WHY WOULD

YOU DO THIS? I COULD HAVE DIED! WHAT TRICKERY HAVE YOU PUT UPON ME? I THOUGHT YOU WERE MY FRIEND, BUT YOU ARE NOTHING BUT A QUEEN OF ICE!"

Silo didn't scream, just struggled a bit more in Kitty's tight grasp, she spluttered a word out, "Bigger."

Kitty loosened her grip and dropped her, "What worries you, my lady?"

Silo's hand touched her sore neck and continued up her face to feel her bruises, "Apart from the fact that you tried to choke me to death, you've grown bigger and slightly older as well."

Kitty looked at her dress, which had stretched slightly and was ill-fitting, her whole body was different than how she remembered. It was her turn to feel her face, "I feel no different, my lady," she said uncertainly.

Silo wiped the snot from her nose and mumbled, "When you teleport, you occupy pockets of time, no matter how brief it is."

Kitty's blank expression was enough for Silo to continue, "The teleportation powers that you borrow from time are stored, so as soon as you reappear, that time is added to your own, making you older."

"So, I am to believe that the more I disappear, the older I will become, my lady?"

"Yes, but with training we can change that, you can store time with ability, but you can never turn it back; you need another powerful sorceress to help." Kitty's face was blank, "You create the time and they can go back with your help, one sorceress to teleport with anything she wants and another to teleport anywhere she wants."

Kitty thought for a moment, "How much have I aged, my lady?" She didn't answer and looked bleak, "My lady?"

"Sorry kiddo, my mind was somewhere else, now what did you say? Oh right, umm? Not much, only about six or seven years probably."

Kitty's heart sank, "May god help me, I'm old!"

Silo tried to get back her friendly voice, "No, you're sixteen or seventeen now, you were ten before I think, so yeah, let's say seventeen, eighteen at a push."

"How long will I stay like this, my lady? Forever? Am I doomed for a life as a child?"

"No, only three hundred and sixty-five days probably."

"That long? My life is doomed, my lady," Kitty said solemnly, "So am I a ten-year-old girl in the body of an adult? Will I think like an adult or still a girl?"

Silo was impressed by such a question from Kitty, "Your mind is that of a child and will quickly mature to that of an adult, it will be like eating ice cream too quick, you'll get a brain freeze."

"Isn't that dangerous, my lady?"

"Your mind is more surprising than you'd think, plus you came from another planet, so I think you'll be fine."

"I came from where, my lady?"

Silo bit her lip and silently cursed herself, bitterly regretting what she had said; the girl wasn't ready to know her origin yet, and it was twice now that she had blurted it out, "Never mind."

As the blue smoke dispersed, a spinning black hole was left in the centre of the roof. Kitty looked at it and then it disappeared as soon as her eyes focused.

"My lady, what was that?"

Silo watched Kitty push her hair back over her shoulder and her big, inquisitive eyes grew, a low laugh came from Silo's lips as she was glad the girl was asking more questions.

"You know I said when you teleport you can store time with each jump?"

"Yes, my lady?

"With the time you can't store, it gets collected and spreads itself quickly out making a little gap in reality, but as you can see it doesn't last for very long, we call them shadow holes."

"What would happen if I was to step in such a hole, my lady?"

"Well if you were to enter it, you would be lost anywhere in time, you could be flung forward or back, but chances are you would not be able to come back."

"Do you know of anyone who has entered and returned?"

Silo looked at the spot where the shadow hole once was and her eyes closed with suspicion.

"There were rumours from where I come from about one person who entered and managed to get back out, the amount of time they saw from the future and past drove them mad."

"What happened to them?"

"They came out different, babbling, weaving and shaking from all accounts; their mind was shattered, and they never were the same, wandering around the land cursed and considered a fool."

"Was it a man or a woman? Was it a witch? What new power did they possess?"

"They had something more powerful than a witch or sorceress: they had knowledge of the future."

Kitty settled down at the side of the roof, eyes closed and leaned back, "So I am a witch, my lady?"

The look in Kitty's eyes before they shut was beginning to seem scary, so Silo kept her friendly voice going, "You're much more than a witch."

"Plus, I can disappear and reappear at will?"

"Yes, you can."

"You will help me with this gift I have, my lady?" Kitty was calmer now and was breathing easier.

"Of course I will, kiddo."

"Thank you, my lady." Kitty tilted her head slightly and allowed herself a chuckle and curtsied again, "One other thing, my lady, is there any more potion left? The daiquiri?"

Silo looked around the roof and found the cup, still upright, "Yes, but you don't need the potion to teleport."

"I know my lady, but I just fancy a drink."

"Fancy?" Silo smiled, "That's a new word."

The crowds on the ground were still looking up in awe at the blue smoke event on top of the church roof and some of the more eager onlookers were trying to gain entry by the doors to see more and to confirm it was witchcraft in play. One man, whose head was covered in a black cloak, stepped away from the confusion and ducked into a quieter part of the market, which was hard to do with all the hysteria. He pulled back his sleeve and spoke into a device attached to his arm, "Hello sir?"

The device crackled slightly with static until a voice could be heard on the other end.

"Why did we ever come here? I think it's safe to say we can leave this cesspool of a planet and head off to the next one to find the girl."

Mason pulled off his hood and spoke again, "General Orion, hold tight please."

"Why?"

As the blue smoke dispersed, Mason squinted hard at the church roof and the two figures on top, satisfied he spoke again into his communicator, "I've found her."

Earth 65

"Harley? Harley?" Achilles spoke into his phone again, "Harley, answer me, we're going into the shuttle and Sully's not well."

"I'm fine," Sully growled, wiping away the blood from her mouth.

"Listen Harley, just answer the bloody phone!"

Achilles looked down at the phone in his hand and sighed. He turned to his mates and shrugged his shoulders, "He's not answering, something's wrong."

Lacy checked her perfectly manicured nails before twisting her neck around at the awesome surroundings of the zoo, "He's fine, he's probably found some geeky device which sounds terrific to him, but sad to us."

Achilles rubbed the new stubble on his chin, in slight teenage thought, "No, something has happened, if he did find something geeky, he'd be the first to be texting or ringing to tell us all about it, we have to find him."

Poxon bared his teeth with worry, concerned about his good friend.

"No, Achilles is right, Harley would have made contact with us by now, he would have reported something funny, or at least told me what wasn't?"

"Chances are you're right, Poxon," Achilles said cautiously.

A booming voice from in front shook all of the group into silence and a look from an annoyed bearded man glared at Achilles especially.

"Excuse me, is my safety presentation boring you?"

Achilles looked hard into the man's eyes, holding his stare, before bowing his head, "Sorry sir."

The man took a sip from a bottle of water on the floor beside his lecture, "Don't worry about it, I'm contracted to waffle on about the safety features; if I didn't, chances are I'd get the sack from my bosses." A small selection of the gathered audience chuckled, Achilles failed to join in, "Anyway, like I mentioned earlier my name is Captain Nate McConnell, well just Nate McConnell and I'll be in charge of this jolly boys' outing." Nate took another sip and corrected himself, "Girls' too." He flashed a grin, showing his teeth and reddish gums, "Ok, well I first of all would like to welcome you on all this maiden voyage of the *Utopia,* a new and exciting breakthrough in space travel and to delve into the world of fantastic creatures available to view on our craft."

Sully was still recovering from her sickness. She had no idea why she had puked up blood. She knew she had told her friends that under no circumstances should they call a doctor, but her bravado was failing and she could really do with seeing some sort of specialist now. Until they grew some sort of backbone and *really* did decide to help her, she wouldn't back down from what she thought was wrong. Sully didn't shout, but just spoke loud enough to be heard by Nate, "Can you justify the keeping of wild animals in captivity for the sake of earning a little extra cash for yourself?"

It took Nate a moment to catch up and realise what Sully was talking about, he squinted his eyes to make her out in the packed crowd of students, "I can assure you, young lady that every creature we have on this vessel is treated with care and sensitivity."

Lacy looked around in vain to try and find their form tutor to see if he could stop Sully from causing another scene, "Where is our teacher?" she whispered to Kane.

"I don't know, but Sully is stirring things up again," Kane replied slowly.

Sully ignored her friends' concerns and concentrated her look at the slightly annoyed captain.

"Do you or your crew have a serious programme installed to try and save endangered species?"

Nate lifted a smile, "Our zoo, *this* zoo is a great place to get close to wildlife."

"Close to wildlife? We're on a spaceship."

"Agreed, but many species on the planet are dwindling in numbers, so we have a lot of animals on this ship who are involved in a new breeding programme to bolster the population of unique creatures. If we didn't keep them on this ship, they would all surely be dead."

Nate was finding his stride now and gripped his microphone with confidence, "Now I have to say that for every animal we do save, there are loads of examples where the breeding programme was unsuccessful, does that answer your question?

Sully accelerated her speech, "How can looking at a caged animal teach us anything about wildlife? The creatures are separated from their natural habitat and have no freedom, what sort of a life is that?"

"A good one if all they are facing in the future is death."

All the students were fascinated by the ping pong ball of debate and were happy to strain their necks to hear more.

"But surely we can learn more about these animals on TV, phones or display screens in libraries in their natural habitat instead of watching them in cages?"

Nate craned his neck, "Does everyone own a TV or phone? You forget young lady that some of the students here are from cities where the Internet has been banned due to Big Man in Olympia, so if that is the case, the only way to see these beautiful creatures is in zoos around the district and here on our ship, does that answer your question?"

"Sort of," Sully grumbled, spitting out some blood.

Nate couldn't see the blood in her phlegm from his distance and just thought she was a rude teenager, unaware she was a sick one, "Well thank you for your concern of our animals, I appreciate it, now, are there any more questions?"

The captain raised his eyebrows and waited for a response as the whole student body decided that Sully's negative stance on zoology was enough for them and were just waiting for the ship to take off, "Ok, well let's get this show on the road then."

Nate smiled inwardly to his gathered crew behind him and then back to the students.

"Can we take off now, sir?" an eager freckled girl in the front row asked.

Keeping his smile, Nate shrugged good-heartedly, "The day started bad, got worse, slowly getting better, so yes, let's fly a ship out of here and see some pretty cool animals, shall we?"

The whole room cheered with excited students, as Nate sent a head nod to the engineers standing by his side. The gathered people kept nodding their heads until the whole ship suddenly began to shudder. Smooth vibrations ran through the entire craft as the engines quietly kicked in.

"Shouldn't we be strapped in for this or something?" Kane asked.

"Doesn't look like it," replied Achilles holding his stomach, hoping it would help it from turning cartwheels.

"No, the floor has a suction feature; when we begin to take off it will switch on, so even if you're standing up or decide to sit on the ground, you will not be able to move as the G-force is quite incredible." explained Nate.

"What if we're wearing heels, Captain sir?" Lacy asked, pointing to the staggeringly high shoes she was wearing.

Nate gave an extended pause and smiled again, "Those heels are fine, young lady."

The vertical acceleration at first was effortless as the rocket boosters were activated. Shock waves were blasted through the air by the incredible energy rush. As the ship raced through the skies, the students were pinned hard to the floor as the acceleration became more intense. They were thrown forward and then back, but remained rooted to the floor due to the suction.

"I feel like Poxon is sitting on me," Kane grimaced.

Poxon felt too sick to retort as the sensation of being thrown from a mountain was a little too much to bear and just gave a delayed thumbs up. In moments it went from daylight to darkness and the students were finally in space. Travelling at now a breakneck speed, *Utopia* soared above the planet.

As the students endured another explosion of force as the booster rockets were dropped, a few decks below the sway lizard roared in agony; the pressure of lift-off was too much for the lizard. All the other creatures in their cages were sedated or still in stasis and were unaware of the change from a spaceship docked on a planet to one now sailing above it.

The creature rammed its huge head against the walls of the ship in pain, continuously bashing each and every cage it passed, the creature was frustrated. It wanted to mate, it needed a partner and it was afraid.

The ship's engines drowned out the roars of the lizard, it was struggling to breathe and to stay on its feet; the suction floor was useless against claws. As the dinosaur staggered through to the next corridor, it passed a giant water tank. A massive panther shark swam to the front of it. It had gone unnoticed by the lizard as the effects of the shark's sleep stasis began to wear off. The great water beast just managed to catch a glimpse of its snake-like tail swaying idly behind it. The shark rose to the top of the surface and as its black eyes looked around. It bared its needle-like teeth and then it sighed:

"Dude, this is not good."

Earth 13

Silo rubbed her sore jaw and worked it from side to side, Kitty's little eyes stared hard at her teacher.

"I'm seventeen years old now my lady, what did you do to me?" Silo moved her hand towards Kitty's shoulder to give it a reassuring rub, but the young girl pulled away with a scowl, "I was loyal to you and willing to listen, but this talk of shadow holes and sorceresses is beyond me now."

Knowing that shoulder rubbing was out of the question, Silo merely rubbed the back of her own head instead, "I'm sorry kiddo, but you knew what this was all about."

"No I didn't my lady, in fact why am I still calling you that? A 'lady' is a Queen, a princess or at least a woman with riches, but you are just a painted woman with blue in her hair."

"Right, calling me a 'painted woman'? Slightly racist, but I guess I see your point."

Kitty closed her eyes and breathed hard, "What is the point, Silo?"

Silo thought for a while, it was strange hearing Kitty speak to her without calling her a title, she was maturing quicker than she had thought, "You have an amazing talent, Kitty, one which we've spoken about."

"One which you have spoken about and nothing else; all you have given me is this power of bewitchery and tomfoolery. I have done everything you've asked me to do and yet it appears you deem it necessary to keep me in the dark about this power I now possess, a power which makes my stomach dance around my ears."

Silo still couldn't get used to how Kitty talked, whether it was due to her new age or her environment. Kitty felt uncomfortable and rubbed her stomach. Silo's own stomach clenched and she rubbed it also, copying Kitty. They were both finally away from the church roof and prying villagers' eyes.

"Ok, let's get out of here."

Silo took over and teleported Kitty away to a forest clearing nearby. Even though Silo was an experienced sorceress, teleporting still felt like travelling blindfolded and backwards on a rollercoaster and she gave her troubled stomach another rub before speaking to Kitty after the smoke had cleared away, "One day when you're ready, then I'll explain everything to you."

Kitty's big eyes blinked back, unconvinced.

"I do not believe you my lady, or Silo, or whatever your name is, all I want to know is the truth. I followed you because you said I was gifted with some special 'ability', is that the word? You made me follow you."

"I did, and this is for your own good."

A twist of wind blew hair into Kitty's face, she brushed it away and carried on, "For what? My face is pale and bleak from the lies you have told me."

Silo coughed and suddenly got the giggles, "Sorry, but I really love the way you talk."

"I'm glad my words please you my lady, but they are words of truth and not lies."

Flapping her arms and looking at the high trees, Silo walked in a circle, crunching over twigs, "Do you trust me, Kitty?"

"From what I've seen my lady, your intent with me has not been terrible or relentless."

"But?"

"But how am I truly to know what is going through your mind? So far, witchcraft has taken me from my uncle's cart and I ended up in the sea, plus you pushed me off a church roof and now I can teleport? Is that the word?"

"It's not witchcraft and yes, the word is teleport and vanish. You are a Vanisher."

"What am I, my lady?"

"A Vanisher."

Kitty clenched and unclenched her fists, Silo was slightly concerned as Kitty was still scowling, "So through teleporting at such great lengths has aged me as well?" Silo's giggles had stopped and she nodded solemnly, "Fine," Kitty said, "So you have taken me away from my family to teach me the ways of such trickery, you won't tell me why we can't stay still for very long or who the man was in that ice cream carriage? Just that some men will want me to use my power for evil and that's it?"

Silo nervously played with her blue hair and sent Kitty a well-intentioned smile, "All I'm asking is to trust me. If you don't, then feel free to walk or teleport out of here right now. Look, I will explain everything to you later, if you just wait and be patient, but if you go, you mustn't let anybody—and I mean *anybody*—see you use your powers."

"Why, my lady?"

"This world isn't ready to see the power that we have at our disposal; it would have cataclysmic consequences if we were spotted using them by anybody just for a second."

"I don't know what those words mean again as you tend to talk such tripe, but what of the display on the church roof? Surely the market traders saw such an event? And what do you mean 'this world?' There are no other worlds apart from this one."

Kitty had caught Silo off guard with her own words and it had made her think, "Ok, I'll get back to you on that but as for the church roof? Good point, I hadn't thought of that."

"So, what of it, my lady?"

Silo continued walking in a circle, pondering, "Nothing, we should be ok. I don't think they saw too much, just a load of blue smoke and fireworks, they might think it was a hanging or execution or something."

Kitty flicked her back, "I wouldn't jest on such things, my lady, an execution is a grim sight to behold."

"Have you seen many?" Silo asked.

"Too many for eyes as young as mine." Kitty examined her hair again, "Although not so young now."

Silo felt her own hair and realised her hat was gone.

Some people had begun wandering through the forest, which gave Silo cause for concern. She ignored her missing headgear for a while, "We have to leave here now, we will continue this conversation later along with more training."

"Fine."

Silo's eyes widened, "Seriously? You're coming with me?"

Kitty shrugged and walked over the broken twigs as well, "My faith in you is misplaced and I can see your soul is broken and tortured, but I do trust you."

Silo was silent as she processed Kitty's words, "Really?"

"Yes, really."

Kitty's quick smile made Silo do the same, she held her right arm aloft, "Hi five?"

Kitty shook her head, "I do not understand, am I stupid for not knowing what this means?"

Silo's smile held, "Of course not, just slap my hand."

The nervous girl wiped her forehead, "Is it some trickery? Will we be bonded like a spell?"

"Just slap it."

Kitty looked at Silo blankly, before closing her eyes and sending an awkward slap to Silo's outstretched hand, she opened one eye cautiously, "Are we twinned with magic now? Will I become as arrogant and bitter as you?"

"Let's just go and try and find my hat," Silo said.

"Why bother? It was a silly hat anyway."

Silo simply snaked her arm through Kitty's and led her away, still beaming.

Mason held out his gun and pointed it at the two figures in the distance.

Orion gently lowered it with his own, "Not now, not yet."

"Why's that? It's set to stun anyway."

"It's too soon," replied Orion.

"What are you talking about? I thought you understood where I was coming from, to make her teleport our planet's inhabitants away from the sun's flares."

Orion looked around to see if they were being followed themselves and spoke quietly to his remaining soldier, "There's nothing I want more than to take that girl now and force her back to Rayash."

"If it's still there," Mason added.

Orion went quiet and then continued with eyebrows raised, "Of course it's still there."

He watched as Kitty carried on walking unaware in front of them, "She has the ability to become the most powerful sorceress in the universe."

Mason crossed his arms "Are you sure about that?"

"Look at her! Magic-wise she doesn't know if she's coming or going, we have to stay on her and watch her gain confidence with her abilities."

"Sir, We don't have time, our planet is dying, we must do something now! We've been searching, no sorry... hunting this girl for years, lost our loved ones, we've travelled and spent time on so many planets trying to find her and now that we have, you want her to walk out on us? Is that what you're saying?" Mason said, raising his gun again.

"That's exactly what I'm saying, solider, so stand down."

Mason kept his gun raised, quivering slightly, "I have a shot sir, I can end this right now."

Orion spoke again, firmly, "Stand down, solider, we'll handle this another way." Mason's arm didn't move, "I won't repeat myself again, Mason."

With a huge sigh, Mason turned back to Orion, "Ok, what did you have in mind, sir? And not to step out of line, but it had better be good."

"I see things differently than you, Mason."

"I've noticed sir, so what's the alternative?"

"As I said, we wait until she gains confidence in her new powers, wait until she becomes more powerful than us two idiots can possibly imagine and then we can strike."

Mason squinted at his boss, "If we wait until she becomes more powerful, how are we meant to stop her?"

Orion studied Mason's eyes after they opened again, hard and intrusive, "We let her come to us, we watch her become the ultimate sorceress and then we take her."

"How do we do this?"

Orion narrowed his own eyes at Mason, he reached into his back pack and pulled out a warm bottle of water, offering it to the quizzical man, "Trust."

CHAPTER SIX:

Divide And Conker

Earth 65

Space cruiser: Typhon
Class unit: 5680
Identification Model: Utopia
Classification: Zoo registry
Storage intake: Chamber infinite 11098
Captain: Nate McConnell
Location: cargo hold

"So, what does this button do?"

Cameo knew she had a reputation for being a little too friendly with the boys in her year, she wasn't particularly proud of it, but it got her what she wanted. She wasn't a pushover when it came to the opposite sex and if she wanted to mess around with one or two guys, then she knew how to protect herself, "I said what does this button do?" she repeated the question.

"Ow! Would you keep still?" An uncomfortable groan came from an older male voice.

Cameo sat awkwardly on the man's lap as they both sat on a chair positioned in front of a massive control desk, "You didn't answer me?"

The man slapped her hand playfully, "You're going to get us into trouble, we're not even supposed to be in the cargo hold; if the zookeepers or Captain Nate come back, they're going to create a stink if they find us."

Cameo turned them both round in the chair to show him the view from behind. Cages of various and exotic animals were lined up in the hold as Cameo held her nose in protest, "You weren't joking about the smell, it stinks in here."

He stroked her thigh slowly and sighed, "You forget that this spaceship is a zoo? Well a learning centre developed for an enterprise and journey of self-discovery."

Cameo giggled, "You sound like a commercial."

"It's what the captain told us when we came on board, it's funny how you remember the little things."

"So why did we have to meet in this smelly animal place then?"

The man gently pushed her off his lap and started to button up his shirt, "We have to meet somewhere where nobody can see us."

Cameo pursed her pink lips and smiled, "I don't know why you're bothering with all this cloak and dagger stuff, there's nobody left in the college we're fooling, they all know about us."

He looked at his phone and checked for messages as it was turned off while he was otherwise engaged with Cameo.

"The less people know about us the better," he replied, his eyes slowly drifting back to the girl, "I have a lot at stake here, you knew that when we started this."

Cameo stretched and began to wander towards the animals, the man watched her cute petite frame saunter to inspect the cages. Her devilish green eyes darted left to right as she studied the creatures in their lock-ups. Cameo was stunning, she knew the fact but didn't play on her looks; if men wanted to be with her, it was her who called the shots, not them. It seemed to be working as she had bagged herself an impressive specimen. She put her fingers through the cage of a young male Belinge tree jumper cat, who cautiously walked over to the wriggling fingers of the person disturbing his sleep and rubbed his soft head against the painted black fingernails of Cameo. She managed to crouch and poke her hand in further to stroke the now purring cat, who was now content that this new interference to its cage would not cause a problem.

"Do you love me?" she turned to ask the man.

"You know I don't," he answered.

"Good! Just hope you weren't going soft for me," her words drifted off.

"I'm still married you know, and I still love my wife."

He followed her to the cages, caught her around her waist to her surprise and squeezed gently. She turned around and kissed him on his neck.

"How old is you wife now?"

"None of your business."

"Thirty? Forty?" He squeezed her again and she moaned dreamily, "I'm just saying."

"Well don't, she's great and I love her dearly."

Cameo flicked her hair back in his face, "Well obviously you do or else you wouldn't be here with me." She looked to the floor with a smile, "Do you want to go again?"

"I have to take a piss."

Cameo sighed, head still looking at the ground, "How romantic."

"Besides, I have to get back before the briefing starts, the captain is going to start his waffle and I have to be there."

Cameo felt eyes on her and glanced around at the caged animals and then back to her lover, "Do you have to leave now?" she asked.

"You know I do, I have to get back to the college class a.s.a.p."

"Why?" her voice sounded like whiney child.

The man spotted something on the floor and picked it up, dismissing it as dust and then turned back to Cameo, "Because I'm your teacher."

The new substitute teacher led the added group of college kids out of the ship's foyer and into the first display of animals on view. She was annoyed that one of her fellow teachers had left her on her own to deal with the added number of rowdy students; she was pretty pissed off to put it mildly.

"Are you paying attention at the back?"

Miss Dwells hated being on tour guide duties but had no choice. She was a good teacher, very young just barely older than most of her charges, she had revised her notes a dozen times before the trip. She had been given a layout of every animal section before the ship was even finished and knew exactly what to say and when to say it, but she had counted on having a colleague by her side when the trip started.

"Sorry Miss," Achilles gave a half-hearted apology, he whispered next and ignored Miss Dwells' minor protests.

"This is bollocks, I haven't got a clue where he is."

Lacy pulled out some bunches for her hair from tight leather pockets, her head rolling from side to side slowly.

"Will you stop moaning, Achilles, nobody knows where Harley is, he does it all the time, this is all new to us too you know."

Achilles shrugged his broad shoulders, which were big for an eighteen-year-old's. He stood taller than his college friends, his bold brown arms squeezed out of an extremely tight t-shirt and he folded them in annoyance.

Lacy was still fiddling with her long black hair that reached the small of her back, she prodded Achilles giggling as she did so. He wriggled his own back to shift her off. His frown deepened, "Get off of me Lacy, you know what I mean."

"Don't let Harley or Cameo spoil things for us, this trip is the first of its kind and we're the first college to be given a grand tour, you should be more grateful."

"Grateful? Grateful for that annoying stink? Grateful that none of the teachers seem concerned about kids going missing on this dump, and, by the way, two of them are our friends, and grateful that for some reason nobody can reach home?"

Lacy prodded him again, her voice with more concern than last time she spoke, "Because we're on a space cruiser, nobody can reach Heffernan City or Olympia."

"You know what I mean, stupid," Achilles snapped.

"Hey! You cut that shit right out."

It took an insult to Lacy for Kane to join in the search and the conversation, "Just chill out, Achilles, she's only saying."

"Shut your noise, Kane, your missus is annoying but she isn't as bad as you, you're only with her because her dad is rich."

"I AM NOT!" Kane rubbed Lacy's arm in an assuring manner, "You know I'm not, don't you?"

Lacy gave him a quick peck on the cheek, "I know you're not, babes."

"Cheers, honey."

Kane walked on at the front as Lacy gave a sneaky glance to Achilles and whispered to him, "He is really."

"I know," Achilles replied just as quickly.

"Would you all just shut up for one moment please?"

The group went silent as Sully spoke, the girl at the front of the group and the only person that they all listened too, even Achilles.

"It's happening again."

Sully doubled over in pain and again released a burst of vomit and blood onto the floor, her eyes wide open.

"Excuse me Miss Dwells? I think I need to see a doctor."

The rest of the gathered students watched Sully's lips part and turned away in disgust, "Euughhh!" The girls in the groups screeched and backed away, "That is so disgusting Sully, I mean could you be any more gross?"

Sully ignored the red-haired girl in her class and emptied her stomach once more.

"Oh, good God!" Miss Dwells exclaimed, "Ok, everybody remain calm. Sully how are you feeling?"

"Literally puking my guts out, Miss, cheers for the concern though."

Miss Dwells looked at Sully who returned the stare coldly, "Right can someone take this girl to the medical bay please?"

"Can't you, Miss?"

"I have my hands full with this class," she told the increasingly annoying red-headed girl.

"I'll take her, Miss."

"Thank you…" She was angling for a name.

"It's Poxon, Miss."

"Poxon, thank you," said Miss Dwells.

"I can get to the medical bay myself," Sully angrily looked into the soft caring eyes of her best friend, "But I would like Poxon to make sure I get there safely."

Poxon rubbed a hand on his already thinning hair and took Sully by the hand, "There's holomaps all over the place, we should be able to find the medics."

Achilles stopped them from leaving and turned his head to the flustered teacher, "I'll go with them, Miss."

"No, it doesn't take two of you to take her to the medic, so far I'm missing a teacher and two other students, who aren't even from my class, so I'll be dammed if I'm losing anybody else on this tour, so hurry up, the sooner you reach the medical bay, the sooner they can find out what's wrong with the girl."

Miss Dwells went back to her study notes, on paper not on an electric device, and tried to educate the rest of the class, pointing uncertainly to a strange looking dog type creature looking forlorn in a cage, "Ok, now who can tell me what this is?"

A few hands with more confidence than her shot up in the air. With the teacher distracted Achilles turned back to Poxon, "Listen, as soon as we can get away, we'll come and find you, keep your phone on and let me know where you are, we have to find Harley and Cameo, it's unlike them to be away for so long."

Poxon tipped his head towards Achilles, "Do you think Cameo is with our form tutor?"

Achilles folded his arms and rolled his brown eyes, "I think it's a pretty safe bet."

Professor Lionel Gregory ran his finger down Cameo's arm and she shivered slightly, "Cut that out, besides I thought you wanted to head back to the briefing."

The teacher continued to escort his student through the massive corridors of the *Utopia*.

On either side were dozens of animals locked in cages, some were barred, others had toughened glass, but each specimen was getting more attention from Cameo than her lover. His warm hands stroked her shoulders and this time she shrugged them off.

"What's the matter with you, Cameo? You moan about not spending more time with me, so when I sort something out where we finally can? You get all funny about it."

She turned around and peered at him with deceptive eyes, "Oh yeah! You've really pulled out all the stops for a romantic day out at the zoo."

"Well this was the only time I could get! My wife is back next week and…"

"Don't care about your old cow of a wife." Cameo turned back to the animals, and raised her voice slightly as the creatures did the same, "Please don't mention old misery guts in front of me again, besides these little buggers look like better company than she'd ever be."

"Don't call her that."

Lionel had a quick intake of breath and wiped his sweating brow, "She's ill and it's not my fault, the doctor's don't know what's wrong with her and we have the kids and she's put on weight and…"

"Shhhh!" Cameo put a finger to his lip, "I'm young and beautiful and don't care about your wife and kids, the only person I care about is my dad, he went missing six years ago thanks to Big Man and his games and I want him back so much, so waffle on as much as you like about your fat wife, I don't give a shit."

Lionel wrapped his arms around her neck and nuzzled it gently, closing his eyes, "You are such a bitch."

"I know," was all Cameo would say.

"I'm late enough as it is, I've probably missed the briefing and my class will be bloody annoyed, but it was worth it to spend time with you."

"Oh please! Could you talk any more cheese? And that terrible smell is back again."

Lionel kept his eyes shut and continued to nibble Cameo's neck, "Must be the animals, we are at a zoo don't you know?"

"No, it's not that, can't you smell it? It was in the cargo hold and now it's back up here."

A smile split his face and he purred, "I'm the only animal around here."

Suddenly her body was thrust against one of the cages and the teacher's hands started trembling all down her side, a teasing smile spread on her face, but she knew it wasn't the right time for more hi-jinks with her tutor.

"Lionel? I told you to cut it out! We've got the rest of the trip to fool around."

Lionel's hands were still rubbing up and down her body, she was getting slightly irritated, "Have you gone deaf? I told you stop it." Lionel still wasn't listening, "I said STOP IT!" Cameo spun around angrily and confronted Lionel. His arms were fumbling at her side as she looked up and gave an ear-piercing scream, louder than all the animals in the cages put together. Lionel didn't respond though; his head was missing. In a few quick, yet silent steps the sway lizard was upon them, biting his head off and trying hard to swallow it.

She fell backwards and continued to scream in terror as the headless body of her lover fell the other way. The dinosaur had momentarily forgotten about her and was busily chewing away on Lionel. She looked at the huge clawed feet and was mesmerised by its enormous tail, and once Cameo had taken in what exactly she was looking at, her mind cleared and the panic set in once again.

Holding in the urge to scream, she turned around in her very tight leather trousers and wobbly legs and began to run for her life with her high heels in hand. Cameo could no longer hold in her fear and screamed in terror as she bolted down the corridors. The sway lizard's head was still deep in entrails, lifting it up to allow itself to try again at nibbling a piece of Lionel's tough thigh. The dinosaur left it and was about to move on to another part of Lionel, when he saw the frightened girl tear down the corridor. The creature was still hungry and ignored the body of Lionel, it could somehow tell that the figure running in front of it had a better taste and started to chase after her.

Cameo was attempting to make it to a flight of stairs but knew she wouldn't get there in time before the monster behind her would grab her like Lionel. She had to find a hiding place quickly. Still clutching her high heels tightly and with tears streaming down her face, she darted to her left and ran into a creature containment unit. It was a water creature of some sort as there was a giant pool in front of her. There was a locking feature on the doors and Cameo quickly studied the buttons trying to work out the combination to close the doors. Shaking with fear as she frantically pressed the buttons for the door, Cameo, unlike before, could now hear the footsteps of the approaching dinosaur.

She gasped in relief as the chamber doors finally began to move and slowly close, leaving her in a crumpled heap on the floor. She was breathing heavily with her shoes clutched tightly to her chest. Cameo knew she had to stay still as the roaring of the creature outside was becoming unbearable to withstand and she shivered silently, hoping that it wouldn't break through the doors and get her.

As her heartbeat slowed down, she saw that there was a massive shark swimming in the tank in front of her. A shark in a tank was less dangerous than a dinosaur pounding the doors outside to get in and she attempted to breathe easy. Suddenly the waters of the pool began to move. She could see the shark swimming furiously in a circle and her eyes narrowed at its antics. Strangely, the shark began to thrust itself wildly against the sides of the tank. Cameo saw, to her surprise, arms growing from the shark's side and legs appearing from its bottom. The shark started jerking violently and its new arms reached out towards the side of the tank and hauled itself out. Its body took on a human-like shape and still continued to shake as it dropped to the floor, dripping with water. Cameo slowly rose on her bare feet to see the massive shark now walking towards her.

Her head gave a slightly nervous quizzical tilt as the shark's mouth opened, "Dude, not sure if you know? But your mascara is running."

Cameo didn't have time to thank the shark for its words; by the time her head hit the ground, she had already passed out.

Earth 13

Silo rubbed her hands against her face and sighed in desperation, "What don't you understand, Kitty?"

Kitty's face turned into a cold chill, "I don't know, my lady, what troubles me is why you would concern yourself with my wellbeing?"

Silo could see that Kitty was becoming edgy and wanted answers, "Could we wait, kiddo? We have to continue with your training, your guidance."

"No, I have been patient long enough with you and will endure your trials no more."

"Just a few more exercises and then we're through, I promise."

Kitty paused and spoke with authority next, "I will journey with you only for a while, my lady, but you must tell me what the manner of this quest is about soon: you have my trust, but not yet my faith."

The older girl wriggled her lips, "It's not unfortunate that I am with you, it's an honour."

"What makes you say such words, my lady?"

"Because I know what you are and what you will become. Look, I know it's frustrating for you not knowing who I am and why you have such strange powers."

Kitty threw a hard stare, "The thought did cross my mind, my lady."

"Just give me a little more time, let me train you and then everything will be fine."

Kitty kept her look, "If I keep my promise to you and let you help me with my witchery, honour me and keep yours to tell me what this is all about?"

"Let's just concentrate on getting you used to your powers and we can discuss me giving up my life to protect you."

"I beg your pardon, my lady?"

Silo narrowed her eyes, "Doesn't matter, come on, let's get this show on the road."

She was tired of saying it and at the moment tired of Kitty's moaning.

"Does this mean you are in good spirits now, my lady?"

Silo reached into her bag and took out a bottle of water, tilting the bottle back, Kitty watched as she swallowed the liquid.

"Yep."

She then threw the bottle in the air and stuck her tongue out in mild concentration. A shot of blue flame shot out from her hand and struck the water bottle in two and both parts fell close to Kitty who watched open mouthed as they landed, "Right, your turn now."

"I cannot speak my lady, well I know I'm speaking now but I cannot speak of what I have just witnessed, how can I repeat such an act?"

"You've just got to concentrate. It's like the teleportation powers you have: clear your mind of everything."

Silo's hands began to purr like a hungry cat eating its meal, they vibrated and hummed and then two balls of pure fire appeared in both hands. She twirled the balls around effortlessly and then one more appeared and she tried to juggle them and failed. The balls fell to the ground still glowing as they rolled behind some trees and exploded, making Kitty jump and Silo smile.

"I shouldn't have pushed you off that roof, I apologise again for that, but I knew how powerful you are, which is why I did it."

Kitty was still distracted by the balls and paid no attention to Silo, who carried on nevertheless.

"You are not a witch but a sorceress, there is a big difference. A witch's magic comes from dropping various animal body parts into a cauldron, chanting and hoping for the best."

"All witches, my lady?

"No, there are good witches and some who are tricksters and charlatans, relying on people's stupidity and naivety, but you are a sorceress, your power comes from within, the magic is a part of you. It's the strength of goodness and character that will make you the most powerful sorceress to walk any land. With my help, with my guidance, we can make it happen. Your good heart is a great advantage over those who will come to twist your power and turn it against you. Just stick with me kiddo and you'll be fine to face your own destiny, what do you think?"

Kitty was still dumbstruck by the fireballs that were still sizzling in the trees after the explosion. As the fires slowly came to an end, Kitty spun round excitedly to Silo, still unaware to what she was saying, "I'm sorry my lady, what were you saying?"

Silo studied Kitty's face and smiled at her innocent expression, knowing it was real, she said her signature phrase, "Doesn't matter, let's get—"

Before she could finish, a startled cry from behind her made Silo fall back into the trees and swear loudly, more for the state of her now muddy clothes than what she saw flash before her, "HELP ME PLEASE?! GOD HELP ME!!"

A horse and cart hurtled past the girls with the rider's legs entangled in the reins, his head swung back and forth peppered with mud and blood. He desperately tried to keep his body horizontal and struggled to release his trapped feet.

The cart was full of straw, covering conkers, rocking wildly as it left a yellow trail in the ground. Kitty whipped her head round to Silo, "MY LADY! WE HAVE TO DO SOMETHING!"

Silo watched Kitty's mouth moving, but wasn't listening to the words coming out. She knew she had to save the rider from falling without revealing her powers, Kitty also.

As soon as the horse was almost out of sight, increasing its gallop due to fear more than anything, Silo turned quickly back to Kitty and put her hands on her shoulders, "Ok, here's what we're going to do: we have to get on the back of that cart and slow that horse down."

"How, my lady?"

Silo pointed in the cart's direction, which was now out of sight.

"You're going to teleport the both of us into that pile of straw where he can't see us, and then I'll take the reins and pull the cart to a halt, but you mustn't let him see you use your power."

"You won't have to worry about that, my lady, as I'm not going to do it."

"WHAT!?"

Kitty didn't have time to admire the way she had finally silenced her new mentor, "I cannot even see the cart now, my lady, how can I even attempt to teleport at such a speed."

Silo didn't have time for subtlety and showed it, "Listen, that cart is going to crash and probably kill the rider and anybody else standing nearby, we will not allow this to happen. Now close your eyes and clear your mind." Kitty did so and held her breath, "You've seen the cart, you don't have to teleport 'blind', just picture it in your head and we'll make the jump."

"What if I miss?"

"You won't miss, I have faith in you, Kitty, just close your eyes and let's save the day." Silo gave her a hug and held tight, "You ready, kiddo?"

"I am, my lady."

"Don't worry, I'm sure you're going to be..."

Before Silo could finish, there was a thunderclap of air from Kitty and suddenly she found herself covered in straw laying down on the back of the swerving cart.

"...fine," Silo finally said, actually looking around in happy disbelief. Next to her was Kitty slowly coming to terms with her new ability, her eyes followed the rider of the cart who was still hanging upside down and was now unconscious.

A horrendous grinding noise from under the cart made Kitty turn her head in curiosity.

"This cart isn't going to last for that long, my lady, it's starting to break away, we have to slow the horse."

"How do we do that without revealing our powers? That man could wake up at any second." For the first time Kitty saw slight panic on Silo's face and understood her even more, "I grew up around horses, my lady." Kitty slowly edged towards the front of the wobbling cart, "So we do this quickly."

The young sorceress spotted an opportunity as the cart took another literal turn for the worse. Kitty jumped onto the horse and grabbed what was left of the reins snapping them hard in a straight line towards her chest. The horse still wasn't slowing down, so she anchored one hand on its neck, letting the rein slide slightly which began to do the trick and the horse's speed began to decrease. The rider's body swung back up and bashed against the horse's belly, causing it to rear up and send him tumbling into some hedges, waking him up in the process. Kitty knew the horse was scared and tried to stay calm, patting its side and whispering nice things into its ear. Finally slowing down to a canter and breathing heavily, Kitty twisted and turned the reins until the tired horse came to a standstill.

Kitty didn't whisper this time, she simply shoved out a harsh breath and then spoke gently, "Good boy, good boy."

A groaning sound came from the hedges behind her which made Kitty dismount and turn inquisitively. Silo still appeared to be buried under a mountain of straw, her groans weren't as loud as the ones coming from the bushes, so she headed off to check.

A young man, staggered towards her like a drunk on a weekend night out. His face was bloodied and parts of his hair were missing, conkers lay strewn around the muddy path. His body was fit and tight, his clothes were in tatters, but she didn't seem to mind. Kitty would usually avoid such encounters with boys, they were immature, useless and she had no time for them. But as she had aged through teleporting, she was somehow drawn to this one, especially his deep yet dazed eyes.

"Are you troubled sir?" Kitty asked with genuine concern.

Even though he was in agony, his tired features softened when he saw Kitty, but then quickly turned to anger, "WHAT THE HELL WERE YOU THINKING OF? YOU COULD HAVE KILLED ME!"

Kitty yelped in shock, "I'm sorry, sir?"

"YOU COULD HAVE RUINED EVERYTHING! YOU COMPLETE AND UTTER BASTARD!"

Kitty could feel her temperature rising, "WHAT DO YOU MEAN?" she snapped.

The angry expression from the man didn't change as he stormed towards her, "I THOUGHT I COULD TRUST YOU!"

Before Kitty could speak again, the man brushed past her and went straight to his horse, stroking it tenderly, "STUPID, STUPID BOY!"

He noticed the pout from the beautiful young girl and was rocked by the look on her face, "FORGIVE ME MY LADY, MY HORSE WAS STARTLED BY SOMETHING BACK IN THE FOREST CLEARING. I DON'T KNOW WHAT IT WAS, BUT IT SEEMED LIKE SOME SORT OF SMOKE."

Kitty's lovely face twisted slightly, "Why are you shouting?"

"I'M SORRY? I CAN'T HEAR YOU?"

Kitty usually didn't understand how the human body worked, but took a guess that being trapped underneath a galloping horse and having his head dragged along the ground had damaged his eardrums.

"It is fine sir, you're just shouting a bit."

She heard a groan coming from the cart as Silo rose from the straw and swung her legs from underneath her, "Are you well, my lady?" Kitty asked with concern. Silo checked her sides and rubbed her legs.

"Yeah, all good, kiddo."

Kitty's features softened when she heard Silo's voice, "There was doubt in my mind that you were safe, my lady, but my heart sings that you are unhurt."

The man's blurred gaze caught hold of Silo and his eyes suddenly widened, "WHAT IS THAT?! WHAT TRICKERY IS THIS?! THAT WOMAN HAS A FACE LIKE CHARRED WOOD, IS IT A WITCH? WHY IS HER FACE SO BLACK? WHAT VILE CREATURE IS SHE?"

Kitty's face hardened quickly and she glared at the young man, "You're still shouting."

Earth 65

Sully stroked her side, "My back hurts as well, can you look at that for me?"

"Why me?" Poxon asked.

"You want to be a doctor, right?

"I want to be a vet, big difference."

"Would it help if I went down on all fours and barked like a dog?"

"Only in my dreams," Poxon whispered.

"What did you say?" Sully stared at him in a challenging manner.

"Nothing," Poxon said, his head still in dreamland.

Sully eventually did bend down on all fours and was sick again.

"Are you sure you're going to make it to the medical bay?"

"If you stop talking and start leading, I'll be fine, dumbass."

Even when she was hurling her guts out, Sully was still pompous and arrogant, so that was a relief for Poxon.

"Ok, well I think we're almost there, all we have to do is get you well again and find Cameo and Harley and then we can finally start to have fun on this trip."

For the umpteenth time, Sully wiped vomit and blood from her mouth. She tried to follow Poxon's train of thought.

"Puking up aside, you may have a point - it would be cool to actually try and have a nice time today." Poxon nodded quickly and speeded up his steps.

Katie Kang could hear voices outside her medical centre. She had been sat there for a while on her own, whilst her colleagues dealt with the college kids on the lower decks. She was a nurse and was very bored. She wanted to hear excited voices for once, like the kids seeing weird and wonderful creatures for the first time, but all she usually heard was people moaning and crying.

It was her job, so she couldn't really complain or regret not going to the bottom of the ship for the captain's speech, but seeing as she had no patients turn up, the kids must have been having a good time. She really wanted to be on a beach somewhere nice and hot and with no sick people around her. Katie felt slightly irritated as a knock on the door took her away from her lovely beach.

"Come in," she said, her voice trying to show a sprightly feel.

Poxon nervously pressed the 'open' button on the door and it slid open smoothly. He helped Sully in, whose stomach was shifting in pain more regularly and was greeted by a bored Katie, "What seems to be the problem here?"

"My friend is ill, she has been coughing up blood in her saliva and constantly being sick, I'm not too sure if it's haemoptysis, she has had prolonged coughing so it may just be a horrible chest infection."

Katie leaned back in her chair, suitably impressed, "It seems you should be doing my job, young man."

Poxon looked to the floor, embarrassed, "I know a bit of stuff, ma'am."

Sully glanced at the nurse, expecting some sort of help, "Have you two finished? Kinda dying here."

"Yes of course, could you pop up on the table for me please?"

Sully slowly lifted herself on the treatment table, swinging her leather-clad legs neatly on the side. Katie looked at Sully's tight exposed midriff and felt a tinge of jealousy; even though she had been working out at the gym, her stomach was nowhere as firm as her patients. For a slight moment Katie was glad this eighteen-year-old girl with a super body was ill.

"Could you stick out your tongue for me?"

Sully did so as Katie looked firmly inside, "Hmm," Katie said slightly confused, something Sully picked up on.

"What's wrong?"

"Nothing, but I'm just going to give you a full body scan just to make sure."

Sully could tell something was wrong from the tone in Katie's voice, "Full body scans aren't given to people unless they're really ill?"

Katie simply pointed to the trail of blood on the floor, "You're ill, trust me," she said.

Sully looked up at her nurse with tired eyes, "I don't feel so good."

"I know."

"No, I'm feeling worse."

Katie looked at the results from the computer.

"What's wrong with her, Nurse Kang?" Poxon asked, taking the time to read her name badge.

She rolled her eyes, still looking concerned about the information coming back off the screen, "I'm not sure, the results are coming back as inconclusive."

Sully's tough exterior started to crack, starting with her voice, she squeaked from the table, "Can you please tell me what's going on? I'm beginning to feel worse."

Poxon began to fidget, he was more worried than the nurse was; this was meant to be a fun trip but two of his best friends were missing and another was seriously ill. Katie shook her head, annoyed and impatient, too many questions coming in too fast, especially from teenagers even though they were only slightly younger then she was.

She reviewed the details again from the screen and began to get overwhelmed. The tired nurse straightened up and rubbed her face, taking a step away from the table.

"Well this is what I don't understand, the scans aren't detecting a heartbeat."

Unexpected fright flowed through Sully's body, but she tried to remain calm and began to gently kick her legs like a bored child.

"Excuse me?"

Katie ignored Sully and assumed with every confidence that the scans were wrong, she made a disgusted noise and tapped the scanner with her forefinger.

"Well, this is stupid, so stupid, I don't get it," Katie fumed.

Sully's voice was as expressionless as her tired face, "Are you sure you're using it right?"

Katie's face hardened as Sully's was back to being unwavering, "You trying to wind me up?"

"Nope, honest genuine question. I'm sitting here taking the piss out of you because you're saying I have no heartbeat? Your nursing skills are freaking amazing."

"Are you for real? Who says 'freaking' anymore? What are you? Twelve years old?"

"Old enough to kick your arse," Sully spat.

Poxon surprisingly stepped in, his teenage voice was strong and compassionate, "Ladies please?! This isn't the time or the place for this. Nurse Kang, could you please help my friend?"

Squeezing her eyes tight, Katie sighed loudly, "I'm sorry, I shouldn't have snapped at you, just had a late night and a long day."

Sully's face relaxed, she liked Katie, she had something about her, something spunky.

"It's cool," Sully smiled, slightly red-eyed.

Katie's eyes focused on Sully, "Well, let's check your eyes and see if they're responsive."

As Sully stayed sat on the table, Katie took a little torch from her pocket and shone it in Katie's eyes, still jealous of her tight stomach.

"So, apart from feeing dreadfully ill, how are you finding the trip on this new zoo?"

Sully leaned forward as Katie kept on examining her, "Well I've had better days if I'm honest? Once in a life time trip to travel in space and see all these funky animals and I—"

Sully suddenly stopped, closed her eyes and gave a mighty yawn, the mouth stretch seemed to go on for ages, when she had finished Sully snapped her lips again, her mouth tasted strange. She looked for Katie to give her an apologetic smile, but the nurse had disappeared. *That's odd and kind of rude,* she thought. The funny taste in her mouth made her lick her lips, she seemed to be in quite a daze and began swaying slightly, light-headed and tired, at the corner of her eye she saw Poxon waving his hands frantically. *What's he on about?* she thought dreamily.

"WHAT HAVE YOU DONE?! WHAT THE HELL IS HAPPENING?!" Poxon screamed.

Sully still wasn't sure what was going on and drew in a short breath, "What's wrong with you, nerd?"

"ME?! WHAT'S WRONG WITH YOU?!"

She stared hard at her friend and her eyes finally drifted to the floor.

Katie was on the floor, twitching and convulsing. Sully looked hard and saw blood splattered all over the ground. There was a big hole where Katie's throat had been and blood was oozing down her chest. Poxon's face was lined with tears, "PLEASE STOP!"

Sully forced herself to calm down and spat out the odd taste in her mouth, although it did taste a lot like white wine; she had tasted wine with her parents with meals before they had disappeared and she had enjoyed the taste, albeit it a little salty. Feeling her lips, the salty liquid between her fingers was blood, Katie's blood. She closed her eyes as the remaining blood trickled down her chin. Sully wiped it off and tasted the juice once more... and began to like it.

Sully was no longer scared, just feeling extremely confident and thirsting for more blood. The body of Katie had stopped twitching and it slowly began to rise, swaying awkwardly and covered in blood; no sense or feeling, just an empty shell of the nurse and the human she used to be.

Sully helped the body to its stumbling feet and held it stable. Katie's jaw tried to move as if it was chewing something. Sully took a long look at her face and gleefully licked the blood from her cheek; the taste was odd before, but now she was loving it.

She wiped Katie's blood-smeared cheek and looked to Poxon.

He was shivering fearfully and backed away from Sully towards the door, "I'll get help, I'll find the others, I'll find the captain and make things better again."

Sully confidently smiled and gently pushed Katie in Poxon's direction, the animated nurse ambled towards him, her bloody arms outstretched wanting him and his body.

"Poxon!" Sully growled, her voice was gravelly like a sore throat.

She was smiling now, with cheekiness and guile, "Don't go Poxon, stay with us." Her smile grew, "Stay with us if you want to be fucking amazing."

CHAPTER SEVEN:

A Good Day To Try Hard

"I don't believe this!" Miss Dwells stood rocking on her painfully high heels in annoyance, "So two more students have left us, is that what you're saying?"

Achilles wriggled his jaw, he was just as annoyed as his teacher, "Yeah, I didn't see them slip away either."

"Who are they?" she asked, looking down at her list of notes.

"Lacy and Kane have slipped away, Miss."

Miss Dwells pulled a face, "Oh, those two lovebirds? Why would they want to leave my tour?" Her face stayed the same as she looked at Achilles, mentally cringing, "Oh, I get it."

"Shall I go after them, Miss?" Achilles was eager to leave the boring tour as well.

Her red lips twisted up into a fake smile, "You lot make me laugh, you really do, you had a chance to embrace an opportunity to learn about different creatures from all over the world and you instead want to run away and fornicate."

A wave of sniggering came from the students as Achilles put his hand up to ask a question, "Excuse me, Miss, we *are* still here. We haven't left you."

The teacher was deadly serious, "I'm sick of this! It's been one hell of a long day and this job would be great if you kids started to take things more seriously, so now

I have to find another two students, the other teacher who was meant to be supporting me has disappeared and left me on my own."

Miss Dwells' nostrils began to flare and Achilles knew she was highly annoyed, "What do you want us to do, Miss?"

She replied with a pitiful expression, "Class, just stay with me please, that's all I ask."

Achilles saw how the class were beginning to get just as bored as he was. He wanted to sneak away and find his friends but knew it wasn't fair on the teacher. He listened hard and stared intently at her tired face, growing more stressed by the second. He calmed the class down with a wave of his hand. Far more efficiently than Miss Dwells ever could, he then pointed to a caged spiked dog, pacing up and down, "What animal is that, Miss?" he asked.

Miss Dwells smiled as her face loosened and she eagerly consulted her notes.

Having already been pulled away from the group by his inquisitive girlfriend, Kane wasn't impressed by the dark dirty tunnels he was now looking at instead of the animals he was mildly interested in, "This place sucks, Lacy, why did you take me down here?"

Lacy dragged her reluctant partner further down the corridors, looking for better entertainment, but Kane wasn't impressed.

"Lacy, the tour wasn't that bad? Why are we down here?"

Lacy pushed him up against a wall and savagely kissed him before turning around to see if they were still alone, "Don't be such a wuss, babes, you have to embrace it and not follow others." She reached her hand up his shirt and gently tickled him on his back, making him jump.

"What did you have in mind?" he asked slowly, his hands back on his girlfriend, making their way down her fit body.

Lacy removed them and put her own hand in her pocket and pulled out a few tablets, "Let's make this trip special."

Kane rolled his eyes, "Really? Do we have to? This trip isn't that bad, surely."

His girlfriend slipped a pill into his mouth and closed it for him, she then popped one into her own mouth, "Let's just make it a little bit better, shall we?"

Kane swallowed the pill and went back to kissing his girlfriend.

The sway lizard found it easy to walk along the corridors, they were quite big and allowed its large frame to fit through. It did leave a trail of Harley's blood on various stairwells but that was not its concern; that was old blood and it needed something new; the creature was hungry again and still desperate to mate.

It showed a total disinterest in the dark and gloomy tunnels all around it, but it could smell something ahead, it was blood – blood meant flesh and flesh meant food.

It sniffed the air and grunted, the pain of being alone was becoming unbearable but the need to eat was of a more pressing matter. Nodding its head in the air, the dinosaur moved closer towards the possible meal. Poxon knew he was carrying a little more weight than he should be, his friends teased him about it and before his parents disappeared they encouraged him to join a fitness class, he laughed it off at the time and said he'd do it later.

His parents were now gone, some of his friends had vanished and Poxon felt totally alone. Apart from one friend, Sully, who he had just witnessed bite a massive hole in the throat of a nurse and now the supposedly 'dead' nurse had got up and was chasing him along with his strange friend with teeth issues. Now he wished he had listened to his parents' advice as he huffed and puffed down the corridor.

"WHY ARE YOU RUNNING, POXON? WE ONLY WANT TO PLAY WITH YOU?" Sully shouted.

"PISS OFF AND LEAVE ME ALONE!"

That was not good, he thought, running and talking at the same wasn't the brightest idea when being chased by people who wanted to eat you.

There was a joviality in her voice, but it seemed fake and forced. She sounded like a sleeping child who had just been woken up, tired and tetchy, but the more she taunted, the faster Poxon ran; he never wanted to hear her speak again.

Katie ran alongside Sully, her bloody head bent at an impossible angle. She didn't speak as her throat was missing, but she was unrelenting, uncaring and, most importantly, she was undead.

Poxon emerged from another corridor opening, he climbed upstairs with a speed that was deceptive for his size, he made a determined effort to run through the exit unnoticed, he sniffed his nose and rubbed it weakly, he was tired and running wasn't for him, he couldn't breathe but didn't want to die.

Sully loved the taste of blood from Katie, it was gorgeous and she needed more. It was a shame the new blood had to come from her friend Poxon, he was annoying and insignificant in their group, but she had always found him quite cute and he didn't mind that she lied and pretended to read books just to impress him; it was a shame she had to kill Poxon.

"THERE'S NO USE IN TRYING TO ESCAPE FROM US, POXON!"

"WOULD YOU PLEASE SHUT UP!" Poxon snapped back, knowing it was another mistake to talk to the woman trying to kill him, but her quotes from silly horror films were getting on his nerves. He didn't know what had happened to Sully but it seemed she spoke more now that she was dead than she ever did alive.

He wasn't sure if she was dead or not. The virus she caught had obviously spread, making her drink the blood of nurses, but hopefully there was a bit of life left in her, but not too much as she bore down to eat him.

Sully had finally stopped talking, but she was groaning now, intensely and quite inhuman; that sound alone kept Poxon running but, silent or not, his friend *was* trying to eat him.

He was so out of breath and for an appalling moment he thought about stopping and seeing what would happen if he did let Sully and Katie catch up with him. Running around another corner, Poxon stopped in his tracks. Ahead of him was a problem, a big problem in the form of an adolescent male sway lizard. Poxon was transfixed by its massive jaws and its rough leathery skin. The lizard eyed up the portly teenager, it lifted its heavy head and made a high-pitched squeaking noise like an oily wheel. Poxon took a breath and stepped back, the lizard began a stooping posture and he noticed a fearful ring around both of its eyes as they began to focus on him. He narrowed his own eyes and cocked his head.

"Oh shit!" he whispered.

The sway lizard threw its head back and roared, the sound from the creature encouraged Poxon to screw his eyes shut and dart off in the opposite direction. He ran away knowing he was heading back towards Sully and Katie. He had no choice and was surprised that he only now started crying, oncoming death was in front and behind him.

Poxon knew the giant lizard was frighteningly close, he could hear the enormous footsteps only just a corridor behind, his heart was racing with panic. Deep terror surged through him when he heard Sully and Katie racing forward in the distance. *No way, no way, no way,* he thought, "Not dying today," he said surprisingly aloud.

Ignoring the wet sensation he felt in his trousers, Poxon changed tactics and charged towards the girls. They were probably going to eat him and he was fresh out of ideas. Sully appeared first from around the corner and Poxon was ready for her.

With adrenaline racing through his body, Poxon flung himself at Sully and punched her hard in the face, it was his first ever attempt at a punch in his life and the results weren't satisfactory. Sully's head whipped back from the blow and then a smile appeared on her face, "Well, well well," she wiped the blood from her mouth and Poxon wasn't sure if he had caused it or it was from Katie's throat, either way Sully was impressed, "Not bad." Sully then punched Poxon in the face, causing him to grunt and slam hard on his back to the floor.

"Did you really think that would stop me, my fat friend?

Poxon feebly tried to scramble away on his back and his heart sank further when he smelt what was behind him.

He turned around as the sway lizard stepped into view and simply pointed to it and replied to Sully, "No, but that might."

Sully followed Poxon's outstretched arm and stared at the giant lizard that had just walked into view. It was sniffing repeatedly as it finally had a locked-on scent from the blood on the two girls.

Sully flinched and bit her lower lip, the blood from a creature this size would be an enormous feast. There was no fear at all coming from the teenager as the virus coursed through her veins, she threw her head back and screamed a battle cry. The lizard roared a response and lowered his head in an attacking stance.

Before Sully could attack the beast, Katie ran past her, she too wanted the blood from the sway lizard and raced towards it. Backing away slightly, the young lizard swung its head back and roared again. The nurse with her throat missing lunged with incredible agility high into the air.

Facing her directly, the lizard twisted its neck and caught Katie in mid-flight, its jaws wrapped around her body, squeezing like a giant vice. Katie's abdomen pressed hard through her outfit followed by a flow of blood as her body fell apart in two. Poxon was oblivious to Sully as he puked up violently on the floor. The lizard grunted again and quickly began to tear off the flesh from Katie's body. Sully snarled, eager to take down the lizard who was making a feast from the woman *she* had turned. Poxon looked up to see the expressionless features of his former friend. He wiped the remains of sick from his mouth to say something, but before he could speak, Sully moved swiftly past him to attack the lizard. A smooth growl came from the creature as it whipped its tail around and made direct contact with Sully, sending her crashing into the corridor wall opposite. She fell to the ground with a heavy thud and failed to stir. The sway lizard half glanced at the fallen girl and went back to feasting on Katie, ignoring Poxon completely.

Poxon staggered slowly to his feet and scraped his hand through his hair; the smell from the lizard and his pee-stained trousers were beginning to affect him. He took a nervous gulp as he stood stinking and mesmerised by the loose lizard and then gave enough time to allow one more shiver before racing down the corridor behind him.

"This is such a bad idea," Kane mumbled as he pulled away from kissing Lacy. His beautiful companion didn't say anything, she just looked intrigued by something over his shoulder and pointed. Kane felt a knot in his stomach when he turned around to see what Lacy was looking at. A bunch of blue floating spheres the size of footballs hovered behind him. They moved in bunches at first, pulsating and then moved higher into the air. The balls stayed in the air as Kane rubbed his eyes, he moved forward and tried to grab one of them. As his hands swiped the air, the balls disappeared in a puff of blue smoke, apart from one which flew around the corner still glowing and illuminating the corridor.

"I knew I shouldn't have taken that pill," he moaned.

Lacy's eyes lit up, "You saw that too? These pills are great! Let's follow it."

She grabbed her lover by the hand and pulled him down the corridor, chasing the last remaining blue orb,

"These pills are cool," she beamed dreamily as Kane frowned.

"It's a bad idea, I know it is, we should head back to the others." He knew it was useless to argue against his girlfriend, especially when she had been pill popping.

"Just shut it and keep up," Lacy said.

The drugged-up couple followed the darting ball through further corridors and then past cages crammed with annoyed animals. She continued to chase the orb with Kane, looking behind to see how her boyfriend was coping. Growing up she had watched him go from nerd to cute to now quite hot, which was why she was dating him and not the other geek. Harley and Lacy knew that Kane didn't care that she was rich or that she was slightly spoilt, but she liked his nervous smile, especially when he said he agreed with the majority of her views. She knew he was just being polite and didn't know what she was waffling on about most of the time.

Her head began to feel heavy and it was a strain to keep it from off the floor. Another quick check on Kane proved useless as she couldn't tell if his head felt as hard to carry as her own. Turning another corner, Lacy stopped dead in her tracks as Kane bumped into her. She looked at what was standing directly in front of her and began to gasp in short little breaths. Kane struggled to comprehend the shape as well, his eyes rolled into the back of his head and the whites of his eyeballs showed as the pills took major effect. The 'thing' in front of them took a step forward and Lacy, with a supreme effort, stood the other way as her head was almost at exploding point. The little orb had disappeared and instead was something larger walking towards them.

Lacy giggled nervously and made an attempt to speak to this strange creature blocking her path. She cleared her throat as her body began to tense, "Excuse me sir, but why are you holding our friend, Cameo?"

The creature's eyelids slowly started to move and its black eyes stared hard at Lacy, who now began to sway in front of it.

"DUDE! SHE JUST PASSED OUT IN MY ARMS! I DIDN'T DO ANYTHING!"

Holding up her hands in a calming motion, Lacy spoke again, her lips curled into a smile, "Ok, Mr Shark, that sounds lovely, but can you put my friend down now please?" The shark had carried the unconscious body of Cameo through many of the ship's winding corridors to find help, but knew his appearance would obviously send the wrong message to any would-be saviour, "Dude, there is a massive dinosaur on the loose in this ship, your friend fainted when she saw me and I'm so sorry if I freaked her out."

Kane was in no fit state to put up an argument and tapped Lacy on the shoulder, she causally brushed him off, "Not now sweetie, I'm having a conversation with the friendly shark guy."

Lacy sighed and closed her eyes, opening them again to try and focus on the human-shaped shark creature, "Right, let's get this straight, I don't know how you began walking and talking and I have no idea how you managed to end up with one of my best friends in your arms." She was wobbling again and tried hard to stay on her feet and focused as the shark raised its voice again.

"DUDE! WE HAVE TO GO! I SAID THERE IS A CRAZY MONSTER LOOSE ON THIS SHIP!

"I'm looking at a 'crazy monster' at the moment and he's beginning to freak me out, so drop my friend and please don't eat me."

"DUDE, I'M NOT GOING TO EAT YOU, BUT WE HAVE TO LEAVE, NOW!"

Lacy turned to Kane and squealed in delight, pointing at the shark at the same time, "These pills are freaking great! Can you see a walking talking shark too?"

Kane's drugged up eyes latched on to the shark and he blinked repeatedly just to make sure his eyes weren't lying to him.

"Oh shit! I'm trippin' out, babes, I think there's a shark with legs in front of you. Why is it on land?"

The shark sneezed as Kane grew more accustomed to its appearance and Lacy raised an eyebrow.

"Babes, did you hear that? I think that shark is swearing at us in fish language."

"Dude, I just sneezed," the shark replied, "I have a cold, try spending ages in freezing cold water and see how you like it?"

Kane heard a noise and looked behind him, he started to laugh uncontrollably when he saw another strange creature in sight, "Now this is some scary shit." He cocked his head to one side and looked at the sway lizard which had ambled up behind them, panting heavily, "First I'm seeing a talking shark and now there's a dinosaur behind me, I wonder if it can talk too?"

"DUDE! WE HAVE TO RUN NOW!" the shark screamed.

"Definitely not," Kane said with some assertiveness in his voice, "You seem like a pretty cool guy for a shark, but don't be jealous of other creatures, mate, I just want to see if he can talk too."

"DUDE! DON'T GO THERE!"

Kane ignored the shouts from the shark and stumbled towards the massive dinosaur, "What's the matter, Mr Dinosaur? You've gone all quiet all of a sudden, don't you want to play with me?" Kane asked as he pointed his finger accusingly.

The shark began to wince as the dinosaur stooped over the oncoming Kane, "DUDE! WHAT THE HELL, MAN? STOP!" With a quick flick of its head the dinosaur snapped its jaws around Kane's arm and severed it at the elbow, swallowing the limb in an instant, "DUDE! NO! NO!" The shark cried.

Kane looked at his torn right arm, the drugs were so powerful that the pain of losing an arm hadn't kicked in yet, just the fact of his own leaking blood looked pretty cool to him.

The smell of the sway lizard seemed to bother Kane more than the loss of an arm did, "Hey Mr Shark! Can you smell that shit? What's up with that?"

He began bleeding more heavily as the dinosaur circled him; it wasn't that hungry after feeding on Katie and just saw the little teenager as an irritant more than a threat.

Lacy's pills began to wear off quicker than her boyfriend's and she froze for an instant, her eyes locked onto where Kane's right arm had been and she screamed a guttural cry of terror.

Kane became confused as he saw Lacy fall to her knees in a heap with her hands over her mouth to keep in the oncoming vomit, his own drugs were strong for a moment, which now—like Lacy's—were beginning to fade. Pain and nausea washed over Kane as he saw that the puddle of blood he was standing in was his own, "Oh God, help me."

His usual laid-back voice was now higher through panic, his sobbing head rose from the floor and looked at Lacy crying beside a giant shark on legs. He strangely remembered talking to the man-shark and knew he was a pretty straight-up guy; on an ordinary day trying to wrap around his thoughts that a nerd like him had the coolest girl in the college being his girlfriend was hard to take in but still loved the fact and adored Lacy too.

His attention stayed on Lacy and the shark as his dazed eyes wondered why she was screaming and why the shark seemed like he was getting ready to scoop her up on his shoulder along with his friend Cameo. The only thing he could strangely comprehend was that there was a dinosaur standing above him. Kane wasn't sure if his interest in the creature was due to the pills he took or down to plain curiosity, but he couldn't take his eyes off of the dinosaur's razor-sharp teeth. Drugs or not, Kane felt the pressure of the teeth against his skull. He managed to smile as he saw the shark carry his love, kicking and screaming away from danger, thinking about his lost mum. The smile stayed on his face as it was separated from his shoulders.

Earth 13

"How's it looking, Mason?"

Mason looked through his binoculars and squinted hard, "Can't really see anything, boss." He put them down and motioned Orion forward, "See? They're just talking to that boy by the broken cart, I still think we should grab the girl now boss, we know what she can do and we cannot afford to lose her again."

Orion cracked his knees and made a face to his number two, "We've had this conversation before. That girl, who strangely enough is a teenager now, will have the ability to save everybody on our planet, but we just have to continue to let Silo train her up to become more powerful and when the time is right, we'll grab her and dispose of Silo."

Mason's eyes were downcast, "I know, you did say, but I don't know how."

Orion took the binoculars from Mason, "Like I said, trust me."

Silo sighed heavily again, "Can you please stop poking me?" The young man was so intrigued by Silo's skin that he had to touch it, but her hard stare made him think otherwise for another try, "I'm sorry my lady, but your skin is truly a thing of wonder and is far more interesting than how the heavens have opened up and flowed like horse piss recently, which is what everybody has been talking about."

Silo shooed him away with an impatient gesture, "So horse urine is what passes for celebrity gossip in this place?"

The boy's rapid blinking gave Silo the thought that he had no idea what she was talking about, which she was used to due to hanging around with Kitty for so long. She was getting so annoyed at sighing again that Silo just simply smiled at him, "So, do you have a name?"

The boy looked quizzically at Silo. Kitty stepped in softly.

"She wants to know what you are called, kind sir." The boy froze into silence as he saw how truly beautiful Kitty was. She raised a little eyebrow waiting for a response, "Sir?"

"Forgive me my lady, my heart pounds with pleasure at your wonderful face."

Kitty's face pondered a smile.

"Oh for God's sake," Silo huffed and went to check the boy's eyes, he screamed, dropped to the ground and began to pray.

"Please don't hurt me, my lady!" the boy cried.

"I'm not going to hurt you."

Silo slumped against the cart exhausted and rubbed her temples, "Was just checking to see if you were ok."

The boy looked nervously at Silo then back to Kitty, who gave him a nod and returned his look to Silo, "My name is Thomas Culpepper and I will thank you with what life I have left."

"Ok Thomas Culpepper, well I hope you are feeling better now but we must be making tracks," Silo said in a less than friendly tone.

"Wait! You and your lovely maiden slowed down my horse, I owe you my life, how can I ever repay you?"

"It's fine, don't worry about it."

"I'm not worried my lady, I just want to show you my gratitude."

Silo's face had slipped into an expressionless mask.

"Listen." She paused for a second, "Ummm…"

"Thomas," the boy helped her.

"Yeah, Thomas, listen I appreciate it, really I do but we can't stay here."

"But–"

"No 'buts' kid, me and my…maiden…have to get out of here."

"Where are you going, my lady?"

Silo walked towards Kitty and glared at Thomas through the corner of her eye, "Business."

"What business?"

Sidling up to Kitty, she pulled her aside and whispered into her ear, "Is everybody in your time this nosey?"

Kitty shook her head, remembering what Silo was like, "Don't be mean my lady, he obviously hasn't seen a black lady before? Is that what you are called?"

Silo nodded, "Some might say."

"Well I'm still getting used to everything about you as well, so just be nice to him and then we can get back to training me for the thing which you won't tell me anything about."

"Don't care, let's go."

She pulled Kitty by the hand and walked past Thomas.

As the two made their way down the muddy path, Thomas waited a while and then cautiously made the same trip. Silo frowned and puffed without looking back, "Stop following us."

"I'm not, you just happen to be walking in the same direction as me."

Another sigh from Silo came as all three trudged up the path.

Earth 65

"PUT ME DOWN! PUT ME DOWN NOW!"

The shark looked nervously around as Lacy wriggled frantically on his shoulder. He carefully placed both girls on the ground and backed away slowly. Cameo was still unconscious but Lacy was wide awake; the drugs had worn off and the realisation that her boyfriend wasn't coming back had finally hit her, more so than a talking shark.

"He's dead, isn't he?" The shark nodded as Lacy carried on, "That dinosaur is real, isn't it?"

"Dude, he tore off the arm from your friend and split his head in two, so I would say pretty much."

The shark saw how he was adding distress to the girl and tried to smile, only showing a menacing mouthful of teeth instead, "Sorry, not used to being a shark type thing yet."

She shivered and sighed. Intrigued by her saviour, she looked into his black eyes.

"What do you want with me?" she asked.

"I could really do with a drink round about now, something extremely alcoholic probably."

Lacy nervously twirled a lock of her hair in her fingers, "Can sharks drink?"

"Dude, sharks live in the water."

Lacy slowly rubbed her hands up and down her mouth, wiping away sweat, "I mean alcohol, never seen a shark drink booze before."

She continued to rub her face, getting the sweat from her eyes, "I've never seen a shark answer my question." The tears came again and she them wiped away, something she was getting too used to, "Saying that, I've never had a conversation with a shark. WHY AM I HAVING A CONVERSATION WITH A SHARK?"

The shark shrugged his shoulders and looked up to see Lacy staring at him.

"I'm still on drugs, aren't I?" she asked.

"No dude, you're not, that dinosaur really did kill your friend and I really am a shark."

Lacy finally found her voice and breathed deep, "Are you going to eat me?"

"Dude, I'm a pescatarian."

"What is that?

"Dude, it means I only eat fish."

Lacy glared faintly at him as he scratched his teeth, "Figures I suppose," she huffed. Her confidence grew, "How is this all happening to me? Why is this happening?"

"It's just Slim Pickings."

"How can you say that?" Lacy angrily whispered.

"No, dude, it's my name, Slim Pickings, pleased to meet you."

Unfolding her arms, she gave out one to shake the outstretched arm of the shark. *I'm never taking drugs again,* she thought, "How are you a shark?"

There was a brief silence before Slim Pickings answered, "Dude, I have no idea."

"What do you mean?"

"Where are you from?" he asked.

"Heffernan City."

Slim Pickings pondered, "Ok, did you know what was happening in Olympia recently?" Lacy shook her head as Slim Pickings became more animated, "Dude, the infected zombie-like people killing everybody, did you not hear about that, where have you been?"

Lacy thrust out her lip and pointed to the ceiling, swirling her finger and mimicking Slim Pickings, "I've been on a spaceship 'dude', all I know that it was Apology Day when we left after Big Man's stuff years ago, obviously have no idea what's happened since."

"Sure, it was yesterday I think? Can't remember but Olympia has fallen, dude."

"Sounds familiar," she sighed, she spoke slowly next, still not convinced that the drugs had worn off, "Can you tell me what you're doing with my friend, Cameo?"

"She saw me and passed out."

"Ok, you didn't tell me about your shark business."

Slim Pickings looked at Cameo, still unconscious on the ground and cleared his throat, it was very loud and Lacy jumped, he held up his hands in apology.

"Dude, a long time ago, my dad used to work for Big Man, I won't go into all the details but my sister Amber, my mum and me were involved in a car crash; mum died but Amber and me were kept in hospital, Big Man knew this but kept it from my dad.

Obviously, the dude went off the rails, turning to drink apparently, do you remember the 'Game Show' years ago, the biggest game show in Olympia?"

"That was before the media ban wasn't it? Wasn't that when all those people made the big escape from Gommerstall Prison?"

"Yeah, well cameras from the prison showed my dad and another girl blow themselves up so the contestants or prisoners or whatever they were could escape in a sky ship."

Lacy wasn't expecting this from anybody, least of all a shark, and she moved closer to him, "Go on," she said.

"Well, there was this guy, called himself the Green Man, a tall mysterious dude, kept his face covered up, but he found Amber and me and said we could get our revenge on Big Man. He gave us the same serum those college kids had in the games and got bizarre powers, my sister controlled fire and me..."

"What was your power?"

"I don't know, I was given a whip and that was it, maybe the serum hasn't kicked in yet."

"So maybe you were meant to be a shark?"

Slim Pickings paused, "Dude, I hope not."

"How are you breathing anyway? I thought sharks couldn't breathe on land?"

"Dude, I don't know what's going on with me."

Lacy was interested, drugs or acting she pulled it off brilliantly, "Are you holding your breath? Or breathing through those gill things?"

"Don't know."

"Do you need to swim constantly to breathe and to avoid drowning?"

"Dude, look I don't know!"

"So, are you still holding your breath?"

"Dude!"

Lacy saw the shark was making a sound of impatience and cautiously calmed down.

"So, what happened?"

Slim Pickings hesitated and then carried on, "Everybody who had a gripe with Big Man joined forces and tried to take him down when he left his tower. Olympia was infected by a virus which turned everyone at Dangerfield theme park into zombies, man. We weathered the storm and some other people we were fighting against it at first and then joined together to take down the dragon."

"WHAT?!" Lacy blurted out.

"Did you say dragon?" she stared at him, eyelids flickering heavily as Slim Pickings didn't seem to bat his own, "You did say dragon, right?" she repeated.

"Yep, giant black dragon, wrecked the biggest theme park in the country, Heffernan City? How far is it from Olympia?"

"Twenty, no twenty five miles, I think?"

"Dude, you didn't hear anything, nothing on the news?"

"There's a media ban in Olympia," Lacy said with authority, "Now back to this dragon shit."

"Some other time dude, it's a long story," Slim Pickings slowly replied, "Anyway, as I was saying, there was some major family issues to deal with, so my sister and another girl called Echo flew out of there."

"Echo had a plane?"

"Dude, no, she has wings."

"WINGS! WHAT THE HELL?"

Slim Pickings tried his hardest to look mean, it didn't work on Lacy, but she relaxed anyway, "I get it. It's a long story."

He rubbed his eyes, "We flew for a while, but Echo was tired from the fighting and needed to rest her wings." Lacy pulled a face, really wanting to speak, but let Slim Pickings carry on, "So Echo set us down and I went to stretch my legs, human legs."

"Yeah, I get it, carry on," Lacy shrugged.

"Well, I went for a short walk to exercise and clear my head and somebody crept up behind me and knocked me out, When I woke up, I was in this ship, in a giant fish tank and I was a shark. I wet myself a few times, not that you'd know."

"Have you seen your sister?"

"No but dude, she's stronger than me though, she'll be trying to find me right now, I do want to find her, but I don't want her to see me like this."

Lacy's mouth opened and closed, but she was stuck for something to say, strangely feeling compassion for the shark. She had just lost her boyfriend in the most unimaginable way ever, but she wasn't a monster herself, just confused.

"So, you're definitely sure you weren't born a shark?"

"Dude, I think it's something I would remember," the shark said grimly.

She looked straight at him, "Really?"

"Dude, I'm a waster, a dropout, a bum, I know that stuff but chasing skinny-dipping women was not on the agenda, well not to eat anyway." Lacy pulled a face, "Sorry, you know what I mean." Lacy's face didn't change until Slim Pickings spoke again:

"Listen, I don't know where I am or why I am, all I want to do is get back to normal and find my sister."

Lacy rolled her eyes at him, it wasn't the day she had planned for. A day out on a spaceship zoo with her best friends and boyfriend, she could handle; feeling sympathetic to a humanoid shark was taking some getting used to. She was grateful to be alive and missed her friends but couldn't imagine how scary this was feeling for Slim Pickings on the ship by himself and not the person he was.

Lacy elbowed him in the side, "Ow! Dude what was that for?"

"Well, you haven't disappeared so you can't be a figment of my imagination."

"Dude, did anything I said in the last few minutes get through to you?"

Lacy's lovely glossy lips parted slightly, "Still on drugs probably, anyway we have to find my friends, some of them are quite geeky and would know what's happening right now; if we find them and my class, we could finally know what to do and get out of here."

"Dude, there's still a killer dinosaur on the loose out there as well."

"Yeah let's move, could you pick up Cameo, almost forgot about her."

As Slim Pickings moved to pick up the girl, her eyes flicked open, he noticed and spoke as softly as he could to Lacy, "She's already seen me as a walking shark when I came out of the tank, I think she'll remember me and be ok."

Cameo screamed a mighty cry of terror as she came to and saw the looming face of a shark in front of her. She scuttled away, covered her face and started to beg for her life with intensity.

Slim Pickings rubbed his hands over his face in tiredness and turned towards Lacy. She returned the look through troubled eyes but still gave him a dry smile, "Don't hold your breath."

Poxon thought he'd run twice around the ship already, his tired legs barely kept him up. It was a shame as being on the run from a pretty angry dinosaur had meant he didn't have time to look at all the animals in their unnatural surroundings. That is until he ran past what seemed to be a giant paddock under a massive glass dome. Poxon smiled slightly at the sight before him, killer dinosaur or not, this wonder had to be seen. He shook his head with the smile still stuck on his face. A team of horses were running around in circles; the head of the herd was chasing the others from a slow canter into a gallop. As the horses gained speed, wings which were neatly and strangely tucked into each of their sides unfolded and spread out. Beating in rhythm, they flapped elegantly and made the horses soar towards the top of the dome.

Poxon's head turned skyward and his eyes had time to beam at the sight. The white flying horses were the most beautiful thing he'd ever seen in his short boring life. He and Harley knew their place in the group as clowns and nerds, they were the butt of everyone's jokes and were used to it, revelled in it. But sometimes it was just nice to be himself and wonder at the marvellous things in life, and the flying horses were one of them.

He crossed his arms against his chest and kept on gazing at the magnificent sight in the air, more magical than a firework display on a cold night. A strange energy seemed to crackle in the air, which seemed to intrigue the boy even more, some of the flaps from the wings would generate a thunderclap.

Poxon felt sorrier for the horses trapped under the giant dome than all the other creatures in cages in the zoo. He knew he shouldn't do, but flying horses did look better than spiders in a cage.

He forced his attention back to the wonderful flying horses, trying to get his head away from the dinosaur and his dear friend Sully, who had just torn out the throat of a nurse, and then the same nurse was then eaten by a dinosaur. The horses flying around the dome were pretty quiet now, the thunder from their wings had stopped.

The deathly silence had unnerved Poxon, a powerful growl from a dinosaur was strangely more comforting than uneasy quiet. He knew where the creature was when it was chasing him, but no sounds made him even more nervous. Poxon made a noise in his throat, as if he was trying to clear it for a speech. *Get your head together,* he thought.

Looking at the horses as he made his way out of the giant room, he chuckled as two of them frolicked in the air; it would have been nice to have spent more time with them, not knowing if he'd see any horses again, flying or not. The smile disappeared as did Poxon as he made hasty steps away from the display.

"They're bored now aren't they?" the substitute teacher sighed.

"Shitless Miss, no offence," Achilles replied.

Miss Dwells paused, before speaking, a single eyebrow raised, "Fine, just don't let me hear that language again."

As much as he tried to get the class to listen to Miss Dwells, Achilles knew they were growing restless. He wasn't just worrying about his teacher's feelings with all the other kids giggling whilst taking selfies with the animals, he was also concerned for his missing friends. But for the moment, something else was on his mind, "Um, Miss, are we the only class here today?"

Miss Dwells found it hard to sound interested, trying to waste time looking at her notes, "Don't think so, why do you ask?"

Achilles picked some crust from his eye, irritated that he hadn't washed his face properly this morning, "Well, when we came into the ship via the ground to air transport, there were other ships in the docking station as well as ours, but I can't see anybody else here on the tour."

Miss Dwells was trying hard to feign disinterest, "Sorry, what did you say?"

"I'm saying that the transport ships are still attached to the docking bays and there is no sign of other students, where are they?"

The sudden interest into the other transport ships made her close her notes and listen, "So you haven't seen any other people on this trip apart from us?"

Achilles shuffled his shoulders, "No, have you?"

Miss Dwells became serious for a second, "No, I haven't actually."

The teenager went silent for a while but nodded slowly, "We should try and find the captain Miss, maybe he knows what's happening."

Miss Dwells flicked her head behind to check on the rest of the kids and then her jaw went tense, "What's happening is we will continue this tour and finish this day. I've been left on my own thanks that useless form tutor of yours, Professor Gregory and I won't let his idleness ruin this trip for the rest of us."

"But Miss?"

Miss Dwells heard a whine come from Achilles, which was unlike him, usually he was more strong and confident, it was disappointing coming from him and she let him know.

"My job isn't to worry about potentially missing students, it's to educate the ones here and to pay my bills. Whatever else is going on in this ship, it's none of our business, now enough talk and just listen." She gave him a leaflet about the creatures on their current location and got back to the tour.

Achilles smiled through gritted teeth and slowly followed his substitute teacher. A tall blonde girl nervously kept eye contact with Achilles as he walked past and quickly caught up with him.

"Sorry to disturb you, but I think you're right, I saw the other ships docked at the station when we arrived, but I haven't seen the other students here since we started the tour."

Achilles completely dismissed the girl, "You heard what Miss Dwells said, let's just get this tour over with and go home."

The girl swept her fringe from out her eyes, not convinced, still having a little crush on Achilles she carried on, still with a nervous smile on her face, "The amount of money it takes to sustain this floating zoo would be ridiculously high; it needs support from all school councils, not just one from Heffernan City. One school is not enough to keep the animals and staff maintained for the length of this trip; if our school was the only one booked for this visit, then something is seriously wrong." The girl took a breath, "I think the rest of the students aren't on the ship anymore, but I don't know where they are. No school trip I've been on in the past only had one class on the day, I think they've been fed to all the animals."

Achilles interrupted her, "Where do you come up with this stuff?"

"I watched a lot of horror films growing up, didn't you?"

"No."

"Scared of horror films, were we?"

"No TV."

"Did you live in Olympia, with the media ban?"

"No, my parents disappeared before the ban started, Big Man took them because they were teachers."

The girl's nerves had stiffened slightly, "I'm sorry, I didn't know, you must really miss them."

Achilles ran his hands through his short black hair, tired and anxious, "I've got used to it, listen Dwells is making a move, so we'd best follow to keep her quiet."

Nodding and trying her best to stay cool, the blonde girl followed Achilles and the rest of the class. She stared at the back of his head for a while, mouthing silently what she wanted to say next, then, taking a deep breath, she spoke, "I was just wondering that when we get back to Heffernan City if you would like, if it's ok with you, I mean you don't have to if you don't want to, but if you did…I was thinking if you would like to go out to watch a film or something? Or go bowling, meet for coffee maybe?"

Achilles didn't turn around; his eyes were focused on something else. His reply was distant and slightly wistful, "Yeah ok."

"Really? I mean you don't have to if you don't want to?"

He turned around and offered a sort of smile, "No, it's fine, as soon as we find my friends, we'll hang out, what's your name again?"

"Sayles, my name is, it's Sayles, well I'm called Sayles and I'm babbling, sorry."

The nicer guy in Achilles, not the cool one came out and he turned around to the nervous girl, "What time does this tour finish?"

Sayles looked at her watch, "I'm not sure."

She circled round and confronted Achilles bravely, "Look, I know I'm not cool or anything and don't hang out with you and your cooler mates, but if you're just being mean and going out for a date just to make a fool out of me, I don't want to know, alright?"

"Cooler mates?" Achilles said, ruffled for the first time.

"So, it's a date then, don't be late," Sayles gave him a mock scowl, confidence growing.

Achilles was getting used to smiling again, "I wouldn't dream of it, it's not cool."

The thing which had earlier caught his attention became clear as they walked forward. The other students had missed it, but Achilles picked up on the small object on the ground.

"What's that?" Achilles asked.

Sayles grinned, knowing that the boy she had a crush on was speaking to her as a friend, she slowly shook her blonde hair, "Not sure."

Achilles watched the class walk on and then bent down to inspect it.

"It's a phone, somebody has lost their phone." He picked it up and inspected it slowly, "It looks familiar."

"Let me see please."

Sayles took the phone from Achilles and began to fiddle around with it. Accessing the password in moments, she handed it back to him, "There you go."

Achilles' fingers probed the phone, trying to work it out, "It's Harley's."

"Harley? Your friend?"

"Yeah, he must have dropped it."

Miss Dwells called from the front, "Hurry up you two."

"COMING!" they replied in unison like children.

Achilles looked at the contact list to confirm it was his friend's phone and then went into the photo section and then he froze, "My God!"

"What is it?" Achilles thumbed through the photo section, speechless and visibly shaken, Sayles kept pressing, "Achilles, please show me."

His panic was turning into a slow breakdown. Sayles took the phone from him and looked at the photos, her face twisted in shock.

"Oh no."

She held her breath in silence, which seemed like an eternity, before handing the phone back to Achilles.

"That's Harley isn't it?"

Achilles slowly nodded. He strained to look at the pictures again, horrible pictures. Harley's camera went off as he was being attacked by the sway lizard. Each attack by the ferocious dinosaur on the poor boy was caught by the camera and Achilles and Sayles tried hard to keep the rising sick from leaving their mouths.

"This must have been the last thing he saw, that creature tearing him to pieces was the final thing he saw in this life; he's dead, my friend Harley is dead."

Sayles tried to widen her eyes in sympathy as Achilles punched a wall in anger.

"What do you think did that to him?"

"I don't know, but it's loose on this ship and I'm going to kill it."

Sayles blinked rapidly, "Are you serious? Whatever that thing was it just killed your friend. It's a dinosaur, a carnivore of some sort, you can't take it on."

"Can't let that happen, don't you get it? Harley was all alone, he died with nobody else around and there's more of my friends out there. I'm not going to let anybody else die today."

Staring hard at the ceiling, Sayles quickly turned back sharply to Achilles, "NO!"

Miss Dwells heard the shout and began to turn back from the front of the class. Sayles noticed and pulled Achilles to one side by his arm, which was like the arm of a blacksmith; hopefully she could touch both of them more on their date, but that seemed a long way away at the moment.

"Listen, we have to tell Miss Dwells about this, you can't do this alone."

Achilles easily wriggled free from Sayles' grip, "Miss Dwells? She couldn't catch a cold, let alone a dinosaur.

I'm doing this alone and if you dare mention it to her, then you can forget about our date."

Sayles' face tensed with anger, which didn't drop, even when Miss Dwells appeared, annoyed at the stragglers.

"I don't know what is going on between you two, but this is the last time I tell you to come with me, I expected better from you, Sayles."

Sayles didn't have time to look sheepish, "Miss Dwells, there's something I have to tell you."

Achilles scrunched his eyes towards Sayles.

"What is it Sayles?" Miss Dwells asked.

Hesitation was with both of the teenagers as the teacher pressed on, "Is there something you want to tell me?"

Sayles broke the silence first, her disappointed eyes locked on Achilles, "No Miss."

"Achilles?" the teacher asked, he felt Harley's phone in his pocket and shook his head.

"No."

"Good, well if we're finished here, I would still like to get off this ship a.s.a.p: that bottle of white wine waiting for me at home won't drink itself."

Achilles managed to raise a smile to put his teacher off the scent and he offered his hand out to Sayles below his waist. She took it and slowly smiled a defeated one back, her lipstick glistened and was inviting Achilles for a kiss.

Something caught the eye of Miss Dwells coming from the opposite direction, a figure running at speed, "Ah, it looks like Sully has recovered from her illness, she's back on her feet and coming to rejoin the tour."

A teenage girl came tearing up from behind, each step was faster, with purpose and desire. Sully was upon them, her mouth was stained with dried blood, which Miss Dwells noticed and tried hard to ignore.

"So, I see you're walking again and not being sick, Sully, how are you feeling?"

Before any of the gathered three could react, Sully punched a hole through Sayles' stomach, her hand easily poking out from the other side. She kept it clenched as she pulled out a coil of Sayles' intestines and watched as her lifeless body fell to the ground.

Sully had blanked out the screaming from Miss Dwells and Achilles, but thought it only kind to answer her teacher's question as she licked the remains of the shredded stomach, her voice was low and devoid of emotion, "Never better."

CHAPTER EIGHT

Single Witch Female

Earth 13

"Can you explain to me exactly what we're doing again? We really don't have time for this."

Kitty ignored the words from Silo and settled beneath a towering tree, shuffling slowly on some dry leaves to keep herself away from the wet.

"We are having a picnic my lady, just a quick rest before we move on for my training."

Thomas Culpepper was still with them and snuggled up close to Kitty with some bread and chestnuts, he wasn't even looking at Silo as he spoke to her, "Training? What is this training you speak of yet again, my lady."

"Look!" Silo snapped.

"I can just about get my head around Kitty calling me 'My lady' I can't have you doing it as well."

Thomas tore a strip of bread from a loaf and handed it to Kitty, who beamed a smile back and popped it in her mouth as Thomas spoke again, still really unconcerned with Silo:

"Then what do I call you then? What about 'The woman in black'?"

Both Thomas and Kitty started giggling, "Just Silo, ok?"

Thomas tilted his head and scratched his chin, "Yes, I will."

Silo saw she was wasting her time with Thomas and turned her attention to the reason why she was on the other side of the galaxy, "Kitty, we have to leave now."

She now looked and acted like a petulant teenager.

"I want to stay with Thomas for my picnic my lady, could you please allow me a little fun before we continue?"

Silo put her hands on her hips and pressed her toes hard into the mud. She wasn't in the mood for Kitty's change in behaviour.

"Listen, I let your little friend follow us for a while and gave you some space as you two played nice, but I'm going to tell you for the last time that we have to leave now."

"Can I just get a little time to myself? I've done everything you've asked me to do since you got here and look at me? I was merely a child when I met you and through your witchery you've aged me into a lady."

Thomas stopped chewing and started paying attention as Silo pulled Kitty away from her picnic with force, "Could you please stop talking? Nobody is supposed to know about your powers or ability, now is not the time."

Kitty wriggled free from her mentor's grip, "You need not remind me of this again my lady. I have heard nothing but tales of how I am needed to train and be prepared, but you haven't told me why? All you have done is to irritate me with such tales of magic and have cursed me with the mark of a common witch. You look at me with a stare as cold as winter, but I cannot do any more for you my lady, I just want some time for myself.

I implore you to leave me alone, you're making my life difficult."

Silo stood still, open-mouthed, it closed slightly as did her eyes until they were just slits, "I'm sorry what did you say? I'm making *your* life difficult! What does your life know about being difficult?" Silo gave a shuddering sigh of displeasure and moved closer to Kitty, "I ask you again, how is your life so difficult? Were you shunned by your own neighbours for being different? Were you taken from your parents as a child having to train hours upon hours by someone you didn't know? Did you have to leave everybody you love to travel miles away alone? Did you?"

Kitty's face turned sour and gave a sharp reply.

"Yes, I have encountered such tales, you did that to me, I have endured all of the things you speak of but the pain you suffered on this land you speak of? You make me shiver like a drenched mongrel sometimes because you are doing the exact same to me."

Silo scowled a look at Thomas, checking to see if he could hear their conversation. He grew bored of women bickering and was more concerned with his bread and how wet his backside was becoming sitting on the wet leaves. This time it was Kitty to check on Thomas and she spoke quietly through gritted teeth back to Silo:

"Sometimes I choke with excitement about the wonders of your land, the tales you speak of make my eyes spin. I am still unsure why you came to me, but I know I have been touched by a witch and I know the power I have."

"No, you don't." Silo interrupted.

"Well let me try on my own, you saved my life and I will be forever grateful, I love you with all my heart, you are my guide, my chaperone and a warrior goddess, but I don't want to be with you anymore."

Silo's look didn't change, "The power you wield Kitty is so powerful that some bad people want it from you. They want it to do something terrible, something that will kill billions of people."

"I don't know what a 'billion' is my lady, I'm sorry."

Silo knew that look on Kitty's face; she wasn't about to move.

"If you go with Thomas, if you don't finish what we started, you won't be able fully control your powers. You could destroy a whole village and you could die, but we will discuss this later, but now we have to leave, I don't feel safe here."

Kitty shook her head forcefully, "Those are terrible thoughts to share my lady, but why you are saying such things, I don't understand," Silo wasn't bothered.

"It's true, you will die. You're not strong enough to take on anybody on your own, especially if the hunters catch up with us, you need to complete your magic with me."

The words from Silo shocked Kitty, but she stood firm, trying to find the appropriate words, "No, I don't need magic to tell me that you're being unkind to me, I thought you were my friend."

"I am your friend, but we must leave now, Kitty."

"No! You are not, you speak to me with a look of pity, as if my mouth was filled with pebbles. I'm not a witch, I have another name and I intend to use it from now on; you can't force me my lady, I'm staying."

Silo closed her eyes at the thought of it.

"You're making a grave mistake, Kitty, we have to leave now!"

"It's my mistake to make my lady, not yours."

Thomas finally made a comment now that he'd had his fill of bread, "If you cared for her like you say you do, you would let her stay with me."

"If you cared to keep your teeth, you would shut your noise," Silo snapped.

"Don't speak to him like that!" Kitty hissed back.

"Well, well, well, now it comes out, the clown has spoken."

Thomas smirked as he left the picnic, "Are you troubled Silo? Things aren't going as planned?"

Thomas kept his smile as Silo's anger grew.

"You did this, you turned her against me."

"I think you did that yourself, Silo. I have known you for barely moments, but you are the most annoying person I have ever met, now I don't profess to know why you are travelling with Kitty: it's quite obvious from the colouring on your face, that you are no mother or sister to her. Leave her to spend time with me." He turned quickly back to Kitty, "Travel with me my lady, come and let's have some fun together, would that satisfy you?" he pressed her.

"Oh yes, that would be such a delight to be with you sir." Kitty beamed.

In all the time they had spent, bonding and training together, Silo had never seen Kitty so happy; her tone was flirtatious towards Thomas.

Not for the first time today, Thomas went back to his picnic and tore off some more bread, this time beckoning Kitty. She slowly followed, her face finally looking apologetically back at Silo. She sat on the grass and pulled a face as the wet mud began to seep into her dress. Kitty saw the disappointment in Silo's face as she snuggled up to Thomas. She slowly opened her mouth as tears formed in her eyes:

"There's no nice way to say this: I truly love you my lady and always will, but you are no good for me."

Training Kitty had been more difficult than Silo had expected. She had been nervous at first but had soon begun to show a more determined and spirited nature, which was on show now. She had tried to mould Kitty into the sorceress she had hoped for, almost succeeding until Thomas came along. Kitty had been a child when they first met and now was a teenager due to her misuse of her teleportation powers.

Kitty was always polite, willing to learn and Silo had her in her grasp of becoming the most powerful sorceress ever, without actually telling her why. But that was gone now, due to teenage hormones. She approached Kitty at her picnic spot and opened her arms.

"I get it, I really get it and understand what you're feeling. I was your age once, a long time ago, you really like this Thomas guy, you think you're in love and have butterflies in your stomach."

"I don't feel unwell, my lady."

"Never mind, but we have a job to do and we can't stay here, you are being hunted."

"My lady, you have mentioned these 'hunters' again, what on earth are you talking about. You never say why they are after me; you are beautiful and confusing, is everybody like that in your land?"

Silo pointed to the sky and held her finger there, "My land? That's where I'm from."

Kitty looked to Thomas and back to Silo, "So now you're drunk as well, my lady?"

"I said I was from a faraway land and I am."

Silo watched Kitty's eyes, listening. Thomas was drifting off to sleep, full with bread in his stomach and unaware of the conversation. Kitty stayed snuggled up with Thomas and frowned, keeping her chin high, "So you are from a land in the sky now, my lady? I can take the witchcraft and even the training for something that I don't understand. But my cheeks turn red for the moment you lied to me." The worry lines deepened on Silo's forehead, "We're not moving from here are we?"

"Not until you tell–"

Before Kitty could finish a bright red streak of laser fire hit a tree branch above Thomas, slicing it in half instantly. It fell before he could grab his bread and knocked him unconscious.

Silo and Kitty spun around instantly to see where the blast had come from. Silo's heart sank when she saw and recognised the two figures entering the forest clearing.

Orion and Mason had followed them from the moment they had saved the life of Thomas from the speeding cart.

For once it was Mason who led, eager to place his eyes on the one who he had tracked across the galaxy, knowing that she was the only person who could save their home planet. He had been tracking, following her for what seemed an eternity and now he could finally confront her with so many questions: why she took the saviour of Rayash and bought her to this sinkhole of a planet.

"THIEF!" he shouted.

Orion calmed down his number two, his only number now, he spoke to Silo with calm authority, "So there you are, Silo, pardon my crude language but it has taken a shit load of time to find you." He cocked his head to the side, "You still going with the blue hair thing? Thought that was just a phase you were going through, looks nice though even after all you've been through, kind of retro? Anyway, I digress, could you please hand over the…" Orion stopped mid-sentence as he saw Kitty quivering beside her mentor, "Well well, look at you, you were a beautiful baby and you've grown up and kept your beauty."

Kitty looked at Silo as she answered, wanting approval, "You have me at a disadvantage my lord, I know not who you are?"

Mason raised his weapon and stepped forward, "Didn't the thief tell you?"

Kitty breathed out hard, still nervous, "She told me that I would be followed throughout my life by hunters, idiots with terrible haircuts and bad breath."

Kitty caught the slightest of smiles from Silo, "I'm assuming it is your good selves, my lords."

Orion cleared his throat and did a slow hand clap, "Young woman, it seems the poison of Silo runs through you, I'm sorry about that, but before we take you, let me ask you one question: did she tell you where you were from?"

Kitty didn't panic, but there was a great concern in her voice as she answered, "She told me that you're evil and you want me to do evil things for you, I swear by the almighty God that will not happen."

A small snigger escaped his lips, "She didn't tell you a thing did she?"

"You have judged me badly, my lord, I trust the lady Silo with my life."

Mason was still angry, "You will pray for a quick death if you do not follow us now."

Orion was concerned how he had to calm Mason down again.

"Listen. I'm sure we can work something out, all we need is for you to come with us and everything will be explained."

"I'm sorry my lord, but I will not accompany someone who I do not know."

"Well from what we've seen, you have accompanied two people who you have nothing in common with, yet still join you on your travels."

Kitty's face was stern and cold like stone.

"With respect my lord, Lady Silo saved me from drowning and my heart flutters when I see Thomas as I fancy him." She looked again knowingly to Silo, "Is that word, right?"

Silo nodded as Orion shook his head and began muttering to himself.

"Ok, as most so-called 'clichéd bad guys' say in this situation 'So be it'."

Mason continued to edge forward, his laser rifle was set to live, as opposed to stun, which Silo had noticed. Determined not to let her get away this time, he interrupted firmly:

"We're wasting time sir, let's just take the girl now."

"You're not taking anybody soft lad," Silo said warningly. Orion waved his arms slowly.

"Let's just calm this down people, we've just come for the girl and then we'll be on our way."

Silo was still looking at Mason's rifle, which was beginning to rise.

She gazed intently into the eyes of Mason and her hands began to pulse with blue energy. Orion made a careful reply as he saw Silo's hands power up.

"Don't you dare, Silo."

"Always do," she smiled.

Silo threw a bolt of built up energy at Orion, the force knocked him off his feet and sent him flying into some trees behind. Before she could conjure an energy field, Mason took his weapon and fired it at her. Laser bolts from his gun hit Silo in her gut. She managed to shield most of them, but some went through her force field and knocked her back on the ground.

"KEEP AWAY! KEEP AWAY!" Kitty roared.

She flicked both hands in contempt and her sorceress power sent Mason tumbling to the ground. Before they could rise again, Kitty bent down to tend to Silo, "My lady, I am here for you, are you hurt?"

"The bastards caught me off guard." Silo gripped her stomach and her wound.

She thought rapidly, "We have to get rid of them."

Kitty stood firm and raised her hands in defiance. She had learnt a lot from her mentor and now was the time to master her teleportation skills, "They hurt you my lady, so now I will send these dogs into tomorrow."

Orion and Mason were back on their feet quickly, with weapons raised, "Take Silo out, but don't harm the girl."

A hail of laser fire came from the eager and desperate hunters, the forest was levelled by their rifles. Silo had closed her eyes expecting a quick death. She had failed to raise her shield and just meekly raised her hand due to the pain. When she opened her eyes, both Kitty and she were sitting safely away from the carnage. They could still see the fire fight around the corner from where they sat.

"Woah," Silo moaned slowly, "You teleported us to safety?"

Shifting awkwardly in her position and breathing heavily, Kitty let go of Silo's arm, which she had grabbed before the soldiers started firing.

"Yes, my lady, you taught me how to do it, to remain calm, to focus, clear my head and defend, not attack."

"Well," Silo said uneasily, "Forget that shit, you saved my life which is more important."

Silo painfully raised her hand from her stomach and lifted it high above her head, waiting for Kitty to respond.

"Hi five?"

Kitty looked puzzled for a moment, then remembered how to complete the move from earlier, slapping her mentors elevated hand with her own.

"Hi five, my lady."

As Orion and Mason's laser weapons continued to rage against the forest, Kitty looked eagerly towards the direction of the gunfire.

"My lady, those were the men you spoke of who wish me to follow them?"

Barely able to move, Silo spoke softly, "Yeah, it's them, they'll soon notice we're gone, like I said earlier, we have to move now."

"But what about Thomas? We can't leave him there."

Silo looked beyond her, still feeling weak, "Yeah, we have to come back later when they have left."

Further down the forest Orion signalled to Mason to stop shooting.

"Calm it down, we don't want to draw attention to ourselves, they've teleported out of here anyway."

"You let them get away," Mason mumbled under his breath.

Orion's eyes widened, "Excuse me soldier?"

"We should have blasted them as soon as we saw them, not mess around playing nicely and now they've gone and it's going to take us years to find them; our planet is dying, Orion, I can't go through this again."

Orion watched Mason nervously fumble with his wedding ring on his left hand and quietly fumed back, "Watch your tone soldier, I'm still in charge here."

Mason threw his head back in a sarcastic gesture and rolled his eyes and looked upwards.

"We've lost the girl, we've lost our only hope. I can't even rely on you to swipe a simple teenage girl, you're just like all men."

Orion's mouth wasn't as wide as he'd thought it would be after hearing such a comment; he blamed Mason's words on exhaustion.

"Ok, I'm going to ignore that, because we're both tired. Look, Silo is injured so the girl can't go too far as teleporting with an injury delays the healing process, all we have to do is get the girl on her own and we can make our move."

Mason lowered his gaze from the sky, his eyes fixed firmly on his boss, "What did you have in mind?"

Before Orion could reply, a thunderous sound of many horses running towards them from the opposite side of the clearing made him stop. He grabbed Mason and pulled him back into what little covering was left.

Many horses galloped past with riders wearing a strange attire; some were armed with crossbows, whilst others had swords hanging from their side. Orion stayed hidden; for whatever reason these guards were riding past, they meant business.

Orion turned to Mason and whispered, "Something is about to kick off, we should stay here for a while until the coast is clear."

Mason was finding it hard to contain his frustrations, "Why are we always skulking about in the shadows? We have the power to take out these men, we should take them down and then go after the girl."

Orion interrupted, "What could you really hope to accomplish? We've already gone in with guns blazing and what good has it done? We make perfect landscape gardeners but still can't find the girl? These soldiers' deaths would bring us nothing."

Mason studied the weaponry of the riders as they sped past. He didn't look at Orion, just grunted a response and shrugged.

"What then?"

Orion picked at some plaque on his teeth, "We have a teenage girl who has the potential to be the most powerful sorceress in the galaxy; we need her to be on point and on our side to save our planet."

Mason opened his mouth and then closed it with a sigh.

"We already know this boss, so what else is new?"

Orion looked over to the unconscious body of Thomas, "She's in love, we'll make her come to us."

"Do we kill him?" asked Mason.

"That's not what we do. Wake him up and follow my trail, I'm going to see what those soldiers are doing, catch me up later."

As Orion quietly shuffled away from Thomas, still trapped under a tree branch, Mason's grim face turned into a smile and pulled out a hunting knife, holding it to the young man's throat and looked back to Orion, "That's why I loved you."

Further down the forest, Kitty's eyes were fixed on Silo's wound.

"Are you crying?" Silo asked.

"I'm not normally a weeping woman my lady, but I'm concerned for you."

Silo looked guilty for her own injury and smiled, "Don't worry about me, kiddo, I'll be fine, but for the last time, we really can't stay here." Kitty wiped away tears as Silo struggled to get to her feet.

"Can we not just simply disappear, my lady? With both our witching powers we can go far away and be safe."

Silo sadly shook her head, "That's never going to happen, they will always find us." She corrected herself, "Find you."

"What do you mean, my lady?"

"Whenever you teleport or use any other of your powers, you leave an energy signature which can be picked up from certain tracking devices, that's how I found you when you were drowning because you had teleported a great distance for the first time. I guess that's how the hunters found us."

"So, whoever these people are, wherever I go, they will come and find me?"

Silo nodded, "They want you for themselves, their need is greater than your existence. They will stop at nothing to catch you and if it isn't those two, it will be others like them. They will always hunt you down, track your family, search out your friends to find you; some may be charming, others may be brutal but they all have the same thing in mind and they will never stop running, never stop looking."

Kitty looked to the sky and closed her eyes, "May God help us." Silo raised an eyebrow, "No, just me."

Kitty began to shiver, and Silo put her arm on hers, making the teenager tense slightly.

"Stay calm kiddo, we have to stay calm and we'll both get through this."

"I think it's time we leave my lady, I don't feel safe here."

Silo tried hard not to break out in hysterical laughter, "Finally! You're listening to me, I've been saying we should leave for ages."

Before either of them could rise, the armed riders had gathered around their hiding place. They formed a circle around the crouched pair, the thunder of the horses' hooves so close made Kitty squirm with discomfort and she raised her hand to teleport.

Silo lowered it hand for her, shaking her head, "No, not now, you can't let these people see you use your powers."

"Why my lady?"

"It would change everything, let's just see what they want and do whatever they say."

Before Kitty could ask again, the outraged captain on horseback shouted directly at the pair, "You two are trespassing on private land, watch at me! Watch at me! Do not move, this is the property of our lord and master, you are under arrest."

He beckoned to another rider who dismounted and cautiously moved closer with a long rope in his hands. The leader bought his horse to a stop, he winced when he saw Silo close up, "May my God take me down, what devilment of a creature is this? Why is she as dark as night? Take them to the King and let him deal with this creature."

As their hands were bound tightly by the nervous guard's rope, Silo looked up at the bearded leader, still swearing at her and spitting his disgust at her appearance, "I'm never going to get used to this land," she sighed. Kitty's face turned pale.

"I guess I have 'I told you so' coming to me, my lady."

Earth 65

"What have you done! What have you done!" Achilles screamed at Sully and looked around wildly as Miss Dwells threw up, emptying the contents of her stomach on the ground behind.

Sully bent down and cradled the body of Sayles, "I liked Sayles, she was always nice to me, she was a good partner in science class."

"Then why did you kill her?" Achilles spat.

Sully ignored the screams from the rest of the class and focused solely on Achilles. She seemed to be in a trance-like fix, licking her hands which were caked in dried blood, "Because she was going to take you away from us, she can't do that, you can't leave us, we have to stick together. Harley is dead, Kane is dead."

She looked at Achilles' eyes, they were beginning to twitch.

"You didn't know about them, did you?"

Sully stared harder, "I can smell their blood splatters all over the walls."

Achilles knew about the death of Harley due to his final phone pictures, but the apparent demise of Kane was news to him.

"You're lying," Achilles replied, a voice full of distain. She replied almost instantly, "Am I?"

Achilles glared with determined eyes, "Where is Kane?"

Sully's voice was solemn, "Like I always said, Kane gets around." She showed Achilles the blood-stained palms of her hands. One of the boys from the class made a clumsy attempt to grab Sully from behind. Easily sensing the attack, she side-stepped neatly to her left and spun around grabbing him by the throat, she lifted the frightened boy off his feet and looked into his terrified eyes, "Really?"

With devastating ease, Sully threw the boy across the room and, crashing against some cages, his body fell at an impossible angle on the floor to the bemusement of the animals inside, "Now, have I got your attention?"

Miss Dwells recovered from her sickness and stood up straight, "Listen young lady, I don't know what the hell happened to you, but I will not put up with this behaviour."

"Behaviour? You're worried about my behaviour? Look at me, just look at me! I think we're beyond detention here, Miss Dwells, you going to give me some lines? Ring my parents who aren't there anyway? What are you going to do?"

Sully ignored her teacher's attempt at seriousness and looked at Miss Dwells, still picking at the flesh stuck to her arms, she raised her voice, "I don't know what has happened to me, but it's brilliant. I feel so alive from being dead, I need blood and I want it now!"

Miss Dwells wiped sick from her mouth and stood firm, "Lower your voice when you speak to me young lady, I'm still your teacher."

"Really? You've done a stellar job at looking after your students." Sully gave a head nod to the body of Sayles on the floor, "The only reason I'm not peeling the flesh from Sayles' bones is that she was always nice to me."

"You killed her!" Achilles snapped.

"A minor mishap on my part," Sully snapped back.

"You gutted her," Miss Dwells added.

"Can we please stop with the character assassination?" Sully wiped her neck clean from blood, "I need to feed now!"

Achilles and Miss Dwells moved closer together and backed away from Sully, ushering the scared college kids to stand behind them, "You stay away from us, Sully," Achilles took another nervous look around at his surroundings.

"Just get back."

Sully was completely covered in blood and relished the fact, constantly rubbing the blood into her slender thighs and edged closer to her classmates.

"I'm so hungry, Achilles, why won't you feed me?"

Achilles was shaking slightly, scared of his former friend and at what she could do, his voice was unsteady and he raised his fists.

"You're not going to kill us."

"Are you certain?" Sully asked, noticing her old friend keeping his distance, "Have you not just seen what I did to Sayles?"

Achilles rubbed nervous hands on his thighs too, mirroring Sully earlier.

"Don't mug me off, Sully, we're tight, we always have been, you look like shit and I don't know what you've been doing but some of our friends are dead, don't you get it? Our friends are dead, Sully!"

Achilles couldn't believe what he had just said and stopped the leg rubbing, he was in shock at what he could see and what he'd just heard, "Do you remember what I said to that captain, who I haven't seen for ages, when we first came on this ship? I said that keeping animals in cages was cruel and barbaric, so I think I should let them go, don't you think? But I am still very hungry, so it's only fair I should have a little nibble to stop my hunger."

Sully looked into one of the cages and saw a number of straw wolves pacing up and down. They were desert hunters, known for their dark-yellowish short hides and sun tolerance. The one nearest the front of the cage growled and bared its teeth as Sully came close.

"These wonderful creatures shouldn't miss out on your awesome tour skills too, Miss Dwells. Speaking of which, best stay off the wine before you take a school trip Miss, your eyes have gone."

The teacher shook her head and looked into the cages as well and slowly shook her head fearfully, "Please don't do this."

Ignorant of Miss Dwells' words, Sully broke off the lock on the door with ease and pulled it open. She stretched out her hand full length to the wolf as it growled even more, Sully beckoned to it, "Come on, boy."

The wolf walked forward, more interested in the blood on her hand then anything she had to say. It licked her hands and edged out the cage slowly followed by the rest of the pack behind, "Good boy, good boy," she said.

The alpha male jumped up on Sully with its hind legs on the ground and its front paws on her shoulders, pushing her back which even surprised Sully. It licked the blood from her face with cute force, "Hey! Stop it you!" She laughed and smiled. The feeling on her face was dying, Sully could barely take in the licks from the wolf, her human side was fading away, but she liked the wolf on her; it made her remember being a teenager again, being normal, being with her friends.

Sully felt the grin fade from her lips as thoughts from the past began to make her sad, her parents had gone and so now were her friends. She pulled back from the wolf and kissed it tenderly on the cheek, "You're free now, boy." Sully moved her lips from its cheek below to its neck, "You're truly free." Her teeth bit deeply into the neck of the wolf who yelped and fell back, it rolled around on the floor, all of its paws flailing.

"What's happening, Miss?" Achilles asked.

"Trouble," was the reply.

The other wolves left the cage and gathered around the male, only one grey wolf remained in the cage, looking on. The wolf was still shaking as the whole class stared in disbelief. Suddenly all its legs stiffened and the shaking stopped.

"She's killed it," Achilles whispered to another classmate.

Sully smiled, her hearing had increased since her infection, "I said I would never hurt you, Achilles and I would never lie to you." She spoke looking away from her friend, Sully was still drawn to the wolf, which had now begun to foam at the mouth.

In a virtual instant the wolf shot upwards from the ground and attacked the nearest wolf, which happened to be one of its sons. The two males fought viciously until the alpha male tore out a chunk from the neck from its young offspring. The teenagers screamed in terror when they saw the blood flow from the wound. It was the new wolf who fell to the ground, shivering like its father did only moments before, but it was up on its feet sooner than its dad; its eyes, like its parent's, glowed red.

It shook its head in confusion and sniffed at its father before growling at the rest of the pack. The wolves backed away, wary of the appearance and movement from the young wolf. Sully anticipated the wolf's actions and stood back as it sniffed the air. It squatted down, wriggling its back ready to pounce and Sully allowed herself a satisfied smile and looked back at the class, "Take a seat people, you are going to love this show."

Both father and son wolves turned and attacked the pack. With powerful speed they tore into their family, their mouths clamped firmly on the throats of the startled wolves, tearing away at flesh with ease. As each wolf collapsed, they were soon up again with Sully's virus in their blood, reanimated and eager for blood; they had the thirst, the lust for more food.

The original wolf with the virus and the young male had decimated the pack of other wolves and now each wolf had the 'scourge' virus. All of the wolves were infected except the grey wolf still in its cage, it simply stayed in the back and watched the action outside with darting blue eyes. The wolves gave a hideous screech which made the college students cover their ears.

"What's happening to them?" Achilles asked.

For once his teacher didn't have to look at her notes to know the answer, "Those wolves are just like her now, infected with whatever Sully has."

Again, Sully overheard their conversation, "If you are going to keep dangerous, wild animals in a zoo, maybe you should have removed their teeth to stop them from chewing down to the skin."

The wolves turned to the youngsters and bared all their bloody teeth as they walked past Sully, their growls grew louder with each step.

"I'm not getting paid enough to deal with this shit," Miss Dwells sighed, "I'm a bloody substitute."

Sully looked over at her friends, Achilles in particular, wiping more blood from her face and stared at him. She shivered slightly, unsure for once, her voice was muffled and quieter, "Like I said, *I* would never hurt you, Achilles."

The wolves were getting ready to kill and the students knew and backed away fearfully, followed by more crying and shouting. Amid the panic from the students', confidence grew again from Sully as her eyes moved from Achilles to Miss Dwells, with a half-smile on her face.

"You know what, Miss? When you came in as a substitute and took our classes every now and then in the past, I could see how unconfident you were; the way you stood, the way you spoke, you were quite pathetic really."

Panic rumbled in Miss Dwells' stomach, "Go to Hell," was all she could mumble in a reply.

Sully cupped her hands to her ear, "Didn't get that, Miss? I didn't catch what you just said? Just like you couldn't understand me in class, I don't know if you didn't understand my accent? Or couldn't get my breakdown of words for certain mathematical theories or equations? So, let me break it down in more simple terms which I think your tiny mind might be able to grasp and I'll try and find a word your inadequate brain may be able to take in regarding this current situation."

Sully kept her gaze centred on her teacher as all wolves had now passed her and trotted closer to the fleeing students, "Run!"

A flood of students tore down the corridors of the grand ship *Utopia*. There was a large number of animals still to be viewed on the tour of the ship. The creatures in the cages watched as the class ran by, terrified and uninterested in them. Achilles powered past the front runners and led his class around the twisty labyrinths of the ship.

"Where are we going?" one of the faster kids asked.

Achilles ground his teeth, unsure of the correct answer and tiring quicker than he'd thought, "I've no idea where to go, we just have to keep running away from those wolf things."

"Wolves, they're still wolves," said the runner.

"Yeah, whatever, just keep running, maybe we can find Poxon, Cameo and Lacy," Achilles puffed.

"Or maybe we can get to the hanger, get a ship and fly us out of here?"

Achilles' eyes turned to the fast runner, known as Arlo, "Better idea, why not ask the pilots to fly us home?" asked Achilles.

"Mate, that should do it," Arlo replied.

"Good," Achilles said, struggling to run and talk at the same time. Arlo wiped snot from his nose and flicked it on the floor as he began to tire as well.

A hideous scream from behind them made their heads turn. It was a cry from a slow runner being attacked by the chasing wolves. The girl lagging behind was called

Molly, she was best friends with Sayles and still couldn't come to terms with her violent death. The wolf pack had easily caught up with her and her cries alerted Achilles and Miss Dwells.

"Molly, no!" Achilles whispered. He stopped running, "Arlo, get the others to safety."

"Where?"

"Anywhere!" Achilles yelled back.

"Get everybody away from the wolves, find a safe place and lock the doors or find out who's flying this ship, use a communicator, just get us home."

"Where are you going?" Arlo shouted.

"Molly's in trouble, she needs..." Before Achilles could finish he saw Molly pinned to the ground by one of the infected wolves.

"Miss Dwells?" Achilles asked, his voice was shaky. He hadn't known such fear in his life, even when his parents were taken, "Miss Dwells? Miss Dwells?" Achilles asked again. He looked over his shoulder and couldn't find his substitute teacher.

Achilles lowered his eyes and saw Miss Dwells speeding around a corner with her high heels in hand. Every concern about her temporary students had long left her mind; safety for herself was all she was worried about. The other students ran past him as he ran back to Molly's screams. She was pinned to the ground with the alpha male on top of her, "Oh my god! Please no!" Molly screamed as the hammering of her heart signalled her impending death.

The wolf clawed at her chest with ease and the panic that had hit her earlier was gone.

Molly feebly tried to push the wolf away from her but was dead by the time it had finished. Achilles looked on and shuddered as he saw Molly's body. It began to shake uncontrollably making Achilles wince even more. Blood was being splattered everywhere as Molly's body shook with a force that shocked the remaining students, who were eager to see what was happening with their classmate.

Sully was extremely happy as she saw what was happening, she leaned back to Achilles and grinned, "You're going to love this."

"You bastard," Achilles muttered. Sully held up her hand anticipating something.

"Wait for it," she said.

Achilles looked at both Sully and then Molly's body. The alpha wolf backed away, also sensing something, as did the other wolves. With ultra-quick speed Molly rose and stumbled to her feet.

Before anybody could move, she leapt at a student who had wandered too close to see what was happening. He thought he would ignore the wolves to try and get a better look. Molly tore out his throat with her teeth, ending his tour permanently. The wolves dashed round the fallen body, tearing at it as the alpha wolf had done with Molly.

The dead boy rolled over and was on his feet as fast as Molly. There was a gaping hole in his left side below the chest, which had been eaten by the infected wolves. He walked towards Achilles, who was now standing alone.

Then the boy's bones began to creak in his legs as he awkwardly picked up speed. Achilles covered his mouth, but as his hand slid down his face he drew in a quick breath of surprise, "No," he whispered.

Sully hustled the wolves around her, along with Molly and the male student. The other students had run away as well as Miss Dwells.

The alpha male barked and allowed Sully to stroke its blood-soaked head. It stood up on its hind legs and set his forepaws on her shoulders to lick her face.

"There's a good boy," Sully beamed again, she liked saying it to the wolf. She turned back to Achilles, "So what's it going to be, my lovely? Will you join me and together we can find our remaining friends and cleanse this ship and then we can all go back home and find our parents?"

"Our parents are dead, Sully."

"You don't know that. Big Man has them," she snapped back.

"Be like us, hunt like us, live like us, we can make you so special, Achilles. I want this to work so much, come with me and I can show you a life you never knew existed, we can be the most powerful force in the world." She held out her palm facing upwards to Achilles and beckoned, "What do you think?"

"Really?" Achilles asked.

"Yes, think about all that power we could wield, think of…"

Achilles turned and bolted down the corridor following his classmates.

"Typical," Sully moaned.

Lacy and Cameo held hands tightly as they swung around another corner in the endless rows of corridors in the ship, "Is he still behind us?" Cameo asked.

"Which one? Dinosaur or shark?"

"Shark."

Lacy swished her head back, there was nothing behind her. She leaned against a cage of giant winter porcupines, avoiding their quills as she caught her breath and heaved heavily. The shape of Slim Pickings lumbered into her line of sight, more out of breath than she was.

"Yep, he's still here," Lacy said, getting ready to run again.

"Why is he still following us?" Cameo mumbled tiredly.

"Dude, I can hear you," Slim Pickings said, frantically waving his hands to indicate tiredness.

"Sharks have ears? Pretty cool." Lacy grinned.

"Dude, you going to go through this again?" Slim Pickings sighed.

"Sorry, just still getting used to you, walking and talking blah blah blah," huffed Lacy.

"Dude, Lacy or whatever, I saved your life and Cameo's life too, don't you trust me?"

"To put it bluntly, no," Cameo interrupted.

Slim Pickings was struggling to catch his breath, "Dude, did you forget that I saved your life twice?" The shark collapsed against some cages frightening the creatures inside. Cameo surprisingly showed some concern:

"Hey! Shark person, are you ok?" Slim Pickings didn't move, "What's wrong with him?"

Lacy managed to catch her breath and pointed to Slim Pickings.

"He's a shark, on dry land, I guess he's getting tired or dying, probably needs water."

Cameo squeaked with excitement, "Oh! I can help, wait, wait, give me a second." She reached into her handbag and pulled out a full bottle of water. Twisting the cap off with ease, Cameo ran back to the shark, "You're not going to bite me, are you?"

"Dude!" Slim Pickings moaned.

"Ok, sorry, I got it."

Cameo poured the water into the mouth of Slim Pickings, hoping the lack of food and drink wouldn't find him in too much of a bad mood to bite her hand off. She flinched slightly as his razor-sharp teeth began to move, but only to speak:

"Dude, thank you."

Cameo waited until he had continued drinking all of the water and pulled the bottle away, "You ready to man up now?"

"Dude, I'm a shark."

"You know what I mean," Cameo sighed.

She stood up straight and groaned as her back clicked, offering out her hand to Slim.

"Dude, you can't pick me up, look at the size of me."

"I can try."

"Dude!"

"Stop it!" Cameo shouted, "Stop saying 'Dude' every time you speak, stop being so laid back, what's wrong with you? Have you seen what's happening on this ship? People are dying and you just think it's a game?"

Slim Pickings shifted on to his side and rubbed his black eyes, trying hard to take in Cameo's words, "Do you know what happened at Dangerfield theme park?"

Lacy sighed, "Again, really?"

Cameo produced a quizzical look, "Dangerfield? The theme park in Olympia?"

Slim Pickings nodded, coughing a little, "There was a virus let loose in Olympia, I'm not going to explain how or why because I've already told my story to Lacy and

I'm too tired to do it again, but it was brutal. It gave people anger, a rage, a scourge and then they turned into some bloodthirsty zombie things. I was there with my sister. I saw chaos and blood, too much death, there was a woman running away with her kid, he couldn't have been more than two or three years old and the mum held on to him tight. She was running fast, dodging the carnage and violence around, I called to her, waved her over to me to find safety."

Cameo's eyebrows deepened, "Wait, a woman holding her kid is going to run to a walking, talking shark for safety? That doesn't make sense."

Slim Pickings looked to the ceiling and breathed hard, "I wasn't always a shark. I was a human back then."

"Go on then," Cameo pressed.

"Well she saw me beckoning to her, there was some fairground undercover marquee stuff behind me and she would have been safe…"

"Would have?" Cameo's eyebrows were now raised.

"While she was running, she turned to the kid, I could see her looking at him, she was scared but the boy wasn't, he was relaxed which seemed strange given the situation. She got to the shelter and I waved at her again, she waved back, and she wasn't scared anymore because she knew she was about to be safe." Slim Pickings stayed looking at the ceiling.

"Do you need more water? It's all gone," Cameo replied, the earlier distrust in her voice was slowly fading.

"No, I'm good."

"Well, what happened?" Cameo pressed.

Slim Pickings slowly shook his massive head, his eyes squeezed shut, "She was still smiling when she looked to her son, their eyes locked on each other and the mum was…"

"Mum was what?"

"The mum was still smiling when her son leaned forward and tore her throat out, he must have been infected or bit or something, but that kid killed his mother in a heartbeat. She fell forward onto him and crushed her child, but it was still eating away at the mother's face from beneath her." Cameo's eyes focused fully on the shark, looked down at her heels and then back to Slim Pickings, she didn't have the faintest idea on how to respond, "So that's the reason why I try not to let things get me down too much. After witnessing that and loads of other deaths on that day and today, I don't have a choice."

"You going to sleep with him too, Cameo? We do have a dinosaur chasing us you know?"

Cameo ignored Lacy's voice and looked back to Slim Pickings. She offered her hand out for a second time, "Ready dude?" she said, grimacing as she attempted to pick him up.

Slim Pickings smiled a mouthful of razor-sharp teeth and for once Cameo didn't flinch.

"Dude, I'm ready."

Cameo pulled with all her might and Slim Pickings helped to raise himself off the ground. The two walked up to Lacy, who had controlled her breathing. Cameo playfully slapped her on her bottom, "Bitch."

Lacy quickly slapped her back, repeating the action, "Slut."

The two friends embraced each other tightly and longingly. Cameo looked tired but managed a smile for her friend, "We will get out of here." she said.

Lacy murmured softly in a reply, "I know."

Slim Pickings was alert again and walked quickly up to the girls, "Dudes, can I get a hug too? I need some loving!"

"No!" was the reply in unison as the girls unlocked themselves and put their hands on their hips jokingly, it was the first time they had smiled together in ages.

"Dude, it was worth a try," Slim Pickings winked in return.

"Ok, we have to find the others, we have to tell them what's happening with this loose dinosaur."

Slim Pickings rubbed tired eyes with the back of his fin and responded to Lacy.

"Dude, what can we do against this creature? We've all seen what it's capable of and it's not pretty. I'm sorry about what it did to your friends, but it's a massive beast, is there a captain on this ship?"

Lacy's eyes rose, "You now what? I forgot all about him."

"About who?" Lacy turned to Cameo to and was not surprised by her lack of input, "Oh I forgot, you were otherwise engaged on our briefing when we came on board."

"What's that supposed to mean?"

"You know exactly what it means, you were off partying with our teacher while the rest of us had to deal with this monster."

Cameo produced some backbone, "Oh wait, why aren't you with the others? Why do your eyes look so hazy? Because you and Kane must have left them to do some drugs to have your own fun, hence why you haven't got a clue what is happening or where anybody is: don't judge me about morals when you have none for yourself. I just saw my teacher get eaten, for god's sake!"

Slim Pickings stepped in, "Hey ladies, weren't you hugging each other a second ago?"

"That was before I knew what a hypocritical skank she was," snapped Cameo.

"Dudes, enough! Ok I get it, you two have issues to sort out but now is not the time. There is a killer dinosaur on the loose and I don't know about you but I'm going to get off this ship, find my sister and if I've got time, find out why for some reason I'm now a shark, with or without you, understand?"

Slim Pickings walked past the girls and cautiously out to another new corridor; his words weren't wasted on the girls who looked at each other in disbelief. Lacy spoke first:

"Do sharks have balls?"

"It would appear so," smiled Cameo.

"He was such a wimp at first, I thought it would take ages to find them," she added.

"He did save my life though, so makes him better than any man in my opinion."

"So where do we go now?" Lacy asked.

Cameo walked to an information pod, the computers were meant to show the maps and locations of everything in the ship. She pressed buttons and swiped her hand on the screen, "Nothing, the info isn't working, all location points are down."

"So where do we go now?"

Cameo pondered for a while and then spoke again cautiously, "I have an idea where we can go and be safe."

Slim Pickings came closer and scratched his nose, "Dude, what are you talking about?"

Cameo went back to her serious low tone of voice, "The maps are down I think? But each computer has a functioning communicator, no sorry, functioning locator to the captain's quarters."

"How did you know that?" asked Lacy.

"I do listen to Poxon and Harley sometimes," she replied with a distant smile.

"So, what do we do now?"

Instead of replying to Lacy, Cameo swiped the screen again, "Yes! I've got it, these maps are operational now." A red dot appeared on the screen and started to flash, "Ok, there are the captain's quarters, if he isn't there, I bet there is still a way to contact Heffernan City and get us out of here. Right let's go."

Cameo took off down the corridor without waiting for her friends.

"I SEE IT NOW, CAMEO WAIT!"

Slim Pickings' dark eyes grew, "Dude, that girl must be a thief, I've never known anybody run that fast."

"Yeah but what good is speed if she gets herself killed, you up for some running?"

The shark rolled his eyes, "Dude, looks like I'm a thief too."

"MISS DWELLS! MISS DWELLS WHERE ARE YOU?"

Strangely, Arlo found himself grinning. He would always try to laugh when he got nervous; it was one of his little quirky characteristics, laugh in the face of danger and stick your tongue out whilst concentrating. *What would Achilles do now?* he kept thinking.

The screaming had stopped from the students as they all paused for a breath, looking frantically behind them.

"Where is Achilles?" some of the students asked.

"He should be with us," others said.

Friendly and slightly hesitant, Arlo answered, "Listen, he was right behind us, I'm sure he's coming soon, we have to find Miss Dwells and the others."

Arlo was trying hard to stay calm and collected but it was hard to do so with a group of people who moments ago never knew he existed. He could never be like Achilles. He was strong and brave, and everybody loved him and respected him, they listened to every word he said. *Why would they listen to me?*

He was snapped out of his thinking by a timid girl's voice, "Arlo, why don't we hide in one of the rooms?" Arlo turned to the voice, it was a small classmate called Lyssa, who had deep brown eyes and a mane of brown hair to suit, "I don't hear anything, it's gone all quiet, maybe we can hide in one of the training rooms until those things go away?"

Arlo's eyes sparked up, "Yes! That's a great idea, are they locked?"

Foster, another student similar in build to Achilles stepped forward, "Let's just go and kick some doors down shall we, Arlo?"

He knows my name! Arlo grinned inside, "Yeah ok, sounds good, let's go."

Lyssa threw her massive mane of brown hair behind her head, "Ok, you're in charge now, tell us where to go."

Stepping confidently into Lyssa's view, Arlo mustered up an encouraging grin. *There're listening to me.* Arlo's eyes focused solely on Lyssa, "Ok, let's go to the conference rooms, it's probably safer there anyway."

"Hasn't the captain got a room somewhere? I swear I saw something about it on the guidelines when we came in." asked Foster.

"Yes Foster, yes of course the captain's base! Why didn't I think of that before?" Arlo said it out loud this time.

"What about Achilles?" Lyssa asked.

"Once we get to safety, hopefully he will catch up with us, we won't leave anybody behind."

"You sound like you're in charge," Foster said.

"That's because I am," Arlo replied quicker than he thought.

With everybody on board, the new group ran down more corridors and around more of the zoo's displays with the creatures inside the cages unaware of the students' plight.

As they passed the creature exhibits and headed towards conference rooms, Arlo led the way and made sure to glance his neck back and check behind the students as they ran. The group span around yet another corner at speed.

"We've been running for ages. Do you know how to get there?" Lyssa's voice was sounding more frantic and Arlo knew. He was looking more flustered and was unable to control the panic which had now claimed almost all of his classmates. One girl fell down close to Arlo, he turned back and helped her to her feet, "You ok?

She shook her head dolefully, "I'm scared."

"Me too," he replied, maybe a tad too quickly and not the words the girl wanted to hear, her mouth fell open.

"So, what do we do?"

"Keep running, that's all we can do."

Cameo had lost Slim Pickings and Lacy, she had turned too many corners and running in bare feet was faster than she'd anticipated.

"Shit," she mouthed.

She whipped her head back around her and it was just the sounds of the animals baying in their cages,

"Guys, where are you?"

She couldn't hear her friends' footsteps behind her, no awkward clumps from Slim Pickings or gentle strides from Lacy, just nothing.

"Guys?"

Cameo heard a new sound, loads of different footsteps running at speed towards her.

"Lacy?"

There was no reply, but the charge of feet was still there. They didn't seem to be stopping any time soon, so she carried on running. This ship was full of corridors, it had more fork turns than it had creatures in cages. Never studying, never listening, Cameo thought she'd never had to, being one of the most attractive people in Heffernan City, people usually bent over backwards to give her what she wanted. This wasn't the case now: most of her best friends were missing and some she knew were dead. She was now relying on a giant walking, talking shark to help her and a girl who was so loved up on her boyfriend and drugs that she didn't have a clue about her own reality.

Shaking her head whilst running, Cameo had reached the captain's quarters without knowing. She made her way to the entrance and concentrated. *Oh cool, here it is,* she thought.

Cameo pounded on the door with dainty little wrists, anxiously looking around her for any unwanted attention.

"Hello? Is there anybody there?" There was no answer and she tried again, banging harder this time, but still nobody there. She leaned against the door and pressed her ears against the metal surface, listening intently, "Please open the door." Cameo stood back as she heard a sound from inside. She bit her lip and then chewed it as she heard the door's opening mechanism click and work. The door slid open and Cameo grinned when she saw who was standing on the other side, "Oh wow, it's you, thank god you're here."

The figure on the other side eyed Cameo up and then beckoned her in slowly. Any tinge of panic Cameo had disappeared as she entered into the room; she gently smiled, "I didn't know you'd be here, do you know what's happening out there?"

The figure nodded and spoke softly, "I've had a slight inkling."

Cameo looked around at the room, it didn't look like anything she was expecting "I have some friends on the way, they'll be here shortly. How can we get out of here? The ship is in danger, there is a dinosaur on the loose." Her eyes fluttered when she listened to what she'd just said and couldn't believe it herself, "It killed some of my friends, it's killed Professor Gregory too."

The figure's eyebrows dug deep into its face, "Really? He's dead?"

Cameo nodded, "Ok, would explain a lot."

Cameo stepped closer to the figure, completely confident and safe, "You don't seem surprised that there is a dinosaur loose?"

The figure put their hands around Cameo's waist, "It's a zoo, a lot of crazy stuff can happen and apparently is, just so long as we get all the kids out safely then we'll be fine."

Cameo playfully wriggled free from their grasp, "I know, we have to contact the pilots and get them to fly this ship back to Heffernan City, I can't find any of the other college kids here or their teachers, they must be around somewhere."

The figure pulled her back, "I've been waiting for you, why didn't you call me?"

"I was with the professor, you knew that," Cameo protested mildly and spoke again still looking around at her surroundings, "I couldn't see you because you were doing your job, but I really wanted to,"

The figure grinned, "You should have looked harder."

"I tried, I didn't have the time," Cameo said brightly.

The figure placed their hands on Cameo's face and caressed her cheeks slowly, "Well it's just us two now, this is what I've been waiting for."

Somehow Cameo forgot about her other friends and finally dropped her guard, "Now isn't the time or place," she giggled.

"We'll make time," the figure said, putting a finger to Cameo's lips, "You have no idea how long I've waited for this moment," the figure said.

Cameo spun around with her back to the figure, she began to unbutton her top as she allowed herself to be held by their arms, her top fell to the ground as the figure held her tight.

"God, I've wanted this for so long," she purred.

"I need you so much right now," was the eager reply, breathing heavily on Cameo's neck.

The figure reached into their jacket pocket and pulled out a syringe filled with a green liquid and lifted it up quietly, squirting its contents out gently for a test. Cameo backed up further into the figure, feeling safe and secure.

She nestled herself into their front and brushed away hair from her eyes, awaiting a kiss on her neck.

She lifted her eyes and fluttered their lids, dreamily smiling with complete happiness. Cameo was happy in fulfilment and bent her neck back and licked her lips eagerly. The figure teased their finger down the curves of Cameo's body, making her shudder in excitement. The figure then aimed the syringe towards her slender neck whilst holding her waist tight in their other hand.

"Do you like what you see?" she asked with a grin.

The figure slammed the syringe into Cameo's neck, emptying the green liquid quickly and released her from their grasp as she wobbled on her feet. Her eyes looked hurt and betrayed as she finally fell to the floor succumbing to the contents of the syringe and the figure gave an apologetic shrug.

The figure waited until Cameo had stopped twitching and then pulled her body onto a table in the corner of the room. Strapping her arms in tight with restraints and the same with her legs, the figure then injected her again with the serum. Cameo's body violently convulsed and shook the whole table. She started to bleed from her mouth and eyes, while the figure stepped back and with a grave expression and looked at the results of the serum. When Cameo's broken body stopped moving, they wiped their eyes sadly, "I liked what I saw."

Arlo turned to face Lyssa, his face tangled with frustration, "Where is the captain's room? I can't find it, this is getting bad."

Lyssa looked behind at the other bewildered students who were also tired. She went back up to Arlo and shushed him with a finger to her lips, "You know that and I know that, but they don't need to, they're scared enough as it is without you going on about it."

Arlo shook his head as Lyssa went quiet, "I just wanted to have fun, I just wanted to come on this ship and forget who I am and have a different day than normal."

"Normal?" asked Lyssa.

"What is the reason you're speaking to me, Lyssa?"

Lyssa arched an eyebrow, "I'm sorry?"

"You thought I knew what was going on? Why ask me that?"

Lyssa's eyes scanned behind and then shot back and forth between Arlo and the students, speaking as if she was being prodded by a big stick, goading her to talk, "Well you know stuff, you have information on various things."

Arlo wasn't convinced, "Go on."

"Is now really the right time?"

Arlo mirrored Lyssa and looked behind too, "Now is as good a time as any."

Lyssa cleared her throat as Arlo looked up at her, "You were always reading comics, had your head in a book and was always so quiet, I assumed you were a geek."

"So just because I was reading you automatically thought I was some sort of nerd?" Lyssa just nodded, slightly embarrassed as they continued walking, "Did you ever just stop to think that I just liked to read? Or that I was quiet because I just liked my own company? I'm not a super-geek genius, I'm just scared like the rest of you guys, I don't know what to do, I don't know where we are or where we're going." Arlo was about to wipe a tear, "I'm not Achilles, I'm not as strong as him, I'm not as brave as him and he left me in charge."

Lyssa put her hand on his shoulder, gently pulling him back before they turned another corner. She empathised with him, "Like I said, everybody is scared but Achilles left you in charge for a reason, he has faith in you, I have faith in you, you're not a coward, Arlo."

"Never said I was," came the quick reply.

"No, I meant that you don't back down from things, I don't think you ever have."

"How would you know?"

Lyssa nervously shifted from one foot to the other, "I got it wrong about you and I apologise about calling you a nerd: you're a good guy and Achilles will come back for us, he'll sort things out."

"Doubtful honey," said a voice which Arlo heard clearly, but it wasn't Lyssa's.

He could hear her screaming and it was the most horrific sound, more so than usual as she had screamed quite a bit recently due to certain events, but this was different; it seemed to hang in the air for ages, lasting forever. Arlo looked at Lyssa and heard her long drawn out scream, he could hear the rest of the students shouting and pointing at him, which he thought was strange.

His eyes began to shut. *Don't want to go to sleep, why am I so tired?* Arlo opened his eyes and glanced at his stomach, there was a hand sticking through it, which was pushed through his back and covered in his own blood. He gave a look behind and saw Sully wave at him, with her free hand. She struggled to pull her other hand free from Arlo's insides as he had one last thought. *I wish Achilles was here.*

With a final yank, Sully removed her hand from Arlo's stomach, and as the only thing keeping him on his feet was gone, he fell down dead.

Sully gave a sad look at Arlo's body, but quickly grabbed the still screaming Lyssa by her mane and pulled her closer. She was surrounded by the bloody infected wolves and some more students who Sully obviously caught up with and gave them her virus.

The infection was deep within most of the students; they had black, dead eyes and were covered in their own blood, caked onto their now pale skin.

They swayed in unison and couldn't speak, some had their throats torn out by Sully as she tried to turn them in different ways, but the infection made them mute anyway.

Becoming harder to control as they needed more blood to satisfy their rage lust, Sully seemed to be their leader but even she was having trouble keeping them in check. She was the strongest of them all, the other infected knew that, but only for a while. The wolves growled and made their way around the remaining unturned pupils. Cries of distress came from them as the wolves closed in. The quiet grey wolf hung behind observing the events, it took few steps back but failed to join its fellow wolves in trapping the tearful kids. Sully still held the struggling Lyssa in her hands, "You see? This is what you're missing out on, the power we have and what we can do."

Lyssa tried hard to turn her head and eyed Sully, "How long is this going to take you, bitch?"

Sully gave a nod to the infected and the wolves to attack the remaining students. Lyssa watched as the wolves and infected set upon her screaming friends. Sully softly brushed Lyssa's hair behind her head and gently tore a chunk of flesh from her neck, swallowing it whole. She watched as Lyssa's lifeless body collapsed to the ground and made an attempt to wipe all of the blood from her mouth, "Not long."

CHAPTER NINE:

A Tail Of Two Cities

Earth 13

Kitty awoke with a start; her head was jerky and she was unfamiliar with her surroundings. She knew she was under some covers, lying in the most gorgeous bed sheets and that was it. Her eyes nervously flicked from left to right and she slowly peeked her from beneath the luscious fabrics, "Hello? Is there anybody there?" There was no answer and Kitty tried again, still holding the fine sheets, "Hello? Where am I?"

"You are safe now, my lady."

The other voice made Kitty jump and she pulled herself fully from the bed and saw a woman waiting patiently by the room's only door. She had long straight black hair covering bony shoulders and a very pale slender neck. The clothes she wore were of fine quality and fitted her well. She curtsied slowly and spoke softly, "The King is ready for you now, my lady."

Kitty bolted upright, "What did you say, my lady?"

The beautiful woman in the dress looked shocked, "Why are you calling me 'my lady' my lady?" she asked.

"Because you are a lady, my lady," Kitty replied.

The other girl shook her head.

"No, you're the lady, my lady. I don't think that I am a lady, my lady."

Kitty opened her mouth, paused slightly and then shut it. She looked around at her surroundings and spoke again, "I asked you before, where am I? Who are you? And don't call me my lady please."

Kitty saw now how annoying it must have been for Silo. The other woman's eyes went from wonder to cynical, "You are in the court of his Majesty the King and he wishes to see you now."

Her eyes fixed solely on Kitty like a snake waiting to strike, the young woman's mouth twisted and continued, "My lady."

Kitty's face changed from one of puzzlement to shock, "The King! Which King?"

"Our only King, my lady," the woman said, still staring hard at Kitty.

"I am in the King's quarters?"

"No, you are in your own room."

"Why? What have I done?" Kitty's voice trembled. The woman noticed and ran to the bed, kneeling at the side and reached for Kitty's hand.

"You have done nothing wrong, my lady."

"Then what am I doing here?" Kitty pulled her hand away, "I asked who you were as well."

The woman chewed her tongue before answering, "You fainted my lady, you've been unwell for some time, but my heart sings with joy to see you awake again. My name is Mary, I am your chief lady-in-waiting at the King's wishes."

Kitty's eyes widened, "Lady-in-waiting? I am to have a lady-in-waiting? But what have I done to deserve such a luxury?"

"You caught your Majesty's eye when the guards bought you and Silo in here."

Kitty leapt from the bed in an instant, "Silo! My lady Silo, where is she?"

"The King demands an audience with you first, my lady."

"I don't care! I need to see my friend."

"But my lady?"

"I said, where is she?"

Mary went to hold Kitty's hand again but remembered the reaction she got before and stopped, "She is in the tower, my lady."

There was a silence, finally broken by Kitty, "Take me to her." Mary stood away, "Now," Kitty said brutally.

Mary walked to the front door and banged it three times, "She's ready," she said sternly.

The door slowly opened and another lady-in-waiting was standing nervously on the other side, struggling with carrying some clothing plus curtsying at the same time.

"Give them to me please," Mary gestured impatiently to the girl. She handed Mary the clothes and backed away slowly. The head lady-in-waiting held aloft the dress to Kitty, "Is this ok, my lady?"

Kitty remembered the clothing worn by Silo and how it looked so beautiful and fresh. She would have longed to have worn a garment like the one presented to her only a few months ago, but she was now just interested in wearing something decent and seeing her friend. She gave Mary a defeated smile as she eyed up the dress, "It's fine."

Kitty tried to get out of bed but stumbled on her feet like a newborn deer.

As she fell to the ground, all of her ladies-in-waiting gasped and helped Kitty back into bed, "My goodness, why can't I stand up?"

Mary shooed the others away, Immie and Jane stood by the corner of the massive bed awaiting further orders. Mary pulled the covers back over Kitty and gave her a 'Mother knows best' look, "You've been unwell for some time, my lady, you must stay off your legs and let me look after your tiredness until his lordship is ready to see you at his table."

"I don't want to see the King! I just want to get my friend and get the hell out of here!"

The ladies-in-waiting gasped again, this time at Kitty's language. Mary ushered them with a hand signal to be quiet.

"My lady, I will send a message to the King, it's obvious that you're not ready to join him and his guests, I will tell him that you don't require his company right now, make sure he knows your awake and I'm sure he will join the house in splendid rapture at your breath of new fresh air."

"Listen, I'm happy the King wants to meet me, I'm delighted that he finds a mere slip of a girl like me interesting, but in the words of my friend Silo, 'I'm outta here'."

Kitty ignored more gasps from her ladies-in-waiting and braved her legs wobbling from beneath her, the struggle to rise to her feet was unbearable. Her eyes glanced over at her ladies-in-waiting, they looked troubled and scared, more from Mary than anything else, who spoke sternly to Kitty.

"I have no time for fun and games, my lady, you will stay in this bed and rest until I speak with the King, he has trusted me on taking care of your welfare, although God knows why, he has done nothing but take care of you and your first response in waking up is to simply leave? I am trying hard to conceal my displeasure at your actions, my lady, but it is very hard to do so."

Kitty arched her back and rubbed it in pain, the lady-in-waiting called Immie went over to help her, Kitty ignored Mary's icy looks and thanked Immie, still wondering about Mary.

"What is her problem? I fainted for a bit apparently, why is everyone acting like cunning snakes?"

Immie whispered slowly, "Because you were asleep from collapsing for some time, my lady, we have to get you fit and ready for the King."

It dawned on Kitty that something was far from alright. She remembered what Silo had told her about speaking too fast when she was excited or nervous as it may cause her power to leak. She had to concentrate hard all the time now and was finally learning.

On any other day she would have been pleased at how well she was doing and knew Silo would have been too, but she wasn't here and Kitty needed answers. She spoke slowly but firmly, "I want to see Silo."

Mary groaned politely, but spoke quickly through being so impatient, "Now come along, my lady this is turning into a silly game."

"I won't ask you again, take me to see my friend."

"I've told you before where she is and that you cannot see her, you've been asleep for quite a while." She smiled and held it for longer than it was necessary, "Quite a while," she replied.

Mary's surprisingly calm voice was getting too much for Kitty as she walked over to her, shooed Immie out of the way and tenderly stroked the young girl's hair and her tone became lower.

"You were so lovely when the guards bought you in, you looked so calm and innocent, some of the other girls said you looked crafty when they began to tend to you, even while you slept, but I knew you were different."

Mary's smile became crooked.

"We peeled back your eyes, our doctors said that you were in God's hands now and we could not help you, we had our priests have all the house say their final prayers to you, but I knew there was some fire from the good lord still in you and I begged our King not to let you die. So, you were bought in and we let you rest until you fully recovered, every day I visited you faithfully."

A swell of sickness quickly formed in Kitty's stomach, she stuttered a bit, "Every day? How long was I asleep for?"

"My lady, I don't think now is the time for you–"

"HOW LONG?"

Mary rose to her feet and politely curtsied to Kitty, she headed to the door and turned the handle, hesitating with a long smile back on her face, "Six months, my lady."

"No!" Kitty gasped.

"Seven or eight? I can't fully remember, my lady."

Kitty collapsed into the waiting arms of Immie in shock. Before she could speak, Mary opened the door and was almost on her way out, "Now get ready, my lady, your husband is waiting to finally meet you."

"My husband?"

Mary swung around back from the door, her iron eyes locked hard on the numb face of Kitty. She fiddled with her wedding ring, twisting it slightly, "Why the King of course, my lady, not yet but soon to be married, any minute now."

Immie struggled with Kitty's body as she had passed out again.

Silo watched her guard look in bemusement at her appearance. He sniggered and pointed at her from outside the prison doors. She looked down and scowled at her outfit and her hands, thinking and chin-wiping slowly. It had been many months since she had been slung in prison. She had no idea where Kitty was or how she had been treated. Silo thought that the simple fact that *she* was still alive meant that Kitty was as well. *I could easily teleport out of here and show this monkey what real power is.*

Shaking her head, Silo sat back on the straw-covered floor, which had a foul smell of faeces to it. She had got used to it now, the first few weeks were the hardest, but after a couple of months, it became the norm.

She knew that if she ever used her power in front of them, it would have giant repercussions on the space timeline and possibly destroy the galaxy. That was what she was taught, whether it was true or not, she dare not try. The wound on her stomach was still hurting, the bleeding had stopped a few months ago but it still caused her discomfort.

A young girl called Immie had come in to dress her wounds; she was a very shy girl and didn't talk much, even when questioned.

Through head nods, quiet smiles and whispered tones, she did say that Kitty was alive but in a deep sleep. Silo thought that somehow between being captured and now, there had been a shift in Kitty's power; when she had fainted it was like she was charging herself up like a battery, nothing Silo had seen before.

Silo had stayed safe for many weeks now, knowing the chances were that Orion and Mason were waiting around too, biding their time as they knew also that Kitty would be more powerful after her sleep and would be easily able to teleport a planet, no matter the cost to the rest of the galaxy. She had to find them first before they reached Kitty.

Silo had explained part of her story to Immie, not the fact that she and Kitty weren't from this world, but that she was herself a lady-in-waiting of sorts to Kitty and needed to be updated on her progress. Immie was happy to do so, quietly through her jittery winks. It had to do, as Silo knew it was time to see her friend Kitty. The guard banged on the door, breaking Silo out of her thinking. She stopped herself from teleporting and gave an awkward smile to her captor; she had to think of another way to escape. Rising from the straw, Silo stared hard at the guard and smiled.

Her hips slowly began to move, to the left and then the right. She was starting a little dance, moving gracefully as she could with a damaged stomach around the shit covered floor, trying to be seductive whilst her nose tingled with the awful smell. She had waiting long enough, it was time to go, "Do you like what you see?"

The guard made no effort to hide his distaste for her, "Foul witch! How dare you spin your witchery upon me."

Silo could never get used to how much people prattled on in this timeline and working with Kitty brought the fact closer to home; something which she missed dearly from her young protégé and nobody else. She knew Kitty was safe thanks to Immie but still had to see her.

The dance wasn't working so Silo tried the old fashion route, "Let me outta here! Let me outta here now!" she demanded.

The guard walked toward the cell door and pressed his face up close to the bars, "It is with God's will that you should be kept in here for the rest of your wretched life, you filth."

Silo stared back hard at the guard, "Ok, I get that, but you have to tell me what happened to the girl I was brought in with. Is she alright, is she safe?"

Silo knew Kitty was alive, but had to call the guard's bluff.

"She is of no concern of yours, witch, and you have harmed yourself."

Silo inhaled sharply and looked down at her stomach, she was bleeding again, "Could you at least stop with the witch calling and tell me where she is?"

"Never, witch!" the guard snapped back.

"Did you not just get my memo about not calling me a witch?" Silo asked.

"Do not anger me witch, you will regret trying to go to war."

"Go to war? All I want to do is get out and you smell of cheap beer and that's the only thing I regret right now - not finding where you keep your hidden stash."

"You are a crass cow," the guard said shortly.

"Plus, you're still single I'm guessing?" Silo shrugged.

"You are a witch and the devil's whore!"

"I take it back, you're married."

Silo took a step back and looked around at her surroundings, knowing she had to get out and find Kitty quickly, "So you think I'm witch, right? Well witches have loads of power and can grant any wish you want."

The guard shot a steely look at Silo, "What do you mean, filth?"

Silo went down on one knee and kept her head bowed, "If I had the disgusting power of a witch, I could make your greatest desire a reality, anything you want I could grant you that wish. I am yours to command, my lord."

Silo shook her head and stood up, going back to her seductive dance routine. Wriggling her hips trying to remember how she did it before, she put her hands on her cheeks and dragged them slowly down to her chest, "Do you want to command me, my lord?" The guard was flustered, "I'm the sexiest witch you'll ever meet and you will let me out of here to make your dreams come true...gold, diamonds, castles, it's all yours if you tell me where the girl is and let me loose."

The guard bowed in return, "Forgive me cruel witch, but I don't know the meaning of 'sexy'."

"Yep, definitely married," Silo replied. "If you tell me where she is, my powers will fulfil your greatest destiny."

"What do you mean?"

Silo wriggled again, "Open the door, tell me where the girls is, and I'll give you anything your heart desires."

The guard's eyes lingered on Silo's figure and then fumbled with his set of keys as he looked for the one that opened the door. The lock clicked as the guard entered the right key from his chain, he pushed the door gently and stood back, his eyes left Silo and looked nervously on the floor. Silo was eager to use a spell on him, but knew any sign of the guard knowing about her powers could wreck the very fibre of reality. Breathing hard, she walked forward.

"Well then witch, what about your promise of riches and treasures for me?"

With a crooked smile, Silo waggled her forefinger in his face, "The deal was, my lovely, for you to tell me where the girl was and then you get what you deserve."

"Will I get a new rhythm of life, witch?"

Silo could see the guard's lips moving in prayer and walked forward towards him:

"Where is she?"

The guard looked to the ceiling and then back to Silo, snorting as he did so, "The King has taking a liking to the young girl and she is to be betrothed as his new bride immediately."

Silo stepped back, terrified.

"Who is the King?"

The guard looked shocked, "He is our lord and saviour, he is a patient King, his wisdom is second to none, he is a good man and I'm honoured to serve him, he has taken quite a liking to the pretty young girl, she is to be his bride."

Silo coughed and screamed at the same time, "What's his name?" Silo stressed.

"King Henry."

"So, my friend, the girl Kitty, she is the new Queen?"

"No, they are not married." Silo blew a sigh of relief, "They are to be wed later today."

"WHAT!" Silo yelled.

The guard glared angrily at her, annoyed at why she was asking such a stupid question, "Yes, today of course, you foolish witch, the ceremony is happening later, she will be our new Queen, obviously our King watched over her while she slept, but talk flies like a restless robin in this place, and the word is that as soon as she is up, she will be wed."

"Where is she?"

"She'll be with her new ladies-in-waiting in her bed chambers probably, getting ready."

A horrid fear struck Silo and she flinched at every step the guard made as he entered the cell, "I gave you the information you wanted cruel witch, now give me the power I crave."

Silo shook her head, thinking how scared Kitty must be. Her eyes gleamed with fake delight as they locked back on to the figure.

"Yes, you are spot on, I made a promise and I'll honour that for you, being a witch of course."

Silo's look lingered on the guard as he pressed again, "Am I ready, witch." His head began to bob up and down like an excited child.

A pause came before Silo answered, "Ok, come closer and I'll give you what you want." Silo took a deep breath with her hands on her hips, then she slowly raised them to caress the guard's face.

"My God, I've never known such a touch from a woman."

"I'm sure." Her voice rang with confidence, "Here's another decent touch from a woman."

Wandering hands moved down from his face, and tickling his sides, he shivered with excitement.

"Does that feel good?" The guard nodded dreamily, "Thank you for giving me information about Kitty kind sir, I appreciate it."

"Silence your tongue woman and give me what I deserve."

Silo ignored him and put her hands back on his face, one behind his neck and held on gently, "Fair enough. By the way you know that stuff I said about giving you all the riches in the world and making you more powerful than you could possibly imagine?"

"Yes, witch?"

Silo suddenly gripped the back of his neck tightly and bought her right knee up to his groin with powerful force. The impact made the guard double up in pain as he bent forward with the blow. Silo connected with a tight elbow to his jaw just to make sure as the guard hit the ground unconscious, "I lied."

Dragging his body back into the cell, Silo took his keys and examined it for any other items of use, the whole day hadn't worked out as she had planned and was fast becoming a huge disappointment. She stood up and stretched her back, looking down at the guard:

"One word of advice, matey, never ever trust a desperate woman."

Before Silo could leave the cell, she too was clobbered on the back of the head by someone behind her. She fell into a heap next to the guard and stirred no more. Her attacker watched for a while to make sure she wasn't dead, she was still breathing and that was enough. Mason's eyes couldn't leave the body of Silo as he rubbed the handle of the gun that knocked her out, "I couldn't agree more."

Earth 65

Poxon was hit with the realisation that he'd passed through these corridors before. *I must have run around this entire ship,* he thought. He felt sick, not just in the feeling of running around too much, but he still hadn't found his friends or any of his classmates. They were here somewhere on this ship and he had to find them before the dinosaur did. His fingers wiped the sweat from his eyes for what seemed to be the umpteenth time today. There was no sign of the creature behind him and he really needed a wee, not down his trousers like last time.

He was past scared now, he'd been on the run for so long all that was in his body was determination...and still far too much wee. Yet another corridor loomed in front of him, which split into a fork at the end. *Ok, here we go again.*

Running down the corridor, Poxon made a turn to the right. It was a calculated guess, but sooner or later he'd hope it would be lucky for him. A stench hit him as he ran further, and it was a smell he had encountered before. *Oh no*, he thought.

The smell was that of pee from the dinosaur, so either the creature really needed to go like Poxon did or it was marking its territory, making it extremely close. An ugly and unwelcome sound bellowed from the opposite corridor making Poxon's stomach twist. At least he'd made the right decision in not choosing the left turning, but the cry of the dinosaur was still a sound he didn't want to hear right now.

He picked up the pace and headed around another corner, and then wished to god he hadn't.

The floor was littered with bodies, the bodies of college students. Bright new ship walls were now covered in blood, splattered in the once eager students' remains. This wasn't the work of one creature, the students had been torn apart by more than one thing, a pack of animals had done this. *A pack of something*, he thought. Poxon couldn't look at the awful sight for too long but something else in the far end of the corridor had caught his eye. A man was sitting against the wall, covered in massive cuts and bruises, blood flowed openly from all his wounds. He was rocking uncontrollably and his teeth chattered away. The man was in severe shock as Poxon made his way through the bodies and knelt beside him, "Are you ok, sir?"

Poxon recognised the man and tried again, touching his shoulder gently. The man recoiled and slid further down the wall, his eyes wide and focusing heavily on the student.

"Captain McConnell, are you alright? What happened here?"

The captain of the once proud ship *Utopia* didn't even register Poxon's words, he was still shaking and sweating.

Poxon had had enough of being ignored, from years of hanging around his friends to being a disappointment to his parents, this moment now was a chance to change, his voice was raised but he didn't shout, "I said what happened?"

The captain's voice was jittery and full of panic, "It wasn't supposed to be like this, it wasn't me, it wasn't me!"

Leaning closer, he pulled Poxon closer towards him and wailed in pain, dropping one arm to the ground. Poxon grimaced, putting his hand to his mouth as he noticed Captain McConnell's right arm; there was a stump where his hand should have been and he was bleeding profusely from the wound. He continued to drag Poxon to him with his left:

"I was just trying to make things right. It wasn't my fault."

"What are you talking about, Captain? Who did this?"

"There was so many of them, they attacked me, vicious little creatures, I hid away, had to hide."

"So many of what sir? Did someone let out the animals? Are they loose?"

The captain shook his head violently, "No, not the animals."

Poxon asked again, knowing his next question would get dismissed quicker than the first, "Was it a dinosaur?" He paused, waiting for a rebuke.

"No, it wasn't the dinosaur."

"Wait? You said *the* dinosaur not *a* dinosaur."

Nate McConnell coughed up blood and it ran all down Poxon's top. He began to scream in pain and further panic set in, it was becoming too much for him.

"We have to get you to a doctor, I'll take you to the sick bay."

Poxon then remembered what happened the last time he took someone to the medical bay and thought otherwise, visions of Sully and how she murdered Katie the nurse flooded back into his head.

"We did the dinosaur, we did everything."

Nate's eyes began to fade and this time it was Poxon who shook the captain, "What do you mean? What have you done?"

"I was just trying to help, I didn't think it would go this far." Blood and sweat poured down the face of the captain, "We only wanted to get away, build to run, that's what she said: we had to run, that's what she told me."

"What are you talking about?"

The blood seeping through the captain's top was all over Poxon, he hadn't much time and they both knew it.

"Please Captain?"

Looking at the bodies scattered around him, he thought about Sully again, "Who did this? Was it a girl? Was it one of the students?"

As Captain Nate McConnell breathed his last, the hands that gripped Poxon fell to the ground and he sadly looked up at him, struggling to speak before he died, "Not one student, it was all of them."

Poxon leant down to see if the Captain's heart had truly stopped. He put his ear on Nate's chest, it failed to move.

Standing back on his feet, Poxon swallowed, his throat was dry, and he remembered he hadn't had anything to drink since the class was given bottled water when they'd arrived on the ship earlier.

He closed his eyes and opened them again slowly, looking at the Captain's body and thinking he might get sick at any moment. It was time to get back to what he had seemed to be doing for ages, looking for the rest of his friends. Poxon was tired and more than a little bored with trying to find them. *Are they out looking for me as well?* he thought.

He was almost crying, he hadn't cried so much in one day in his life. Nate's body looked calm as Poxon studied it again, "I'm sorry, Captain," he whispered.

"It's fine, kid," came an unexpected reply.

"BLOODY HELL!" Poxon screamed, "I THOUGHT YOU WERE DEAD!"

"Sorry to disappoint you," the captain struggled to speak in between blood spits.

"You almost gave me heart failure, scare me again like that and I'll be lying down there with you."

The captain's eyes never left Poxon's as he stared wide-eyed at the youngster and then they finally started to close for good, "She's coming, tell everybody she's coming and you can't stop Ni—"

"Who is coming? Who is Ni?" Poxon asked.

"It doesn't matter, kill yourself now, you'd be better off dead."

"Why? Who is she? Who is she!" Poxon tugged at the captain's collar.

"If you want to be safe from her? Stay dead." Nate McConnell coughed up some more blood and then died.

Poxon realised that speaking to the Captain wasn't going to answer him anymore, he controlled his breathing steadily as he sadly had got used to death today; looking at the strewn bodies of the other college kids on the floor, he was a professional.

His mission remained the same: find his friends and get home, he wasn't even concerned about this 'Ni' person.

He dragged the captain's body out of sight, which took a lot out of him. He couldn't move the rest of the dead students' bodies and left it at one.

"Survival is a hard job these days," Poxon spoke out loud, forgetting he was alone, "Oh yeah, I forgot." Another corridor loomed ahead, "Shall we carry on then, Poxon?"

"Yes, let's."

It probably didn't help matters that he was talking to himself and answering back as well, "Ok, alright then, another corridor? Wow! Who would have thought?"

He bowed and waved a courteous stance to allow himself through, giving a sad glance at the dead bodies on the floor, he shook himself for a moment and carried on speaking, "After you, Poxon."

"Why thank you, kind sir."

"Let's save the ship and be a hero blah blah blah."

Poxon got the whole sentence out of his system before heading off again, never looking behind him. He turned a few more corners, thinking about talking to himself again. And then he froze. Ahead of him stood the quiet grey wolf, watching him intently.

Poxon had been through enough today to be stunned, but he still acted with caution. He raised his hands slowly, "Easy boy."

The wolf stepped forward a few paces and then bared its teeth, a low growl followed, "Easy boy," Poxon repeated, a tremble in his voice this time. It was snarling viciously as its gaze never left the boy, "Stay away," his voice trailed away helplessly and his body began to shake. Poxon's words were useless as the grey wolf ran towards him, gaining speed. He simply dropped to his knees and prepared for the inevitable, "It never rains, but it pours," he huffed and closed his eyes.

Achilles wondered where it had all gone wrong. His parents had been stolen from him, his close friends Harley and Kane were dead, he'd seen a girl he really liked gutted in front of him by another friend who had been infected with some sort of virus which had made her a killer, and a bigger bitch than usual. The college trip to the floating space zoo had been a definite disaster and all Achilles wanted to do was find his remaining friends and get back home. His lips tightened when he thought back to how Harley had died and the pictures he'd seen of his death by a dinosaur, and he still wanted to find it to get his revenge.

There still wasn't any sign of Miss Dwells, she had disappeared ages ago and was nowhere to be seen. He cursed under his breath as he found himself alone again, thinking back to this morning when he had been surrounded by his friends and was looking forward to the trip.

There was a strange smell in the air and it wasn't from the animals on the ship; it was damp and mouldy, making his nose twitch. Shaking his head, he couldn't shake the faint humming sound he could hear. It sounded quite high-pitched and then quickly ended on a lower tone. Concerned just for a moment, Achilles went to the nearest door and tried to slide it open, as he had done with countless other doors earlier, waiting to see another long corridor before him.

As the door opened, and he walked through, something heavy hit him on the base of his neck. His legs buckled from under him, and he fell heavily onto his hands. Another blow to the back kept him floored until a female voice he recognised spoke.

"WAIT! I KNOW WHO IT IS!" Achilles tried to turn over but someone had their knee in his back. He struggled to glance up and just about made out a girl's legs. She was barefoot and holding some high heels in her hands, but that was as far as his neck would allow, "Please," he struggled to speak.

The girl waved the knee from Achilles' back and he rolled over as the pain set in. Lying on his side he looked up through tired eyes and at the female voice, she ran over and tried to haul him to his feet.

"OH GOD! I'M SO GLAD WE'VE FOUND YOU!"

The voice caused more pain to him as she hugged him with extreme tightness, "Oww," Achilles moaned.

"Oh shit, sorry."

She released him and he sat back down and had time to fully focus on the female voice. Achilles saw Lacy beaming back at him, clapping her hands nervously. He launched himself from the floor, ignoring the pain and gave a massive bear hug, "I thought I'd never see you again," he tried hard to stifle his tears.

"It's ok, it's ok," she whispered. Tears welled up in her eyes also as she gently pulled back to look up and down his body.

"Something terrible has happened," he said.

"I know, something terrible is happening," Lacy corrected him.

"There's so much going on, I don't know where to start."

Achilles gave a sniff, catching the terrible smell, which was still lingering, as was the humming.

"Kane is gone, he's dead," he said solemnly, trying to forget either.

Lacy stayed quiet for a while and then answered, "I know, I saw it, a dinosaur killed him, sounds mad but it's the truth."

"I believe you, I saw pictures from Harley's phone of a creature, it had its jaws around him." Achilles sniffed again, "Harley's dead too."

Lacy tossed her head back and tightened her eyes in grief, "I don't think I can take much more of this pissing day."

Achilles moved closer to Lacy and held her arms, rubbing them in comfort, "Something else has happened, Sully has something, a virus I think, but it's turned her into some sort of violent killer zombie. She was puking up blood before and smelt like rotten flesh but now she is infecting all the creatures from the zoo, wolves and probably much more, she's killed Sayles and—" Achilles stopped talking instantly, "Shit," he muttered.

"What is it?" Lacy asked.

"I think there's something else big in the room, can you smell that?"

"Oh wait, Achilles, hold on." Lacy clutched his arms anticipating trouble, "Just hang on a second there, babes."

Achilles slowly turned around at looked at the shape behind him.

Slim Pickings moved backwards towards the wall, raising both hands in a calming manner, "Dude, just relax."

Achilles hesitated and then murmured softly, "What the shit is that?" He stared again, "What the shit is that?" he repeated, still not believing what he could see, "Lacy?"

"Achilles, wait."

"RUN!! GET OUT OF HERE NOW!" Still groggy from his attack he made a feeble attempt to push the shark away, "LACY! COME ON! IT'S NOT SAFE!"

Fresh vomit erupted from Achilles' mouth and all over Lacy's hair as he pulled her away by the hand and ran further down the corridor, wiping sick from his mouth and looking back at the dumfounded Slim Pickings. He found a large computer terminal and hid behind it, hand still gripped firmly to Lacy's. She struggled to pull her arm free and finally yanked it angrily from Achilles' grasp and stood up, walking towards the giant man-shark.

"What the hell is wrong with you?" she hissed at her old friend.

"Lacy, it's not safe! Come back! It's going to eat you."

Both Lacy and Slim Pickings gave him an almighty dirty stare.

"Dude, you'd better just calm down," said Slim Pickings, getting a tad irritated.

"I know," agreed Lacy, sidling up to the huge shark and rubbing his arm apologetically, "You alright babes?"

Slim Pickings nodded his head, "The dude is just scared, it's fine."

Lacy pulled out chunks of sick from her hair, huffing angrily at Achilles, "Look what you've done!"

Achilles nervously rose from behind the computer terminal, ignoring Lacy's bad hair day and pointed repeatedly at Slim Pickings, ducking back down when he saw the shark again, "IT CAN TALK TOO? WHAT THE HELL!"

"ACHILLES!" Lacy shouted like a tired parent, "COME HERE NOW!"

Achilles shook his head like the child of said parent, "IT'S A SHARK! IT'S GOING TO EAT ME!"

Lacy shook her head in disbelief, "Was I like that when we met?" she asked Slim Pickings.

The shark thought for a moment and then smiled, "A little bit."

She shrugged her shoulders with embarrassment, "Sorry!"

"Dude, it's fine, getting used to it now."

Frustrated about her friend hurting Slim Pickings' feelings, Lacy turned back to Achilles, still hiding behind the terminal, "Achilles, please come out, he won't hurt you."

Caution mixed still with slight fear, Achilles peeked his head up and he saw Lacy's face harden, "You spoke about Sully being a zombie? A dinosaur killing our friend Harley? With everything that has been going on, are you really surprised about seeing a walking talking shark?"

"But, but, but it's got legs and–"

Lacy was losing her patience.

"No, seriously Achilles, get out here…NOW!"

Achilles silently made his way from behind the computer terminal and looked directly at Slim Pickings, "You're not going to eat me?"

The shark shook his head, "You're not my type, dude."

Achilles wasn't convinced, "Just to let you know, I know how to take care of myself."

"I'm sure," Slim Pickings replied.

Noticing how close Lacy was with him, Achilles walked up close to Slim Pickings, dropping the bravado in complete awe of him and meekly held out his hand.

"My name is Achilles."

Slim Pickings did the same and shook his hand, "I got that already dude, nice to meet you."

Achilles held on to the hand and sniffed hard, "It's not you then."

"What dude?"

"That smell, thought it was a shark thing, but it's not, can't you smell it?"

Slim Pickings' huge nostrils flared, "I can smell a whole load of puke."

Lacy gave a playful slap, "Anything else?"

"There's a faint smell of something, can't quite describe it, smells odd."

"What about you, Lacy, what can you smell?" Achilles asked.

Lacy simply gave a point to her hair, which was enough proof for him.

Achilles looked at how relaxed Lacy was with him and tried hard to lower his guard.

"So, were you born a shark then?"

"Nope, I was human, took a special serum which is a long story, it made me a tad stronger, but I wasn't a shark, this whole shark thing is all new to me."

"So, you don't eat humans?"

"Dude?"

"Sorry," Achilles said with an inquisitive grin. Letting his smile fade away, he tried again, "So how did you get here?"

"Here? I just walked."

"No, I meant, how did you get on the ship? Were you here from the beginning?"

The shark blinked quickly, "Dude, that's the big question and I have no idea how I got here."

Lacy pulled her head away from the shark, "Is there anything you remember about this morning?"

The usually laid-back voice of the shark became even more slower and solemn, "After the chaos with what happened in Olympia, the infection and the dragon, I just wanted to get out with my sister, so after I came to…"

Achilles interrupted him, "DRAGON? YOU SHITTING ME?"

Lacy stared at Achilles, making an inverted comma sign with her hands, "Don't ask, it's a 'Long story'."

"What happened? What, you got knocked out?"

Lacy held her stare and simply shook her head at him and Achilles got the point, still unsure he spoke slowly, still trying to understand.

"Ok, so you were a human, took some stuff which made you slightly stronger, met a dragon, survived a virus, somehow you got knocked out, woke up on this ship as a shark with a killer dinosaur on board. Is there anything else I should know?"

Slim Pickings thought for a while, "Dude, I have hay fever too."

Achilles groaned, finally getting used to the shark's wisecracks. Slim Pickings felt a rising in his throat and it wasn't just the sickly smell becoming worse.

"Dude, you mentioned about your friend being sick earlier?"

Achilles tried to ignore the humming, getting slightly louder.

"Yeah, she went crazy, vomiting and shit."

"Was she bleeding from the eyes, coughing up blood?" Achilles nodded with enthusiasm, "Plus couldn't be reasoned with?" added the shark. Achilles continued nodding, "Dude, your friend has killed as well?"

"Yeah, she killed some of our friends plus she infected some wolves on the ship and that's it."

Slim Pickings' fist smashed into the side of the corridor in anger, which, even in her brief time of knowing him, Lacy thought was out of character. The terrible smell had hit her now, more prominent now than the sick in her hair.

"What's wrong?" she asked, wiping her nose.

"Dude, your friend, you said she infected some wolves too?"

Achilles spoke with a steady tone, "Yeah, she let some wolves out from their cages bit one and then the rest got infected, so we just have to avoid them and her and find our way to the pilots."

Slim Pickings shook his head, "Dude, you don't get it, she won't just stop at the wolves, I've seen how this infection spreads, remember?"

"Me too," Achilles butted in, "Sully was my friend! I saw what she did."

"Is doing."

The shark's reply was so quick it caught Achilles off-guard, "What did you say?"

"Dude, she didn't just infect a few wolves and called it a day: she is making her way through the ship infecting everybody and everything she comes into contact with. She wants to make everything her own and she will release and infect every creature on this ship, I've seen it! No begging, no bargaining, no regrets, she will kill everyone."

"So, what do we do now?" asked Achilles.

The usually dopey look Slim Pickings had, even for a shark, was gone, "Dude, this was a college trip right?" Lacy nodded, "Have you seen any other students apart from the ones in your class?"

"We saw the other college cruisers docked to the ship when we came on board."

Achilles spoke after Lacy, "Thing is though, we never saw any other students, it was just our college class here."

The shark shifted its weight as they walked further, "Dude, that's interesting, where are all the other students?"

"I don't know," Achilles gave a concerned look to his friend, "So the only students we've seen are the ones from our class."

"Dude, who are now all infected."

"We don't know that, shark boy."

"That's not my name and I think I'm older than you, look I've seen a whole theme park taken down and infected within minutes by this virus."

"Really? That's something I haven't heard in the last five minutes, do fill us again, I'm sure we can find the time."

"What's your problem, dude?"

"My problem is that's I've just seen pictures of my friend getting torn apart by a dinosaur and another has been infected with a virus that gives her a blood lust and the rest of my friends are either also dead or missing and to top it all off I'm having a conversation with a shark."

"Your turn to repeat that, dude, I've already heard you say that."

Confusion hit Achilles as the realisation struck, "I can remember myself saying that as well, I spoke about the virus, you spoke about the theme park, why is it all familiar?"

"Guys?" Lacy grunted, "We have to keep moving if we're going to get out of here."

Achilles held a look at Lacy and then followed the shark around the corner. Lacy sized up the pair of them and watched as they walked out of view. Sighing heavily, she walked off after them. She really wanted to get off this ship and she really wanted to get that annoying tune from out of her head. She hummed it quietly as she caught up.

Earth 13

"Where is the King now?" Kitty asked.

Mary finished off working on the gorgeous wedding dress, still not totally happy on the fit. She adjusted some fine pearls to hang lower before she answered, "He is expecting you to join him at the ceremony my lady, everybody will be waiting."

"Please, you must grant me an audience with him immediately, this isn't right."

Mary ignored her and carried on with her adjustments, "The King has fallen in love with you, a mere slip of a girl has taken his attention away from his people, you will be merely a girl Queen playing with a life you are too young to understand, his face is down turned whenever he cannot see a flicker of movement in your eye. It is amazing how sometimes our faces betray us. I have seen my lord in anguish at your suffering in sleep, where you have failed to raise an eyelid on him since your awakening."

"I don't know the King, but I must speak with him."

Mary was finally growing tired of Kitty's whining, "I am responsible for your wardrobe, I am responsible for your well-being and I am your advisor: you must marry this man, for the good of the country."

"Why?"

"The people are suffering; there is no money in the land; farmers can't afford livestock; children can't eat and are dying in the streets; taxes have gone up to fund another useless war; people have nowhere to live and are sleeping in the gutter."

Kitty heard and sniffed in defiance, "With all due respect, you live in a castle; you have endless riches around you, what have poor people suffering got to do with you?"

Mary stopped fiddling with the dress and sighed, "The people need inspiration, they need something to live for; they have lives that don't matter to man nor beast, but a royal wedding can give them hope." Mary gathered herself and spoke politely again, "To put it plainly, when you have nothing to strive for, a royal wedding will just give them something to do. You're a child from the street, they can relate to you, a common girl in the place of the palace, marrying the King? At the end of the day they have their fingers crossed or fingers in their ears." She glanced at Kitty as the tears began to roll down her young cheeks, "May I?"

"May you what?" Kitty asked

Mary bowed her head and wiped the tears from Kitty's face, "The King is a good man, a trusting man, I can no longer please him with my lies about your condition. For the good of his people, to get the country loving him and to take their mind of the shitstorm that is their lives. He needs to marry a common girl, quickly."

Kitty was impatient and jumped back in, "Shitstorm? You swore."

"Does it offend you, my lady?" Mary stood rigid, waiting for an answer.

"No, it's something my lady Silo would have said, but thank his lordship for his concern though truly I do, but I'm not going to marry him. The last wife he took went to the gallows, I will not have the same fate happen to me, where is Thomas?"

Mary's eyes looked to the ground, "What are you talking about now?"

Kitty grew more agitated, "You took away my lady, MY ONLY LADY! The thought of her dying is something I can never want to believe and now you've taken away another person I know."

Mary smiled a subtle grin, "There is no denying that you are the most beautiful creature I've ever laid my eyes on, but you are also the most naïve."

Kitty cursed herself for not listening to Silo more, "I don't know what that means."

Immie and Jane were still present, the two girls looked at each other, in both their young faces they knew that his conversation wouldn't end well. They had seen their chief lose her temper before, and it wasn't a pretty sight.

"It means that you have to think about others for once and the good of the people, your people now; the King wants you as his bride and it's time to be a dutiful wife to our lord and master."

Kitty's face twisted, breaking her pretty looks, "Where is Thomas?"

Mary turned to Immie and jokingly whispered, "My lady asks a lot of questions, doesn't she?"

Immie nodded, slightly intimidated by Mary.

"My patience grows weary of you, good woman," Kitty's voice raised a little.

She hesitated before she spoke again, making sure her words were right, "*You* irritate me greatly."

"As do you, a woman who is without child and as young as yourself does not want to be Queen? You have an audience with the King, so why do you delay? His Majesty is waiting to receive you now."

Kitty answered as she looked to the ceiling wistfully, "I will be happy from the bottom of my heart as soon as I know both my friends are safe."

"Your young man friend is here, he was given a job as a grounds man and still serves us to this day, and obviously you know the location of your painted whore Silo."

"DON'T CALL HER THAT!" The shout from Kitty was intense, but merely made Mary smile deeply.

"Forgive me my lady, I did not mean to cause offence. I should have taken a warning from your cold eyes that

I should have not spoken ill against the lady in prison, but you must stop behaving like a spoilt fool. You will not see your friend in prison and you will let the King take you for his wife; reel in your black tongue and listen to reason for once. There is something wicked in you, Katherine, and your beautiful face of arrogance for not taking the King? It wounds this whole house deeper than we'd thought."

Mary felt Kitty's eyes burn into her, "How do you know my name?"

Before Mary could answer, the main door opened and all the ladies-in-waiting dropped on one knee immediately, Mary followed quickly.

Kitty spun her head around and gave a tiny smile when she saw who entered. A tall, bearded man dripping with the finest furs stepped in; his face was completely clean, no spots, no stained food and no scars either, just a very fine face. The red beard was cut exquisitely and was a complete square to complement his fine chin. He carried no weight like many men of his age; he looked old, around thirty maybe. Kitty froze with curiosity as the handsome man strode further inside, and she sniffed a little. *He doesn't smell! He washes himself!*

Whilst Silo had been training her, she had always said that you should never ever judge someone on their appearances, but this man looked 'fit' which was another thing Silo used to say about seeing a handsome man, so a slight contradiction on Silo's part.

"My lady, are you ready?" the man asked.

His smooth, low, charming voice broke her out of her daze. She didn't recognise him but knew from the riches on his fingers and chains around his neck that he held some power in court.

"You tease me your Grace, I am not sure what you mean?"

"You have my warmest wishes, my good lady. You are a good girl, but you still struggle to know the face of this kind stranger? Was it that you were raised in a barn that you don't know the man who stands in front of you?"

"We were actually, and it served my family well until our dogs took it over, the smell was too much: a dog is a man's best friend but not a woman's."

All the nervous saliva in Kitty's mouth was still there as the man threw back his head and let out a belly laugh.

"Have I displeased my lord?" Kitty asked.

"I have only seen you awake for mere moments, my lady, but already you make my heart dance with joy and laughter. It is with you every step of the way on your path to recovery."

God! Is that how I sound? Kitty thought. *Maybe Silo was right, we do speak like...*she paused...*dickheads.*

"Are you sure your eyes don't deceive you, my lord? I'm quite little and not that fetching to the eye at all," Kitty replied to the man.

"You are most beautiful, my lady, a thief of hearts. You are the most delightful creature I have ever laid my tired eyes on, your face is a dream to view."

Kitty's eyes grew bigger in the man's compliments and her little stomach fluttered a little; she couldn't help but smile, even the ladies-in-waiting giggled from bended knee.

"You are irresistible to me my lady, pure perfection in a woman."

Kitty's smile beamed and even she had to giggle and feel embarrassed. He was still looking lovingly at Kitty's eyes when he spoke boldly, "So as I am your lord and master the King, I know you, Katherine Howard, and you *will* marry me now and do exactly as I say."

Kitty's smile dropped lower than her ladies-in-waiting, she looked to the girls who had slowly risen to their feet with the King's permission and then back to the ground and whispered out of sight:

"You had to go and ruin it."

Earth 65

The sway lizard roared again at the artificial lights of the ship. It was blinded, and it wanted to rest now, but there was nowhere to go. It wanted to get into some of the smaller conference rooms as they looked dark, but its size wouldn't allow it. Sniffing heavily in frustration, the dinosaur carried on down the long corridors, a familiar scent had made it quicken its pace.

Cameo's eyes wouldn't open. She tried hard to, but something sticky wouldn't allow it. She was lying down on a comfy table it seemed, a shiny one with handles at each side as she felt around nervously. *A bed?* she thought. *That's strange.*

Cameo tried to think of every possible explanation to why she would be there, but she couldn't. She woke up with a fuzzy head and that's all she knew. Her eyelids were struggling to break the crusty substance keeping them closed and she tried to use her fingers to scrape them clean, but she couldn't move her hands; they were in restraints. *Why am I chained up?* Cameo moved her hand and snapped the restraint that was easily holding down her right and then the one on her left. Her legs were also in bonds and she pulled them both free, her eyes were still hurting. The pain was excruciating as her fingers rubbed against them, "OOWWW!" *Voice sounds odd*. Her eyelids immediately came free from the goo but Cameo still couldn't see clearly. She remembered leaving her friends now, she had left Lacy and the scary-looking but friendly-sounding shark to find the captain's quarters to see if they could get out of this ship; it was slowly coming back to her now, as was her eyesight. A flurry of movement caught Cameo's improving sight; there was somebody else in the room, "Hello? Is there anybody there?" It hurt to speak. She went silent as a statuesque figure stepped out in front of her, "Oh it's you! I thought you had left me."

The figure waited for a while and then answered, "I would never leave, you mean more to me than anyone."

"Even him? The guy in the desert you spoke about?" Cameo asked.

The person didn't answer as Cameo struggled to speak again, "Why am I on this table thing? I can't see, it's so dark."

The voice of the other person was trembling, "You're safe here, that's all you need to know."

"I can't see you, something is wrong with my eyes and my legs hurt." Cameo twisted slightly, "There's something digging in my back."

The figure in front of Cameo began to wipe their own eyes, slightly wet; they didn't know what felt worse, knowing what they saw or knowing what was about to happen.

"I'm sorry, I'll give you a moment," were the final words they said to Cameo as they began to walk out.

Cameo's expression changed, not listening, "This thing in my back is annoying..." She looked thoughtful as she wriggled on the bed, "My cheeks are sore." She nervously tried to touch them, "That's not right."

An uneasy quiet fell over the room as the figure had their back to Cameo, not quite leaving. A slight panic rolled over the student, "I don't know why I'm here, please don't leave me." Glancing behind her to her right, the pain returned in Cameo's eyes, "I think I can see now." Cameo finally saw what was sticking in her back and a rush of sick erupted from her throat. She threw up violently all over herself and the table. The figure waited for a moment and left as Cameo started screaming hysterically.

Sully was used to hearing the screams now, some even sounded familiar. Her infected wolf pack had the run of the ship and most of her classmates were either dead or infected. The ones who were left ran for their lives, terrified of her, but there was nowhere else left to run; their teachers were missing, and the transport ships had gone.

She didn't care about them, Sully just wanted to get her revenge on the yellow dinosaur that had got the better of her.

Her wolves were ready. They—like her—were blood hungry; they had fed and turned most of what their new mistress had given them. Sully wanted to find Achilles more than ever now. She wasn't concerned with the other friends, the skanks and nerds, the virus spreading through her veins had made her so powerful. She even thought that she didn't need her wolves.

Her body shook with laughter with the plans for what she was going to do when she finally did catch up with Achilles.

There was nobody around to hear her private joke, only one wolf who tenderly licked her hand as it felt she was in distress as her body still rocked from her own humour, "It's ok boy."

She remembered how to say that, as she stroked the wolf with its head still bloody and matted. Sully found some words harder to say then others since her transformation. Maybe she did need her friends after all. She hadn't heard laughter in ages and she was kidding herself if she didn't want to see them goofing around and being sluts next to her like old times. Her friends may yet play a part in her plans. She had lost her parents and she was not going to lose them as well.

Infecting Achilles was going to be hard, he was tricky like a confident eel, but she had to make him her mate if they were going to take over the ship and fly it to Gommerstall Prison to find all of their parents. She could do anything she liked and nobody would be able to stop her; if they weren't there, then she'd force the ship straight to Olympia and take on Big Man himself.

If Sully was going to get her parents back, she had decided that she'd needed her friends after all. She wanted to hear their laughter for one last time—dead or alive—whether they liked it or not.

Her wolves were getting restless, "Do you smell something, boys?"

The wolves circled around her, whining and wagging their tails excitedly. They had a better sense of smell than Sully and they had caught a whiff of something. A sneer appeared at the corner of her mouth, "Go get them." Sully sniffed the air herself, "Not Achilles, he's mine."

The wolves gave a howl and then tore down the corridor. Sully watched them leave and for once had a tinge of nervousness in her red eyes, "Don't hurt him."

Achilles let out a frustrated smile as he was finally getting used to the shark's tall tales. He walked ahead of Lacy and Slim Pickings and felt sorry for Lacy having to listen to his stories, which strangely seemed quite familiar, but at least his silly talk helped him to take his mind off the strange tune in his head.

"You ok back there?" he asked as they passed down another section of the ship.

"Dude, we're fine."

"I was beginning to think you two had got lost back there."

"No, just listening to Slim talk about the virus attack on Dangerfield theme park in Olympia."

"Again? Tell him we're bored of his shit now."

"I heard that dude," said the shark.

"You were meant to," Achilles huffed.

"There's still no sign of Cameo or the Captain's chamber," he said.

"We know," Slim Pickings and Lacy said in unison.

"Do we know where we're going yet?" Lacy asked.

"No," Achilles whispered, "I haven't a clue." They came across another door and Achilles looked at the sign on the front, "It's a water filtration plant. According to the maps we have to go through here to reach the Captain's room."

"Do we have to go through here? Is there not another way?"

"Sorry Lacy, but this is a short cut, so we could skip it, but it means a few more corridors to get where we're going."

Achilles too had concerns about their direction, with the tune still floating in his head: this was the only way. He waited until the other two caught up as he stood by the door and peered through the misted window.

"Dude, shouldn't we research this room before we go in?"

"You know what?" Achilles said to the shark, his voice uncertain, "I think you might be right, we should keep walking."

"Dude, that's a good idea."

"Achilles," Lacy interrupted, "Can you smell something?"

"Actually, I was going to mention that, yeah I can. And it's not the sick in your hair."

Lacy looked at his bulging muscles from beneath his tight t-shirt and focused back on his face, "Thanks, but really, you can smell it?"

Achilles squared his lips and flared his nostrils, "It's getting stronger."

Slim Pickings stepped forward, investigating the smell too, "Dude, there's a virus, it's spreading around the city of Olympia, it's turning everybody there into some sort of zombie creatures."

Lacy gasped, "Oh my god! That's terrible! What happened?"

"Dude, well there was this virus, it's spreading around the city of Olympia, it's turning everybody into some sort of zombie creatures."

Lacy gasped, "Oh my God!"

"That's terrible," Achilles finished her sentence for her and spoke, his eyes directed solely at Lacy and spoke sharply, "You've said that before, not just now, you said it earlier."

"Yeah?" said Lacy flustered, "Why are you saying this?"

Achilles paused, "Because I've heard it all before."

The tune in Lacy's head was growing, making her more confused, "I don't understand what you're saying, Achilles."

Slim Pickings leaned into the conversation, not close enough to be rude, but just enough to get the feeling between the two.

"Dude, we have to keep moving and get out of the theme park, the big black dragon will be after us."

"Dragon? There's a dragon on this ship?" Lacy said worryingly, "Why didn't you tell us about a dragon?"

"Dude, we're not on a ship, isn't this Dangerfield theme park in Olympia? We have to keep moving and get on that rollercoaster ride and get out of here."

Achilles spoke softly, still confused, "Shark, we're not in Olympia: we're in space on a floating zoo."

Slim Pickings hesitated as Lacy began to wobble on her feet, slightly woozy, "Oh, ok what about the dragon chasing us?"

"Shark, there is no dragon. There is a dinosaur on board but the dragon was back in your city apparently."

"What dragon?" Lacy asked.

"Dude, why do you keep calling me a shark?"

Achilles was nodding his head with meaning, "Can anybody hear that humming?"

"Dude, I said why are you calling me a shark?"

"Is nobody going to discuss a dragon chasing us?"

Achilles shook his head, dazed and finally raised his voice, "LOOK, YOU'RE A SHARK! WHICH IS WHY YOU LOOK LIKE A SHARK. AND LACY, THERE IS NO DRAGON CHASING US, ONLY A DINOSAUR!"

All of a sudden Lacy turned to her friends and started giggling, "Dragons don't exist, Achilles, they're like unicorns." Lacy began to sway as the tune beat heavily in her head, "Wait? Do unicorns actually exist?"

Slim Pickings put his hands on his hips and glared at her, "Dude, don't be silly, unicorns don't exist."

"Good, I thought I was just being dumb," Lacy said.

The tune was in Slim Pickings' head, it made him pause for a bit until he spoke again:

"Dude, unicorns are extinct."

"But dragons aren't?"

"Dude, dragons are what?"

"Extinct?" Lacy still had bits of vomit on her, and she was still picking them off slowly, "So dragons aren't extinct, but unicorns are?"

"Dude, why do you keep mentioning dragons?"

"Because shark, you keep saying one is chasing us, but it's not a dragon, it's a—"

Achilles couldn't figure out what to say next, he chuckled softly trying to remember what words should be coming out of his mouth, still shaking his head.

"Wait? What was I saying again?"

"Dude, you were saying that there was a shark chasing us?"

"No, I was saying that you are the shark."

"Dude, really?"

"Look at yourself."

Slim Pickings followed the eyes of Achilles down to his own hands, "OH MY GOD! I'M A FREAKING SHARK! LOOK AT ME! LOOK AT ME! LOOK AT MY GLEAMING WELL BRUSHED WHITE TEETH, WHICH TO BE FAIR LOOK PRETTY BAD ASS IF I'M HONEST."

"Nobody says 'freaking' anymore, unless you're from Billinge City."

"Dude, are you calling me a freak?"

Achilles smiled nastily, "If the shoe fits." He paused, "Wait it can't fit as you're a shark."

Achilles' smile remained, "Boom!"

"Dude, why are you being so mean to me?"

"I think nature beat me to it."

Achilles was laughing heavily and swaying more, he bit his lip with his lower teeth as he failed to contain his glorious humour. Lacy dropped to the floor and scrambled around trying to get to her feet amid fits of laughter. She stood up only to fall down again.

Slim Pickings approached Achilles with his chest pressed forward and all of his stunning teeth on show, "Dude what you said to me back then."

Achilles stumbled forward, half expecting trouble, trying hard to contain his giggles.

"Dude, it was freaking awesome!"

The two fist bumped and the fell into each other's arms.

"Dude, you're the man."

"No, you're the man."

Slim Pickings pointed to his face, "Dude, not anymore!"

Their fits of laughter continued.

"That's a good one, mate," Achilles' eyes were watering from laughing so hard.

Lacy managed to raise herself from the floor and danced around in a circle around the boys, the humming tune in her head was so loud, and as she glided around them she couldn't help but hum the tune out loud.

The boys stopped laughing, "That tune you're humming, where did you hear it?"

"What? You ruined my dance!" she deadpanned towards Achilles.

"Dude, I know that tune, it's been doing the biz in my head for some time now, bruv."

Lacy's glare shot around to Slim Pickings, "I told you about calling me 'dude' and now you start calling me 'bruv'? I'm not a man, you dick!"

"Well stop humming my tune then, bitch."

"What did you say to me?" Lacy slowly spoke, enunciating each syllable so the shark could understand.

"You heard," Slim Pickings grinned, he hummed the tune out loud as well.

"Bastard." Lacy uttered the word with pure contempt.

"Well at least he didn't say 'dude'," Achilles chipped in and then burst into giggles.

Before he could say another word, Lacy lashed out with a powerful backhand striking Achilles right in the jaw. The big teenager with bigger muscles stood still and then began to shake, fighting the urge to cry, "You hit me! You hit me!" Achilles felt his jaw and still went back to his tune.

"YES, AND I'LL DO IT AGAIN, YOU STUPID SHIT! God, that felt good." Lacy's heavy breathing stepped up a level, the release of energy was fantastic. She turned to Slim Pickings, "Right, Shark man, you're next."

Slim Pickings backed away, his hands covering his huge head, "Not the face! Not the face! And not my hands, I want to be a DJ."

"Nobody uses their hands to DJ anymore," snapped Lacy.

"I'm old school, babe," Slim Pickings tried to humour her.

He flicked and twisted his hands to indicate his moves on an old-style turntable, "Do you get me?"

Lacy kneed Slim Pickings in his groin, "Oh I'm just getting started," Lacy said quickly.

As the shark dropped to floor in pain, Lacy turned her attention to Achilles, his face still ached, he put up his hands in defence, "Don't hit me!"

"Too late," Lacy replied and walloped him again to the face.

"Stop hitting me," he implored.

Lacy's eyes showed no response as she continued to pound upon Achilles, each blow connecting neatly across his sides and face. She hummed the tune so loudly, that even Slim Pickings had to join in as he rolled around on the floor in pain.

Her anger increased as did her physical punishment on Achilles, "YOU GETTING ME NOW, ACHILLES? YOU LIKE THIS SHIT HUH!?"

"Stop it please!" he begged.

"NO!"

Achilles curled into a ball as Lacy began to kick him. His cries began to fade as Lacy's ferocity increased. With seemingly no energy left, Achilles took a blind kick at Lacy's legs. It worked as she fought to keep her balance, wobbling from side to side as her legs finally gave way. Lacy's head connected heavily with the ground. She lay there motionless for a while and looked to Achilles, who had uncovered his head, and Slim Pickings, who had stopped laughing and humming.

"Ow!" She felt the back of her head and looked at her fingers; there was no blood. She eased herself up onto her feet and swallowed, struggling to comprehend what was going on. The two boys were silent and just stared at her. Lacy decided to break the uncomfortable silence herself, shaking her throbbing head.

"What just happened?"

"Dude, I'm not sure, I think you went psycho on us." Slim Pickings rubbed his sore groin area as he got to his feet; he was almost back to his usual self, a tad serious to start with.

"Yeah in fact, you did attack us dude, you went ballistic on our cases."

"I did? I don't remember?"

Achilles also rubbed his bruised sides as Slim Pickings felt his head, "Did I go for a swim? My face is soaking wet."

The tune had numbed everyone's hearing and they tried hard to recover their senses.

"Why were you humming that tune?"

Achilles arched his back, "We all were, it's still stuck in my head, you didn't kick it out of me just yet."

"Dude, what exactly happened to us? One minute we're trying to find a way out of this place and the next I'm laughing so hard I could have easily given myself a heart attack, and Achilles over there looked like he was ready to go nuts on you from the foetal position."

"Shut up, Shark," Achilles snapped back.

Lacy's eyes rapidly blinked as she finally realised what had happened.

"Oh my God," she mumbled. She went into her pocket and pulled out some small broken tablet capsules. A rising tide of dread hit her, "OH NO, NO NO!" she pulled a scared face and began to panic. Her expression was confused, she reached out to Achilles, but he moved away, more annoyed than frightened.

"What is that?" he asked.

Lacy looked at the capsules. She wasn't scared anymore, but her face was deadly serious, "It's a pill, Kane got it for me, it's called 'Ying Yang'. It's a very dangerous pill, we decided not to try it as the effects would be devastating, well more than that, it would shit things up."

"Dude, well that idea went swimmingly," Slim Pickings said.

"What does it do?" Achilles stared at her.

Lacy went quiet.

"Answer him now, dude."

Achilles looked at the shark.

"Was that too much?"

"Little bit," said Achilles.

"Sorry dude, not used to playing 'good cop, bad cop'."

Lacy finally found her voice and it began to crack, "You break one pill open and it releases some sort of chemical thing that gives you the ultimate high. It makes you feel like you can take on the world, but the comedowns are deadly, your emotions go sky high, you can be ultra-happy or..."

"Turn ultra-violent," Achilles ended.

"Yeah, sorry about that. It was like I could see what I was doing, but couldn't control my actions and the scary thing was I was actually enjoying it, I didn't want to stop."

"Dude, so you turned into a bully, I couldn't stop laughing, and tough guy Achilles over there turned into a little baby."

The look he flashed to Slim Pickings was Achilles back to his grim self as he spoke next, "Anything else we should know?"

Lacy wrinkled her brow and sighed loudly, "It's also an hallucinogenic, you start seeing things, crazy things, stuff you can't be sure if it's real or not."

"Like dinosaurs," Slim Pickings whispered.

"Or talking sharks," Achilles' voice was haunting.

"I've told you before dude, I'm real."

Achilles walked over and prodded him, "See? I told you, dude."

"Yeah, but you could be what my mind wants me to see and not reality, I mean a talking shark, really? How do they come up with this stuff?"

Slim Pickings ignored him and turned his attention back to Lacy, "So you think that this whole scenario is in our heads and not real?"

Lacy took some time to compose herself.

"One pill can give you the ultimate trip, it can bend your mind and…"

"Dude, we've heard this all before, what are you trying to say?"

"I'm saying that one pill could change your reality for a while, like I said just break one open and you start seeing things, it apparently only lasts for a few hours."

"How many were in your bag that broke?" Achilles asked, his blood pressure rising. Lacy felt hot and sick, "HOW MANY?!"

She looked at Achilles and bowed her head, "Twenty."

There was silence for a while and then Slim Pickings dropped to his knees with his head in his hands, while Achilles rubbed his eyes and opened his mouth, "I TOLD YOU! I TOLD YOU TAKING THOSE DRUGS

WAS BAD AND YOU DIDN'T LISTEN TO ME, YOU DIDN'T LISTEN TO A WORD I SAID AND LOOK WHAT'S HAPPENED! I MEAN ARE KANE AND HARLEY REALLY DEAD? ARE WE REALLY ON A SHIP? I DON'T KNOW!"

"I'M SORRY!" Lacy cried as she too went on her knees.

"I didn't mean to do this, I'm so sorry!"

Achilles was relentless, "You're sorry? Well that's just great isn't it? You plan to take a shedload of drugs, never ever thinking about the consequences; you've always been selfish Lacy, always thinking of yourself."

"Dude, that's a bit harsh, man."

"What do you know, shark boy? You only met Lacy..." Achilles stopped in mid-flow, thinking he had all the information he needed, "When you came onto this ship, you were a shark, right?"

"Yes, dude, so?

"So?! So, if you were already a shark when you came on board or taken on board, whatever it was, how could it be the drugs?"

"Dude, you've lost me."

Achilles dropped his mouth, his expression blank, he spoke very slowly, "God help us! Listen, I won't say it twice."

"Dude, you are though."

"Ok, three times. What I'm trying to say is that you were a shark when you first got here right? So, if that was the case, how could you think that the drugs had anything to do with it?"

Slim Pickings' huge mouth widened with slow acknowledgement, "Ahhh, yeah, I get it."

He turned to the still sobbing Lacy, "So what's that about? How could you guys think that you're seeing a shark now, when I was one already before I even met you? Could the drugs even do that?"

Lacy didn't respond, she just kept crying.

"Dude?"

Lacy wiped her eyes, "I don't know, maybe? The capsule could have broken when we entered and wherever you were, you could have been affected too."

A hint of desperation entered Achilles' voice, "So the whole drug bag could have broken at any time, is that what you're saying? So this entire trip still could be an hallucination?"

Lacy shot a beleaguered look back to her old friend, "Yeah, so that could be the case."

"Dude, if we are hallucinating, why can't I get this tune out of my head?"

Lacy avoided the shark's dark eyes as Achilles moved closer to the shark and nodded.

"The tune you were dancing to earlier Lacy, we can all hear it."

He hummed it, followed in tune by Slim Pickings and then Lacy finally looked back up and joined in. The three hummed in unison and looked around nervously.

There was a fierce edge to Lacy's voice as she hummed louder. As Lacy's voice increased, the others started to decrease their own.

"Listen, just listen for a minute."

Slim Pickings heard what Achilles had said, and stopped humming, "Dude, I can hear something else."

"I know, just listen for a bit longer," Achilles said, he noticed the shark's lower lip starting to tremble, Lacy was still in a daze.

"Lacy! Stop humming."

"But?"

"JUST DO IT!"

Lacy did as she was told and stopped. As all three went quiet, the sound of humming still continued but not by them, it grew louder down the corridor. She jerked rigid at the sudden noise increase.

"What's that sound?" She was readily interested now. The humming was different now, it was low and deep but was suddenly rising in intensity.

"I don't get what that noise is?" Lacy was concerned now, as they all were.

"Wait? It's coming closer."

Lacy went back to crouching, trying to hear better and holding her breath, "Oh my God!" she gasped.

"What, dude?"

A howl rang out from somewhere behind them as Lacy's tears glistened, "The humming, it's not the drugs - it's wolves!"

"RUUNNN!!" Achilles screamed.

Lacy didn't move until Slim Pickings grabbed her by the arm, "Move it, dude."

Hastily making their way down the corridor, Achilles backtracked, "STOP, STOP!"

"What is it, dude?"

"Turn around, Shark! We're running towards the wolves."

Slim Pickings held back his new fleeing friends, "We can't, they're coming from behind us too, mate."

"We're dead," Lacy mumbled.

"No, wait, we can hide in the water filtration plant. We get in there, lock the door and hide."

"What if it doesn't work? What if they find us?" Lacy sniffed to Achilles.

"It will work," Achilles' voice had more doubt than Lacy wanted to hear, her confidence was growing as Achilles' own faltered.

"Ok, let's go back, quickly."

"Dude, why didn't we go in there in the first place?"

"You were waffling on about the virus in Olympia as I recall," said Achilles.

"Dude, I recall that's when you began crying about the smell."

Suddenly a surge of anger hit Lacy, "ARE WE REALLY DOING THIS NOW?! MY BOYFRIEND IS DEAD, MY FRIENDS ARE DYING, AND I WILL NOT STAND HERE—DRUGS OR NO DRUGS—WAITING TO GET EATEN BY WOLVES WHILE YOU TWO..." Achilles and Slim Pickings ran off before she had finished her speech.

"Pricks," she muttered.

Earth 13

"My friend is still imprisoned in the tower, your Grace, I cannot pretend that she is being well looked after and I would like to see her if I may?"

The King walked next to Kitty, side by side in the massive royal gardens with his guards in front and behind them. Kitty had her ladies-in-waiting, Immie and Jane, walking nervously between the guards.

The King felt his beard and twisted it slowly, "Do you pray for her, my lady?"

Kitty forced a smile, "Prayers won't get her out of prison, your Grace, only you can do that."

The King's eyes looked up and started rolling, "Why do you persist on such matters? When you are my bride I hope that such determination will be used in different areas."

"You still think that I will, your Grace?"

"Your pretence that you won't amuses me."

Kitty maintained her expression to the King, "At any other time my heart would sing at the thought of being Queen."

"So, what has changed?"

A little smile crept onto Kitty's face, "Let's just say it has been a rough few days, your Grace."

The two people looked at one another and quickly turned away.

"This day will be a better one for you my lady, all you have to do is to say yes to being my Queen, you are a good girl."

Kitty quickly changed the subject, "I must thank you, your Grace, for the beautiful ring you gave me, but I cannot accept it."

"Does it not please you? The finest diamonds are encrusted in it."

"Yes, you are too generous, yet you still continue with this talk of me being close to the throne, it is quite unsettling."

"If I don't?"

"I'm not sure, your Grace."

The King stopped walking, "That wouldn't be in your best interests, my lady."

"Is that a threat, your Grace?"

"I would put a hold on your tongue and keep it in your mouth, it will do you no good severed from your body."

"Forgive me, your Grace." Kitty looked to the ground embarrassed and then felt her neck in worry.

"You must forgive me my lady, I have not quite mastered the art of sarcasm."

Kitty took one step forward and then paused, "I am intrigued by your fascination with me, your Grace, I mean you don't even know who I am, yet you want to make me your bride?"

"I thought the mention of ruling the country by my side would be enough."

"My best friend at my side is what I would prefer."

The King scowled, "Come with me, I have two surprises for you." He grabbed her by the arm and pulled her backwards past the guards and through the winding paths of the garden, the journey took them up a constantly higher ground.

"Where are we going, your Grace?"

The King didn't answer but just kept gently leading her around the twisting hedges, always going up. She had only just met the ruler but somehow felt safe in his company. It wasn't just the armed guards trying to keep up with them a few steps behind, it was just his overall personality, his demeanour. Kitty was allowing herself to be led and knew Silo wouldn't be impressed if she could see her now, thinking of her mentor and friend in prison snapped her out of her daydream.

The King suddenly beckoned to someone waiting at the sides of the garden. The person ran quickly up to the couple. Nervously keeping an eye on all the armed guards, Kitty glanced over her shoulder and instantly recognised the quick-footed figure.

"THOMAS!" Kitty ran up to the young lad and threw her arms around him, as he was in easy grabbing range, "I'm so happy to see you well! How are you?"

His eyes skipped over to the King looking at him and then back to Kitty.

"I am glad you are well too," he said eagerly.

"I thought I would never see you again," Kitty beamed.

Thomas laughed, still keeping one eye on the King, "My lady, you are so full of life and joy. I knew I would see your joyous heart again."

Kitty nodded with excitement, but composed herself in front of the King and curtsied.

"What happened to you?" she asked.

"I followed you here after the crash and when I arrived, I found out you were injured and in a deep sleep, so I pleaded with his Majesty if I could stay here, just as long as I knew you were well again. I needed to see if you would wake and the King was gracious enough to let me work on his grounds for him; he is a very good man and you would do well to marry him, he loves you so much."

Kitty could feel tears forming and wiped her eyes before they could roll down her cheeks, "Thomas, have you seen my lady Silo?"

"You don't need her," he said too quickly for Kitty's liking, "She won't go, she refuses to leave you, she is always wrapped around you like a snake."

"Because she's my friend." Kitty shook her head in disappointment, "She saved your life, we saved your life!"

Thomas look confused and hesitated, "Well I will always be grateful for what you both did, I know this to be true, but she is still no good for you, the King is the only person you need right now in your life, not her." The King raised an eyebrow as the chatting pair forgot he was there, "I have to go my lady, but I wish you well and I will see you again, let what I said sink in for a second: let Silo go."

Thomas bowed and walked away, constantly looking back at Kitty, her eyes fixed also on him. She was hurt by his words but happy to see him again.

"Are you done?" the King asked bluntly.

Kitty brushed her long blonde hair from out of her eyes, "Your Grace, have I offended you?"

He smiled grimly, "You like the young lad, don't you? Should I have cause to arrest Thomas Culpepper?"

Kitty's face dropped, "It was a joke, my lady, still working on sarcasm. I have another surprise for you, my lady, one I think you would enjoy more than a lovesick puppy like Thomas Culpepper."

"Where are you taking me now, my Grace?"

"Be patient, my lady." *If you don't tell me where we are going I'm going to teleport you off this castle and watch you bounce down the steps like a ball*, she thought, "Not long now, my lady."

Kitty's face softened slightly, "Fine."

"The tone in your voice tells me otherwise."

"Can I ask you a question, your Grace?"

"Of course, child."

"What really happened to your wife?"

The King pulled her closer and whispered into her ear, "I loved all my wives, they were good clean souls who worshipped our God and me, but some things just don't work out and you just have to let them go."

"With divorce."

"Yes."

"Plus a beheading."

"Sometimes."

Kitty began to tremble slightly, fearful of him for the first time, "Will this fate befall me, your Grace?"

The King shook his head, "There is little chance."

Kitty looked at the sky, there was little sun and a cold wind whipped around her, the evidence from the heavy rain before showed on her gown as she had to traipse through the now overgrowing grass, "I am cold, your Grace."

"This won't take long, my lady."

The certain comfort she had in believing in him was starting to fade. Before Kitty could add another doubt to her mind, the King spoke again, "Here we are, my lady."

Through the rising gardens, the King and Kitty reached the top of his castle, a beautiful sight on the best of times, but on this cold, gloomy day the mist finally began to part and Kitty gasped at what she saw below her, "A beautiful Queen must have a beautiful kingdom, my lady."

Kitty held a hand to her chest as her eyes widened. Hundreds of people had gathered at the foot of the castle, only allowed in to celebrate what would be a fantastic wedding day. As soon as they saw Kitty looking down from the castle peak, they screamed with delight. The towns folk cheered and cried with joy, throwing their hands in the air. It was a sight for Kitty, seeing the whole castle gates flooded with people waving and clapping at her.

"Is this for me, your Grace?"

"Of course it is my lady, these people are yours to govern, yours to love." He pointed to the sky and the huge crowd roared their approval from below, "They have come to see you my lady, they have come to witness you become my Queen and my wife, they want you."

As the sun finally crept out from behind the clouds, Kitty shaded her eyes, "They don't even know me, why are they cheering?"

"They cheer because they followed your plight, they knew about the sick girl I took in and how you were asleep for ages. They knew about your weakness and loneliness and how I cared for you."

"I wasn't alone, and…"

The King had fun interrupting her, "Look at the wretched lot; they have nothing to give, nothing to live for. I thought me as their lord and saviour would be enough in their lives, but it would seem not. I try to stay thankful for them and courageous, but it seems I am not enough. They want a Queen, a young Queen, something to live for, something to rise from their slums and give them hope in their shitty lives, I am but a careless King."

"This isn't possible, your Grace."

Kitty's face was turning cold as the King bought her forward, "They need a new woman, someone they can trust."

Kitty looked away forlornly, "I don't want to be Queen."

"YOU WILL DO AS I COMMAND!" snapped King Henry.

Kitty stood back and wiped her face as she saw the true colours of the King surface. His face immediately dropped to one of concern, "I'm sorry, I shouldn't have said that."

"Your Majesty…"

"No, please let me finish, you are not in terrible danger if you choose to be my wife, you will want for nothing; houses, and riches, a life of pure luxury."

"That is not for me, your Majesty."

His voice darkened, "Then you are ignorant as well as rude."

"Not 'Mrs Ignorant' though, your Majesty."

The King threw his head back and roared with laughter, "I respect you even more now, child, you have a fire in your soul which I would not dream of trying to put out."

"So, what now?" Kitty asked heavily.

"Now, we will go and dine with our wedding guests and welcome you as my bride, as you are a good girl."

Kitty's face fell, "Your Majesty, did you not hear my words?"

"I did my lady, but you forgot that I am King and as King I must make my people see the good in me, and marrying you will help that cause."

"You know my answer your Majesty, I'm a woman of my word."

"So am I."

Kitty raised an eyebrow, "Of my word I meant, not the woman part obviously." the King hurriedly corrected himself.

For the first time since Kitty had heard him speak, the King was flustered. A slight drizzle of rain hit his face before hers as the sun still shone hard, he bowed his head to protect his face from the wet, "She can go."

Kitty froze, "What did you say?" The King was silent, "Your Majesty?"

"If you become my bride today, if you marry me now, I will release your friend from prison."

The shocked teenager became suspicious, "What's the catch?"

"What language do you speak, child?"

Kitty remembered her 'Silo' language and glanced across the sky, "I mean what do I have to exactly do for you to release Silo, your Majesty?"

A flit of irritation hit the King and he regretfully shook his head, "Lying becomes part of the job as King, but I'm not lying now, wed me now and I will release Silo is it? Strange name for a painted whore."

"Don't call her that, your Majesty."

"You put your friendship with her above being my Queen?"

Kitty made a point of looking directly into the King's eyes, "My ladies say that since I awakened, I'm the prettiest girl in court."

"Your ladies-in-waiting are right, your beauty can turn a man's heart upside down and you have turned mine my lady, like I have said before, you're a good girl."

"Are you still cross with me, your Majesty, for requesting Silo be released?"

The King took her hand and kissed it.

"Your wish is always my command, my lady. Now go to the tower and release your friend. Tell the guards their heads will replace the ones on spikes at Traitors' Gate if they fail my demands, be a good girl."

"You keep saying that."

"Because you are, a very good girl."

"Thank you, your Majesty."

Kitty curtsied quickly and sped off with her new ladies-in-waiting, Immie and Jane, in tow. The King watched all three girls run away excitedly, the ladies now leading Kitty as she was unfamiliar around the castle. He waited until the girls were out of sight, paused slightly and then bowed his head, "You can come out now," he said bitterly. A figure in a black cloak stepped out from behind a stone pillar, he eyed up the King and bowed as he rubbed his head.

"Are you content?" the King asked. The shadowy figure removed his hood and stepped forward.

"Yes, your Majesty."

"So, as you've given Katherine Howard to me, Silo is now yours."

The King looked around, "I thought there were two of you, where is the other one?"

The cloaked Orion copied the King's actions, trying to find his partner, Mason, "Not sure your Majesty, I'm sure he will turn up."

"So, the painted wench, what would you do with her?"

As Orion pondered, Mason finally appeared from out the bushes and heard the King's question, "I'm sure we'll think of something, your Majesty."

Earth 65

Slim Pickings couldn't help but look over his shoulder, convinced there would be a wolf or even dinosaur making their way behind him, "Dudes, we're not clear, I can hear them following us."

"You're saying 'dudes' now? You're going plural?"

The huge shark's eyes looked Achilles up and down, slowing from running as they reached the door, "I have no idea what that means, dude."

"Plural, means more than one."

"No idea what that means."

Achilles hesitated before catching his breath, "Doesn't matter, let's just open the door."

Achilles guessed a familiar code and the door slid across.

"1234 works again!" he smirked.

Immediately they were knee-deep in water. There were three other tunnels in the room, pumping water throughout the ship. It was dark and smelled dirty and foul as the old water was being purified. As the three moved deeper into the massive room, their clothes were soaked through, "Hey shark, you should feel right at home now," Achilles said.

"Not really, dude."

"Why?" asked Lacy.

"I can't swim."

"I thought you said you were in a tank when you were brought on board?"

"Dude, that's right, as a shark, not a human."

Lacy hesitated, her petite nostrils flared with the awful smell, "Wait. I thought you were a human, not a shark?"

Achilles stuck in next, "So, if you changed from what you are now back into a human, you still can't swim?"

"Dude, I am a human, not a shark."

"I'm sorry to break it to you, Slim Pickings, but you are a shark right now."

The shark shook his head confused and looked to Lacy, "Dude, your pills are really pissing me off!"

Achilles listened as the silence was broken with wolves barking, "Shit, they're close."

"No, they're here," replied Lacy, "We have to go, we have to keep moving."

They waded deeper into the new tunnels now and reached another giant opening, with scaffolding all around the walls of the unfinished part of the room.

The sound of the wolves grew closer as it was apparent now the three were trapped. Lacy forced herself to stop and try and catch her breath, "Where do we go now? We can't go back the way we came, those things are in here with us."

Achilles drew himself slightly away from the water and puffed out his chest, shivering from the cold, but still defiant, "I'm sick and tired of running, I've been running for ages now." He shifted his legs and pulled out an iron bar from the water below him, "I think it's time we made a stand, right now with the wolves and everything. You ready for that, shark boy?"

Slim Pickings looked around and saw a crow bar left behind from one of the workers, under the water. He fished it out and swung it around wildly for effect.

"Guess we're about to find out, dude."

Achilles looked around wildly, "Right, there are three tunnels and three of us, so we watch each one, back to back, nothing gets in here without us knowing."

"They're wolves with a killer infection and we just have iron bars, how can we stop them?"

Achilles gripped his bar hard and looked to Lacy, "We do it together."

As the barking increased, they heard loud splashes as the infected wolves were definitely getting closer; the water was slowly rising and the smell was worse. Achilles whispered to the others, "Stand by each entrance," he pointed.

"Shark, you go over there, Lacy you take the left tunnel, whatever comes through, you batter it hard and quick."

"What if it's someone we know from class?" Lacy asked nervously.

"I can't kill them and what if we're still hallucinating? That's murder."

Achilles shook his head, "Our friends are dead Lacy, those things, the wolves are coming to kill us, and they will if we don't strike back."

All three settled in their positions watching their own tunnels and each other's. The sounds of splashes were almost on them, but the barking had stopped. Heads looked nervously around and the iron bars were raised high above their heads. Achilles shivered with the cold and started shaking even more when something moving slowly in the water caught his eye. A wolf had slipped in through another entrance that all three had missed, even Slim Pickings' finely tuned eyes had failed to spot it.

The big alpha wolf with infected red eyes paddled its way towards the shark who was busy guarding his own tunnel. Achilles caught a glimpse of the wolf and suddenly tried to shout, but fear had hit him, "Shark, shark!" Achilles tried to shout, but Slim Pickings couldn't hear his frightened voice. Achilles ducked around a corner and tried to catch his breath. He couldn't speak now; he was terrified and words weren't coming out of his mouth.

He swung his head back round and saw the wolf paddling expertly towards Slim Pickings and was almost upon him. Achilles clutched the iron bar close to his chest, rooted to the spot. He couldn't even whisper now as tears of fear rolled down his cheek. The wolf was an excellent swimmer and silently through careful paddling made its way to Slim Pickings' back. He was none the wiser as the wolf opened its jaws behind him and twisted its head to take a bite and then it growled; that's when Slim Pickings heard it.

"Dude, no." Slim Pickings closed his eyes, hoping for a quick death.

"LEAVE HIM ALONE!" Lacy swung her bar hard down on the wolf's head, "YOU GET OFF HIM NOW!"

Another heavy blow shattered the head of the wolf, brains flew all over Lacy. She could feel the vomit leaving her mouth and quickly turned her head as she emptied it in the water beside her. Before she had time to wipe her mouth, another wolf was swimming up close beside her. She shoved it away, at first tearfully, and then as it moved back in closer she rammed the iron bar twice in its mouth, twisting it until the wolf's jaw snapped in half. Lacy pushed the bar with all her might until it exited through the top of the wolf's head.

The first wolf's body floated for a while on the surface, a big bloody hole was where its head should have been and the second wolf's head was still stuck to Lacy's bar. She wriggled the bar free and dropped it into the water, "Oh my God! Oh my God!" Lacy began to hyperventilate.

"Look what I've done, look what I've done!"

"DUDE! YOU DID IT! YOU KILLED TWO OF THEM!" Slim Pickings yelled.

Lacy collapsed into a heap into the water, exhausted and still frightened. Slim Pickings splashed over and scooped her up, "Dude, that was pretty bad ass!"

"I killed them, I killed them!" Lacy gasped.

"I think they were already dead anyway."

The waters were rising as the filter system became jammed with the dead wolf bodies. More wolves began to enter the room, their red eyes illuminated the darkness as they paddled closer towards the three, "We have to get out of here, they're getting in, dude."

A surge of confidence hit Lacy as she looked back into the water to retrieve her bar. After a short fumble she found it and stroked her thumb against her bar, shivering with anger as well.

"I killed two, I killed two of them, didn't I?"

"Dude, you did really good but we can't stay here."

Lacy didn't want to back down as the splashing grew louder, she pulled on Slim Pickings' skin.

"No, let's stay and make a stand, we have the weapons, we can fight them off!"

"Dude, we can't, there's only three of us and…"

The rising waters were a concern and even Lacy had trouble treading water as it was just above her chest now. She looked to her right; she knew the wolves were heading for them, loads of dark shapes were paddling frantically their way towards them.

"Move out the way, Slim, I'm ready for this."

"Dude, I won't say it again: we have to leave, there's loads of wolves coming in."

Lacy lowered her bar and swallowed hard, "How do we leave, Slim? We're surrounded."

Before he could answer, she turned angrily to Achilles, who had finally made his way over, still hiding behind them, the water almost up to his neck. He was struggling to move, his legs were weak and his arms ached.

"WHERE WERE YOU?! YOU WERE SUPPOSED TO HAVE OUR BACKS! WHAT WERE YOU DOING?!"

Achilles' eyes were darting everywhere in panic, "I don't…I don't know."

"YOU DON'T KNOW?! THIS WAS YOUR IDEA!" Lacy screamed.

"Lacy, this isn't helping, dude, we have to leave now."

"He brought us in here and now he's crying like a little bitch!"

"I'm sorry, I just froze, I couldn't move, Lacy," Achilles spoke, his voice barely a whisper.

"Dude, don't worry about it."

"WHAT?!" Lacy yelled, her hands splashing and struggling to keep her a float.

"I said it's fine, Lacy."

Slim Pickings didn't say 'dude' so Lacy knew he meant it and kept quiet. The smell was terrible as more and more wolves swam towards them. Lacy's heart sank when she could clearly see the figures of some infected students behind them. They didn't swim, they just dropped to the bottom of the room and began walking towards them completely submerged. The flooded water began to cover the heads of Lacy and Achilles and just to the chest of Slim Pickings.

"Lacy!" Achilles cried as he watched the water cover her head. The few infected wolves had now become a pack, swimming intently and in a pattern, splintering out left and right to trap the three.

"Oh, shit man, oh no." Lacy's eyes went blank and she sank underwater, "No!" Slim Pickings reached out and hauled her to the surface. Lacy managed a smile with her eyes as she coughed up more water.

"Dude, at least the sick has been washed away."

Lacy didn't answer, there was nowhere to go now and she knew that they were about to die. She dipped her head beneath the water and through the blackness could see red eyes from the infected edging closer.

Achilles rolled over on his back and began to sink too. Slim Pickings heard the splash and went down to find him. Holding both Achilles and Lacy in both arms even he was struggling to stay afloat.

Slim Pickings thought about just holding on to them tighter and just giving up and letting all of them sink like a stone; it would be so easy just to let the infected wolves and students tear them apart. He would never see his sister again. *Sod that,* he snorted.

With an almighty effort Slim Pickings brought Lacy and Achilles to the surface, everybody now struggling for air. He breathed hard into both their mouths to give air into their lungs, carefully trying not to harm them with his teeth, his black eyes opened wide as water dripped from them.

"Right, we're getting out of here, dudes."

Lacy coughed up more water as she struggled to keep her head afloat, "How?"

Slim Pickings had a moment's thought, "Dude, a shark that doesn't swim will drown."

"Anything that doesn't swim will drown," Achilles spluttered.

"I'm going to try something," the shark said.

Slim Pickings clenched his fists and concentrated hard. He groaned with pain as his body began to change, his snout grew larger and his legs disappeared only to be replaced by a giant tail fin, a huge white underside replaced his chest. He thrashed his head wildly as his arms flapped around into fins. The five gill slits on either of his body, now turned to seven and began to move slowly and his skin turned scalier.

Slim Pickings splashed hard, causing Achilles and Lacy to lose their grip. They began floating away before sinking.

"Oh, hell no!"

He clumsily dived beneath the dark water, he frowned a peculiar shark way as the waters went through his nostrils, shaking haplessly to get the water from out his nose. Slim Pickings quickly remembered where he was and twisted his new huge body around and swam awkwardly towards the pair. His new eyes saw the fear in Achilles, friend or not; a fully-grown panther shark swimming towards him was probably not how Achilles had planned his day.

Stretching out to his full length, he whipped his tail around which crashed into a student. Achilles instinctively held out his hand and caught hold of Slim Pickings' dorsal fin and held tight.

Lacy was sinking quickly and Slim Pickings' eyes grew with alarm as he saw black shapes looming up towards them with piercing red eyes that shone impressively in the dark. It was hard to tell whether it was infected wolves or students but he didn't care. It was time to leave and definitely with Lacy, the blackness had her completely enveloped.

Ok. You can do this, he thought.

He had the energy, and with Achilles gripping firmly to him, Slim Pickings dropped further into the waters. He smashed his way through the shapes which were heading towards Lacy; he could make out that they were indeed students. He found it easy to swim through the infected and made a supreme effort to scatter them. He saw Lacy through the dark waters and also armless and legless students struggling to make their way to her. Achilles reached out with great effort and grabbed her, swinging Lacy onto his pectoral fin. Lacy hung on tight, one hand on the shark and the other on Achilles.

Slim Pickings' mouth was agape, and he closed it immediately from the disgusting taste. He wanted to get out of the waters as quickly as possible. He found his eyes drawn to the nearest wall; with no time to choose another way out, he closed his eyes. *Here we go.*

Flicking more shapes away from him with his enormous tail, Slim Pickings used it to propel him towards the wall, his eyes were already shut as he smashed headfirst through it. He wriggled his body and saw that Achilles and Lacy were still hanging on to him. Looking behind he saw he had easily lost the wolves and slowed down slightly, getting used to swimming as a shark.

They were still in the water filtration plant; it was a massive system and Slim Pickings looked again for another way out. He circled around again in the new room until something else caught his eye, more red eyes coming towards him at speed. *Too fast for wolves,* he thought.

The shapes darted quickly through the water and it had Slim Pickings concerned. He froze and tried to shake the sight from his eyes. When they came closer, his eyes finally recognized what they were. He allowed a little moan to leave his throat, "Oh my god."

Sharks entered the room through the hole in the wall, all infected. Slim Pickings had no idea how they had got here, but they were swimming towards them fast. He made his way to the surface for the others to get air, allowing Lacy to utter a deafening piercing scream before they went back under again. The infected sharks were cutting left and right quickly and were almost upon them. Slim Pickings made an effort to break through another wall and neatly swam through the hole; the new sharks followed, low and fast. They remained right behind him and he was panicking. The more he turned sharply, the more Achilles and Lacy struggled to hang on. His head was starting to hurt with all the wall banging and he was struggling to come to a conclusion with the chase.

With every wall he battered through, the infected sharks swam after him and gained more on them as well. Slim Pickings couldn't let up, knowing that a single drop in speed would mean the infected sharks would catch up, but he was beginning to tire. The shape to his right was gaining on them, it was a larger black shark and swam quicker than the other infected ones.

Slim Pickings smashed through another wall and veered sharply to his left. He roared with pain through the water as he knew he was starting to falter. Lacy clung on desperately, trying to will her friend onwards. She couldn't hang on for much longer and was starting to fade. She could barely make out Slim Pickings' eyes, which were half open and starting to close. She banged on his side and let go briefly with one hand and point upwards with the other.

More infected sharks joined the chase as Slim Pickings saw what Lacy was pointing at, an opening above him and an artificial light shining from the gap. He remembered it when they had first entered the main room. There was scaffolding all around the walls as maintenance was still being carried out on the new ship. He had smashed his way in a circle all around the flooded filtration plant.

The only way out was up through the hole, but he had to make his exit work or else the infected sharks would be on them.

Achilles climbed higher onto Slim Pickings' back as the shark started its ascent, gripping the fin tightly with both hands as Slim Pickings shifted vertically to reach the opening point.

The large black shark was also rising into the gap, swimming far more quickly as Slim Pickings was weighed down with Achilles and Lacy, who had stopped banging his side and just prayed her friend would make it to the top.

He really wanted to enjoy the swim as it was his first time as a full shark, just to take in the silence of the water and explore it without being chased, only the vibrations of the chasing sharks and his own heart beating against his chest was all Slim Pickings could feel. He flipped his tail one last time as they shot upward and finally broke the water's surface. *Dude.*

Like a cork from a fizzy wine bottle, Slim Pickings flew from the opening and concentrated on turning back to his half-human self. As he was spinning through the air his pectoral fins changed back into arms and he flung Lacy into the scaffolding. She hit it hard but was intact as she rolled into a steel bar, winding her heavily.

The black shark soared through the air and snapped its jaws tight, missing its target by inches and falling down into the gap.

Achilles had slipped from his back and Slim Pickings managed to kick him into the scaffolding level below. Like Lacy he rolled like a bowling ball down the narrow wooden planks; he too had the wind knocked out of him when he came to a stop at the metal support.

Lacy scrambled to her feet and looked over the side to see where Slim Pickings had landed. He'd crashed onto the floor, just by the water's edge of the opening.

He attempted an army roll but his dorsal fin prevented him from doing so. Struggling to his feet, he ran and took shelter at the bottom of the scaffolding. He watched as the other infected sharks shot out of the opening and simply fell back into the water with an almighty splash, the water hitting Slim Pickings in the face.

Wiping it off, he gingerly made his way out from his hiding place and looked up at the scaffolding above him to see if the others were ok.

"Hello?"

Both Lacy and Achilles looked over their respective edges; the voice sounded tired and familiar, but it was not Slim Pickings. All three followed the voice as it called out again.

"Is there anybody there?"

A huge grin appeared on Achilles' face and Lacy squealed in delight and clapped her hands, wiping a tear away as well. Poxon appeared from around the corner, he was bloody and staggering heavily but it was definitely him.

"POXON!" Lacy shouted.

"IT'S YOU! IT'S REALLY YOU!"

A regular expression came across Poxon's face, a huge smile.

"Yeah, it's me."

Achilles waved frantically from his station and Poxon returned the gesture. Poxon's eyes widened when he saw Slim Pickings standing at the foot of the scaffolding, he wasn't frightened at all, "Ok, a giant shark or humanoid Selachimorpha, most interesting."

Slim Pickings stepped forward and Poxon stood still, "Dude, you aren't scared of me? You do know I can talk, right?"

Poxon nodded, "Thanks for telling me sir, I've seen a whole load of things today, many of which I can't and will never fathom, let's just put you on that list shall we?"

Slim Pickings looked up to the scaffolding to the others, "Dudes, you know this guy?"

Lacy couldn't contain her joy, "YES! HE'S OUR FRIEND, THE ONE WE TOLD YOU ABOUT, HE'S ALSO SOMEONE SLIGHTLY CLOSER TO ME!"

Slim Pickings looked back at Poxon in disbelief, "Ah, ok, I thought the dude Kane was your boyfriend?"

Lacy smiled, "It's not like that at all, he's my–"

Achilles leaned over his support, interrupting, "WHAT HAPPENED? WE'VE BEEN LOOKING FOR YOU EVERYWHERE!"

Poxon smiled, but didn't shout, "You wouldn't believe me if I told you."

Lacy's magnificent smile soon disappeared when something at the corner of her eye caught her attention, "Oh my God."

She screamed with all her might below, "POXON!"

Poxon looked up at Lacy and then followed her line of sight to what she was shouting at.

When he saw, he sighed and looked away.

Slim Pickings arched his head to see what the fuss was about and saw why Lacy was extremely agitated, "Dude, oh no, dude."

A grey wolf silently entered the room, it sniffed around heavily and kept on walking.

"SHARK! DON'T MOVE!" Achilles shouted from his scaffold tower.

"Dude, thanks for that."

"Don't move," Achilles whispered again.

Poxon removed his glasses and wiped the dirty lenses on his shirt, "Oh right," he said as the massive wolf came further.

The wolf sniffed Poxon up and down as he calmly allowed it to do so.

"POXON!" Lacy screamed.

The wolf looked around the water and then made its way to Slim Pickings. It stopped right in front of the big shark, unafraid of its appearance and began to growl. It was so loud that it echoed around the walls of the room. Achilles and Lacy unsteadily began to make their way down from their towers, tears fell from her eyes. The wolf growled even louder and bared all its teeth to Slim Pickings, stepping closer.

"Dude, wait there."

Lacy shook her head terrified as the wolf inspected Slim Pickings. The shark took a step backwards, breathed in and opened his mouth to the wolf, "Dude, this may sound strange, but can I ask you a stupid question?"

The wolf stopped growling and stepped back, licking its lips and then opened its mouth after a yawn and spoke, "I'm counting on it darling."

CHAPTER TEN:

A Clear And Pleasant Danger

Earth 13

"Well kiddo, you took your time."

Kitty beamed and ran to the cell where she heard that voice, "MY LADY!"

Kitty reached her hands through the tiny gaps in the door as Silo did the same. They held on, not wanting the other to let go. Immie was joined by Jane and they stood behind uneasily next to the guards.

"My heart sings to see you alive my lady, I feared the worst when they said you were being kept down here."

"Took your time getting down here though," Silo sounded tired and Kitty was genuinely hurt.

"My lady?"

Silo still held her hand but pointed with her fore finger, "Immie and Jane over there told me how long you've been awake."

Immie shied away behind Jane as Kitty glared at them and then back through the prison door.

"They are quite a pair, aren't they?" Kitty said coldly.

"Those two girls have been my eyes and ears in here, they are good girls," Silo said as she picked out dirt from her own eye.

"So it seems, my lady," said Kitty still staring at the two in the corner.

"You don't get one without the other, where there is Immie you'll always find Jane."

Kitty grew bored of how great her new ladies-in-waiting were and tried again with Silo.

"The King was..."

Silo cut her off, "So you had to ask his permission to see me? It seems some people are being bullied into silence these days."

"Why are you being like this? I haven't been well and the King..."

"Enough with the King!" Silo snapped.

Kitty thought she would get a lovely greeting from her friend after being away for so long, this was not the response she had been expecting. She turned to her ladies-in-waiting, "Could you leave us please?"

Immie and Jane made a curtsy and left quickly. Kitty eyed up the guards suspiciously and released her hands from Silo, "What is wrong with you, my lady?"

Silo retreated into her cell, "Wrong with me? What's wrong with you? Do you know how long I've been here in this prison?"

Kitty still kept her look on the guards, barely blinking, "Could you leave us as well?"

The guards didn't move and Kitty tried again, her brow deepened as did her voice, "Do you want me to tell my future husband, your King, that you've disobeyed my command?"

A slow unease drifted along the prison walls and then the guards finally left. Kitty peeped her head around the corner until the guards were out of sight and then walked back to the cell. Her face reflected the disappointed look of Silo, who spoke first, "So Immie was right, you and the greatest man in the country are to be married."

Pushing her tongue against closed teeth, Kitty rolled her eyes, "Should have known it was her, big mouth."

"She's a good girl and more importantly she does what she's told."

"Then maybe you should make her your apprentice!"

Silo watched Kitty pace up and down nervously, "Look kiddo, I don't want to fight, I..." She paused, "I've missed you."

Kitty ran back to the cell door and attempted to hold Silo's hands again, "I've missed you too."

She double-checked the guards had left again but still whispered, "Why don't you teleport out of there my lady? You have the power."

"I can't, you know that."

"Why?" Kitty asked quickly.

"I've told you before, you haven't listened to me, kiddo, constant use of my power will upset the space time continuum and jolt this planet from its time. Even though I'm trained in these arts, I cannot take that chance. I must stay here and accept my fate, whatever that may be."

"You can't stay here! Those men are still after us."

Silo's eyes became alert, "Shit, forgot about those two."

Kitty opened her hands in a pleading nature, "You see my lady? That's why I need you, I can't face them on my own."

"I've taught you all that I know, you don't need me, just remember to always defend never..."

"ATTACK!" Kitty spat, "I KNOW MY LADY! THAT'S ALL YOU'VE EVER SAID SINCE DAY ONE!"

Silo shook her head, "I just want the best for you."

"WHY? ARE YOU MY MOTHER?!"

Silo hesitated and then sat back down on the straw, head in her hands. Kitty never gave her a chance to talk, "I'm sorry, I didn't mean to say that." Her expression didn't change, "I wanted to tell you something my lady, the King does want to make me his bride, he is smitten with me and the only way he will release you is if I marry him." Kitty wiped all of her face, "You know why I did that, my lady? The reason why I have given myself to a man I do not know?" Silo shrugged and that was too much for Kitty as she snapped her head back to the cell, "I DID IT FOR YOU! I HAVE KEPT MY HEAD UP AND TAMED MY WORDS TO MARRY THIS KING SO MY DEAREST FRIEND CAN BE RELEASED AND THIS IS HOW YOU TREAT ME? ALL I WANTED IS FOR YOU IS TO BE FREE!"

"No," Silo said, a little shocked, "You do not have to marry the King on my account. I will stay here and I'm bound to be released soon and being that there is nothing more I can teach you, I'll be on my way."

Kitty's anger increased, "I DON'T UNDERSTAND. WHY WON'T YOU FIGHT? WHY WON'T YOU HELP ME?"

"BECAUSE I CAN'T!"

"What do you mean?"

The bleakness in Kitty's voice made Silo continue, "It seems Mason was a better shot than I expected."

Silo pulled back her top and showed Kitty her wound caused by the gunshot, "Not looking good I'm afraid, kiddo."

Kitty gulped as she saw the hole in Silo's stomach.

"I've been keeping myself alive, just about with what power I have left, but it's fading fast, I'm fading fast,

I haven't much time and I can't teleport or use any of my powers. It hurts, everything hurts."

Tears immediately streamed down Kitty's face, "No, no, no, no, no! We have to do something."

"There's nothing you or I can do, it's just my time."

"NO!" Kitty yelled, "I won't allow it."

She squeezed her eyes shut and concentrated, her fists clenched and shaking. A small blue energy glow snaked around her wrists briefly and then was gone. Kitty tried again and this time nothing happened. Silo looked at Kitty's quivering hands from behind her cell door.

"Even though I said not to teleport, you can't anyway, you are not focused."

Kitty nodded vigorously, "Right my lady, I will try another way."

"No!"

Silo clutched her stomach in pain, "You can't and mustn't do this."

Her gaze wandered around the cell and back to her stomach, "There's nothing you can do."

Shuddering, Kitty let out a deep breath, "I'll marry him then."

"What?"

"I need to find Thomas my lady and get you both out of here. If the only way the King will let you go is if I marry him, then so be it."

"No, just go, run away and hide, the hunters will be after you and you need to get away."

Kitty was growing more agitated, "What if I try to reason with them my lady? If we meet at a time of my choosing, surely they would leave me alone if we could..."

Silo was tired of constantly cutting her off, "YOU CAN'T!" Silo went quiet again, "You can't reason with them. They, Orion and Mason, will stop at nothing to get you to teleport our planet Rayash."

Kitty's eyes narrowed, "What did you say my lady?"

"Our planet, the planet of Rayash."

"I don't understand, this is my home, this rock is where I'm from, you called it Earth?"

"It's one of many 'Earths' but you are not from any of them."

Both women's expressions had fallen.

"You are in frail health my lady, I think your words are unwell."

Silo bowed her head, "No, I'm fine and you are not from this world."

Kitty's eyes flicked up and had meaning in them, "You lie my lady, you told me I had a gift, that I was a sorceress?"

"You do have a gift and you are a sorceress, but not one from this world, you aren't human."

Kitty started to shake with nerves, "I thought you had a tender heart, I thought you were my friend, but now I see you have layer and layer of deceit running through you."

"That's not true," Silo said defensively.

"THEN WHY ARE YOU DOING THIS TO ME? WHY ARE YOU SAYING THIS?"

"I didn't ask for any of this," Silo huffed.

"So, tell me then, or are you too familiar with a life of lies!"

Kitty's voice was full of venom, which was too much for Silo, "KITTY! I'M NOT MAKING THIS SHIT UP!"

Silo was clear headed and direct, "You really want the truth? Shall I tell ya?"

Kitty was silent as Silo shifted on her straw bed, "In the beginning Rayash was a beautiful planet, lovely wildlife, fantastic people, a planet of sorcerers, living in peace, everything was fine."

For once, Kitty butted in, "Until what?"

"Until our sun started to die. Solar storms ravished the planet, turning it into a wasteland which soon it would destroy everything. Your parents, your true parents, were scientists and powerful with magic. Your mum was a Vanisher of the strongest kind and when you were born it was written that when you reached adulthood, you would have the power to teleport the whole planet away from our dying sun."

"Written? Written in the stars?" Kitty asked.

"No, written in some science journal. Anyway when the government found out that a child potentially had the power to save the planet, they got involved and came after your parents. It was passed as law that you had to give up your child for the greater good of the planet."

"So why didn't they let me?" Kitty said, strangely politely.

"Do you remember when we stopped off in a tavern after we sorted out those muggers in Pollard street?"

"Yes, we went there for a distasteful drink."

"Well, in the back room they played a game, with a giant table with six pockets and balls, you had to hit the balls with a stick into the holes to win the game?"

"Yes, I remember, my lady."

"Well, imagine if those balls were planets, you could teleport the white ball from safety but you would come crashing into other planets in a new solar system; the white ball would be safe, but the other planets would be destroyed due to your slip stream of teleportation."

"Like a 147?"

"What's that?"

"Doesn't matter, my lady."

"So that would mean you would save millions of lives on Rayash, but kill billions on other planets, plus the strain of teleporting a planet would kill you. So, your parents decided to send you away in a survival pod for a new life on another planet, the government found out and sent an army of soldiers to stop them." Silo paused.

"Please continue, my lady."

"The soldiers came into the science temple where your parents were, your mum was about to give birth and all she had for protection were the sorceress midwives, who fought hard and managed to keep the soldiers at bay whilst your parents sent you away with one midwife for protection in the pod."

"What happened to my parents?"

"They died."

"Couldn't you save them?"

Silo gazed at Kitty and then her prison surroundings, "No."

Kitty's head was shaking and she wiped more tears from her eyes, "The army?"

"They followed the pod, with General Orion in tow, but it seems only he and his lieutenant, Mason, survived and are still chasing you."

"My lady, if the planet is dead, why are they still after me to save it?"

"The state of travel through planets and solar systems can have an adverse effect on ageing and dramatically slow down the time process, so even though you are a teenager on this planet and grew up here? Rayash still lives, so what are years on this Earth are only hours on Rayash. Orion wants to take you back to Rayash and teleport it away."

Kitty looked to the ground, "My lady, I've never seen this planet you speak of and you say it was a wasteland now? So surely if I was to teleport it away, wherever I ended up, wouldn't it be still be ravaged by their sun and not fit to live on?"

"It's what I just said," Silo sighed.

"No, I did listen to what you said earlier, you said teleportation is a movement of objects between one place and another, whilst not disrupting time or the physical space between them, so how have I aged when I teleported? And what..."

"I DON'T KNOW!" Silo snapped.

"I don't make the rules, I just carry them out and I help mothers give birth and that's all I do, it's all I ever wanted."

Kitty stayed quiet, quickly thinking, "So you are not a true sorceress?"

"Nope."

"You are merely a midwife?"

"I am a midwife, not *merely*, and a sorceress apprentice; midwives do more for us than you can possibly imagine."

Kitty licked her lips slowly, "So you have already dishonoured me with your lies, and you are a foal teaching me to ride a horse." She licked her lips again and spoke with grit, "My lady..."

"Take it easy," Silo said, "Your powers manifested as a baby, you teleported away before we hit this Earth and I spent years trying to find you, walking around the country, tracing your energy signature and when I finally did find you, all I had to do was keep you safe and watch you grow. But then Orion and Mason came and I had to train you so you could protect yourself." Silo shifted with pain and clutched her open wound, "All I ever wanted to do was protect you. When I found you, we became close, we bonded, you are my only friend, you are my sister."

Kitty turned away and looked down, "So I am not from this land, my lady?"

"No."

"This world is not my own?"

"I'm sorry kiddo."

"So, my family, my life everything I grew up with was fake?"

"Kitty, wait."

"NO!" Kitty spat to her mentor, "This land is not mine? The bed I lay in, the friends I played with? They were not my own?"

"YES! THEY WERE YOUR FRIENDS! IT WAS YOUR BED! BUT YOU WEREN'T BORN HERE, YOU ARE AN ALIEN!"

Silo reluctantly spoke, her voice was weak, "I can't apologise again."

"You are not sorry, you are nothing to me, just a liar and a cheat."

"Kitty, please?" Silo begged.

"Everything you told me, everything you taught me was a lie, my family, my history, my life? It wasn't real." Silo couldn't speak, "So be it," Kitty said, she arched her back and picked at something in her eye, "Guards!" she called and walked back over to the cell door, Silo rose from her straw bed and watched Kitty speak.

"May God watch over you Silo and serve you well and I will stick to my promise and marry the King so you will be released. But on doing so, you will leave this city and never come back. I will deal with the people after me, you've taught me enough with deception, I will pray for you as I know you will be in constant danger."

"Kiddo, wait."

"No, you don't have the right to call me that anymore."

The guards walked back up to the prison cell, eyebrows raised between iron helmets,

Silo reached out and put her fingers through the cell window. Kitty did the same and their fingers entwined for a moment and her eyes looked longingly into Silo's. She pulled away and straightened the length of her gown and looked to the roof.

"No, don't touch me."

Earth 65

"DUDE! IT'S YOU!" Slim Pickings picked up the grey wolf and squeezed it hard until it yelped in distress making him think again about his grip as he released it. As the wolf dropped to the ground, it shook its head and stared at the students, standing defensively and watching open-mouthed in its direction.

The wolf eyed up the shark who still had a massive grin on his face. The group watched in anticipation as its mouth opened and the same voice which shocked them earlier, spoke again, "Thank you, I don't want to die with a nerd on my face."

"DUDE! I NEVER THOUGHT I'D SEE YOU AGAIN!"

Licking its left paw, the articulated voice continued, "Thank God you're here, I always hoped at my lowest point in life you would be the true hero to turn up and save me."

Slim Pickings got excited and rubbed his head, "Dude, really?"

"Sarcasm hasn't introduced itself to you yet has it darling?"

Lacy's stomach flipped and a dumb nervous smile hit her face, as she whispered to Achilles, "It's still talking!"

The wolf walked over to her and whispered as well, "I know, isn't it wonderful!"

Lacy stepped back, "It's just that I've never seen a wolf do that thing you're doing now, the thing that I can see happening, the thing that..." She paused and tried to stop babbling, "I've never met a talking wolf before and..."

The wolf interrupted, "If it makes you feel better, I've never met a talking wolf either." It relaxed its hind legs and sat down, "Well I guess you would like an explanation to why you are looking at a wolf talk so elegantly, but then again you have in your number a walking, talking shark, a dumb shark granted, but he is a shark nevertheless."

Lacy's breathing slowly returned to normal and she even noticed Poxon and ran up to him, equalling the crushing hug Slim Pickings gave the wolf earlier.

"I thought I'd never see you again!"

Poxon pulled out of the embrace with a smile, "You do know I'm still your nerd brother, right?"

Lacy pulled him back, "Shut your noise you little dick."

They hugged each other and nothing around them could take away the moment. Achilles was welcomed into the hug by Poxon, "My man," he smiled.

Lacy's smile folded, "Kane, Harley. In fact, everybody..."

"Not now," Achilles said, "Let's just enjoy this."

Lacy thought it was the best thing he had said all day and said nothing more. Their embrace was interrupted by the wolf's crystal-like voice:

"You do know that I'm still here, right?"

Lacy still wasn't sure if she was still hallucinating and spoke with caution, "So who might you be?"

"I might be the beautiful daughter of the richest TV magnate in Olympia."

The wolf looked up, "Until fate stepped in and dealt me a cruel hand."

Achilles nervously moved forward and still couldn't believe he was about to address a wolf, "Listen, we are having a very hard time taking this entire day in from what we've seen and who we have lost, so if you could cut us some slack and get to the point?"

The wolf looked at Poxon, "Yes you were right, I see what you mean about him."

"What did you say about me?" Achilles snapped, "In fact how did you two even meet?"

Catching his scent and attempting a smile, the wolf ran its eyes over Achilles and then back to Poxon, "I think you should explain, darling."

Poxon stepped forward, "Ok, well the infection, from what I could gather, is an extremely virulent toxin, an intrusive and hostile virus which affects both animals and humans causing extreme mindless rage in both hosts. It's highly contagious." Poxon stopped to take in his nervous frustration at explaining the situation, "From what I've seen already, the virus takes over the host, the time differs with various hosts, full infection could take a matter of seconds or hours in some cases."

Poxon was still having trouble at explaining the situation:

"A bite or a scratch or them vomiting on you will lead to spasms and in some cases haemorrhaging internally turning the host into a bloodthirsty, rage-filled monster."

"The infected, from what I've seen, have no knowledge of their past life and are just in an incontrollable rage to cause violence and death."

Poxon stopped and his eyes looked skyward, "Except Sully, our friend, who shows traits of infection, but she has gained a stronger intellect and heightened agility."

Achilles cursed out loud in recollection, "Yes! I've seen her. Sully has changed; she has the infection, but she can walk and talk like a normal human being though."

"Jealous, are we?" said the wolf.

The wolf was ignored quickly as Achilles continued, "She has turned and murdered some friends of mine, good friends who didn't deserve to die like that." Achilles thought back to the death of Sayles and didn't want to clear it from his head just yet until something else popped in, "If Sully is some sort of host Queen? Can we capture her and force her to turn the others back to normal?"

Slim Pickings suddenly went serious, "Dude, you saw what was chasing us, there's no way those people are coming back to life again...again."

Poxon picked up from where he had left off, "From what I have seen from Sully, and not the other infected, she displays touches of territory strongholding and extreme self-preservation. She is able to think and kills with thought and not instinct; she doesn't become disinterested when she kills, it's for a reason." Poxon tapped his head, still in deep thought, "Always for a reason."

Still thinking he looked to Achilles, "Given the circumstances and it may be a cruel question, but did you know Sully had the hots for you?"

Achilles shocked himself by laughing, "What? No! She's my friend, we've been tight for years, she doesn't fancy me!"

The wolf sneered, "Silly boy, silly teenage ignorant boy, are your hormones racing so hard that you can't see the obvious?"

Achilles' muscles tensed, "DO WE KNOW WHO THIS IS YET?"

Lacy, like everybody else, ignored the wolf, "It has a point, Achilles."

"Thank you," said the wolf.

"Shut up."

Lacy brushed her hair over her shoulder, she couldn't ignore it any longer, "We've seen quite a lot of shit today, so I guess it's time we do this."

She paused in mid-flow, hoping a moment's silence would prepare for her next question, "Who are you?" she asked the wolf.

The wolf padded in between the group and sat down, business-like and calm, "Wow look at all those depressed eyes; it's like a doctor's waiting room in here."

"Could you please answer the question?"

The wolf looked at Lacy and then at Slim Pickings, who nodded at her and pulled a face, knowing that the shark was on her side.

"Olympia is dead. The virus that is on this ship was created by Apollo or was it Ares? Either way, they are my brothers. Anyway it was created to prove a point to my father, Big Man, you may have heard of him? Anyway, to cut a horribly long story short, my father created a serum to enhance the DNA of some kids who he wanted to fight in his splendid 'Game Show'. I and the goofy shark over there had the serum, although he wasn't a shark the last time I saw him, which is peculiar. So, my brother Apollo gets jealous of our father's fame and creates this virus and spreads it throughout our capital and takes our father hostage in his own tower. Some delightful survivors of Olympia teamed up to take him down, but my father is still incarcerated by my brother, so the only person who I know who could save my dad is my head teacher, Elias Glaucas, currently last seen escaping the prison city Gommerstall prison in a supply ship which exploded and crashed, probably killing everyone on board. So, I leave a transvestite whom I only just met to look after my very angry green-haired sister who now hates me by the way for lying to her and so off I go as a wolf, because for some reason I can turn into a dog and a wolf and werewolf: is that what it's called, Poxy?"

Poxon nodded, not bothering to correct her.

"Anyway, as I was saying, I'm walking to Gommerstall…"

"Dude, do you know how far it is from Olympia to Gommerstall? It would take months to get there on foot."

The wolf glared at Slim Pickings.

"I haven't eaten shark for a while, wonder if it still tastes delicious?" Slim Pickings went quiet.

"I thought you were trying to 'cut a long story short'?" Lacy asked.

"Yeah, you sure talk a lot for a wolf," Achilles added.

"Bones interest me, do you mind if I chew on yours?"

Achilles went quiet and let the wolf continue.

"So, somebody knocks me out from behind, I wake up, I'm tied up and see experiments in a makeshift lab, students being turned into animals. I'm guessing the students who came in those college ships that are still docked to the zoo station are all either dead or infected or animals now?"

"STUDENTS?!" Achilles shouted.

"Oh, I have your attention now? That's sweet and I am getting bored. Yes, I believe the ship collects people, turns them into creatures, for what? I have no idea, but I escaped, wandered around for a while before I met up with Poxy over there and now the only way I can get off this god forsaken ship it seems is to rely on..." the wolf rolled its eyes to the group, starting with Lacy, "A Skank, Slim Dickings, fat nerd." Looking at Achilles, it continued, "Nature has already made a joke on you, so it's not fair for me to jump in."

The group surveyed its sarcasm, "My name is Aphrodite Wylde, daughter of Big Man, and I'm slightly annoyed that the beautiful fur coat I'm wearing may be permanent.

"Dude, you can't change back to a human?"

"No, and it seems you can't either."

"Dude, how did you recognise me?

"Because you're the only cretin on the planet who says 'Dude' in every sentence. Listen, I don't care about the students or the animals or you lot if I'm honest, all I want to do is find the person who captured me, make them turn me back to a human, torture them for a while and then get going to Gommerstall and it's looking like all I have is you bunch of reprobates to help me, ridiculous."

Lacy interrupted with a bored sigh, "Anybody tell you you're a complete bitch?"

"They wouldn't dare," replied Aphrodite.

This made Lacy laugh softly and speak to her brother, "I haven't seen Sully yet, but who did she kill?"

Poxon's fingertips probed his chin, "After you left, Sully became ill, violently ill, she was coughing up blood and everything, so I took her to the nurse."

"Dude, which one? I'm guessing a ship this big has loads of nurses on board."

Aphrodite took a step back, "Wow! Look at you desperately trying to be helpful when you have the brain the size of a peanut. I'm impressed, what else can you do?"

"Dude, I can flush the toilet."

Slim Pickings showed his giant teeth in his permanent grin, "Dude, I know you, have you buried any shit recently? Would you like a toilet roll?"

Aphrodite sized him up, "Wow, finally showing some balls are we? Do sharks have balls by the way?"

Lacy nodded her head in agreement and looked at Slim Pickings, "See? I told you."

"Dude, this whole thing is bigger than you now, so get back licking yourself for a bath and listen." Slim Pickings glanced back at Poxon, "Go on dude."

"Katie, her name is..." he stopped. "Her name was Katie. Sully's condition got worse and she was the nurse who was dealing with her. Sully suddenly went wild and tore Katie's throat out, but Sully was still able to speak and was coherent."

"What did she say? Lacy asked.

"Come with us if you want to be amazing? She swore in between that sentence, but I didn't think it was relevant to go into that much detail."

"Still get hives on your skin when people swear at you, bruv?"

Lacy scanned her brother's eyes with a smile, "I don't understand it! I get itchy bumps everywhere on my skin when somebody swears or curses and I know it's not hay fever."

Poxon composed himself and looked into Achilles' eyes, "Katie was the same nurse you gave 'eyes' to when we came on board?"

"Yeah, so?"

"Anybody else?"

Achilles thought again.

"Sayles, Sully killed Sayles right in front of me, gutted her."

Poxon scanned the pain on Achilles' face.

"I liked her, we were going to go out when we got back home."

"So, Sully saw her as a threat and killed her."

"I guess so."

Poxon tightened his jaw before he spoke, "It's obvious that Sully wants to mate with you and she will stop at nothing to do so. I'm guessing she wants to start a new infection with you and spread throughout the country."

A flashing red light on an information computer terminal caught Poxon's eye. He walked over and swiped his hand on the screen as everybody else still had their eyes on the wolf. Poxon's eyes grew wide and he rubbed his chin again with his free hand.

"Hmmm, ok well this is interesting."

Lacy took her eyes off the wolf to look at Poxon, "What is it?"

"I'm looking at the scans of the ship which include the animal cages and their security locks. Wait, I'll put the display on hologram, so you can all see."

Poxon tapped at the console again and a holographic display illuminated the room. He began pointing like a teacher in front of a board in class, "Right, so we are here, through here is the Captain Nate McConnell's quarters."

"Good, where is he by the way?" asked Achilles.

"He's dead, can I carry on please?"

"Dead?"

"Yep, saw it myself. Anyway, as I was saying, this is where we are and these big squares here are every animal cage in the ship. Now, when the locking mechanisms are fully functional, they show up as green as they are all under lockdown."

Lacy nodded silently and then pointed to the map image herself, "So why are they all red?"

"Because red means that all the cages are open, every animal on the ship is free."

"Oh my God, was it an accident?"

Poxon looked at the console, "No malfunctions, all locking mechanisms were working fine but were released manually recently. I can patch on the security cameras and see who freed them from the main hub." The group stared at the image in disbelief on the hologram, as Poxon made a nonchalant glance back to the image,

"Yes, as you can see it's Sully releasing the animals, not sure when she did that as the timers aren't working."

"Dude, can you check on that computer thingy to see if the animals are infected?"

For some reason Poxon chuckled at Slim Pickings' question, "Actually, I can, the cameras can zoom in onto them, plus some of the more endangered species have motion trackers on them."

"Any sign of the dinosaur?" Lacy asked.

"Oddly enough, no," Poxon replied.

"Ok, here is the combined feed to all security cameras for the..." Poxon stopped and muttered under his breath, "Shit."

"You just swore, what about your hives?" Lacy asked.

"I don't think it matters anymore," came Poxon's solemn reply, "See for yourself."

Images from all around ship showed the animals free and now infected. Creatures of all shapes and sizes darted in and out in front of the cameras. There was no sound, but everybody could see complete carnage; the infected animals attacked everything on sight, even the herbivores lashed out and began to feed on others in their way. Every muscle in the group tensed as they saw animals tear into frightened students fleeing for their lives. Jaws quickly opened and tore flesh easily from tired student backs. Heavy animal claws raked against terrified innocent faces. Poxon suddenly rattled his head, "Oh, I forgot, I can get sound if you want."

He was becoming accustomed to controlling the console and did it all too easily, swiping away for the security cameras to add sound to their watch, "Ok, here we go." The sound around the room was deafening. An infected giant sabre-toothed tiger cornered a crying girl, she pleaded with the giant cat to stop, "PLEASE! GOD NO, PLEASE DON'T!"

Without a pause the tiger snapped its jaws around her head and pulled it clean from her shoulders. The tiger roared and flexed its tongue to soak up the blood spurting from the hole. Lacy put her hand over her mouth and then retched violently. The animals ran amok through the corridors. The students darted left and right to escape them, but it was no use. The virus had spread throughout the ship and nearly every caged animal had the infection. Classes of students who came on board to learn about endangered species, now found themselves becoming the same.

They froze, they hid, they ran, but were easily found by the infected creatures. Creatures raised their heads and picked targets easily from the selection of prey on offer. Guttural growls unlike any the watching group had heard echoed around the corridors as the infected animals took control. The cries continued from the students.

"PLEASE LEAVE US ALONE!"

"DON'T LET THEM NEAR YOU!"

"SOMEBODY HELP US! PLEASE!"

The screen showed a giant snake-like creature slithering across the high ceiling of one of the corridors as the students ran away beneath.

A boy stopped below it to catch his breath as his classmates ran past. The snake raised its head and then looked at the boy, who hesitated in fear as he glanced upwards.

It struck with powerful accuracy, coiling around the screaming student and hoisting him to the ceiling.

He tried to struggle but the snake flared and hissed soundly. It pulped the unfortunate boy and carried him through the ventilation shaft.

One person walked through the oncoming rush of students, a girl whose face was bloody but beautiful and she had something in her hand; it was a fruit. Poxon swiped the screen again and the camera zoomed onto the girl. It was Sully, her eyes glowed red as she noticed the camera watching her.

She quickly grabbed a fleeing student in her left arm and twisted the girl's torso like rope. Sully bit into the now dead girl's neck and tore a chunk out of it before dropping the corpse on the ground still holding her fruit. The infected animals simply ignored her, she had complete control over them. The virus running through her veins had given her a power and strength she could only have dreamt of.

She took a bite out of the peach and noticed one of the security cameras focusing on her. Sully dropped the rest of the peach on the ground and blew a kiss to the camera, before pointing to her eye, making a 'heart' sign with her hands before mouthing the word 'Achilles'. She grabbed another fleeing student and snapped their neck before throwing their body at the camera, destroying it. Lacy dropped her head and wiped away her tears, "Ok, that's enough." Poxon was engrossed in the screen and didn't answer his sister, "I SAID ENOUGH!" Poxon turned off the camera feed without looking at Lacy, he chewed on his lips as he thought, "I think she said, 'I love Achilles'."

"Yeah, I think we got that, Poxon."

Achilles lowered his voice, "So what do we do now?" he asked. "She knows we're here, she is leading all the animals to our location. She's coming for me, isn't she?"

Poxon looked around at Achilles, "That seems to be the case."

Lacy pulled Achilles to one side and whispered in his ear, "Do you think we're still hallucinating?"

"I'm not sure, that was a lot drugs you had and now we're seeing talking wolves and zombie animals?"

Lacy sniffed, "Ok, well, stay close to me, very close to me and Poxon as well; we're leaving this ship, with or without the others."

"What about the shark?"

"Shark or not, drugs or not, he saved our lives and he's coming with us."

"Right, shall we put it to a vote?" Achilles raised his arm.

"We're not at school, put down your hand, no we're leaving now."

Poxon overheard their conversation as well as Aphrodite, "There's something you need to know."

He walked back to the console and got familiar with the controls again, "I did a scan on the five drop ships still attached to the main zoo hub. Sully or someone else has destroyed the start-up codes, so we can't use them."

"What about the ships we and the other students came in?"

Poxon turned and squinted at the screen as he tried to answer Lacy, "They've been jettisoned but again I don't know who by."

"So, what you're saying is there is no way off this ship and Sully and every infected animal are making their way to us now?" said Aphrodite, "Not to be rude, but why don't we just give this Sully what she wants, I mean I'm sure this young man is delightful but maybe turning him into a zombie would work wonders for his social life, not that anybody would notice."

"Are you for real?" spat Lacy.

"Real as a talking wolf can get," replied Aphrodite.

"That is a headlong fail all round, there is no way we're giving our friend up to those creatures."

Slim Pickings also overheard the whole conversation, "Dude, you've seen what happened in Olympia, what those 'things' can do? Why would you want to send one of your friends to their death like that?"

"Firstly, you have to calm down and gargle, and secondly, do I actually care about him? He could be on fire and I wouldn't care, but if this woman only wants the muscle boy, she may let us go if we give him to her."

"Dude, what'd you say? Let us go? Where can we go? We are on a ship floating in the middle of space, we can't get off it and chances are I'm gonna have to fight my way through a shit load of zombie bastards again! Sometimes I think you're as a sharp as a marble."

Achilles yelled to Aphrodite, "Oh mate! He just owned you!"

Aphrodite growled slowly, "I'm impressed, ok dipshit, how do we get off?"

"We don't."

Lacy's words made everyone hit silent, "What did you say?" asked Aphrodite.

"I thought we had a chance, I thought we had a shot at finding the pilots or captain, an escape ship, but there's nothing now."

"Wait, but the pilots would have surely seen what we just had on the security screen? They must have sent out a distress call for us."

"Then where are they, Achilles? Why isn't anybody coming for us?"

Poxon had a strange sense of calm before he spoke, "Going by normal protocol, if the pilots are under threat, then the cockpit goes into lockdown, nothing would we able to get into them, so help still could be on the way I think."

"You could do us all a favour and think quicker?"

Poxon's eyes wandered over to Aphrodite trotting around in circles, "What do you mean?"

"I mean that you are our chief nerd, so surely you can hack into the cockpit computers and talk to the pilots?"

"DAMMIT!" Poxon cried.

"What? Did she upset you, bro? asked Lacy.

"No, she's right, she's spot on. If I can patch into the pilots' computers, maybe I can try and speak to them, see if it can visually track us and they can let us into the safety of the cockpit."

"What if that doesn't work?" Achilles glared.

"The pilots have a better chance of reasoning with us than they have with the infected."

Poxon examined the screen again, swiping and tapping away, "I think I can do this, but it may take time."

"Dude, time is something we don't have," Slim Pickings challenged.

"For once, and it pains me to say this, but I agree with the shark," Aphrodite added.

"All you have to do is let me see if I can contact the pilots, just keep this room safe for me, about twenty minutes maybe?"

Before another word was spoken, one of the walls which was being supported by the scaffolding began to crumble and then collapse. A yellowish snout appeared through the hole, followed by the shuffling frame of the sway lizard. It tired slightly as the weight of the wall shifted briefly on to its back. It roared with pain and defiance as it finally struggled its way through.

Expressions of fear ran across all their faces as the creature stepped into the massive water filtration plant. They all stared in terror and disbelief as the creature shrieked again. Aphrodite surprisingly stood her ground, with a mixture of growling and barking at the dinosaur.

Its huge head lowered to investigate the wolf and then it roared again, with huge jaws open. The dinosaur was close enough to the group that they felt its rancid breath in the air.

"Ok, everyone, don't move." Lacy said quietly.

"Are you shitting me?" whispered Achilles.

"Look, it's eyeing us up, it hasn't struck yet. Pox, where is the Captain's quarters?"

Poxon moved away from the console to join his sister, keeping his eyes fixed on the lizard, "We're close, it's in the next corridor."

"Right, stay close and quiet and as soon as it turns away, we'll make a run for it."

"Not to be rude darling, but I'm guessing it can out run all of us, why don't we make a diversion, one of us distracts it while the others escape."

Aphrodite turned to Slim Pickings, "I wonder if it likes shark meat?"

Slim Pickings was too terrified to reply, Lacy turned to Aphrodite, "No lip from you, wolf, we're making a move on my mark, will it chase us, Pox?"

Poxon's breathing began to get haggard, "Too scared to think, sorry."

Lacy took control again and narrowed her eyes as the others were still trying to digest what was happening.

"Sod it, run!"

The group all took a violent quick turn to the next opening in the endless corridors in the ship and began running.

The sway lizard roared again and took chase after them, breathing heavy and stepping in perfect time as its head bobbed along the flooded chamber. Before the group had a chance to fully escape, a figure stepped forward from the distance of a sub corridor.

"WAIT!" the figure yelled.

Everyone stopped and stood still for a moment, the voice sounded even more aggressive than the creature chasing them. They looked back frantically and then towards the figure in fear, caught between the middle.

"Miss Dwells?" asked Achilles.

The substitute teacher's appearance was greeted with stunned expressions.

"MISS! GET OUT OF THE WAY NOW!" screamed Lacy, looking back fearfully at the chasing dinosaur.

The sway lizard's tongue shifted left to right as it finally caught up with the group. Lacy screamed in terror as the creature caught up with them. Miss Dwells threw her hand in front of her, "STOP!"

The lizard bellowed angrily and stomped past the frightened group and headed towards the teacher. She took a few steps back and shouted again, "I SAID STOP!" The dinosaur loomed over Miss Dwells and inspected her with a heavy sniff, her eyes locked onto the lizards and she pointed to the floor, "Drop."

Instantly the sway lizard fell to ground and began to playfully rub its nostril into the floor.

Miss Dwells walked up to the heavy breathing creature and rubbed its underbelly. It wasn't covered with leathery scales and the lizard enjoyed having it rubbed, its huge hind legs shook with fulfilment. Its huge tongue lopped out again and playfully licked Miss Dwells, who pushed it away with a grin and a giggle. The dinosaur was breathing differently, heavy content panting like a happy dog. Her smile disappeared when she saw the intense stares coming from the confused group, "I guess I owe you all an explanation."

Earth 13

Kitty watched as Immie and Jane fussed around her dress. She tried to stand still on the small stool they gave her, but her ladies-in-waiting prodded and poked so hard she was tempted to use her powers and teleport the girls away from her onto the roof of the castle, but she remembered the words from her mentor that she should only use her powers to defend and never attack, even if annoying ladies-in-waiting were wearing her down to her last nerve.

"Have you finished yet?" she sighed.

"Almost done, my lady."

No sooner had Immie replied, Jane accidentally tore off a button. Immie stomped her foot in anger at her friend, "Oh no! What have you done?" she cried.

"I'm sorry! It just came away in my hand," Jane's face instantly turned pale.

"Your folly is going to ruin my day," Kitty said in hopeful jest, but it was deadly serious for Jane.

"Forgive me, my lady, I meant no harm." Jane shivered in fear and backed away as Immie began crying.

Kitty raised her head to see Jane cowering in the corner, her mouth turned as if she had swallowed something bitter.

"Please forgive me, my lady, please I beg of you. I didn't mean it!"

Kitty was shocked at her reaction and raised her hand and made a gentle tapping motion in the air, "Hey it's fine, do not make yourself ill over one dress." Kitty thought about what Silo would say now, "Just chill out babes and everything will be smooth."

Kitty's words were confusing, but they calmed Jane and she smiled, which didn't last for long.

"Interesting choice of words," came a voice from the open door of the room.

There was a scared silence from Immie and Jane and they both stared blankly as the King entered the room with his cohorts, "I have never heard such strange words uttered, where did you say you were from again?"

"Around," Kitty said quickly, "I get around." Kitty still couldn't believe how handsome this man was and still showed her shaky nerves when he was near her. The King walked up to Kitty and inspected the broken button on her dress. He shook his head in slight confusion, before taking the button and fiddling with it before it finally slotted into the hole.

"See? No harm done." He looked at Jane, "Don't sit in such a wretched way young lady, everything is fine."

Jane curtsied slowly to the King, still keeping a nervous watch on him.

"Yes, your Grace," she replied meekly.

He approached Jane and went to stroke her face, she flinched as if he had held a knife to her throat, "Do not worry child, does your Queen mind?" He looked at Kitty, "Do you?"

Kitty looked perplexed, "No, it was a mistake, it's fine."

"Good, so let us be married then."

"Wait, your Majesty, where is Silo? Is she here? Can I see her?"

The King held out his hand and Kitty took it and stepped cautiously off her stool.

"I want to see her now, your Grace."

"You will be my Queen, just come with me, join your adoring public, your friend is outside waiting for us to be wed."

Kitty threw him a long suspicious look, "She is here? Are you sure?"

The King looked at Kitty, unimpressed, "Are you calling me a liar?"

"No, your Grace, I meant no disrespect, I just need to see my dear friend, I miss her so much."

The King kindly kissed Kitty on the cheek, "I thought she would be held a prisoner until I knew what to do with her, but she is a friend of my Queen and I declared her a free woman."

"So, you have judged her and allowed her to be at our wedding?"

Looking down at his splendid shoes, he rocked in them before answering, "Yes my lady, she is outside now, once we are wed you can join her."

Kitty almost slapped his arm with joy, but squealed in delight instead and ran outside. Immie followed and Jane went to do the same until the King held her back. His attention shifted abruptly to her. Kitty had already left the room to join the screaming public outside. Immie waited for her friend but was ushered away by the guards present. The King hesitated before closing the room door with just one guard left, "Now what are we going to do with you?" he sneered.

Jane watched the King's deep eyes and fear spread slowly across her face.

"I don't understand, your Grace?"

The King laughed, pleased with himself, "I think you do. These are troubling times with the people young lady, they need a Queen to unite them and make them feel better about themselves and I cannot allow anything to go wrong today." Jane backed away fearfully as the King moved in closer, her eyes began to tear up, "So you see, you're attempt to destroy her dress would put the wedding back and I will not allow it."

"It was an accident, your Grace," Jane reiterated.

"It doesn't matter, it's unquestionable that Katherine belongs to the throne and nothing will stop me marrying her, not even a poor wretched whore like you. I doubt you'll be coming to the wedding."

The King was in Jane's face and he stroked her cheek and whispered in her ear, "I know you were giving information to that 'thing' in the prison, my guards saw you and Immie talking to her and I will deal with her later. Silo has some hold over my Queen and I won't allow it. You have betrayed me, Jane, and I'm very disappointed."

"No, your Grace I didn't, I would never."

"Shhhhh," he pressed his finger to her trembling lip.

"It doesn't matter anymore, I think it is time for you to leave, which is a shame as I will miss our companionship, you were one of my favourites."

"Please your highness, I didn't mean any harm."

The King ushered the guard away, who left quickly. He watched him leave and continued to stroke the frightened girl's face.

"Now, what are we going to do with you?"

Jane screamed for help, but nobody came as her cries were drowned out by the screaming public outside. Kitty looked on in awe at the crowd as she made her way out to the clearing. Immie walked on behind her slowly, still waiting for the appearance of her best friend.

Earth 65

The punch from Lacy was hard and direct on the face of Miss Dwells and it knocked her off her heels. The dinosaur stirred but the teacher waved it down as she felt the taste of blood in her mouth, "Ok, I'll give you that one, you know if we were at college now you would probably be suspended."

Lacy spoke through gritted teeth for fear of pissing off the dinosaur, "You think this is funny? Is this some sort of sick joke?"

"I can explain."

Lacy was ready to punch her teacher again and couldn't contain her anger, "EXPLAIN? THAT THING HAS KILLED OUR FRIENDS, IT KILLED MY BOYFRIEND AND YOU KNEW WHAT IT COULD DO, YOU BROUGHT IT ON THIS SHIP? HOW COULD YOU DO THAT!"

Miss Dwells spat out the blood and wiped her mouth, "I'm sorry about this, all of it, I didn't mean for this to happen."

Aphrodite padded forward looked up at Miss Dwells, "Hello?"

"Yes?" replied the teacher.

"I said Hello?" Aphrodite said again.

Miss Dwells blinked heavily, "I heard you the first time, what do you want?"

"You're talking to a wolf who is talking back to you and behind me is a shark who has feet and is walking around, now doesn't that seem strange to you?"

"I've got a dinosaur letting me tickle his stomach, nothing actually feels weird anymore."

"Not in the slightest?"

"Not from you anyway," Miss Dwells coolly replied.

"Have you finished playing nice with her?" Lacy asked Aphrodite, as she fixed a cold stare to Miss Dwells, "Who are you really and what do you want with us?"

"I'm your teacher and…"

"DON'T LIE!" Lacy snapped.

The sway lizard craned its neck and let out an annoyed shriek.

"I wouldn't raise your voice around me, he already doesn't like you for punching me."

"Will it eat me?" Lacy's voice had a slight tremble.

"No, he just ate."

Lacy's glare returned, "My boyfriend."

Miss Dwells' voice started out completely calm as she heard the strain in Lacy's voice and straightened up and then it cracked slightly, "My name is Dallas Dwells." Slim Pickings sniggered before apologising and letting the woman speak, "I'm from the city of Karrick."

"Karrick? That's thousands and thousands of miles away, it's almost on the other side of the planet."

"Thanks for the geography lesson, Achilles. Unfortunately I'm not your geography teacher so I don't give a toss what you think." Dallas continued, she hoped, with no more interruptions, "This wasn't meant to happen. I only meant to come on board, take what Captain McConnell had left me, and then leave in one of the student ships, but that didn't happen since somebody jettisoned all the student ships and the drop ships, so I'm stuck here."

"This still doesn't answer the question of what you were really doing on this ship?"

"I have a sister, a very powerful sister, and she is after me and she will stop at nothing to find me."

"What did you do?"

"Why do you assume it's me?"

Aphrodite licked her teeth and continued, "The fact that you say you have a dinosaur for a pet, but it really seems that it is your protector. Karrick is on the planet hundreds of miles below us, yet you still don't feel safe. You have no fingernails left from biting them from nerves. You aren't really a teacher judging from your tone with the students and attitude; you couldn't teach a dog to bark. You've been shaking like a nerd on a first date ever since we met you, so what's the story?"

Dallas stared at Aphrodite with sad satisfaction, "You're good."

"I used to be the hottest girl on the planet, now I'm a wolf and I'm bored."

Aphrodite's voice was tired but still continued, "Karrick is not a great place to live; slavery and hunting still exist."

"In some parts," Dallas said.

"You were a part of this?" asked Achilles.

"I was, my family, my sisters...we hunted men, we kept them as slaves as the whole island did and if any women tried to help men escape? We would kill them too; all tribes, all creeds, all races were united in our hatred of man."

"Ok, not something I would put on my CV, but again, how did you end up here?"

Dallas lifted her chin and answered Aphrodite, "A ship crashed into a mountain on our island, it was escaping from the prison city Gommerstall."

Instantly Aphrodite's ears pricked up, "Gommerstall? A ship escaped from there about six years ago, but blew up in mid-flight. Was it the same one? Were there any survivors?"

"As soon as the ship crashed, a scouting party went out to see if there the crew were alive."

"What did they find out?" Achilles pressed.

"The ship went into sleep stasis and tried to keep some of the prisoners alive, but most of them died on impact."

Aphrodite made a nervous growl, "There was a man on board, his name was Elias Glaucas, did he survive?"

Dallas went silent.

"IS HE DEAD!?" yelled the wolf.

"Yes," came the sombre reply. "Not from the crash though."

"Fine."

For once Aphrodite's voice had lost its edge, "Then my father is truly lost to me. The only person who could have saved him is Mr Glaucas."

"What are you talking about?" Lacy asked.

"Dude, it's just some hassle back in Olympia, it's not important," Slim Pickings added.

"Not important? This is my life we're talking about, it's Olympia and my dad and brothers."

"Dude, this isn't about you, it's bigger than you now."

Aphrodite went silent and turned to Dallas, she opened her mouth as her fangs hurt slightly, "Please continue."

"I was with the scouting party and we made contact with the survivors, it was a long trek back to our base and we ran into some problems transporting them to my sister." Dallas didn't speak for a while, "Something happened, something big and my sister…" Dallas paused again, "She was our leader, our saviour and I betrayed her."

"What did you do?" Lacy folded her arms, "What did you do to the people who would be slaves you mean? That's what they could do right, on Karrick? It's pissing disgusting"

"I agree, I don't always see eye to eye with my island's view on things, especially slavery, that's not a nice thing."

"That's big of you," huffed Achilles.

"Listen, I'm going to wrap this up now as we don't have much time, I fell in love with one of the prisoners and went against my whole life, my upbringing, what I believed in for love, I took them away and tried to rescue them and get them back home to Olympia."

"Who did you fall in love with?" asked Aphrodite. Dallas didn't reply.

Lacy hesitated, she was still uncomfortable with the slavery issue, "What was the outcome?"

"Stop asking so many questions, Lacy," demanded Dallas, her eyes sank thick and fast. Lacy surged with confidence now and walked over to her teacher, tilting her chin up with a finger, "Listen, this story is getting really boring now, those infected kids are heading towards us now, so either you speed up or get out."

Dallas shook Lacy's hand away from her head, "I betrayed them over the one thing they hate more than anything and now they're coming after me, all of them, the whole island."

"You said that happened six years ago, so you've been on the run for all this time?"

Dallas nodded at Poxon's question and her nervous laugh came back, "It does take a while to travel from Karrick to Heffernan City but that's another long story. All you need to know is that my sister is coming for us."

"Us? We didn't do anything."

"Doesn't matter, Poxon. Anybody I come into contact with, she will kill. You can't reason with her, you can't bargain with her, you can't bribe her, the only thing you can do is pray for a quick death."

"Little melodramatic, darling, don't you think?"

"You're just a wolf; she'd tear you apart before breakfast. She has a following of hunters called the 'Worthy'. Where she goes, they go."

"So we've gathered that you're slightly chicken and run out when the going gets tough, but that still doesn't explain how or why you are here on this spaceship."

She paused with an aggravated face, trying hard not to strike Aphrodite.

"Yes, I did run, I ran and hid for years. Another girl from the tribe helped me escape and together we left for the capital, Olympia. A war was coming and we had to be ready, we needed an army."

"Dude, are you serious?"

"Deadly serious," Dallas replied to the shark.

"Not to alarm you guys, but the infected are heading this way, now."

Poxon's shoulders sagged again, "We can't stay here."

Dallas was oblivious to Poxon's claims and carried on regardless, "Our Captain, Nate McConnell, worked for Big Man in the 'Game Show'. He befriended me when I came alone to Heffernan City. I wasn't in a good place and he found me and took care of me, I will always love him for that. He helped me hide and get a job as a teacher, that's where I met some great kids, who I knew would be able to help as well."

"Really? Seems they'd let anybody teach these days plus I don't recall him being in the labs, just drips and nerds worked there, I've seen the captain and he was quite fit."

"So, you are Big Man's daughter? He must be so proud."

"You do know you're talking to a wolf, darling."

Dallas pointed to the sway lizard, "You attack me, he attacks you. I'm warning you."

"No, you're annoying me, big difference."

Poxon spoke up again, "Is anybody listening to me? Those things are closing in."

Everybody ignored him.

"Do you remember those poor children who Big Man gave his serum to, so they would fight for his pathetic TV shows? Well Nate and his team took blood samples from all of them and began the cloning process."

"Cloning process?" Poxon and Aphrodite spoke at once.

"Yes, but only one was a success, a pretty young blonde girl who had the power to make time bombs. He was meant to be working for somebody else in the lab, Big Man's son or something? But the clones are ours, I have a friend there helping, her name changes from time to time."

"How many clones are there?"

Dallas's attention moved swiftly to Lacy on her question, "Hundreds of them, waiting for our command."

"Command for what?" Lacy asked.

"War against my island."

"You bitch," Aphrodite's voice grew with distain, "So if I finally do find a way back home, I have to rescue my father from his two freak sons, deal with a zombie apocalypse in Olympia, try to stop a march of time bomb clones, plus an invasion of bitches from Karrick. As well as having to find my sisters, one of whom is a dragon and the other hates me."

"And a partridge in a pear tree!" Slim Pickings smirked, "Sorry dude, couldn't resist it."

Lacy shook her head, "For the last time, what are you doing here?"

Dallas groaned quietly, "Nate McConnell was also a pilot and a Captain, he was placed on a Typhon zoo ship, a new ship a new space flight to show college students the magnificent creatures of the planet. We had a year to plan and invite kids from every college in the country. We had an idea to see if we could use the students on board for genetic experiments. I managed to speak to some and see if they would like to take part in a magnificent project."

Achilles showed further interest and his eyes dipped, "Genetics? That's what Harley saw, that's what he said before that bastard creature tore him apart and don't deny because I saw the pictures on his phone before he died. I thought he was just waffling on about typical geek stuff, but he was right, wasn't he?"

"He was and I'm so sorry for what my dinosaur did; I know words can never bring your friends back. He was my pet back in Karrick, he was special, very special and we smuggled him on board for my protection. We got separated and he got scared, hungry and frustrated."

"Frustrated? He killed our friends and I swear if we get out of this ship alive I'm going to take out my frustration and take pleasure in knocking the shit out of it."

Aphrodite heard Lacy's words and flopped to the floor, she rolled around on her back twisting and turning, rubbing her head on to the ground and scratching her paws on the metal surface.

"What are you doing?" Lacy asked.

"I can't laugh so I'm clapping, this is the only way I know how."

Everybody went quiet, standing nervously listening to the silence, nobody wanting to ask the next question.

"Dude? What did you do to the kids?"

Dallas looked at the scarred face of the shark, she studied its black eyes and her own eyes widened, "Wow! I forgot you could talk? We didn't think that it would work on you, but that's great news, thank you."

Slim Pickings' nostrils flared as he heard the words from Dallas, "What did you say?" He could feel the anger bubbling under his skin, "Dude, I was a man and now I'm a shark, if you know who did this, please tell me?"

Dallas wiped a tired hand against her face, "We did. We had some spare time and we saw a lonely wolf walking across the plains, so we picked it up to see what we could do with it."

Aphrodite's back began to rise with anger, "So you experimented on me? Ok, I kind of understand that to make me more perfect, but now can you turn me back to a human?"

"No," said Dallas defiantly.

Poxon's eyes were in constant movement, "We have signs from the east and the west block, the west profiles are approaching fast. Get prepared people, as we're about to have company." Yet again, Poxon was being ignored.

"Dude, you didn't answer me, what did you do to the kids?"

Dallas' hands dropped to her sides, "Nate was dealing with the experiments. We were doing so well until he left and he never came back, so I had to continue on my own with the remaining students we had. I'm not a scientist so the procedures were different, the students were different. I tried my best, but it just wasn't the same."

Poxon looked up and down on the screen, "He's dead by the way, I did say? Oh, you weren't here yet, yeah the infected students killed him and they're still coming and something else as well."

"No," Dallas sniffed, "No, no, no, this wasn't meant to be, everybody I meet ends up dead, why does this happen?"

"I bet you're a bundle of laughs at weddings." Aphrodite tried to hide her sarcasm, but failed.

"Does nothing ever bother you? How do you sleep at night?"

"Red wine and ridicule," Aphrodite said.

"Still, you might have to put it in a bowl this time," she sighed.

Lacy spoke firmly next, "Listen, you're a fraud, it's an act. You didn't care about the Captain, you only used him to help with your experiments. You used him like you used every student on this ship to get what you want. You're pathetic and a shit teacher."

Aphrodite wagged her tail, "God I love her."

"Now answer my shark friend," Lacy said, "What did you do to the students?"

Poxon turned a semi-circle from the screen back to the group, "Listen, I don't know if you're getting this? But we have incoming from opposite sides of the room now we're stuck in the middle, so if you have a plan to get out of here you better start thinking now."

Dallas wiped her eyes and headed to join Poxon at the computer terminal. She swiped a few screens and the huge door connecting the captain's quarters to the water filtration unit began to open.

"Miss Dwells! What are you doing?!"

"Protecting us."

A huge scraping sound was coming from the end of the corridor. Something big was scratching its nails against the corridors, huge footsteps headed towards them. Achilles backed away from the awful sound, "This doesn't look good."

Poxon looked at the screen, "This doesn't look right either, multiple signs heading our way."

The scraping sounds started to include groaning with them, strange snarling noises as well. The sounds made the sway lizard stand up and roar in their direction, its tail swished hard anticipating trouble. Poxon was nervous also.

"There are no doors leading off apart from the main two, with things coming from either end, we're trapped here."

"What about those doors over there?" Achilles pointed to some in a corner.

"Blocked, we can't get out that way."

The noises shuffled closer as Poxon breathed hard, trying to keep it together. Dallas tiptoed across to the open corridor and peaked her head through to hear the oncoming noise. She reared back when she saw what was approaching and confidently took a side step away, "Like I said, protection."

A huge reptilian head appeared from the open corridor. It was broad and had a wide snout with loads of teeth. It resembled an alligator, but it had a human bottom half, filled with armoured body plates and working upright legs, a flat tail came from its rear and dragged along the floor. The massive head sat on the shoulders of a tight male chest and entered the room, looking around with purpose. Lacy opened her mouth to scream, but everybody else was already running away before she could.

"WHAT THE HELL IS THAT!?" cried Achilles. The alligator entered the room and peered around, the remaining students and Slim Pickings were struggling to get the other door open. They didn't want to go back under water, the infected wolves and sharks were probably still in there, there was nowhere else to run. Lacy tried to pull at the slide doors, "OPEN THE BASTARD DOOR!" she screamed.

The alligator creature sized them up and then turned behind him, waving its hand back towards the corridor. Suddenly more creatures appeared, shuffling awkwardly towards the group; they were human animal hybrids of all sorts. Cheetahs, rhinos, elephants, all manner of mixed up half-humans and animals entered. It was clear that the door wasn't going to open and Lacy turned around to face the bizarre creatures, still hoping that she was hallucinating. She froze, helpless, she couldn't move for pure terrifying fear as the animals moved closer. The leading alligator sifted past all the other students. Achilles, Aphrodite and Slim Pickings made half-hearted attempts to stop it but it simply pushed them away and went for Lacy. Its huge snout sniffed around her small head. She felt numb and couldn't move.

"DO IT! GO ON AND KILL ME YOU SHITTING FREAK!"

The alligator pulled back and opened its many teethed mouth, "'Allo."

Lacy's mouth went as wide as the alligator's, "You can talk?"

"You used to sit next to me in home economics? Albeit I looked slightly different."

She slowly walked towards it, "Sorry? I don't remember you."

"Yes, you used to copy my recipe for fairy cakes." The teenage girl was clueless and shook her head, "I made lemon kippers for you to pass our first cooking exam." Lacy grew embarrassed as the alligator spoke on.

"I made you salmon in a sweet and sour sauce plus prawn curry with sticky rice, just so you would get through the course and notice me, but you don't know who I am, do you?"

Lacy put her hands over her mouth and then used one to wipe away a tear, "I don't know who you are, I'm so sorry!"

The alligator tried to smile, but it was all awful teeth, much like Slim Pickings when he tried, "That's what

Miss Dwells said you would say, you were the cool kids in class and ignored every one of us. We were in your classes from day one and you never knew we existed. We carried your books and did your homework, we even carried your beer for you and you can't remember any one of us?" As the huge bunch of mixed up animals moved in closer, Lacy eyed up the alligator and stepped up closer. Its hot, dustbin of a breath would normally make her physically sick, but she wrapped her arms around it. She spoke slowly and closed her eyes with the hug:

"It is good to see you again, Eric."

Eric's dead eyes flickered and he really tried hard again to smile. He actually did like Lacy, she always said 'please' and 'thank you' for his paperwork.

"By the way, that was a badass recipe for the salmon." She took a step back, "What did they do to you?"

"Miss Dwells said she had an experiment on the ship for us, something that could make us better, stronger and..." Before Eric could finish, a female voice screamed above his.

"LOOK WHAT SHE DID TO ME!"

From her right side Lacy caught a movement. From the corner of her eye she saw a figure bound over the rest of the creatures and huddled in a corner, shivering and breathing heavily.

Poxon ignored the acrobatic creature and the rest of the mutated newcomers and kept his eye on the terminal, a red light flashed rapidly in the corner of the screen, it began to pulse and move towards their location.

"Much as I would really want to talk about each and every one of your mutations, and I'm not joking, but we are about to be joined by Sully and every infected thing on the ship, student and animal. We have to make a stand now."

Lacy was more concerned about the creature in the corner, "Hello? You can come out, I won't hurt you."

"SHE LIED TO ME, SHE LIED TO US ALL!" The voice sounded familiar to Lacy as the shape stayed in the shadow.

"They are sixty feet away," said Poxon, "Can any of you guys fight?" he asked the creatures, unconcerned by their appearance. Eric shrugged.

"Not sure, do we have to kill anybody to stay alive?"

"Well unless we can find a cure, everybody and everything heading this way is technically dead anyway, so fill your boots."

Poxon looked at the massive frame of Eric, not intimidated at all, "Did you ever get to read issue 20 of *Power Chick and the Illegals*? The one where her brother turns out to be Dr Midlife Crisis, her arch nemesis? Fifty feet by the way."

Eric clapped, "Mate, you remembered I read comics! Cool, but no, I missed that issue."

"Well, if we get out of here alive, you can have mine."

Eric nervously picked at his claws on his hand, "So what you're saying is that you really hope we die?"

Poxon smiled, "Bang on mate, nobody is touching my comics, forty feet now, what the shit?"

Lacy closed in on the figure. She looked at it with a strained expression, "Please come out?"

"Thirty feet." Poxon looked around frantically for another escape route.

"They're almost on us."

"Then we finally fight and be somebody," Eric said forlornly.

"I THOUGHT SHE LOVED ME!" the figure screamed and leapt from its hiding place. It sailed through the air and nimbly landed in front of Dallas. It had a long slim body with brown fur poking out from beneath skin tight black leather trousers, it looked odd with webbed feet and hands with sharp claws wearing a very expensive outfit but the creature wore it well.

"Oh my god," whispered Lacy as she finally recognised the creature. Its head was weasel-like, but as light hit the creature, it resembled an otter more than anything. The trousers were ruined at the rear by a long tail which the otter was leaning back on for support. Deep black eyes looked directly into the eyes of Dallas.

"Do you like what you see?" asked the otter.

"I'm so sorry, Cameo," mumbled Dallas.

"CAMEO? THAT'S CAMEO?" Achilles couldn't believe what he saw.

"Dude, they turned you too? That's so not cool, she was stunning," Slim Pickings sighed.

"I thought you liked me?" hissed Cameo to Dallas, "Then you turned me into this bastard thing."

"God, Cameo, how many people were you sleeping with?" asked Lacy, ignoring the fact that her best friend now looked like an otter.

"I thought we had something special," Cameo moaned.

"Two teachers on one trip? That's progressive of you," Lacy's teeth grinded hard.

"Twenty feet now!" shouted Poxon, "Do we have any ideas?" His voice was shaking uncontrollably.

"I have one," Cameo chuckled. With a quick flick of her elbow, Cameo knocked out Dallas.

"NO! YOU STUPID BITCH!" yelled Aphrodite, "HOW CAN SHE TURN US BACK TO HUMAN IF SHE'S OUT COLD?!"

"Not my circus, not my monkeys," Cameo frowned.

"WHAT DOES THAT MEAN YOU LEFTOVER TRAMP?!"

The sway lizard made a startled growl and went for Cameo, sweeping past the startled animal students.

"No dude," said Slim Pickings quickly. His heart beating frantically, he shoulder-barged the dinosaur, knocking it to the ground, "She's my friend." The big shark shook its head, slightly dazed, "Dude, isn't life pretty?" he said and then collapsed next to the lizard.

"SHARK!" Achilles yelled.

The teenager went over to his new friend and held his massive hand. Joined by Cameo, Achilles recoiled at her look.

"Good to see you too, Achilles."

"What happened to you?" his eyes couldn't leave the new form of Cameo.

"Shit happened, now help me move Slim."

Aphrodite growled with raw ferocity and leapt at Cameo. They both fell to the ground wrestling furiously with each other, Lacy and Achilles ran over and tried to pull them apart.

"Ten feet now, what the fu—" Poxon was almost hysterical.

The lizard got itself to its feet and roared again. Looking at the fallen figure of its owner, it seized its chance for revenge and ran towards her.

"Not today," Eric said.

He whipped his huge tail around at the oncoming beast, and for the second time in moments, the dinosaur fell as Eric struck hard. The alligator boy looked at the lizard on the ground, "Stay." He looked around him, "Nobody around to hear my gag, perfect."

"Five feet, no! They're right outside!" Poxon yelled. He was staring wide at the chaos behind him.

Lacy and Achilles were struggling with Aphrodite to get her off Cameo as Slim Pickings lay on the ground. The sway lizard was up on its feet again and attacked Eric, the other student animals rallied around their friend and made a wall around him, defending Eric from the lightning attack of the dinosaur. Poxon had nothing left has he counted down, "Four feet. PLEASE STOP IT!"

Nobody listened to the frightened boy as they continued to fight amongst themselves.

"Three feet. Two feet. One foot." Poxon wiped his mouth slowly as something heavy banged against the door from the other side and was relentless. He crept underneath the computer terminal and began rocking with fear. He couldn't help but look over his shoulder at the door, knowing that at any moment the room would be filled with the infected. The bravado about dying before losing his comics was gone.

"SULLY'S HERE, SHE'S HERE AND SHE'S GOING TO KILL US!"

Poxon burst into tears and backed further under the console, shivering with fear, "Sully's here and she's going to kill me." Nothing could stop the flow of tears down his face, "She's going to kill me."

CHAPTER ELEVEN:

Return Of The Loving Dead

Earth 13

Kitty wandered amongst the wedding guests, she didn't know any of them and they tried to make out that they knew her. They gushed about her dress and jewels, but Kitty didn't care about any of it; her mentor and friend was the only person she wanted to see right now.

She was desperate to find her and leave the castle, all that needed to be done was to marry the King and then she and Silo could escape, run away and be safe. Somewhere she could complete her training and be just as powerful as her friend. This was becoming a hard task at the moment; she couldn't find her.

Kitty's dress was becoming annoying, it was dragging and keeping her back. Immie and Jane were nowhere to be seen and this was also worrying for Kitty.

"You look anxious my lady, surely this should be the happiest day of your life?" The familiar voice made Kitty jump as she turned to around to see her future husband with a huge entourage behind him, "Forgive me, my lady, I meant not to startle you."

Kitty bowed and then curtsied, in a slightly muddled fashion.

"No, your Grace, just a bit nervous about what's going to happen to me."

The King smiled and shook his head, "You will be a great Queen, the people outside will love you as much as I do."

Kitty was about to smile when another noise made her jump, "What was that, my lord?"

"Why they are the church bells, my lady, signalling our impending marriage."

The nervous girl attempted to smile again, "I cannot find my friend, Silo, you said she was released but she isn't here."

"Your friend is no longer in prison, I set her free."

"So why isn't she here then, your Grace?"

The King rolled his eyes around in frustration, "Can we please forget about her for today? She has left, she isn't coming, she was invited but she didn't want to come."

Kitty took a small breath, "Is that what she said, your Grace?"

"Yes, she was disappointed in you for choosing me over her and she stormed out."

A tear formed in the corner of Kitty's right eye, "Why would she do that to me?" she sniffed, "I miss our companionship."

"You have mine now, my lady."

"But…"

"You will be my Queen and that is the end of it."

Kitty wiped her eye, "What about my ladies? Jane and Immie?"

"They have left too my lady, they decided that a life of adventure with Silo was a better one than here with you, I'm sorry."

Kitty's legs buckled slightly. She regained her poise and leaned forward to the King, breathing quickly through nerves and anger, allowing herself a pause before speaking.

"I am ready to become your Queen, my lord, to serve you and the people."

The King held out his arm and the girl snaked hers through and allowed herself to be led to the church.

It was a glorious piece of architecture, the beautiful smooth walls of the church had various flags hanging from them. Kitty didn't know what each flag stood for, but she liked the pretty drawings on them. The ceiling was extremely high as she craned her little neck back to see its magnificent splendour. The King gently pulled at her for her attention as the clergyman was about to start proceedings. Dressed in robes equalling the length of the Queen's, the clergyman started proceedings.

"We are gathered here today in the house of our Lord to join in holy matrimony and witness the union between…" The clergyman hesitated in mid-flow.

"What is it?" asked the King.

"Your Majesty…"

He nodded his head in Kitty's direction to get the King's attention, the girl was looking right past the clergyman's shoulder and at the onlookers gathered to the side.

"My lady, what is the matter?" she simply ignored the King and carried on walking away. The perplexed clergyman shrugged his shoulders as the King's confused face mirrored his own. Something had caught her attention which was far more important than getting married. A man in the crowd saw Kitty approach him and bowed nervously.

"My lady?"

"Sir, you do realise who you stand in front of?"

"Yes, my lady."

"Then please tell me, where did you get that hat?"

Kitty strode slowly up to him and stood right in his front, her teeth bared. The hat belonged to Silo, her treasured possession, the second thing behind Kitty which she couldn't live without, "You had better speak to me right my good sir, where did you get that hat?"

"It was from, I mean it came from someone, I can't really say who," he stammered.

"I SAID ANSWER ME!" she screamed.

"MY LADY!" shouted the King.

"NO! YOU DON'T GET TO SPEAK TO ME."

The crowd stood aghast at the young girl's words to their King, as did he. Kitty turned back to the man in the hat, "I will ask you again and God help you if I get the wrong answer."

Tears appeared in her eye, followed by a grab to his throat.

"The dark woman," he said quickly.

"What did you say?"

"The woman with the painted skin, the hat belonged to her, his Majesty the King gave it to me."

Kitty snatched it from the man's head and examined it, there was a blood splatter on the side. She held her stomach, feeling physically sick and almost retched. She whirled around in anger to the King and held the hat aloft, "Where is she?"

The pure venom in her voice stunned the crowd. The King gave a crooked smile and stood behind the clergyman.

"You continue to grant me so much attraction to you, but it is time to stop with such foolishness, my lady, now get back here and become my Queen."

"I WILL NOT!"

"You are becoming childish, my lady," the King sighed.

Once again Kitty's voice kicked forward, "Do my childish antics bother you my lord? I will stop in haste if you tell me where Silo is."

"SHE IS GONE!" he yelled. There was complete silence in the church. Kitty's stomach turned again as the congregation began to turn on to her, "WHERE IS SHE?!" she screamed. Kitty tried to push past the people to get back to the King, "LET ME THROUGH!" With a nod from the King, the crowd held her back, "SHE'S NOT HERE, WHERE IS SHE?!"

The crowd did their job well, making a wall between Kitty and the King. They held her tightly and slowly pushed her towards him, "WHERE IS SILO?!" Kitty yelled again to the King.

"I see you have her hat, a gift for you indeed my lady, I would treasure it always if I were you."

Kitty's stomach rumbled with fear, "What do you mean, your Majesty?"

The King's face brightened, "Silo won't need a hat where she is heading." He smirked, "If you'll pardon the pun."

"I am here for you my King and I will be your loving Queen, just tell me where she is?"

The King didn't answer right away, his eyelids lifted, "Asleep, for good." Kitty collapsed into a heap on the ground, nobody went to her aid as the King grinned.

"I know her to be a witch; she is cursed my lady. I know this to be true as I was warned about her and I will pray for her soul." Kitty rose to her feet and clasped her hands to pray. She looked around at all the people gathered around her and then closed her eyes and concentrated, "Forgive me, my lady."

Blue smoke swirled around her and then she teleported away. The congregation screamed in terror as the King raised his hands defensively and stood back.

"Good God!" was all he could say.

Kitty reappeared at the execution tower, which was part of a trinity of buildings built close to the castle. The church and the execution tower were all within a stone's throw of each other. Kitty was getting used to her powers and teleporting seemed so natural to her now as Silo said it would be after time.

There was a big crowd gathered at the tower, people who would rather see an execution rather than a wedding, but it seemed to be a private show as many of the towns folk weren't allowed in and had to watch the wedding instead. She slowly walked past Traitors' Gate; the awful smell of the recently dead made her hold her hand to her mouth. There were massive spikes in front, giant sticks in the ground with severed heads stuck on the top. She waded through the moat around the tower, trying not to look at the heads of the dead, but one head looked familiar.

She hauled herself up from the water to take a closer look, it was harder to do in her wedding dress and the stench and dirt clung on to her clothing as she approached from behind.

"No, please no."

The head of Thomas Culpepper was placed at the centre of the spikes, it was a ghostly white, not how Kitty remembered him from the conker cart. She doubled over in shock and clutched her stomach tightly before the sick could rise.

She wanted to scream but somehow she knew things would become worse as she moved further.

Kitty's rising emotions got the better of her as she headed towards the gathering of selected people. She saw a raised scaffold platform covered with straw, a minster of the church stood by praising the people and the King. He waved his hand and looked solemnly at the figure below him.

A body lay slumped on a chopping block in front of Kitty's eyes, its head was missing but the beautiful body lay still on the block. An executioner stood wiping his blade from the bloody body, swirling his axe triumphantly to the crowd who cheered at his handiwork.

Yet again Kitty had to push past crowds to fully see what was happening. At the bottom of the scaffold was a young girl with a sack, she was crying uncontrollably as she cradled the sack in her knees.

It was Immie, she cried with raw emotion and rocked back and forth with her tears. Kitty trembled as she approached her lady-in-waiting. Immie screamed with more grief when she saw Kitty, "Please, please go away, my lady!" she sobbed.

The sack was leaking blood, it was all over Immie's dress as the crowd cheered and roared their approval. Kitty's eyes flicked up to the bloody body with the stump where its head had been. She looked back to the sack and Immie and then back to the body on the chopping block.

"What's in the bag?"

Immie turned away, still shaking, "Go away, my lady."

Kitty shook her head as tears streamed down her face again, "What's in the bag, Immie?" Her words weren't calm anymore. The crowd clapped at the executioner as he lapped up the applause. She recognised the dress from the executioner's block and shouted at Immie, "WHAT'S IN THE BAG?!"

Immie threw her little head back and screamed a guttural cry of anguish. Kitty backed away, fearfully shaking her head.

"NO, NO, NO!" she screamed as the realisation smashed home that it was the body of Jane laying neatly on the chopping block, minus her head. Kitty pushed past the crowd and cradled the weeping Immie. In deep shock her lady-in-waiting shivered a look up at Kitty, "They killed her! He killed her, my lady!"

Kitty wiped Jane's blood from Immie's face, it was time for her to step up and be an adult, she was scared of taking charge. Silo told her what to do usually but she wasn't here, "We have to leave, now Immie, we can't stay here."

Immie desperately tried to keep the bag away from Kitty.

"WHAT DO I DO?! WHAT DO WE DO?" Immie yelled, taking her turn to wipe the blood splashes from her mouth.

"We need Silo. We find her and we'll get out of this place. I can protect you and she can too, we just have to make sure she is safe. I think the King has done something."

Immie looked up at the scaffold and her heart broke again, she spoke in a mournful tone and pointed up, "My lady." Kitty's eyes followed Immie's finger to the scaffold and they grew wider, "No."

Silo was being escorted to the scaffold by two guards of the King. Her uniform was gone, she was barefoot and wearing a black dress. They hauled her up the steps and pushed her onto a block next to Jane's body. Her face was bloody and had been severely beaten; the wound on her side had healed, but had already caused irreversible damage to her. Kitty instantly became as lost as a little child, just like the day Silo found her.

"What are you doing up there, my lady?" she asked slightly confused. She looked up at the block and tried to climb it, she was trembling more now, "Please come down from there."

Silo was prodded by one guard's axe to kneel down at the chopping block and that finally shocked Kitty into action, "SILO!" she screamed, "GET UP! TELEPORT!" Silo's battered face acknowledged Kitty with a hurt painful smile. She shook her head forlornly, her powers were gone due to her injuries. Kitty exchanged a horrifying look with Immie, "Stay calm, my lady, I'll get you myself." Kitty closed her eyes and concentrated on teleporting up to the scaffold. When Kitty opened her eyes, she was still in the crowd, "What's happening?!" She tried to teleport again but her powers weren't working, she was panicking fully now, "WHY ISN'T IT WORKING?!" Silo kept her head down on the block, she struggled to look over and caught Kitty's eye, "You have to concentrate, kiddo," she whispered strongly against the crowd.

Kitty clenched her fists and closed her eyes to teleport trying to filter out the roar of the people eager to see an execution. She failed again and fell to her knees. Tears poured down Kitty's face, "I CAN'T! I CAN'T DO IT! PLEASE GOD NO!"

Silo spat out some blood and smiled, growing ready for her fate, "It's fine, thank you, Katherine Howard."

This was the only time Silo had said her full name, "For what?" Kitty sniffed.

"For being my only friend," was Silo's reply.

Kitty sobbed uncontrollably, "YOU LET HER GO!" she cried to the executioner, her words were wasted, "DON'T LEAVE ME! PLEASE DON'T LEAVE ME!"

The death drums from the band standing to the right of the tower started to roll, there wasn't much time. Kitty yelled to the men gathered in the crowd, "HELP ME! SOMEBODY HELP ME!" Nobody did. Kitty was directly below the scaffold block, her eyes were streaming, "I DON'T KNOW WHAT TO DO!" The executioner let out a tired sigh.

"You are holding us up, girl."

"Please good sir, I beg you, please spare her."

There was no response from him and Kitty's voice changed, "DON'T YOU TOUCH HER! DON'T YOU DARE TOUCH HER, YOU BASTARD!"

He looked at the baying crowd and then back to Kitty, "Tell your friend to make peace with her God."

The crying girl moaned in frustration, "Her God? There is only one God, sir." The executioner hesitated as one of the masked guards stepped forward and stood just behind him and nodded. The executioner just about saw the guard and nodded back, the executioner removed his hood as did the guard. Mason waved his massive axe above Silo, taunting Kitty as Orion the guard rubbed his eyes. The two hunters who had been chasing her and Silo across the country and the planets apparently had finally found them. Kitty couldn't believe what she was seeing.

Then as easily as removing the hood, Mason changed his face; it was pure sorcery, like Silo and now herself. It was a strange and wonderful sight to see. Mason's face took the shape of many people with ease. Orion was unaware of Mason's ability as he had stepped back slightly from the chopping block to calm down the crowd, the faces continued to change until Kitty's face looked even more stunned.

Mason's face morphed into Mary, the chief lady-in-waiting, who had probably heard her whispers and concerns to Jane and Immie. It was then quickly followed by Thomas Culpepper, the boy she had a crush on and the one she told her true feelings about the King to. She had been truly set up, and now Silo was about to pay the ultimate price for her loose tongue.

"You were Thomas Culpepper?" Kitty asked.

"Yep, actually I killed him at the site of the cart crash. Orion doesn't know that so let's keep it between ourselves. It was clear he had feelings for you, so I took his face and messed the King up. He thought Thomas was really after you, so the lad you really liked at the castle grounds... was me all along." Mason's face settled back to its normal state and he spoke again, "You mentioned one God? Not anymore."

Silo heard the voice and recognised it immediately, trying to look up from her block.

"Good one," was all she was prepared to say to him.

"This can end now," Orion said. He had missed the face changes of Mason, "Everything alright, Mason?" he asked. Mason shrugged with a smile.

Kitty had never heard Orion speak before, it sounded quite warm and she liked it, which was a shame as he was unintentionally trying to kill her.

"Come with us, join us in trying to save your true world. You don't belong here, your powers are beautiful and could save billions of people."

Kitty was about to turn away, but his voice had a hold on her, "If I came with you and saved our home world, would you release Silo?"

Studying the fear in Kitty's eyes, Orion didn't hesitate to answer, "If you leave now with us, leave the King, we'll take Silo with us. We just wanted to scare you into saving our planet, we were never ever going to kill Silo, why would we kill one of our own? We just used her to find you."

"Ok." The tone in her voice suggested that she believed him, "I'll do it," Kitty said.

"No!" Silo felt the urgent need to remind Kitty again, "If you do this, if you go back with them and teleport Rayash, many planets will die just to save our own, could you live with that?"

Kitty stood and spoke defiantly, "Yes, if it saves you and my true people."

Silo groaned in frustration on the block, "Please don't do this, kiddo."

Kitty moved to the foot of the scaffold and looked directly into the eyes of Silo, "Then help me my lady, I don't know what to do, I will not lose you." The younger girl felt her stomach gurgle, "I need you."

Silo gave a strained smile, "I'll let you into a little secret." Her smile disappeared and tears finally began to form, "I'm scared." Kitty attempted to touch Silo, her hand stretched as far as it could go at the foot of the scaffold.

"Don't be scared, let me be scared for you." A lapse in concentration made Kitty smile back to her mentor. Mason swirled his axe high in the air, confusing Kitty and Orion, but Silo smiled a response.

"Don't defend." The smile hung for a while as she noticed the glint in Mason's eye and put her head back on the block, "Attack."

"What do you mean?" Kitty said, she could not stop weeping, "I will save you, I will get you out of..."

Kitty was too busy talking she didn't notice Silo's head tumble past her. Immie quickly gathered it up and put it in her bag with Jane's, she was hysterical. Kitty squinted, trying to get a closer look at why Immie was screaming holding a black blanket, she carried on talking.

"Don't worry, everything is going to be..."

She noticed Silo's bloody body and went into shock, wiping her runny nose, "That's not right, that's not right, I'm seventeen years old I think? That's not right."

The axe from Mason had taken Silo's head off with one clean blow. Then she finally realised what had just happened. Staring at Mason, Orion stumbled back and mumbled, he didn't want this.

"No, wait, what did you do? She didn't need to die."

Kitty threw her head back and screamed at the top of her lungs falling to the ground, "NOOOOOOOOO!!!!" The whole crowd stopped cheering, they had never witnessed such raw emotion from a girl so young. Kitty's face had changed, gone were the pretty innocent eyes of a Queen, but were replaced with a red glow, her mouth was twisted, ugly and bent.

She got to her feet but carried on rising. She was floating in the air. Now in complete control of her powers, she was teleporting so rapidly it had now given her the gift of flight. A blue light wrapped itself around her like a giant snake, pulsing with pure energy as it slithered around her body. The crowds of people gathered for the execution screamed and ran away, having never experienced anything like this at all. A witch was in sight.

The King had left the church after hearing the noise and ran to the execution block with his followers. He stumbled into the clearing and yelled at the clergyman who had also joined him, "GOOD GOD MAN, WHAT IS THAT?!"

"A good girl," Kitty said coldly. She flicked her wrist and a bolt of plasma neatly flew from her hand and struck the clergyman in his chest, sending him spinning to the ground.

The King was shouting at his guards, telling them to back off. He had no idea what he was dealing with, confusion and panic spread through everyone. Kitty breathed in hard and tried to push back what was happening in her mind. She suddenly threw her hands by her side and roared into the skies with her confident powers, she flew with ease up and above everybody else.

She saw the King trying to drag away Immie and her bag; she implored him to stop but he knew what he was doing, he was about to make her suffer permanently for helping Silo and ruining his marriage. Kitty instantly swooped down and gathered the King in her arms and flew with him skywards, holding him tight.

"Stage one," Mason muttered as Kitty and the King soared higher into the sky.

"I know you, your Majesty, you are the one who brought me here, you are the one who dealt with trickery with the two fiends who have been hunting me across the land. They promised you riches beyond belief if I was to marry you. They promised you to be the ruler of this world if I was to become your bride. You are the one who let poor Thomas and Jane die for information about me. You are the one who killed my best friend, my partner, my mentor, my beloved Silo, who was being held against her will. Now I'm sure you took part in her beatings when she couldn't defend herself and you laughed at her death and now attempt to harm my good lady, Immie. I was about to become your Queen, Queen to a murderer, what say you?"

The King wasn't fearful of Kitty or her powers, just angry, he struggled in her grip but wisely stopped, seeing how high they were off the ground.

"You are a witch, you are a common whore and cursed, but you are my wife and you…" He looked to the people below who seemed like ants, more so than usual, "YOU WILL DO EXACTLY WHAT I SAY!"

"You are a bully my King, you are a coward and stupid like all bullies are."

"I AM THE RULER OF THIS LAND, YOU ARE MY WIFE AND YOU MUST KNOW YOUR PLACE, YOU WILL SET ME DOWN NOW AND LISTEN TO ME, YOU WITCH!"

There was dead silence as Kitty's eyes glowed and she tilted her head, getting used to her powers now, "Really?" she asked.

"I AM THE KING OF THIS COUNTRY, YES I HAD JANE AND THAT PAINTED BITCH SILO KILLED BECAUSE I AM THE LORD OF THIS LAND, WHAT CAN YOU DO? YOU STUPID, PATHETIC LITTLE GIRL! YOU ARE A COMMON WENCH AND LUCKY TO BE MY BRIDE, WHAT CAN YOU DO?"

"What can I do?" Kitty asked.

"YES WOMAN! WHAT CAN YOU DO?!"

She discarded him like a ragdoll. The King didn't stop screaming as he fell from her hands. Kitty never took her eyes off him as he disappeared from her sight, "I can fly, your Majesty." It was quite a while before he landed, and Kitty could only assume he had made a bloody mess.

"Stage two," Mason said, Orion grabbing him by the arm.

"What is going on here?"

"What needed to be done sir, the King is dead."

Orion looked wordlessly to Mason who spoke instead, "You better hold on to your stomach, General Orion, because it's about to become a bumpy ride." Mason removed a rifle from beneath his executioner's robe and aimed it a Kitty. He took a few loose shots at her in the sky, which she dodged easily thanks to her training with Silo.

"COME AND GET US, KATHERINE! WHAT ARE YOU SCARED OF? ARE YOU GOING TO GO OUT CRYING LIKE A BABY? JUST LIKE SILO?"

"That should do it," Mason smirked.

There was an ear-splitting roar of sound as Kitty hurtled through the air like a powerful blue javelin towards the two men, her fists thrust out before her.

"You ready, General?" Mason asked.

"No," came the reply.

"Doesn't matter."

Mason looked at the blue blur hurtling towards him, "Because here we go."

With unimaginable force, Kitty flew into the castle, with the blue smoke hanging behind her. She was teleporting out of pure anger and hate, without slowing down. There was a mighty thunderclap of sound and then everything was gone.

Kitty, Mason, Orion, Immie along with the castle, the church and the executioner's scaffold disappeared, replaced only by Kitty's signature teleport smoke.

The clergyman emerged, wandered from the debris of the buildings that didn't teleport completely, with Kitty.

He looked around at the mess and his heart relaxed when he saw other people who had survived the assault from Kitty. He rubbed his chest, still hurting from Kitty's plasma strike, tatters from his robe hanging from his shoulder. He trudged down the path and pulled out a small object from his belt. It was a small device, a miniature construct. He placed a long wire from the machine into his ear, fiddling around with the piece until it nestled neatly inside.

He pressed a button on the side of the device and smooth music played out through the wire towards his ears. He opened his lips to sing along with the words, head bopping along and his hips swaying in rhythm to the song. He realised swiftly that he was singing out loud and looked around to see if he'd been noticed, "God I love this tune."

Earth 65

"WHY ISN'T ANYBODY LISTENING TO ME?" Poxon screamed. Lacy stopped fighting with Aphrodite, and dragged the wolf away from her neck.

"Get off me you tramp, my brother needs me."

Lacy ran over to the computer console to find Poxon shivering beneath it, "C'mon bruv, we're getting out of here."

Poxon smiled at his twin, "No, we're not, we are all going to die, but thanks for thinking of me." He realised after he had spoken, that the wrong words had come out, "Sorry, I didn't mean to upset you, but Sully is outside and she's very annoyed."

Lacy finally heard the banging from the outer door and wiped her chin with grave concern, her stomach was doing cartwheels with nerves.

"Ok, listen, you've heard of saving something for a rainy day?" Poxon nodded, "Well it's pissing now outside." The sudden shattering of glass from the outer door shocked Lacy into movement, "HEYYYY!! EVERYONE STOP RIGHT NOW!"

The sway lizard slowly got to its feet, as well as its owner Dallas, who went to pet it on the snout. Lacy targeted her, Cameo and Achilles, "I SAID LISTEN!"

Most of the room turned around, the animal students and Aphrodite took their time.

Lacy angrily pointed to the pounding on the door, "DO YOU HEAR THAT? IT'S THE SOUND OF ALL THE INFECTED ON THIS SHIP TRYING TO GET IN HERE TO KILL US, THEY DON'T GIVE A SHIT ABOUT WHERE WE CAME FROM, THEY DON'T CARE ABOUT WHY WE ARE HERE, DO YOU THINK THEY GIVE A SHIT ABOUT COOL KIDS AND NERDS?"

Achilles dragged his hand down his face in slow despair and rubbed his other arm, which had bite marks from Aphrodite, "We can't get out, the escape ships are all gone, we've nowhere else to go."

Lacy proceeded to look around the battered room and the amazing individuals locked in with her; she lowered her voice slightly, "Our parents were kidnapped and we don't know whether they are alive or dead. We miss them dearly, but we carried on and went to college and fought our way forward with decent grades to get on this ship, and now we're here and no infected beings are going to stop us from getting out."

Aphrodite looked at the door, which was taking a pounding from the other side, and then back to Lacy with great uncertainty.

"How do you suppose we do that, darling? I mean look at the reprobates we have gathered here, hardly an army, more a freak force."

Lacy was momentarily distracted by the sound of the banging and turned her attention back to the wolf.

"We knew about you, Aphrodite Wylde, we knew from Heffernan City, all about you being the biggest bitch in Olympia City and having the most deceptive beauty and now you're a wolf, are you going to let some dead students stop you?"

Lacy crossed her arms as the shark Slim Pickings woke up and slowly got to his feet.

"You, Slim Pickings, before we had even met, you had already saved the life of my friend Cameo and then you carried Achilles and me through the water filters on your back as a true shark. Plus, you've dealt with these things before in that theme park you kept telling us about and that's when you were human."

She then turned to Dallas, her eyes kicked the teacher sharply into touch, "I don't give a shit about your sister or about her vendetta towards you, but that bastard pet of yours killed my boyfriend and some of my best friends today and you have turned my class into half-kids, half-animal creatures just to protect yourself? You're a selfish bitch and when we get of here I will put so much hurt on you and make you suffer so much, it would be scary and rated 'X' in a horror film…or at least get you fired, any one of them would do, but right now we need you and your dinosaur."

Lacy was tired of addressing individuals and turned to the collective, "AS SOON AS THAT DOOR BREAKS DOWN, LOADS OF…"

"WE GET IT!" Cameo shouted. She was still getting used to how her voice sounded as an otter and put her hand on her throat and spoke softly, "Stand together and fight together, we might have a…"

The massive door finally came crashing down and Sully stood in front of a whole bunch of infected students and animals. Her eyes studied Cameo, "I recognise the outfit and the voice sounds familiar, so is that the college bike known as Cameo? I love the new look personally, but I don't think otter chic is in this season, looks like your screwing days are over, bitch."

Before Cameo could answer, part of the ceiling collapsed under the weight of the infected creatures trying to gain entry. As everyone scattered for cover, dozens of infected creatures clung upside down to the remaining ceiling and crawled like bats inside, then they all dropped, landing on top of the changed animals.

It was student versus student, the infected clawed savagely at the animal students who fought back with all their might.

Aphrodite and Slim Pickings smashed away through the infected party. The wolf leapt around the giant room attacking the infected students, striking hard with speed and killer accuracy and then checking her fur for blood.

Eric the alligator blocked out the screaming by whipping his tail around and knocking over a bunch of kids he actually recognised from his book club, his lizard eyes squinted with regret, which disappeared when they didn't stay down. He tried again and knocked them into a wall, their heads shattered like pumpkins against a brick wall. Eric didn't have time to mourn as he heard too many ear-piercing screams from behind him.

A girl who had the horns of a gazelle had impaled one of the infected successfully and was struggling with them, trying to keep them away from her. Before she could do anything else, they leaned forward and bit into her cheek, tearing it right open. She gave a hideous cry and fell to the ground as the infected creature chewed on her face, still attached to the poor girl's horns.

The sway lizard protected Dallas from the oncoming horde. Like Eric, it whipped its tail around to send the infected spinning to the ground. Its jaws clamped hard around one student's neck. The infected student struggled for a while and then went limp.

Achilles watched as the body fell to the ground minus its head and thought about Harley and if that was how it killed his friend. He then shook those thoughts away, knowing he would deal with the dinosaur himself later. Right now it was about staying alive and punching and kicking his way out of there.

Lacy reached for any weapon she could find on the floor; iron bars were strewn everywhere. She picked one up, feeling the weight in her hand and swung it around viciously, it sat well and did its job.

She wasn't too sure if she was hallucinating from the drugs, but she had to beat these creatures off for the sake of her life and Poxon's as well, "GET AWAY! GET AWAY FROM US, YOU BASTARDS!"

Poxon was still shaking underneath the computer terminal, Lacy bent down hurriedly to speak to him, "Pox, we have to go, we have to get out of here."

He sniffed, still traumatised from what he could hear, the screams of pain were deafening.

"We're going to die aren't we?"

Lacy whispered in her brother's ear through clenched teeth, "We will if you don't fight, I need you to be strong for me."

Tears were still in Poxon's eyes, "I can't, I'm scared!

"Shh…" she said, gently rubbing his shoulder, she could feel how tense it was, "Then we'll be scared together."

"What do you mean?"

Lacy crouched even lower under the terminal and pointed behind her, "You do know there's a battle going on behind us." Poxon didn't move, "Ok, can't believe I'm doing this now but never mind, when we were kids and if I had a nightmare or some kid even attempted to bully me at school, I always thought, 'What would Poxon do?' I mean you were smarter than me, more polite, and you always knew the right thing to say to comfort me when I was scared, even when Mum and Dad were taken from us, you stepped up and became a man, so that's when I changed." Lacy flicked her head back to see if any of the infected were close to their computer terminal. Satisfied they wouldn't be disturbed just yet, she carried on, "I knew that one day I would have to be strong for you, so I toughened up, changed my look, built a wall around myself and let nobody get in emotionally, saving up all my anger and hate, because I knew that one day I would have to be your rock, the one to save you, the one you would turn to on our darkest day."

Poxon quickly shook his head, "That doesn't make any sense."

Lacy looked back and quickly forward, "Confused?" she asked.

"Yes."

"Scared?"

"No."

"Good, job done. Now stand up and fight." Poxon got to his feet, wobbly at first from crouching for so long, he became stable and then picked up another loose iron bar from the ground, "You ready?"

Poxon nodded.

"Good, aim for the head."

Poxon glared at his sister and she mockingly raised her hands, "Sorry, forgot I was talking to the biggest nerd in the galaxy."

A blur of movement filled the room.

"Fight!" was all Poxon said as he attacked the nearest infected student. The animal students were fighting hard against the infected. Various hybrids were struggling but putting up a brave fight.

A porcupine girl shot her quills at some creatures, all aimed at their heads putting them down permanently. Two students with magpie heads and wings but human torsos swooped in and constantly picked up the infected, dropping them from great heights, making sure their heads splattered on the ground. But they were tiring, even Aphrodite was backing away, sizing up the situation.

Suddenly the sea of infected students parted, allowing Sully to enter. She scuttled down one of the suspension cables like a lizard and back flipped into the centre of the massive room with grace, she oozed confidence and beauty even though she was technically dead.

"ACHILLES! I WANT YOU NOW, WE HAVE PLENTY TO EAT, YOU CAN END THIS IF YOU GIVE YOURSELF TO ME."

Achilles stepped forward himself, breathing hard to hide his nervousness, "Why don't you leave us alone, Sully, we haven't done anything."

"No, they haven't, but you have, you always did have something I wanted...your heart."

Achilles saw the blood pulsing through Sully's now naked body; she didn't need clothes, she was magnificent and dead, "Just leave us be, Sully, just go away."

"Where can I go, my love? We're on a spaceship in the middle of nowhere."

"Did you disable the drop ships? Did you jettison the ships that could get us out of here?"

"Of course I did, my love, I didn't want you to leave me so soon."

The main room was filled with the infected now, they were only being held back by the will of their Queen Sully. The animal students had nowhere else to go, backing away from their former friends. Sully's skin rippled with blood, "You come with me, be my mate and we take this ship and rule the galaxy with our children. Nobody will stop us, nobody can beat us, with this virus running through our veins we are unstoppable."

"Family."

Sully bared her teeth for the first time in a while, she was confused, "What?"

Achilles strode forward, his eyes locked on to her, "Look around you, look at everybody on this ship, we have had the most trying of college trips today, we've lost some good friends, lost our teachers, classmates turned into animals and the rest into zombies." He shot a dirty look to Dallas, "We have no escape ships, stranded in outer space and no idea how to get home."

One of the infected wolves moved close to Sully, she stroked it gently and it nudged her for more.

"What are you talking about, Achilles? Better make it quick."

"What we've been through today has been absolutely shit and I don't even know if I'm still trippin' but look around this room, you may see a bunch of crazy ass animal kids, you may see a stuck-up talking wolf."

"Charming," Aphrodite huffed.

"Cameo, one of your best friends is now an otter girl," Achilles continued.

"Cheers for reminding me, dickhead," Cameo sighed as Achilles cleared his throat.

"What I'm trying to say is everybody here has been through shit today and we're still here, we're still fighting, we're still strong, because we're family, and that's what you don't have, and we do. You don't have to do this, just calm down and we can try and figure this out, come with us and try to get back home, you're my best friend and I love you."

She shrugged but her voice was sincere, "So you don't want to be with me?"

"No, I don't," Achilles said defensively.

Sully gave him a sour look, "Are you sure, my love?"

He gave an awkward smile, "No, sorry."

Sully smiled back at him and Achilles quickly turned away, "So you say this room is filled with family?" Achilles nodded hard. Sully kept stroking the wolf, "All I see is a room filled with dead people."

"Dude, there already are…"

Sully spoke quickly before Slim Pickings could again, "I mean *more* dead people"

Slim Pickings looked at Cameo, confused.

"She means us," Cameo said.

"Oh, I get it, dude."

"Don't do this," Achilles felt his stomach twist with nerves.

She flicked her hand and the wolf ran forward, attacking the animals. All of the infected surged towards the animal students. Achilles punched one in the face and then smashed it in with an iron bar. He backed away into the wall of animals, safe for a while; the room was massive but the infected were moving in closer.

As the infected stormed in, Lacy cracked her forehead against one of them, her vicious head butt sent the zombie creature sprawling onto the ground, and she battered its head in with her bar and swung it around viciously. There was a hardness in her eyes; she wasn't going to let anything come between her and her friends. Lacy delivered blow after blow to the infected, screaming like a wild woman, the others took note and started fighting back. Achilles bobbed and weaved his way through them with his iron bar breaking heads open as he did so, while Cameo was getting used to her otter claws, slashing away at the infected. She managed three or four steps forward before she was finally driven back, she liked the feeling and attacked harder on her return.

Sully urged her walking dead forward without participating in battle herself. She looked at her former friends battling side by side with the genetically engineered animal students and a dinosaur ripping her army to shreds.

Her mouth twisted as the students were holding their own against her dead, her side were losing, "I WILL ASK YOU AGAIN, ACHILLES, THIS FIGHT CAN END IF YOU COME WITH ME NOW."

Aphrodite padded up to Achilles and sat right beside him, looking straight at Sully, "I have no words for how much I loathe you, even though I like your style, but we've won darling, so be a good girl and call off your nasty dead people for us."

Sully smiled, "I like you, you're funny, be my pet, come with me and help rule the galaxy and also sit on my bed late at night and in the morning and lick my face, I want you to love me as Achilles doesn't."

Aphrodite scratched herself and gave a slight show of her fangs, "As tempting as that seems darling, I'm going to see how things pan out with these nerds, plus there's the whole thing of you being insane and dead."

Sully gave a faint laugh, "You think you've won do you?" She put her fingers to her mouth and whistled hard. The piercing sound bounced around the room followed by silence, "You had your chance," Sully whispered. On Sully's signal, a mass of the infected stormed through the broken doors.

Her eyes flashed a rage fire as they leapt and bounded towards Achilles and the others. They gave an accompanying howl, which was more monstrous than anything the animal students had heard before. They covered their ears with webbed hands, hooves, feathers, anything to block out the horrific sound. There was nowhere left to run, and they knew they were all going to die so they crouched down to the ground.

Achilles gave Lacy a long, glazed look, she returned with a dented smile and held out her hand. He took it and offered his free hand to Slim Pickings who did the same to Cameo until all of the remaining animal students were holding hands, hoping for a quick death from the infected. They huddled together, some crying, others silent in defeat. They all closed their eyes and gripped hands harder.

Slim Pickings wondered about his sister for a moment, knowing that he would never see her again, the giant man-shark began to close his eyes like the others, "Later dudes."

Before his eyelids closed, a blue light flickered high up from the ceiling. Slim Pickings blinked as he tried to get the bizarre blue light into focus. The light was darting all over the ceiling and glowing brighter by the second, "GUYS, I THINK YOU BETTER TAKE A LOOK AT THIS."

Everybody opened their eyes immediately, knowing if Slim Pickings hadn't used 'Dude' something was very important. The ceiling was lit with disorienting colours, they flashed and flickered and it was quite a light show. It had stopped the infected in their tracks as they too were fascinated by the many colours on the ceiling.

Three blue flashes of lightning illuminated the room and suddenly it wasn't just occupied by the infected. Suddenly a huge black hole opened in the ceiling, the blue lightning bolts crackled and then roared around the room as the whirling hole grew bigger. It was a massive cavern of a hole and started to spread quickly like a wave of darkness.

"What the hell is going on?" a bemused Achilles asked Lacy.

"God knows," was her reply, shading her eyes from the blinding blue light.

Another massive flash of lightning, right in front of them made everybody look to the ground. When they opened their eyes, the lightning had stopped, and some massive buildings were now in front of them. As the energy swirl dissipated, it looked like an old church had miraculously appeared. The building seemed to be completely intact and it sat in the middle of the room; the other building was different, it had been split perfectly in half. It pressed hard against the side of the ship and the walls began to creak; if they were to break, the whole student community, animal and infected would be sucked out in to space.

Next to the church was a primitive construct made of rickety wood with some strangely-shaped blocks in the centre. An axe lay blood-stained to the side.

Lacy's eyes widened when she realised there were people next to the wood construct. A girl in a strange-looking dress had a big sack and tried to keep it safe, the sack appeared to be bleeding as the crying girl pulled it closer to her. More people appeared from the church wearing strange garments and they all started to scream as well.

The space ship rocked slightly, the weight of the church and other building was taking effect, and nobody could imagine in their wildest nightmares what would happen if the ship crashed, and it seemed that was about to happen.

From the wooden tower, a female figure stunned everybody by gently rising to the ceiling, blue smoke swirled around as she floated to the church roof. She turned her head nervously and then started to descend back down to the floor with ease.

Achilles' heart pounded when he saw the face of the apparent magician. She had long blonde hair and a red, vintage, out-dated dress. Her terrified eyes shot left to right as she took in her new surroundings. As she reached the ground, she ran over to the girl with the sack and hugged her tightly. The infected heads lolled over and studied the new being and then ran to attack.

"NO!" the girl screamed. Her hands glowed blue and she shot a bolt of pure plasma fire at the first infected student running towards her, which took off its head easily.

"Woah!" all the college kids gasped and shared baffled looks. As more infected rushed in, the girl in the red dress took to the air, making a massive booming sound as she flew up.

"This is awesome!" Poxon grinned, completely forgetting about the oncoming horde; he was transfixed by the flying girl. A blur of red and blue came swooping in from above and more plasma blasts came from her hands, striking with extreme accuracy at the infected.

She didn't know what these creatures were, and she felt even more confused and scared when she saw the mixture of teenagers, bizarre-looking animals and monsters in the corner of the room. They frightened her just as much as the ones who were running towards them, but the ones in the corner were holding hands and cowering. She didn't know if they were praying, but they weren't going to die, not if she could help it.

She descended down to head level and knocked some more heads clean off the necks of the infected with her powerful flight.

Lacy saw the tide was turning in their favour, and turned around to the others, "Ok, I give up, this day can't get any weirder. I have no idea who that crazy flying girl is, but she is helping us so let's give her a hand." Lacy stood up and reached for her iron bar, shaking her head as the flying girl soared above them, "Never taking drugs again I swear." A grin spread across her face as she raced towards the ruined buildings inside the ship. She swung her bar against the face of someone who was already missing their lower lip, and the rest of their head fell apart. Still weak and scared, the animals put their fears away as they watched the girl in red take down the enemy. They got to their feet and followed Lacy into battle. The ship was unsteady now with the added weight of the large church, and began to slightly tip to one side.

The flying girl looked to the ground in between, shooting plasma blasts. She saw that the scary looking animals were helping her and then she thought back to what a friend had once said about 'Never judging a book by its cover' and supporting those who were a little bit different, weird and a little bit strange.

Her deadly plasma beams were wiping out the infected and the strange looking animal people were doing their part too. The girl with the sack was a frightened bystander now; she stayed by the wooden construct, huddled with the leaking bloody bag.

Sully could only watch as her army of the dead were being wiped out by this remarkable flying being. She, like everybody else, couldn't believe her eyes and shook her head in wonderment as the girl streaked across the giant room.

Sully's dream of finally getting Achilles to love her was blowing up in her face and she hid inside the church to watch from a distance.

Pulse blasts from the girl in the air had all but levelled the infected; the ones which were left were mesmerized by her light show. The girl noticed this and concentrated hard to make some fireworks spin out of the room through the gaping hole where the main door used to be.

The infected spun around and chased after the dancing light away from the animal students. The flying girl landed quietly next to the crying girl with the sack.

Immie backed away fearfully as Kitty Howard dampened her powers and went to comfort her. Kitty cradled her and the sack containing the heads of Jane and Silo. They didn't speak, just held each other and Kitty started to cry too.

Lacy motioned to Slim Pickings and Eric to hang back for a bit and then motioned to Poxon and Achilles to come with her. The trio walked up to the two girls in strange dresses huddled on the floor. Kitty's eyes looked them up and down, still fearful even though she had witnessed them fight on her side. Her eyes locked onto the frame of Achilles as he stepped forward. Poxon's eyes were fixed onto Immie.

As Achilles stood over her, Kitty stood up with purpose and looked him in the eyes. She remembered what Silo had said after a successful training session. She was scared. She didn't know where her power had taken Immie and herself. She was powerful after teleporting the church, half the castle and the execution scaffold to this strange place. Kitty closed her eyes, hoped and lifted her hand in the air, "Hi five?"

Achilles looked to Lacy and Poxon and then grinned, "Fuck yeah."

He slapped Kitty hard on the hand followed by Poxon and Lacy.

"So you can understand the words we are saying?" Poxon asked.

"Yes, your grace."

"Your grace?" Poxon said nervously.

"I'm sorry, I meant, sir?"

Lacy bit her lip with concern, "I've seen a lot of strange shit today, so this doesn't surprise me, what the hell are you? Who are you?" Before Kitty could answer, the deluge of questions began, "How can you fly?"

"What planet are you from?"

"How can you shoot fire from your hands?"

"How did those buildings get here?"

"Can you save us?"

"Got a boyfriend?"

Aphrodite stepped forward and freaked Kitty out even more as she opened her mouth.

"Love your hair."

The talking wolf was enough, Kitty was trembling already but now she was terrified.

She began hyperventilating.

"Ok no more questions guys," Lacy said to the group. She bent down next to Kitty, giving an awkward smile to Immie.

"Take your time and just breathe slowly, breathe like me."

Kitty mirrored Lacy's breathing technique but her panic was still evident, "My lady, you have a terrifying wolf that can talk amongst you, what witchcraft is this?"

"That's Aphrodite. She was human but got turned into a wolf by witchcraft as you say; she's a bitch, but she's our bitch and won't hurt you. But, speaking of witchcraft, you just suddenly appeared in our ship with a church and half a castle I think? Plus, you can fly and shoot laser bolts from your hands, so if anybody deserves an explanation it's us."

"Does she not frighten you, my lady? The beast who can talk like a woman?"

Lacy pointed to the animal students behind her.

"Take a look in front of you, all these strange-looking animal beasts speak like women and men and will be labelled as freaks when we return home, but they have fought alongside me, protected me and they are my friends and I'm sure as hell going to protect them should they need it, you should—"

"Never judge a book by its cover," Kitty finished, "My lady you're right and I'm sorry, I was taught better by my mentor."

Kitty looked at Achilles, "My grace, my mentor was a black person as well by the way, as are you."

Achilles shot a confused look back, "Thanks for letting me know," he replied with slight sarcasm.

Kitty curtsied as his tone went over her head, "You're most welcome, your grace." She took a little breath, "My name is Katherine Howard, a Queen of a far-away land but originally from the planet Rayash and now living on a planet that I don't know the name of, Earth I think? Not sure which one as I'm told there are many. I'm not a witch, I'm a sorceress, a Vanisher apprentice to my lady Silo, her head is in that bag. I can teleport and shoot class ten plasma beams from my hands and eyes. This girl is Immie, my lady-in-waiting." Kitty laughed in her nervousness, "I left my King on our wedding day after he had my best friend killed and I teleported away." Kitty then broke down again, "I pray for forgiveness for my sins, I pray for my lady Immie as she does not know where we are, none of us do." She paused and thought over her next words, "We are scared shitless. Are they the right words to say, my lady?"

"Good enough," Lacy sighed and stopped, "Did you say the head of your teacher is in that bag?"

"Yes, my lady."

Lacy tried to pick out Dallas from the crowd, "Wrong teacher," she huffed, "This day can't get any weirder," she added.

Poxon snaked in between the girls, "You are from Earth? Well so are we and you say there is more than one?"

"Apparently so, your grace."

"Fascinating...and you can teleport, transferring energy from one point to another without touching the space between those two said points."

Kitty's voice was trying to be steady, "Yes, your grace. I was told by my mentor that I'm a sorceress who has the ability to teleport myself and others through displacing alternate dimensions through my will and reappearing in other locations."

"How many people can you teleport at one time?"

"Well, in my training I only teleported one person, my mentor, your grace."

Poxon pointed to the church, half the castle and the execution tower, "I think you do yourself a disservice."

"Yes, your Grace, I've never done that before, my powers are emotion-led, so the more upset or angry I get, the further I can teleport and the more..." Her voice trailed away, "People." Kitty threw a shocked look at Poxon, "They tricked me."

"Who are you talking about?" Poxon asked.

Before Kitty could answer, a pulse blast exploded from the wooden execution tower which everybody had ignored, it was fired from a rifle and the compression blast struck Kitty directly in the chest, sending her flying into the animals gathered behind her. Two figures jumped down from the block and removed their guard outfit and cloak respectively. Mason and Orion strode purposely towards the animal students, unconcerned by their appearance. They were now wearing full body armour, "I believe she was talking about us." Mason kept on walking, with his rifle still smoking.

"She's finally figured out how her power works and we got her so mad."

"Watching her best friend's head fly from the chopping block pretty much did it." Mason loved the sound of his own voice, "We've travelled thousands of miles to find this girl and now we will be taking her and be on our way if you don't mind."

Lacy had slight contempt for the newcomers, "Well actually we do mind as this girl has just saved our lives and you've just shot her."

"I didn't shoot to kill, I just stunned her, I need her alive," Mason said, failing to holster his rifle. The ship juddered to the left and began to slowly descend.

Lacy turned around sharply, "People have been appearing and disappearing from this ship all day, it's been a strange one at that, but I don't take kindly to giving up girls to men who have just shot them."

Mason wasn't stopping, "Right, I'm going to change the terms, give me the girl now and I'll let you live."

Orion pulled up his number two, he was tired, winded and weary, "What are you talking about? We didn't come here to kill children."

"We already have, you fool," Mason still held his rifle.

"Watch your voice, lieutenant, I am still your commanding officer."

Mason's face twisted with contempt, "That doesn't mean anything here, we're not on Rayash now, I've led this mission to find the girl, not you."

"I mean it, soldier," Orion's brow was furrowed.

"You do know I killed Thomas Culpepper."

"You said it was all down to the King," Orion looked up, alarmed.

"I sliced his head off at the cart and kept it to put on the pike for dramatic effect. Do you really think that backwater dumb idiot King would have hired the boy his Queen had a crush on, unless I suggested it?"

"YOU DID WHAT?" Orion shouted.

Lacy whispered to Aphrodite and backed away, "This doesn't sound good."

"I know darling, it sounds great, they are so going to fight."

Lacy rolled her eyes and slipped away to check on the stunned Kitty. Orion stood close to Mason, "You killed that boy, I thought it was all down to the King?"

"Nope, all me" Mason beamed.

"Why did you do it?"

"It was clear that the girl had feelings for him, so I used him to get her to the palace. The more Thomas asked about Katherine, the more the King grew more jealous and wanted him dead, all too easy. Plus, seeing Thomas dead helped with Katherine's rage and increased her powers."

Orion's face was closed and dry.

"If you killed Thomas earlier at the cart, how could he appear again at the palace, I saw him there."

"Did you really see him though?"

Mason's grin was so evil it sent a chill down Orion's spine, "The girl isn't the only one here with abilities."

Mason slowly waved his hand in front of his face, it rippled like stone dropped into a pond and then another face was in its place, Thomas Culpepper, "Ta-da!"

Orion held his stomach as it churned with sickness, he stumbled backwards and stuttered.

"One of them?"

Mason turned to Orion with a scowl, "I cannot believe that you are my husband, I cannot believe that I'm married to someone so stupid."

Orion felt his throat constricting and rocked to his left side, "What?"

"You know that on Rayash, the men wear their wedding rings on their right hand and the women wear theirs on the left?" Mason said. Orion was too shocked to answer. Mason held up his left hand and wriggled his index finger in front of Orion, "All this time and you didn't notice?"

Orion's eyes went soft.

"One more trick."

Mason did the same face reveal as before like Thomas Culpepper, but instead one more familiar, "Hello my love."

The face rippled again and in the place of Mason, Orion saw Bailey, his wife. This time the whole body changed, not just the face. Orion couldn't hold the contents of his stomach in anymore and threw up to his side. He wiped his mouth and looked at his wife, "Where is Mason?"

"Is that all you have to say to me? Not 'I missed you' or even 'I love you'."

"WHERE IS HE?!"

Bailey raised a finely-plucked eyebrow to her husband, "Since you asked so nicely I will tell you: he's dead."

"WHAT?!"

"When you ambushed me on that rocky planet and you snapped my neck? You actually snapped Mason's."

"No!" there was a slight panic in Orion's voice.

"Yeah, you should have known that marrying a sorceress would probably come back to bite you on the arse, I'm a shape-changer, you idiot!"

Orion felt that everything he knew was being ripped away from him, "So all that time we travelled together, all the words I said to Mason about how I felt about my wife, that was you?"

"Yep, plus the person who fired that rifle back on Rayash who killed that young private? That was me as well, I needed to make the men uneasy and frightened. They followed you into battle, but the nerves were already beginning to shred."

"You blew up all my men."

"Yes, I did and took the place of Mason, easy life."

Orion couldn't believe what he was hearing, "Wait a minute, you had Silo killed, your own apprentice, your best friend."

Bailey was revelling in her storytelling role, "Yes, now that was the hard part, truly it was but she lied to me, she had lied all along."

There was disgust now in Orion's voice, "What are you talking about?"

"Here's the thing, lover: the chosen child from Rayash, the saviour of our planet, the girl who will teleport our planet to safety from our dying sun, the one who Silo hid from you and fled…"

"YES, I GET IT," Orion snapped.

"There were two."

"Yeah, I know, Silo and the baby Katherine."

"No, two babies."

"What do you mean?"

"God, is it any wonder why I left you?" Bailey sighed.

"Bags packed isn't leaving, you have to walk through the front door first and get the rest of your stuff, which you didn't do."

"Couldn't do as you changed the locks." Bailey calmed down and ignored him.

"Look, Kozak and Tashar had twin girls. The prophecy was that one girl would have the power to teleport, and with proper use of her power she would be able to teleport almost anything she wanted, people, cities or planets. Maybe killing her in the process, but that's beside the point. The other girl would grow up having the power to jump anywhere in time, so imagine if you knew one of your daughters could potentially have the power to teleport anything she wanted and the other could go anywhere in time?"

"Then they could be the most powerful creatures in the universe," Orion mumbled.

"Wow! The penny finally drops."

Orion's eyebrows kept lowering, making his forehead crease, "So if you were protecting the family from me, why didn't they tell you about their other child? Why tell your apprentice and not you? They must have known your heart is happy in betrayal."

"Shut up," Bailey snapped.

"No, they must have seen something dark in you, something which made them put the lives of their newborn daughters with a teenage midwife sorceress."

Orion circled around his wife, "What did they see? They must have seen something, it must have been the prophecy or the...?"

Orion gulped with realisation, "Shadow hole."

"I SAID SHUT UP!"

Bailey's fist flew hard and fast, connecting with Orion's chin. The General wiped the blood from his mouth and smiled "You were the one who came back through the shadow hole, you were the one whose mind was broken."

"YES! IT WAS ME! I STEPPED THROUGH THE SHADOW HOLE AND CAME BACK OUT WITH SO MUCH MORE! I HAVE SEEN THE FUTURE, I HAVE SEEN WHAT I WILL BECOME AND IT'S GLORIOUS!"

Lacy walked cautiously closer to Orion, "That's your wife?"

"Yep, we really should have had counselling."

"You do know this ship is starting to drop right? What with us now carrying a church and half a castle. Do whatever it takes, talk her round."

Bailey heard Lacy, her eyes flicked over to her, "You stupid little girl, talk me round? Shall I tell you what I've seen?"

"Yeah, sure, it's not like this ship is going to crash anytime soon."

Orion saw the look of pure evil in Bailey's eyes, "Why Bailey?"

"I fell into a shadow hole when I was still trying to master the art of teleporting. I was a teenager, what would have been seconds in this world was years in the shadow hole, the future showed me and two teenage girls ruling the galaxy, my two teenage nieces."

"Your nieces?" asked Orion.

"How do you know that?"

"They called me 'Auntie'. They called me by my true name Anne Boleyn Bailey. Look, don't grow impatient with me lover, I'll explain. Tashar was my sister, I saw the future in the shadow hole and saw another reality, one where I was a Queen, I was the ruler. The girls and I had so much power, planets crumbled before us, cities and governments did what we demanded or perish. I lived a life of decadence, but then the shadow hole reappeared and dragged me back. I was gone away from Rayash for ten minutes, TEN MINUTES! I HAD A LIFETIME OF POWER SNATCHED AWAY FROM ME IN A TEABREAK! So, then I knew what had to be done."

Lacy felt the need to remind them again about the ship's descent, her finger pointing downwards, both Bailey and Orion ignored her.

"So, I came back out and nobody believed what I had seen. They thought I was insane and ignored me, not even my own sister thought this to be true. Nothing happened in years so I kept up my sorcery along with midwifery, teaching both to students, until Tashar became pregnant and our sun began to die. That was the sign. She knew this too and got my own apprentice, Silo, to mask one of the girls from me, so I thought she was just carrying one child when it was in fact two."

Orion's mind slammed into reverse, "So you had no intention of taking the girl for the good of the planet, the prophecy said that a child would save us? Teleport our planet away from danger."

Bailey's eyes were glued to her husband, "I don't give a shit about the planet Rayash, it could burn for all I care. I just wanted the girl to take and raise myself and then track down her sister Kimberley Watson."

Aphrodite's eager ears pricked up, "Wait, did you say Kimberley Watson?"

Bailey smiled in amusement, "Oh, a talking wolf, how quaint, I sense that you have an ulterior motive whilst hanging out with these children, believe me, treachery knows treachery."

"If you can turn me back to a human, I would hang on your every word, if not, do me a favour darling and shut up, right, Kimberley Watson is dead, the skank blew herself up trying to escape prison years ago, using little energy balls as time bombs."

"No, you dozy cow wolf: those balls weren't exploding time bombs with fire and stuff, they were *literal* bombs of time."

Aphrodite considered using her claws on the sorceress, but relented, "What?"

"When she exploded, she was sent hurtling through time. She didn't die, she is just lost, lost in time."

Aphrodite sighed, "Is there any way I can get rid of that Kimberley bitch?"

Orion took over, feeling stupid, "So you used me and everybody."

"Pretty much," Bailey answered quickly, "Tashar and Silo knew my motives and hid Kimberley from me. I think Tobin was a distraction, helping her cousin Silo." Bailey paused, "Little bitch. Anyway, Silo went into the pod with baby Katherine, whilst another lone rocket with Kimberley was launched elsewhere, cloaked by my sister and apprentice. They knew what was going to happen, so I had to pretend that I wanted to keep the baby safe, but in all fairness…"

"You just wanted her for yourself," Orion finished her sentence.

"Are we going to go through this again?" Bailey sighed.

"Yes, I used you to track down Katherine. Yes, I had Silo killed. Yes, I knew we would end up on this ship.

And yes, I am going to find Kimberley and we will rule the galaxy."

Aphrodite cut to the chase, "Why is everybody intent on ruling the galaxy? It's like buses, you wait for one and then two nut bags turn up at once." She paused to lick herself, "Ridiculous really."

Bailey picked at her mouth, carefully trying to keep her lipstick perfect. She aimed her weapon at Aphrodite, "I need Katherine alive, but I don't need you."

Aphrodite simply collapsed on to the floor in a subservient manner, laying on her back with her feet in the air.

"Stop being so cute," huffed Bailey, "Shame you're going to die when this ship crashes."

The wolf rolled over and then got to her feet with her tail wagging hard. She stood on her hind legs and offered out a paw to Bailey, who laughed out loud.

"That's quite sad. I thought you were stronger than that, but here you are begging like the bitch you are."

Aphrodite rolled to her feet and began licking her front paws, "I wasn't begging, just stalling actually, darling."

"Stalling for what?"

A neat line of pulse fire zipped over Aphrodite and hit Bailey square in the chest, which sent her flipping through the air like a trained gymnast, landing hard on the ground. Bailey coughed hard, unable to breathe, and gasped for air as she looked up at her assailant.

"Me." Kitty was up and spoke with purpose, her hand still glowing blue from the blast she had fired, "That was for my poor lady Jane."

Bailey held got to her feet, still wheezing and in pain, "You must have felt a lot for her. You do know I killed Silo as well?"

"Don't you dare speak her name, you have no right after what you did."

"So, what are you going to do to me then, child? How will you avenge Silo?"

Both of Kitty's hands glowed blue now, "Believe me my lady, you will know when I'm ready."

The massive shapes of the church and castle started to shift and lean against the side of the ship. Everybody tumbled to the ground and rolled around on the floor, frantically trying to get back on their feet. The ship dipped more and continued its descent to the planet below. It was like a theme park ride as the ship gained speed as it dipped from the sky. The zoo ship *Utopia* couldn't hold the weight of the teleported castle and church and maintain full power at the same time. As the church began to crumble, internal explosions rocked the ship.

Kitty brushed the dirt from her wedding dress and was ready for battle. Bailey acknowledged the young Queen's stance.

"There's no point in fighting me, young lady, you cannot defeat me. Your new friends will die when the ship crashes, join me and we will find your sister and all of us will rule."

Before Kitty could answer, the ship dropped again. Despite struggling through the pain in her side and the confusion of where she was, Kitty managed to look sharply at Bailey, "You must think me a fool, my lady, if you ever believed I would help you destroy so many lives." Kitty ran to Immie, who was still in shock, and stooped to hold her hand, "We are leaving now."

She shouted to Lacy and the animal students, "My lady, you fought bravely to help me, and you have my beautiful thanks. I do not know where you are from, but I will teleport you all to safety."

Kitty gave a respectful look to Lacy and closed her eyes to concentrate on teleporting. When she opened them again, she was still on the ship, "Something's happening, it's not working!"

"You silly girl," Bailey shook her head with a wry smile, "You've just teleported two massive buildings and a useless execution tower halfway across the galaxy, your power needs to recharge, like a battery."

"Like a what?" Kitty replied.

"Doesn't matter," huffed Bailey, "That's why I knew you'd teleport here onto this ship. The planet below is where she was raised, so we're getting close. Your sister and you share a signature power trail every time you use your 'gift'. It was how I found you and I'm guessing how Silo found you too. We're all sorceresses and can track one another when they are sort of near. To find Kimberley we need a massive boost of kinetic energy, which we will get when the ship crashes. When I hold on to you, the charge will teleport us right to Kimberley, wherever she is in the timeline; the raw energy from this crash will be immeasurable and then we can begin to rule as a family."

"What about everybody else?" Kitty asked.

"Everybody else on this ship will die," smirked Bailey.

"Wrong answer."

Kitty launched another plasma burst at Bailey, but the elder sorceress anticipated the attack and deflected the blast with an energy shield, "You're not very clever, are you? Did Silo teach you anything at all?"

Kitty threw her hands together outstretched into a massive plasma clap and the results sent a massive shock wave through the ship and Bailey, sending her crashing into the wall.

"One or two things, my lady."

Bailey wasn't moving and Lacy took this as a chance to try and find out how would they escape. She looked to her brother, her tone was serious with an ounce of doubt, "Are we getting out of here?"

The whole room looked to Poxon for a hopeful reply, "The impact won't destroy the planet when we hit, we're not as high as an asteroid crashing, but the impact will cause major damage to Olympia and surrounding cities."

"Heffernan City?" Achilles asked.

"Yeah, pretty much everything will be destroyed. We're screwed, ladies and gentlemen and animal people."

The battle between Bailey and Kitty intensified, each using different magical powers to defeat the other. Kitty was holding her own against the person who trained her own mentor.

Orion looked sharply on at his wife fighting Kitty and whispered to himself, "Goodbye my beloved Rayash, I failed you. I just wanted to save my people, my planet." The glare he gave Bailey grew harder with hatred as he aimed his rifle to her, "Mum never liked you anyway."

With a roar of pure anger Orion unleashed a volley of laser fire from his rifle. Bailey deflected the blasts, but was still fighting Kitty, and with Orion now entering the fray, she was struggling. The animal students could stand back no more and ran past Lacy and Poxon, trying to help Kitty fight.

Achilles cleared his throat as he observed the massive battle in front of him. He held his stomach as the ship swayed again, and looked at Lacy.

"Not the day we planned for on this college trip, eh? Still think we're on drugs?"

Lacy wiped her nose, she looked bemused, "No, I think this is real, we're going to die soon."

"I had a date with Sayles, I was looking forward to that."

"Seeing as she's dead and you're next? Probably not a good thing to look forward to."

Achilles grinned and gave his old friend a hug, "We still aim low and miss in life, don't we? Still didn't find our parents."

Lacy swallowed swiftly, "Failing for us is just a drop in the ocean."

Poxon cut in quickly, "What did you say?"

"Just a drop in the ocean?" Lacy repeated.

"THAT'S IT!" Poxon yelled.

"If we can change the ship's trajectory into the ocean instead of the cities we would save millions of lives. Ok, there would be major flooding throughout and we still would die, but it means our homes would be slightly flooded, but still standing."

Lacy's eyes remained on her brother, "Can you do it?"

"Maybe I can patch into the pilot's flight path, see if I can divert the ship from our home."

"Why couldn't you do that earlier?" asked Achilles.

"I'm still learning, dickhead." Poxon took a deep breath after swearing and ran back to the computer terminal, dodging the fire fight above his head.

"I KNOW IT! I KNOW IT!" he cried, "I don't need to be in the cockpit, I can do it from here."

Poxon bashed himself over the head to remind himself of his forgetfulness and then frantically started swiping the screens on the console, tapping the onscreen keyboard as if his life depended on it, which it did.

"I said can you do it?" Lacy repeated.

"Quiet," he shushed, "Need to really concentrate."

It was hard to ignore the battle and Poxon kept switching looks to Kitty and back to the screen.

"HURRY!" Lacy shouted.

"I KNOW!" her brother yelled.

"FASTER!"

This time Poxon ignored her and spoke into the small speaker in the top left corner of the console, "Security code 56911491 emergency override transfer full ship control to console number 2991."

Poxon stood back from the console and waved his fists at his side in panic, "Come on!"

The console screen suddenly changed colour and the computerised voice of the ship's computer spoke, *"Status...searching." "Status...searching." "Status... searching."*

"COME ON!" Poxon shouted and bashed the screen with his hands.

"Security code 56911491 accepted, cockpit deactivated, cockpit deactivated."

"YES!" Poxon screamed. He spoke into the terminal again, "Entering new coordinates 0791."

The computer voice spoke again, *"Coordinate details accepted."* Poxon looked to the battle between Kitty and Bailey and breathed hard.

"What did you do?" asked Lacy.

"I changed the ship's coordinates, we're crashing in the ocean, not land."

Aphrodite ran up to him, scaring the teenager with her teeth baring. She stumbled on four feet as the ship rocked again, "So why can't you stop the ship completely, you little nerd?"

"We're about to go into free fall, can't stop the speed but can alter the direction."

"So, we're still going to die?" Achilles asked.

"I'm afraid so," was the reply from Poxon.

"WELL DO SOMETHING ELSE!" screamed Achilles.

Poxon gritted his teeth as the ship lurched and continued its drop, "I'M TRYING!"

Aphrodite was finding it hard to keep her balance as the ship was plummeting, "If you two can stop arguing like two drunks in a late-night chicken takeaway shop we can try to press on, or has that common-sense horse already bolted?"

"What did you say?" asked Poxon.

"Let me guess, you've had another epiphany moment?" Aphrodite asked.

"Yep, horses bolting. It may be a way out of here."

A barrage of laser fire from Orion's gun blasted Bailey's stomach. She fell to the floor and Kitty followed up with a storm of plasma bolts. A bat-like student flapped to the air and unleashed a sonic cry, the deafening force made everyone put their hands on their ears as the blast pushed Bailey back towards the wall. In a blur of motion. Bailey teleported from the ground to the batgirl and threw her to the floor, then continued with her defensive manner deflected laser bolts from Orion and Kitty. Lacy ducked her head as more flying animals took to the air, hammering Bailey with bits of debris from the ship's walls. She shouted to her brother, "WHAT DID YOU SAY ABOUT A WAY OUT OF HERE?"

Poxon was still on the computer console, his eyes concentrating heavily on the screen.

Immie cleared her head and tore off her heavy wedding dress gear and stood by his side.

"Your Grace, we are not safe enough, I know not who you are or where I am? But my good lady is fighting for her life, how may I be of assistance?"

Poxon lifted Immie's hand to the screen and placed her thumb on the corner, "Just keep pressing here," he said. His stomach was in turns, he wished his best friend Harley was here to see how close he was to a beautiful girl, he looked to Lacy.

"I saw some horses with wings, Pegasus I think they are called? If they are uninfected, maybe we can use them to fly out of here."

"WHAT?! RIDE HORSES WITH WINGS?!" Lacy yelled.

"Yeah, or you could stay and die." Poxon's eyes bored into his sister as she looked around the sinking ship and recognised her error.

"Are they close by, man?" Achilles asked.

"Let me look." Poxon swiped the screen again, standing closer to Immie; her hands were caked in blood, she looked terrified yet stunning.

The screen showed a holographic schematic that showed every animal pen of the *Utopia*, dozens of green dots appeared in the projection but many more glowed red, "Everything with a heartbeat glows green. Any person or animal who is dead lights up red but unfortunately the infected, as they have a virus but aren't technically dead, will light up green as well, so it's hard to tell who's who."

Poxon leaned forward, "Ok! Here we are, containment pen 2144."

"Are they still in there?"

Whipping his head back round to Achilles, Poxon gulped, "I'm not sure."

Poxon swiped the screen again, hoping to see a sign of life or movement. He selected the camera which automatically panned left to right slowly.

"COME ON!" Achilles yelled impatiently.

"Wait, hold on." Poxon examined the screen, his eyes squinted.

"YES!" he cried as green dots darted everywhere.

"They're here, loads of them."

"Are they infected?"

Poxon's fingers moved across the screen, trying hard to mask his panic.

"I don't know, but it's our only chance," he replied to Lacy.

The battle between Bailey, Kitty, Orion and the students wasn't helping the ship as it couldn't contain their fire fight along with the weight of the added buildings. Poxon finally withdrew his hands slowly from the console, "Sully didn't release them, I've no idea why not, but I'm grateful as hell."

"Can we still make it to them?" Lacy asked.

Poxon stayed away from the console but closed his eyes to recollect the horses' location. As he thought, a plasma blast from Bailey ripped into the ship's hull, making it rock and everyone fell to the ground heavily. Lacy checked her nose, it was bleeding, but she ignored it.

"This ship is going to crash soon, isn't it? Really, how much time do we have?"

She was looking directly at Poxon who was blinking rapidly as he stood to his feet, as if still dazed from the fall, "Judging by the extra weight we have and structural damage and computer damage and…" Looks of impatience were exchanged among the whole gathering of college students and Poxon changed his approach of speech, "The ship is about to crash into the ocean in thirty minutes, killing us all." He took the hand of Immie who had started crying again, "I can get us out of here in twenty minutes. Let's go."

With Immie still in tow Poxon ran back to the battling animal students and yelled with determined authority, "STUDENTS! WE ARE LEAVING!!"

Immie looked at Kitty who was now struggling with Bailey as the students bailed out and followed Poxon, "What about my lady?"

Poxon shielded his eyes from the glare of the plasma fight, "She will find us, I'm sure of it."

Poxon tried to lead but Immie resisted, dragging her feet, "My King has married the most beautiful woman in the land, she could have wanted for nothing, lived a life of luxury, but she didn't want that and now she stands before me in another world fighting a witch for the honour of her dead friend."

"What are you trying to say?" asked Poxon.

"I'm scared, your grace, and ashamed for being so."

Poxon pulled her close and locked his lips with hers, his tongue fumbled clumsily in her mouth as he held Immie tight.

"UNHAND ME, YOU SNAKE!" she screamed. She pulled away Poxon's hands and slapped him firmly in his face, "HOW DARE YOU, SIR!" she spat.

Poxon rubbed his cheek and looked at his watch, "Are you confused?"

"YES!"

"Scared?"

Immie paused, "YES!"

"Shit, it didn't work," he sighed.

Poxon thought about the same tactic Lacy had used on him, trying to remember her exact words and obviously he had messed up.

"Good, job done. Let's just get the hell out of here. Fifteen minutes."

"Your actions are very strange, sir. Do you have jester blood in you?"

"Nope," came Poxon's quick reply.

Immie thought about a line she had heard Kitty say after talking to her mentor Silo, she tried hard to remember it until it finally came to her.

"Well, you could have fooled me."

"We have a dinosaur, Poxon, how the hell are we going to get it on a flying horse?"

Poxon rubbed his eyes in exasperation as he tried to run, "I don't know Lacy, maybe lay it over two horses? I don't have time for this."

"Just leave it here to die, it did kill two of our best friends or did you forget that?" Achilles snapped.

Dallas heard everything, and came running from behind with Aphrodite and Cameo, "If my boy doesn't make it out of here, then there is no way I'm turning you guys back to humans."

Cameo's otter eyes looked to Aphrodite in frustration as they both ran and feared the worst, "Don't worry, darling, we'll get your little pet out of here, even if it kills us." She looked to the animal students behind her, "More them obviously, I'm not dying for anyone."

Plasma explosions erupted all around them as the students made their way to the bigger hole in the door.

Kitty was fighting to maintain her balance with Bailey, the blasts ricocheted all over the room. Orion had taken up a defensive position and still tried hard to fight his wife, his eyes focused on the tired and battered frame of Kitty. The young girl he had travelled so far to find and the one he had hoped would save his planet, taking her back to Rayash to teleport it away.

He looked at what she had done, teleporting to a world across the galaxy to avenge her friend, fighting a sorceress clearly more powerful than her to protect some kids she didn't know. He couldn't take her back to die, it would be dishonourable for a general to do such a thing.

As Kitty deflected yet another plasma bolt from Bailey and replied with one of her own, Orion saw his chance to speak, "I'm sorry, Katherine."

She could only allow a quick glance, "What?"

"I'm sorry for hunting you, I'm sorry for making these last few months terrible, you didn't need to suffer like this."

Kitty increased her energy shield to allow a moment's respite.

"Did my good lady Silo need to suffer? Did she need to suffer as you hounded us around the country? Did she need to suffer as she never had a full night's sleep without fear? Did she need to suffer as her head left her body?!"

Orion looked wearily around at the fleeing animal students and the creaking body of the ship, he saw his wife about to conjure up another plasma bolt and he knew this was his chance.

"No, but I can make things right, drop your shield."

"Your grace?" Kitty asked.

"Just do it."

As Kitty released her magic, Orion sprung forward yelling an insane battle cry, unleashing all the firepower and energy he had left. He threw assault grenades at Bailey and kept firing his rounds at her. Thoughts of honour and fair play had long left his mind as his rage exploded on how he had been duped for so long by his wife.

His assault had caught her off guard, yet Bailey back-flipped neatly and retaliated with a killing strike of her own. The plasma blast was so strong, it took him easily off his feet and slammed him into a wall, he didn't move after that.

Before Kitty could see to him, Bailey was right behind her. She spun the startled teenager around, grabbed her around the throat and lifted her off her feet. Bailey's hand squeezed hard around Kitty's neck and she couldn't even gasp for a breath. She kicked out feebly at her attacker to no avail as her legs went weak and her head dropped forward.

With a shout of anger and frustration, Bailey slammed Kitty twice against the same wall as Orion and dropped her like a rag doll. Bailey eyed the rest of the students escaping and bent over to the body of Kitty and whispered in her ear, "I'll be back for you later." Bailey teleported away.

As soon as she left, Kitty coughed and spluttered, her lungs aching for air.

Orion groaned and clutched his wounded side, he didn't regret his choice, but he did hurt, "Where is she?"

Kitty's face was battered, her lip was split, and her eyes were cut, "I don't know, your grace."

Orion spoke, his voice was lost, "I think the kids have found a way out of here, I hope they make it."

Kitty's eyes glazed over, "She'll find them, she always does, she always will. I don't think that we can stop her."

He hesitated and then lowered his head, "I tried to do the right thing in life, tried to make a difference as a general, as a husband and I failed on all counts." Orion held his injured side, it was worse than he'd thought, "You're a sorceress, trained by the fun-loving Silo."

"I am proud to say I am, your grace."

"Good, I need you to do one last trick for me."

The *Utopia* rocked for a moment and didn't show signs of steadying.

"Our main thrusters are breaking up," Poxon huffed as he ran, "They are the only thing keeping us in the air."

Lacy completely ignored him as they turned another corner, she really hated running around this ship, "WHICH WAY?!" she shouted.

"LEFT!" Poxon yelled. He tried desperately to remember the route to the horses, "NOW RIGHT!" Most of the animal students ran or flew after Poxon as he led them through the tiny corridor, "WAIT! WRONG WAY!" He doubled back on himself, crashing into some of the following animals, "SORRY! THIS WAY!"

Achilles rolled his eyes in desperation, "ARE YOU SURE?!

"YES! YES! I REMEMBER WHERE THEY ARE NOW!"

A synthetic female voice was heard all around the ship and above their heads. *'Primary engines offline, extensive core damage detected, altitude decreasing, automatic shutdown procedure initiated.'*

"No!" Poxon's face crumbled.

"Dude, what does that mean?" asked Slim Pickings, who had made himself get to the front of the running.

"It means we've got fifteen minutes to get out of here," replied Poxon.

A burst of blue flame suddenly appeared in front of them and all of the students looked aghast at what emerged from the smoke.

"Well, well, well, it's my little chicken shits," Bailey smiled.

"RUN!" Lacy screamed.

Bailey unleashed a series of high intensity plasma blasts at the animal students; some got up, but many didn't.

"STOP IT! YOU'RE KILLING THEM!"

Achilles didn't know half these students; when they were human, he would have ignored many of them on a daily basis, so they changed their whole genetic make-up just to be accepted, to be different. And now they were being murdered by a crazed sorceress, "I'm going to end this now," Achilles said.

"What do you intend to do, darling?" Aphrodite asked.

"I'm going to kill her," Achilles gritted.

Aphrodite smiled a wolf grin, "Ask a stupid question and you get a stupid answer." The wolf stood aside, "Be my guest."

Achilles still had an iron bar in his hand and raced towards Bailey. Without backing down in the slightest, Bailey merely smiled, "How sweet."

She teleported away from Achilles' attack and reappeared behind him, leaving a shadow hole which didn't disappear. She picked him up by the back of the neck like a cat playing with a mouse. Bailey held him aloft and swung him in front of the other students.

"PUT HIM DOWN!" Cameo screamed.

"Ah, an otter girl, I guess job opportunities won't be heading your way soon at any time unless they are for building dams?"

"I'm an otter, beavers build dams, you stupid cow."

"Whatever! Either way, your dozy heroic friend is going to die in my hands right now." Bailey beamed, before anybody could scream, a voice beat them to it.

"No, he's not."

The voice came out of nowhere. It was calm and delicate, and one Bailey hadn't heard before. Heading towards Bailey striding purposefully was Sully, she had emerged quietly from the church and was amongst the students undetected, "You will let him go right now."

Bailey couldn't work out quite what she was looking at. Sully was covered in blood but still had an intriguing figure, nothing Bailey had seen before. She oozed confidence and beauty and her stunning form made Bailey raise her eyes. She held Achilles higher in the air and put her full concentration on Sully.

"Who might you be?" Bailey asked with polite confusion.

"I'm the daughter of beloved lost parents. I'm the bastard who got infected with this shitty virus. I'm the one who has lost and killed so many friends today and I'm the one who will drop where you stand if you don't let go of my Achilles."

Bailey rubbed her eyes and stepped back slowly, "You look purely remarkable my dear, are you sure you don't want to join me?"

Sully stared at her quizzically, "In all honestly I have an army of infected students at my command, albeit chasing a blue light down this ship like puppies after a stray ball. But they would do anything I ask them to, and I would have joined you in your quest for complete galaxy domination, sounds cool…"

"What's stopping you? I can sense the power and self-loathing flowing through your body."

"One thing," Sully replied and pointed at Achilles, "Him."

Bailey tossed her head back and howled a fury of laughter, "This thing? You would give up becoming a joint ruler of the galaxy with me for this wretched creature! You, my nieces and I would be ever ruling, why give that up?"

"Because he's my friend and I love him."

Her voice trailed away as she tried to compose herself. She looked at the animal students, Cameo, Poxon and Lacy, "I love them all, these are my best friends. I didn't know that before, but I do now. Whatever you want to call them, geeks, sluts, bitches, teacher's pets, buffoons, they are leaving this ship, because they've earned the right to." Sully looked at Achilles again, "We are family."

"Do you have all your sisters with you?"

"What?"

"It doesn't matter," huffed Bailey.

Bailey tossed Achilles aside like an old toy, as he stumbled to his feet he saw in Sully's eyes that she was prepared for a fight.

"Please don't," he whispered.

Sully just about read his lips and she whispered back in kind, "I love you."

Sully ran at Bailey, her claws aiming high. Bailey's expression was positive for an attack and she made a plasma energy knife, keeping it low as she raced past Sully and slashed at her stomach. Bailey smiled as she came to a standstill. Turning around to look at Sully, she felt a tremendous pain around her throat. *This doesn't feel right,* she thought. Blood poured from her wound spreading quickly under her head. For the first time Bailey's eyes went wide with fear. She gurgled like she was talking underwater as she tried to speak, "S-s-she c-c-cut me! She c-c-cut me!" Bailey stumbled and fell, still holding her bloody neck, she had time to look up at Sully, "B-B-itch."

She teleported away leaving blue smoke and yet another shadow hole. Bailey reappeared where Kitty and Orion had fallen, she stooped down to hold the teenager, "Y-y-ou're c-coming w-with me," Bailey's voice was fading as were her chances of survival, "W-we t-teleport w-when the ship c-crashes, the kinetic energy will send us through space and f-find y-your sister and t-then we will r-rule."

Before Orion could speak, Bailey teleported Kitty away to the cockpit, her husband simply stood up and ran on towards the students.

Sully collapsed to her knees, Achilles' eyes had seen a lot of horror this day, but nothing could prepare him for what he saw oozing out from Sully's stomach; it was her intestines. She tried to gather them back up, but it wasn't working. She spat out blood and looked at Achilles, "Oh dear, slightly embarrassing."

"No, no, no!" He bent down by her side, ignoring the blood gushing from her front.

Sully gave him a lopsided smile, "When I wanted you to see me naked, this wasn't what I had in mind."

Achilles tried his best to stem the blood flow with his shirt, but it wasn't working, "Like those muscles," Sully said dreamily looking at his arms, her eyes were glazed, "Pick me up in those arms and take me away."

Achilles looked around frantically, "SOMEBODY HELP ME!" he screamed.

Sully put her finger to his lips to shush him, "It's fine."

Achilles looked at her with compassion, "You're infected though, a zombie or something? Surely you can't die?"

"Look at my stomach, it's all over the place. I don't want to live like that and I don't want to come back as one of those mindless zombies. I controlled them and only I can say when I die, and I think it's my time; I'm bored and want to go home." Sully grabbed Achilles by the chin, "I'm in charge and I say when I want to die." Sully's jaw began to fail her as she now had trouble speaking. She still held on to Achilles as she strained to talk again, "I only ever wanted to be..." Sully paused, "Loved."

Her head flopped back and Achilles screamed, "NOOOOOO!!!!" He shook her body as his heart was hammering against his chest, "WAKE UP! GET UP!" Sully didn't move.

Slim Pickings moved through the crowd of students and put his hand on Achilles' shoulder, "Dude, she's gone."

Achilles wouldn't leave her side, "NO! SHE'S NOT!"

"Dude we have to leave. Poxon, how long?"

Poxon looked at his watch and forlornly at Sully's body, "Ten minutes."

Slim Pickings hauled the hysterical Achilles to his feet, "Dude, it's time to go."

Lacy wiped her nose and tried to hold back her tears for Sully. Dallas and Aphrodite remained quiet as they saw the kids grieve for their friend. A massive jolt shook the entire ship and everybody's stomachs twisted like it was their first time on a rollercoaster. The sound of groaning metal from within the ship grew worse. As the ship leaned over again, Sully's body began to roll away.

"CATCH HER!" shouted Achilles.

"Dude, I don't think we should make any sudden moves."

They all clung on as Sully rolled into a shadow hole. The blue smoke swirled around briefly and then the hole and Sully were gone. Everybody desperately tried to hold on to the side as they all looked to the space where Sully had last been.

"I don't think we could have stopped her, it wouldn't have made any difference," Cameo said, she turned to Slim Pickings and gave him a scared smile.

The ship was now about to fall from a great height; the thrusters had stopped and Poxon's expression tightened with fear, "Time's up," was all he could say as the weight of the church and the castle had finally taken its toll on the ship. It rocked again and then the ship went totally dead. Poxon's face turned tense, "Hold on to your stomachs."

Everyone's eyes focused on Poxon as he nervously drew his lower lip in between his teeth and then the zoo ship tilted further.

"AHHHHHHHH!!!!" came the group scream as everyone tried to hang on to something. The force from the deceleration threw them back against the ship's hull. Poxon clawed his way through the corridor, followed by the rest of the animal students; vomit now lined the walls of the ship as hardly anybody could stomach the force. The water from the filtration unit cascaded everywhere, along with broken sprinkler system units sending the students hurtling down the corridors, columns of water swirling around them.

Sliding down multiple corridors, heavier students whizzed past Poxon, unable to follow, and with alarmed cries, went down the wrong way. They were sliding too fast for anybody to grab hold of them and Poxon could only watch them plummet to the deepest ends of the ship and to their doom.

Poxon was still leading the water chute ride down the corridors, leaning left and right as they headed towards the stables.

Immie was frightened, she was in an unknown world, had just lost her friend, and was sliding down a water chute next to Cameo, a girl who looked like an otter. From the corner of her eye another figure swept into view, it was Orion. Struggling with a mouthful of water, she yelled to him, "WHERE IS KITTY?"

Orion just simply shook his head as he rocked through the corridors. Immie didn't say anything else, the terrified look on her face said it all.

Poxon recognised the upcoming corridor and tried to latch on to the opening with both hands, "WE'RE HERE!" he yelled, his body smashed awkwardly against the opening of the new corridor, trying frantically to grip on to the side. Lacy was sliding past her brother at an alarming speed, "LACY!" he screamed.

He flung a hand out to catch her, but it was too late as she slipped by, "NOOO!!"

Cameo was now submerged and in her new otter form she easily swam after Lacy, and in a few powerful tail flicks, was upon her. Cameo swung Lacy back into Poxon's hand and he let out a determined croak as he pulled her to safety, "Thank you," he spluttered. Cameo was too tired to talk and attempted to do a thumbs-up with her claws.

Poxon and Lacy hung on bat-like to the support columns in front of the door. Poxon couldn't speak any more with the water overtaking his head. He pressed the security override code again on the panel set at the door's side. *Come on, open!* The ship's female computerised voice spoke again. '*Access granted for containment unit 2144.*' The doors opened and the students and Poxon tumbled into the stables. The ship was still tilting, and they slammed to the bottom of the containment unit. Water was gushing in and filling the stables. The doors shut behind them as the ship's voice spoke again. '*Automatic shutdown procedure complete.*'

Even with the water rising through the doors, Poxon couldn't believe the wonderful sight in front of him. He thought he'd never see these beautiful creatures again. The winged horses were panicking in their glass-caged paddock, flying higher to escape the water, flapping their wings desperately to escape.

"Ok, I'm going to flush out the water from the paddocks, when the horses are free jump on one and then I'll release the top hatch. I have the clearance codes, it's our only way out of here."

"Dude, I can't ride a horse," said Slim Pickings.

"I can't ride a bike, what's your point?" said Poxon.

"Dude, when you ride a bike and fall off, you tend to get back on. A little different when you're hundreds of miles above the planet's surface."

"Ha! A shark riding a horse, priceless!"

"You do know you're a wolf, right?"

Aphrodite shook her wet fur, "Shit, forgot about that."

"Do you still think this will work?" asked Lacy.

"I do," said Poxon confidently.

Dallas pointed a finger up in the air and raised an eyebrow, "What about my dinosaur?"

"Hold on, hold on," Poxon said, "Lay it down on that big horse over there and tie it down."

"With what?" Dallas asked.

Poxon narrowed his eyes to his teacher, "Your dinosaur, your problem."

Amid the sudden confusion, one of the student animals spoke up, it was the bat-like creature who had recovered from her battle with Bailey, her name was Tessy.

"I'll take him," she said.

"Me too," said another winged student, it was another girl, but only her voice gave away her gender, as she was completely covered in feathers, like an eagle.

"Good, that's sorted," Poxon said.

He released the water from the horses' containment paddocks and they galloped around in circles, snorting hard. Soon their legs were a blur as they raced around the unit in a panic. They were breathing heavily but didn't unfold their wings just yet, their tails blew brilliantly behind them like clothes on a windy washing line.

"Ok, here's our only chance. On their next circuit grab one and hold on for dear life." Poxon had so much confidence his plan would work and that they wouldn't get trampled. The ship was swaying again and didn't have long in the air.

"MOVE IT! MOVE IT!" Achilles yelled.

"One more pass," Poxon whispered, rocking on his heels as if he was going to take a long jump in an athletics final. He watched and hoped his weight wouldn't slow his jump or break the horses' necks, as they raced around the bend, "Get ready," he was still whispering.

The 'chubby nerd' as he was called at college was calling the shots as the lead horse galloped closer, his eyes never left it and he took one last chance, "NOW!"

Poxon made an astonishing leap into the air and landed on the horse's side, clinging on to its neck and smashing his legs against its belly. In panic, the great horse, veered to the left and then the right with Poxon gripping on desperately.

The horse reared up high but Poxon would not give up and tightened his grip on it, it was terrified and bucked again.

"It's ok boy, easy, easy." He rubbed the horse gently on the neck and began to pat it, still whispering.

At first the horse hardly slowed until continuous patting from Poxon finally worked and the horse finally stopped. The chasing pack all came to a standstill when the lead horse stalled. Without the slightest hesitation Poxon shouted behind to the others, "FIND A HORSE AND GET ON!"

The students, animals and humans found a willing horse and climbed onto their backs. Lacy had Aphrodite laying across her lap, "Ridiculous," the wolf snorted.

Orion lifted Immie onto his horse and she struggled to get away, not wanting to be anywhere near him. The students with wings had taken to the air already as Tessy and the eagle struggled with the dinosaur. The horses were uneasy with their riders and made it clear to them by trying to shake them off. The students tried the same tactic they saw Poxon use moments before and began to stroke the horses tenderly and slowly. It worked, and the horses were calmed. Everybody's stomachs churned again as the ship was preparing to tumble.

"ARE WE READY TO GO?" yelled Poxon. A long, long silence passed.

"YES!" shouted Lacy, trying to keep Aphrodite from shifting on her lap.

Before anybody could move, the ship tilted on its side once more. It rocked, and everybody held their breath as the proud zoo ship *Utopia*, unable to carry the weight of the church and castle, toppled out of the sky.

The horses and their riders hurtled towards the massive ceiling, spinning helplessly out of control.

"DO SOMETHING!" Lacy screamed.

Poxon clung on hard to his horse as they somersaulted. He had one chance as they were all about to hit the roof, "COMPUTER!" he shouted, "SECURITY 56911491 ACTIVATE ALL EMERGENCY ESCAPE HATCHES 2144." With alarms blaring and a shift of smoke, several hatch doors slid back immediately, including the main roof hatch. Every horse saw the largest opening and began flapping with confidence towards their escape route. They soared out of the top of the ship in a neat formation and hit the thin air of the atmosphere as the ship fell beneath the clouds.

"KITTY!" Immie screamed.

She reached out her arm as the ship carrying her friend disappeared out of view.

Bailey gripped onto the armrests of her seat. She was strapped into the main chair in the cockpit. There was no sign of the pilot or co-pilot, either they were dead or had escaped but there weren't any bodies around. It was just Bailey and Kitty seat belted into their chairs and plummeting towards their doom.

Bailey was still bleeding from her throat she reached over to Kitty and held her hand, she was anxious and tried to speak, "B-b-before w-we c-crash, y-your power will t-t-teleport u-u-us away from h-here, the energy w-will f-find Kimberley and then we can rule." Kitty looked at Bailey and shook her head, "W-what?"

She shrugged her little shoulders, dismissing Bailey's words completely and then a laugh of bitterness came from her mouth. She almost apologised and replied blankly, "Remember what I said about what revenge, what I would do for what you did?"

Bailey seemed confused, maybe it was due to the blood loss, But Kitty's voice sounded different, harder, "D-d-did to w-w-what?"

"Not what, whom." Kitty's voice was now soft and slow, "Silo," was what she said next. She simply waved her hand in front of her face and Bailey met new eyes and couldn't suppress a shiver down her spine. Kitty's face had disappeared and next to Bailey sat someone with new features, a face which she shared a long history with, it was Orion. Bailey laughed, but it was shaky, she finally knew what had happened.

Kitty, like her, was a sorceress, a Vanisher and one of the many spells she had learned was being a shape changer; she could take on the appearance of anybody she chose. On Orion's request, they had swapped faces. He wanted to make amends for what he had done, his death was the only way.

He gripped his wife's hand, pleased with the swap he had made with Kitty, he had time to feel around his bag and take out a fairy cake with the other hand and gave it to his wife, she gave a bite.

"Hard as rocks."

Bailey looked at Orion and returned the squeeze, knowing her crusade was over and the end was imminent. She didn't scream or sob, she just smiled about Kitty, "Clever girl."

The ship hit the ocean with the full force of a gigantic battering ram. It exploded with a brilliant light and the massive waves from the impact clawed their way to Olympia and Heffernan City, submerging all the districts. The students on their winged horses felt the impact in the clouds above and struggled to remain riders as the horses rocked again.

It was dawn now, and the explosion below accompanied the early light of the morning sun. The students had a full day on the *Utopia* and now their zoo ship and lost friends were gone forever. The horses regained composure and started to head downwards.

The wind whipped around Immie and she struggled to contain her hair and emotions and tried to keep her distance from Orion, which was hard as they both shared a flying horse.

"SHE'S DEAD! MY LADY IS DEAD!"

Orion squeezed her, his legs clinging on to the horse's underbelly. He felt her tremble and so finally dropped his façade, he waved his hand in front of his face and it turned back to Kitty's. Immie stared at the now complete Kitty, which had once been Orion, with her heart in her throat. The anger she expected to rise didn't and thought she'd imagined the whole madness.

Whilst struggling with confusion she still let out a squeal like a stuck pig. She looked at Kitty as if she had grown a second head. Kitty calmed her down and gently stroked Immie's cheek. Immie shook her head not wanting to be distracted, but Kitty calmed her down quickly, "It's me Immie, I'm back."

The hairs on Immie's arm rose and she turned her head to meet Kitty's, "Is it really you, my lady?"

Kitty smiled reluctantly, "We can't go back home. I am the Queen and I left my husband. I embarrassed him, and humiliated him and think I killed him, the most powerful King Henry. I know the future in my land and his followers will kill me if I go back home. I, Katherine Howard, will be beheaded along with my friends and ladies-in-waiting, so we are stuck here, we have nowhere else to go. My lady Silo, Thomas, and Jane are dead."

Immie didn't look at Kitty, she just looked at the early morning sun and shivered with cold.

"So, we are both trapped in this new world then, my lady?"

"I'm not your Queen, you don't have to call me that anymore, I'm no one," she said forlornly.

"You are someone," Immie said, her voice lighter, "You are my new sister."

Kitty looked at Immie.

"God bless you then, my sister," she said.

"God bless you too, my lady." Kitty finally found a way to smile again.

Achilles watched as Tessy and the eagle girl, Natalie, struggled with the dinosaur. He flew his horse in further and spoke to the two girls, "You know you can drop that 'thing' if it's getting too heavy for you?"

Tessy turned her eyes to Achilles, her dark eyes met his, all traces of human were gone from her, "He's a heavy pain in the arse but we got him."

"That bastard thing killed my friends, just drop it in the ocean and be done with it, nobody would notice."

Tessy clenched her teeth against the pain of carrying the dinosaur, "Not an option, we promised Miss Dwells we would keep her pet safe and we will."

Achilles flew to the other side of Tessy and Natalie, gaining confidence with flying his horse.

"Why are you protecting it? Miss Dwells lied to you, she turned you into these strange creatures and for what?"

"For what?" Natalie said, her bleary tired eagle eyes focused on Achilles, "We saved your lives back in that ship, the cool kids needed us nerds to help you escape, and for what? You still don't know anything about us."

"Natalie, stop it," Tessy said, arching her back in pain.

Natalie made an annoyed sound with her beak, "No, he has to hear this."

"Tessy and I were in the same class as you for ages and you didn't even notice us. Do you know who we are?"

Achilles avoided the sharp gaze of Natalie and looked ahead, "It's hard to recognise you as a bat and an eagle."

"You know what I mean."

"No, sorry I don't."

"So, it took Miss Dwells to turn us into animals, so you would notice us?" Natalie said, drawing the attention of Achilles again, "It's what's inside that counts, not outside."

He struggled to make sense of it and slowed his horse down, "Look, just because we were in the same class doesn't automatically make us friends. It was a big class, and do you know what? Some people just don't get along or have a chance to speak to one another. It's not being rude or arrogant, it's just life. Some people, no matter how nice you are, won't be your friend, so just deal with it and do us all a favour and drop that thing, it killed my friends."

Natalie gave a quiet sigh, "It killed *your* friends, not mine." She then smiled, "Deal with it."

Achilles grunted, "I thought my mum was the most annoying person in the world until I met you. Well you just keep your eagle eyes open, as I will kill that monster, whether you like it or not."

"I'll be watching," Natalie said coldly.

Achilles eased his flying horse forward and left the struggling pair. Another bird flew into view; a giant vulture girl swooped in and helped Natalie and Tessy with the dinosaur. She had battered old black wings and a bald head, with no feathers on it, but had the most beautiful voice, "Would you like a hand? Or claw maybe?" the vulture asked.

"Thank you, Zima," Natalie replied, "He's becoming quite a handful or clawful or talonful?"

"I get it," Zima said softly.

As the three girls flapped their wings in unison with the sway lizard, it began to stir and slowly start to awaken and then wriggle in their grasp, "Dammit! It's awake, this isn't good," Natalie said with a dry voice, "It's wriggling too much, I'm not sure on how long I can hold it." There was a terrible strain in Tessy's voice and more on her frail bat wings.

The sway lizard's eyes were fully open, and it peered at the trio of girls flying it away to safety. Its tongue lopped out to the side of its mouth and it gave an almighty yawn and moved its arms forward.

"We might have to drop it, it's going to attack us, maybe Achilles was right."

Natalie listened to Tessy and nodded, "Ok, this thing is awake and a killer, it could turn on us at any moment. Yeah, it's a shame to say this, but we are going to have to drop it before it kills us. On the count of three," Natalie added.

Zima's calm voice spoke, "Are you sure?"

"Yes, get ready," said Natalie.

"One, two..."

The sway lizard growled and cocked its head, it bared its teeth and made tremendous gasps to breathe easier in the sky, it roared with a long hard breath, alerting Dallas, who was about to fly over. Natalie waved her away with a free hand, in pain, "IT'S FINE, MISS DWELLS, WE HAVE THIS!"

Dallas flew in closer for an inspection and saw that the three girls had her pet under control. Satisfied, she flew back to the front without saying a word, just a head nod. Natalie continued, "Ok, on three." A lovely soothing roar came from the dinosaur and then more.

"Best not to drop me from this height, will be rotten luck if you do, dear girls."

The flying girls all panicked and then tried to remain calm with their host, its voice completely freaked them out as they struggled to keep it in their claws.

"YOU CAN SPEAK?" said Natalie, alarmed.

"That seems to be the question of the day, my dear. You young girls may have quite saved my life. Look, I know a charming little pub which serves up delightful food in Olympia, we must go there when we land and please let me treat you all."

Tessy ignored the invite, "I mean how long have you been able to speak?"

"Since I was a toddler dear girl, remarkable ability, you should try it when you've got nothing better to do."

"So, this whole time on the ship, you were able to speak? Why did you kill those students? Does Dallas know you can talk?"

The dinosaur went quiet after Tessy's question.

"I say, I'm most frightfully ashamed and sorry about that. I have this terrible bloodlust which I've been affected with, not my doing you see. Happened back in Gommerstall but I can't control it, some dammed fool put it on me and there's nothing I could do about it. The lovely lady Dallas Dwells is a wonderful creature and unaware of my vocal abilities and I would like it to stay that way for the time being."

"So, you didn't mean to kill anybody?" asked Zima.

"Far from it my dear girl, love the beak by the way, but once the bloodlust starts I can't stop myself, can't even talk when the dastardly frenzy begins. I'm not even a blasted dinosaur!"

"So, what are you?" Zima asked.

"I was a human being my dear girl, let's get that straight but someone played some tomfoolery on me and turned me into this blasted dinosaur. One thing I can't tolerate is bad sportsmanship. The name is Aubrey by the way."

Natalie opened her mouth, trying to make something polite come out, "Well bloodlust or not, Aubrey, you killed many people today and that boy Achilles wants to kill you."

Aubrey tried to find a comfortable position whilst being carried by Natalie, Tessy and Zima. He shifted in their hold and stared out to the sea, "To tell you the truth, it would have been a somewhat disastrous day, my little sweets, if the young fellow Achilles managed to get his hands around my neck."

"You killed his best friends, he wants revenge. I'm surprised you don't kill him next."

Aubrey couldn't help but reply quickly to Zima's soft and caring sweet voice, "I know my dear, but he's my son, which makes this whole day most peculiar."

"HOLY SHIT!" Natalie gasped.

Aubrey's eyes shrunk a little in disappointment, "Language my dear girl, language."

Lacy was still struggling to keep Aphrodite and herself on the horse and fly safely. Whether it was the lack of air or the fear of falling off, the wolf was uncharacteristically quiet, laying in silence. She looked behind her and saw all the other animal students on their own Pegasus; it truly was a remarkable sight and she didn't impress easy. Lacy caught up with her brother and remained silent for a while herself. Poxon spoke first, a thread of contentment in his voice for once, "Beautiful sight, isn't it?"

Lacy's horse was flying so steadily that she took a quick moment to shut her eyes and feel the sunlight on her closed eyelids, "I didn't imagine the trip would end like this," she said.

"It's not the trip I'd wish for," replied Poxon, his voice strained.

Lacy detected the sour note in his voice, "I miss them too."

Poxon turned to his sister, her eyes flicked back open and were sympathetic, "I thought we were invincible, our little gang. I thought that we could take on the whole world and always win."

Lacy's horse shifted, she quickly recovered her balance, "We are invincible, in memories, because memories never die; memories are immortal and that's what Harley, Kane, Sayles, Arlo, Sully…all of them are. Keep that image of them in your mind, everybody will always live. They are immortal in our hearts."

Poxon clutched his horse tighter in his cold hands, "I love you, Lacy."

"I love you too, Pox."

"God, I think I'm going to be sick and I'm not talking about the flying horses," Aphrodite's tired voice made the siblings stare at the awakened wolf. She looked long and hard at Lacy, "You ok, my darling? You're looking quite tired, you look like a horse after an acid attack." If wolves could smile, Lacy was sure Aphrodite was doing it now.

"Right, darling, where do we go from here? I say we should fly to Gommerstall and find my headmaster and my dragon sister."

"Dragon sister?"

"Long story, don't interrupt darling. Yes, find my old headmaster, Elias Gluacas, in the prison city as he is the only man I know who has the brains to sort out this flood situation. Most of the cities will be close to being underwater since the Utopia crashed, so he will have a way of saving everybody; he's the second cleverest person I know. The prison ship crashed six years ago trying to escape but I know he's still alive and Cassandra too."

"Who's Cassandra? And didn't Dallas say Elias was dead?" Lacy asked again.

"She's my sister, the dragon, although she doesn't know she's my sister. Anyway, Elias isn't dead, I know my headmaster, he's alive, nothing would keep him from getting back and seeing his daughter, my sister."

"Wait, I thought Big Man was your dad, not Elias?"

"Elias is the father to my foster sister, Gemma, could you please keep up darling, I'm tired of explaining this to you. So it's settled, we fly to Gommerstall and find my headmaster and save the cities."

Lacy shook her head and slapped the wolf softly on her back, "Do I look like I was born yesterday?"

"Not really, the crow's feet give it away."

"You do know I really need to pee right now," smiled Lacy.

"So, do I," said Aphrodite, making herself comfortable on Lacy's lap.

"I was about to say, the only reason you want us to fly to Gommerstall, which would take months by the way, is so this headmaster of yours, who may be dead, can rescue your dad from his tower, which is underwater by now probably. And why would I want to rescue the guy who put most of our parents in jail? We're not going there, end of."

"Spirited speech darling, but we are going to Gommerstall to bring back my headmaster. My foster sister or freak sister or whatever, Gemma, is also trapped in Olympia and I have to find her. I don't want to, but have to, plus my dad is rich by the way. Whatever you want, it's yours, jewellery, cars, ships, money."

"My parents?" Lacy asked. Aphrodite hesitated.

"We're not going there."

"WHO SAID THAT?" Aphrodite and Lacy spoke at once. Dallas was riding right beneath and was glad the girls hadn't peed yet.

Her horse rose in between Poxon's and Lacy's, shifting them slightly.

"Did you hear our conversation, Miss?" Lacy's eyes tightened with suspicion.

Dallas looked behind to see how the batgirl was doing with her dinosaur; the bat and eagle girls were still struggling and now had a vulture girl joining them, but her pet was in safe claws or talons, giving her time to speak, "I told you, I'm not going back to Gommerstall. Have you any idea what my sister would do to me if I went back? If she's alive."

"If she's alive? What are you talking about, you silly woman?"

Dallas made an effort to catch Aphrodite's eyes and mimicked her, "Long story, darling. Sound familiar?"

Aphrodite sighed, "I can see you're annoyed, sweetie, let's discuss it over dinner, let me check my calendar, oh wait, I can't check, I have no hands because you turned me into a wolf. Is tonight ok though? Oh wait, tonight is looking doubtful, sorry no can do, I can't make it because my city is UNDERWATER!"

"If I go back to Gommerstall, I will surely die and so if I'm dead, how can I turn you back into a human?"

The wolf looked pensive, as pensive as a wolf could look, "Ok, agreed. I will go where you go and stay where you stay; you and that stupid dinosaur aren't leaving my sight." Aphrodite licked her front paws frantically and then bit them, still trying to keep comfortable and safe on Lacy's lap.

"Are your hands hurting you?" Dallas asked.

"Like I said earlier darling, I don't have hands anymore I have paws; if I had hands, I'd be choking you right now."

Frustration twisted the face of Dallas as she looked behind at the flying students, "We do have quite an army though and a sorceress with us. If my sister is dead, we may have a chance against her acolytes to rescue your headmaster, and I know he's dead but if she survived? No chance, this is a nonsense mission."

"Did you see Elias die?" Aphrodite asked.

"Yes and no," was all Dallas could say.

"Good enough for me," said Aphrodite.

"Wait, survived? Army?" Poxon listened and spoke up, "Ok, there's obviously something you're not telling us about your sister and also, they're not an army. It's a bunch of frightened geeks who wanted to be different to stop being picked on and bullied and so their teacher turned them into some sort of freak force. And Kitty and Immie have just somehow teleported though space and don't know if they're coming or going. They've been through enough today and yet again some have died, maybe they…" Poxon caught his breath, "…maybe we just want to go home."

"Hope you brought your snorkelling gear and flippers with you tubby, because that's the only way you're getting back to your mother's basement." Aphrodite said with venom.

Poxon looked at the wolf, "I'm still a kid, that joke would have worked if I was forty and still living at home."

He looked at his watch, "We're directly below Heffernan City, if we're going home we should try and get the horses to dive now, we could go back and help clean up after the flood."

Aphrodite took control of the conversation, "Clean up *after*? It's still flooded, it's a dead zone darling, why would we go there when it's filled with dead people in the water who will come back to life and try to eat us? And what's worse than that is there's probably poo and pee in that water too."

"So, what do you suggest we do?"

Aphrodite groaned and closed her eyes, feeling comfortable again on the flying horse.

"God, I thought nerds were supposed to be clever. Listen, it's simple. We just keep flying to Gommerstall, find my headmaster."

"Probably dead," said Poxon, she ignored him.

"Bring him back to Olympia."

"Flooded as well, like Heffernan City," he added.

"Don't live there so don't care. Anyway, we rescue my dad and also track down my foster sister too."

Dallas chipped in again, "Did you say the prison ship crashed six years ago with teachers inside?"

"Teachers, actors, painters all sorts of culture freaks inside," Aphrodite said.

A realisation hit Dallas and she veered her horse over to Poxon, "I think there's something you should know about your parents," she said, in a manner so direct it made Poxon jerk his head back immediately. Lacy couldn't hear the conversation; she was so content and even happy riding her flying horse. She would just leave her brother and teacher to waffle on. She had a bemused expression on her as Aphrodite spoke again.

"Have we made our minds up? Are we going to help clean up a flooded shit hole with a bunch of carnival freaks or are we going to fly to Gommerstall to rescue my headmaster?"

Lacy gave a tight smile, she just wanted to fly and not answer so many questions, "Ok, I've decided, I think we should fly to a nearby city, maybe Billinge city?

"Billinge is miles away," said Aphrodite.

"So is Gommerstall," came the quick reply. Lacy rubbed her horse's neck and kissed it.

"Billinge won't be flooded. We fly there, rest and regroup, and figure out what we're going to do."

Aphrodite stared at Lacy and wondered what the hell she was thinking. Poxon's enjoyment of flying mirrored his sister's; he had a brief window of exuberance on the Pegasus and it ended abruptly after hearing the words from Dallas. He also took a look behind him, with the many animal students, Kitty and her beautiful companion, Immie. Poxon geed his horse to fly faster, the lead horse flew high above the others and then he made it spin around and face the entire flying force, tension and determination hit at the same time, "No, things have changed. We're going to Gommerstall." He took one more longing look at the students, "We're going to war."

Epilogue One

Sully rolled over on the mud. It was very dry and bits were stuck on her smooth skin. She stood up and brushed it off her. As she looked to the sky, the ship was nowhere to be seen. Her wound had healed and there was no blood on her at all. She had no idea what had just happened, all she could remember is being cut by Bailey and rolling into a black hole. She was dizzy and swayed gently to match the cool wind that was blowing across her face. Her stomach lurched with the sudden change in gravity and her whole body ached. The sun looked different, flares seemed to be launching from the surface and heading towards the ground. The air had a curious sulphuric taste to it, she snapped her lips to get the taste from her mouth, "Hello? Is there anybody there?" No reply came back. Sully looked behind her, there was a small cave with a neat front. Shielding herself from the sun's rays with her hands, Sully made her way to the cave's opening. Sitting down on a smooth rock, she again looked around to see if she was the still the only person there, "Hello?"

Still no answer. The only thing that caught her attention was a little rat scurrying around by her feet. Sully gently picked up the rodent and stroked it tenderly, before taking a little bite from the creature's back. The rat squealed in pain and struggled free from Sully's grip. It rolled around on the mud for a while still squealing in pain.

Suddenly it righted itself and sniffed the air, and hurriedly ran around in circles. Another rat appeared, the distressed sounds from the first brought it out from its hiding place; it was its mate and checked to see if it was ok.

The first rat tilted its head, closed its now red eyes and stood up for a form of attack.

Sully tried to step in between the two with a firm palm, but the first rat attacked the second easily.

The new rat couldn't escape the snapping jaw of the first as part of its neck was torn open. It fell backwards and squirmed on the ground and within moments had righted itself and sniffed around the first one. Both had bright red eyes and ran up to Sully and investigated her, not seeing her as a threat. Sully reached out an arm and the two rats scrambled up and settled on both her shoulders, "Ok little ones, you staying with me?" The rats didn't move, feeling comfortable on their new base. Sully raised an eyebrow. There was a dry muddy trail leading from the cave's entrance through some trees. It was narrow and long but in the distance Sully could just about make out some buildings through the clearing. She raised her chin as her mind was whirling with curiosity about who or what was in the buildings ahead, "Let's take a little look."

Glancing around Sully walked off to see what the planet Rayash had to offer.

Epilogue Two

"Good morning, my dear. I trust you are well?"

Scarcely daring to look up from where the voice was coming from, Bailey kept her head bowed, she should be dead, but it didn't feel like it. *How would I know?* she thought. A strange feeling landed in the pit of Bailey's stomach as the voice spoke again.

"I do hope that trip wasn't too uncomfortable for you?"

"Where am I?" was all Bailey could say.

She finally lifted her head and turned to the direction where the voice was coming from and found an old man with white hair looking back at her. He was wearing glasses and a crumpled t-shirt with shorts and sandals. By his side was a beautiful woman with short blonde hair and an even shorter skirt, who wriggled her painted blue toe nails through her sandals and waved over enthusiastically to Bailey, who could see she had two fangs poking through her smile.

On the other side were two other figures, one was a guard of some sort, dressed head to toe in metallic body armour and a metal faceplate, a narrow slit was all it had for eyes and a massive blue cloak flowed behind it, its shape was masculine.

The other person in the room was another girl with bright pink hair and sunglasses. She looked slightly younger than the blonde and sat, head in her hands, sighing heavily. Her skin was porcelain white, which lit up the dark room. It was clear the girl with pink hair was itching to be somewhere else.

Bailey also saw that that the girl was sitting cross-legged comfortably on what seemed to be a dead body; it was a man face-down to the ground in a bright red suit.

"Could we hurry this up please?" It wasn't the girl sitting on the body who spoke, but yet another person lurking in the background. It was a powerful and impatient voice. Another girl about the same age as the one sitting down, strode forward. She was dressed head-to-toe in a tight leather catsuit wearing massive high heel shoes with long brown hair. Her outfit had a row of knives attached to her belt, with two laser rifles hanging down over both her hips with a strap; her knuckles were bloody, she rubbed them slowly, waiting for a reply.

The old man waved her concerns away and finally got round to answering Bailey, "Ok, so where are you indeed. Well, you are currently being held in a small pocket of time known as a time trap. It's where you can store time just after teleportation to briefly have a think about things, change your original destination or in our case, just simply chat."

"I've never heard of such time power," said Bailey, still looking at the assortment of oddities in front of her.

"Then you're obviously not the powerful sorceress I was led to believe you were."

Bailey took umbrage with the man's comment, still scrutinising her surroundings, "How did you conjure up this up? This collection of deadbeats and weirdos, am I dreaming? Am I dead?"

"A conjurer does tricks, Bailey, trust me, all this is very real."

The group were growing tired of Bailey. The old man had to gesture again to calm them down. Bailey stretched her neck and arms and looked directly into the old man's eyes, "So you had the power to teleport me away from the ship before it crashed?"

"Yes."

"Is Orion dead?"

He hesitated and then nodded, "I could have saved him, but we would have had conflicting views on what we aim to do. His heart died pure and we will give him that honour in death at least. You, on the other hand, are untrustworthy and pure evil but we can work with that."

"So, you can teleport and work with time, what are you? And what do you want from me?"

The old man looked Bailey in the eye and smiled, "I, like you, am a sorcerer. Not from the planet Rayash, but a sorcerer nevertheless. I too fell into a shadow hole like yourself and survived as well, but when I came out I had seen many good sights in the future, some bad as well, and I found I had the ability to alter time, not for long just for as long as time would allow me."

"That doesn't make sense."

"Time isn't supposed to make sense. It uses us every day of our lives until you learn to use it for your own advantage, not to be greedy or disrespectful. And then, and only then, when time trusts you are you allowed to have some fun with it."

Bailey was more confused than ever and rubbed her head, hoping she had banged it and this was all a hallucination.

"What are you again?"

The pink-haired girl whispered to the leather-clad girl, "She sure asks a lot of questions for someone whose life we just saved."

"We're called 'Apeshit'." said the blond girl.

"We are not calling ourselves 'Apeshit', Tara," the old man gave a charmed smile.

"I think that bump on the head from that rollercoaster cart has done more damage to your thinking than I'd expected."

Tara gave a sweet smile back, "Timeslayers?" said the pink-haired girl.

"No."

"Killjoys?" asked the brunette.

"Hey guys, no, look we haven't decided on a name yet." The old man looked back to Bailey, "I have gathered these people from various stretches in time for our little venture."

"Venture? You want me to hang out with these freaks?"

The old man spoke without even looking at Bailey, "I'll introduce you to them all later but for now I think we can have an adventure which will benefit us all."

"Which is?"

"You are looking for another time traveller, your niece, Kimberley Watson."

"Yes," Bailey replied glumly, "How did you know?"

The old man ignored her, "Well, we will help you, so long as you help us. I was present when Kimberley blew herself up and her guardian friend, Nayan, to release the prison ship from the Gommerstall prison vines and try to save her friends. I was preoccupied with my former employer, Big Man, as you may call him, and I let the delightful child Kimberley slip through my fingers, but she is a wonderful creature and I need her to join us to finish the game."

"Game?" asked Bailey.

"Everything is a game. The children on the ship earlier running away from that sway lizard, Sully the virus girl and then your good self; their escape was so inventive and spectacular, the Queen Katherine defeated you with such grace that was a great game to watch."

"Yeah, virus girl ripped you a new throat missy, we loved watching that," laughed the girl with the pink hair.

Bailey shot an angry look at the old man, "You were there? You saw what that bitch did to me and didn't help?"

"I tolerate time, but it barely tolerates me, I'm not a teacher just a pupil of time. That whole scenario, that whole day on the ship had to play out to the full before we were allowed to interfere."

Bailey thought she understood and nodded, "So where do we go from here?"

"Well, my dear, after all your searching with your late husband for Katherine, it seems we have finally found the other twin. She keeps using her time power and each explosion sends her to a different reach in time and she instantly forgets where she came from with each blast, but she is currently on Earth."

"Which one? There are loads, she lived on one of them."

The old man dismissed Bailey's comment with a petulant wave of his hand, "Yes, but this Earth has the most delectable bacon and egg sandwiches, unfortunately mixed with the most idiotic of people. She won't be hard to find when she appears, and when she does, bring her back to me intact."

"What if I say no?"

Tara spoke instead, "If you decline, that will be fine babes because we can put you right back where we found you, can't we?"

"We certainly can, Tara," agreed the old man, "If you don't want to join us, we will teleport away and leave you moments before we arrived to live the rest of your life, all of the five seconds you had left of it on the *Utopia*."

"You're sure Kimberley will be there?"

"Oh, she'll be there, Bailey, don't you worry about that."

Bailey hesitated and then delicately made a manoeuvre around the group to speak to the old man, "So what do I call you then?"

The old man's eyes twinkled and he began to laugh, a huge belly laugh, "My goodness, my dear, I must apologise for my rudeness." He cocked his head to one side, "Jago, my name is Jago."

Bailey rolled her eyes skyward, "Looks like I'm going to another Earth then."

Jago held his smile, "That's what I wanted to hear."

The End